The Aisha
Prophecy

The Aisha Prophecy

John R. Maxim

iUniverse, Inc.
New York Bloomington

The Aisha Prophecy

iUniverse books may be ordered through booksellers or by contacting:

iUniverse
1663 Liberty Drive
Bloomington, IN 47403
www.iuniverse.com
1-800-Authors (1-800-288-4677)

ISBN: 978-1-4401-5534-5 (pbk)
ISBN: 978-1-4401-5533-8 (ebk)
ISBN: 978-1-4401-5532-1 (hbk)

Printed in the United States of America

iUniverse rev. date: 11/17/09

PRAISE FOR JOHN R. MAXIM

"No one does better characterization and plotting than Maxim."
<u>Linda Howard</u>

"John Maxim is superb"
<u>Iris Johansen</u>

"Maxim, who's been writing top-grade thrillers for more than two decades, continues to be one of the form's best kept secrets"
<u>Publishers Weekly</u>

"Dazzling."
<u>Andrew M. Greeley</u>

"Top drawer entertainment."
<u>Kirkus Reviews</u>

"Maxim's super-smart novels simply can't be put down."
<u>Booklist</u>

"Maxim constructs a complex plot, juggles numerous characters, and pulls it all off with a cinematic breathless pace."
<u>Library Journal</u>

BOOKS BY JOHN R. MAXIM

NOVELS

Bannerman's Ghosts

Whistler's Angel

The Shadow Box

Haven

The Bannerman Solution

The Bannerman Effect

Bannerman's Law

Bannerman's Promise (previously published as A Matter of Honor)

Time Out Of Mind

Mosaic

Abel Baker Charley

Platforms

NONFICTION

Dark Star

Visit the JOHN R. MAXIM HOME PAGE for more info.

For the men – and especially the women – of Iran, Israel, Palestine, Saudi Arabia and Washington D.C. who helped me write this book.

None of whom, sadly, can be named here.

And, as always, for my wonderful Christine

ONE

She had asked him to join her for her late evening swim. She held a bottle of wine and two glasses. Her eyes said, "We need to talk."

The invitation was unusual in any case. They'd often shared the pool or soaked in the Jacuzzi, but they'd never done so at night. She would swim alone, all the pool lights turned off. It was her time, she said, to lose herself in her thoughts. They both knew that that wasn't the reason. It was only in the darkness that she'd fully disrobe. Only when her scars could not be seen.

It did no good for him to chide her about a self-consciousness that from his point of view was misplaced. For one thing, he had a few scars of his own including one through his eyebrow that some women thought sexy. She thought he was foolish not to have it removed. She also once suggested that he shave his head. Or at least get those thick brown curls cut short.

"Anyway," she'd said. "you're not that damned sexy. And it's dumb to be so easily recognized."

One can see why any discussion of scars was a subject best avoided at all costs.

Sensitivities aside, she had a wondrous body. It was splendidly muscled like that of a dancer, like that of the natural athlete she was, and yet so softly curved and so utterly feminine. He treasured every inch of it. Especially the scars. Far from being ugly, he saw them as a testament. To her courage. Her indomitability.

He would never intrude on her evening swims. But he found not watching her hard to resist. From a distance. Standing quietly in darkness. He would watch as she swam doing languid laps during which her strokes made barely a sound and her motion hardly even stirred the surface. He would watch her as she rose from the pool, seeming almost to levitate out of the water. She would bend to pick up her towel and her robe, her body glistening with droplets in the moonlight.

Next she'd climb the stone steps that led to the Jacuzzi. Sometimes she would turn her face toward the house and pause before easing herself into it. She would smile. Or she would nod. Not toward him. To herself. She always knew that he'd be watching her, unclothed or not. And they both knew that neither would speak of it.

Tonight was different. Her eyes had said so. Those marvelous amber-colored eyes.

As they walked the winding stone path toward the pool house, she turned to look back at the main house. All the windows of the two upper floors were dark except for a single flickering glow that came from the screen of a computer. "Niki's room," she said. "Niki should be in bed. She spends too much time on that computer."

But the screen blinked off at almost that instant. "She must have heard you," he said, although he knew she could not have. None of the girls could see the pool from their rooms. Except for the one point of vantage he'd found, the whole estate had been landscaped for privacy.

The pool house had been built in the style of the main house, as had the separate garage. Split-timbered Tudor on a base of gray stone. The pool itself was of an equally impressive design. First a mound had been built to house the Jacuzzi. The mound was about eight feet high. The pool itself was fed by a waterfall that seemed to come from the Jacuzzi. It didn't, but that was the illusion. It tumbled over gray boulders and tropical plants that created a grotto effect. The Jacuzzi, built of stone in matching earth tones, bubbled welcomingly as they approached. She reached for a switch that dimmed all the lights. She placed the wine and the glasses on the nearest edge and reached for the clasps of her robe.

The robe was red silk, oriental in style. Full length, high collar, showing only hands and feet. She bent down to gather the hem of her robe and raised it as she stepped into the water. She continued to raise it as she lowered her body, removing it only when her breasts were submerged. She placed it near the towels that he'd brought. She glanced at him shyly, self-consciously as always. She murmured, "I'll get over it. I know I should have by now."

He said, "Whether or not, I'll be here."

He knew that she might never. The scars still ran deep. Fifteen years had passed since she'd suffered the first of them. Back then, she'd left Texas – she'd grown up there, adopted – to learn what she could about her natural parents who had died at the hands of Saudi jailers. She was twenty-two years old. Almost fatally naïve. She'd paid a Saudi to smuggle her in from Bahrain and serve as her guide and translator. The guide took her money and betrayed her. She was quickly thrown into a Saudi Prison, frightfully abused, released six months later. Well… not so much released as disposed of. She been dumped from a truck near the Jordanian border. She'd been left on the hot sands to die. A Muslim doctor, a women, treated her first. Later a team of Israeli surgeons made the more serious repairs. Other Israelis took her in. Still others trained her. They made her into what she soon became.

Those scars were deep but they weren't the last. There was the one high on her forehead the width of her face. A bounty hunter tried to scalp her as he sat on her chest, wanting her conscious as he did so. He was an Englishman, by the way. Neville Bean. Not a Saudi. Neville Bean looked more like a hog than a man and was known for extravagant behavior. He told her that he meant to take her eyes as well. They would make a wonderful trophy. He interrupted his scalping long enough to pry her eyes open for a good last look. He used the butt of his knife hand to do so. Bad mistake.

She bucked and she seized the knife hand in her teeth. In trying to get loose he shifted some of his weight. This allowed her to work one hand free and to reach her own knife that was sheathed in her boot. The story is that she slowly disemboweled him. The story is that she didn't stop there. She then took his eyes like she was coring an apple. Next she released him and pulled him to his feet so that she could watch him stagger blindly about,

4

trying to hold his insides together, all the while screaming in agony.

The story, at least much of it, is nonsense.

Yes, old Neville tried to scalp her; she did best him and kill him, but he would have died quickly with her knife in his brain within two seconds of her getting a grip on it. When you go to kill, you kill. You don't taunt, you don't torture and you certainly don't linger, especially with a scalp that needs stitching into place. The Israelis have denied that they embellished the story, but they surely had no interest in correcting it.

Nor has she, for that matter, ever spoken of it. Not to him. She knows that he knows that she is a professional. She knows that he knows how she works. But she's probably also a little embarrassed that she'd let a creature like Neville Bean get close enough to put his mark on her.

Even so, she didn't really seem to mind that scar. It hardly showed unless she wore her hair up. Israeli surgeons, eventually, made it almost invisible. And one or two others as well.

Much more obvious were the scars from the bullets she took back when he first knew her and was with her. They hit her in the abdomen, right side, tearing through her. He more than avenged her. As did the Israelis. She'd very nearly died, but a fine doctor saved her. Not Israeli this time. Another Muslim. But those scars, unlike the others, could never be hidden even though a one-piece swimsuit would conceal them entirely. The deepest scar was the knowledge that she'd never bear a child. Those scars were why she'd only disrobe in the dark. That was why she would only make love in the dark. It didn't really make sense. But there it was. He had accepted it.

She sipped her wine. She was looking at the house. She said to him, "You know we can't stay here." He nodded. "Not forever, but you heard what Harry said. He thinks we should lie low for a year." He spoke with the barest trace of an accent in a voice that was deep but very soft.

She shook her head. "I don't think he meant here."

"He did indeed," he told her. "Harry made it quite clear. He also said that if we should begin to feel restless, he owns homes even grander in a half dozen countries. Two that I know of come with yachts."

She said, "Yachts come with crews and grand houses need staff. Sooner or later word would get out. Someone would realize who we are."

Possible, he thought. Perhaps even likely. She still had a million dollar price on her head. Himself, he'd probably be worth more than that if he wasn't widely believed to be dead. For that matter, so was she. Killed several times over in this or that country by this or that bounty hunter or fanatic. They've been trying to get it right for fifteen years.

She said, "I want a life. I want a home of my own. The girls especially need a home of their own. They should be going to school. They should be making new friends."

He was silent for a moment. "You've decided to keep them?"

"Certainly Aisha. I'm all she has. The other three... I don't know. Well, actually I do. It might be best for them if I let the Nasreens place them. The Nasreens will give them new names and new papers. They'd be safer than they are with the two of us."

"That is the first time I heard 'us' in your musings. Am I to conclude…"

She waved a hand as if to forestall the question. She said, "The thing is… no one knows what I look like. At least no one who isn't a friend. There's only one fuzzy photograph. They're not even sure it's me. There are descriptions, but they vary so wildly that…"

So wildly as to be useless. He knew that. It's why the Black Angel has been killed so many times. He asked, "Is it me you are concerned about?"

"Yes."

"I could remind you that I have been dead for two years. That I'm considerably deader than you are, my darling. But that isn't what concerns you. What is?"

She didn't answer.

"That I'd leave again?" he asked her. "Or that I won't?"

She brushed her hands across her eyes as if to wipe away tears. They could not have been tears. The Black Angel never wept. It must have been the rising moisture from the hot tub.

She said, "I've never told you how I feel about you. I don't know if it's love, but it might be."

He started to speak. She reached her fingers to his lips. She said, "Let me try to say this. Just listen."

She said, "Aisha loves you. There's no question about that. As far as she's concerned, we're her parents. Yes, we're all she has. We are all she'll ever need. You and she are also all that I have." She took a breath. "But you're a lunatic, Martin. There's my concern. You can be tender and loving. You're honest and true. But you're fearless to a fault, almost gleefully reckless. Look what happens when you're between jobs and getting bored. You go to rough bars and pretend to be gay, hoping that some bully will pick on you so that you can take him apart. I'm not sure that lying low is in your genes."

"This was only once or twice. An occasional diversion."

"Occasional? Shall I cite more examples?"

He poured himself more wine. "May I speak now?"

She said, "No. Here's what else I think aboutus. We've never been a team, we've often gone separate ways, but that's not how people think about us. Being together, staying together, magnifies the chance that someone will make us. If that happens they'll have also made the four girls. I can't forget that we almost lost Aisha that way. There's no longer a bounty on Aisha, we fixed that, but there's probably one on the other three girls. And even if there isn't, someone might go after them as a way to get at me. I mean at us."

"You want me to leave. So, I'll leave in the morning. I'll be out of the country by nightfall."

"Shit."

"Wrong answer?"

"Of course it is, stupid. I'm stuck with you, damn it. How could I ever have another man in my life? I mean a straight one. Steady job, steady habits. How would I ever explain all these scars?"

He shrugged and sighed deeply. This clears it all up. He's a dangerous lunatic. But he's her lunatic. Yes, she could start dating. She would draw men like flies. But explaining the scars would be the least of her problems. She would still always be who she is, what she is. And God help any such man who crossed her.

He said, "So you're willing, I take it, to settle for me. I'm overwhelmed by such selfless devotion."

"Oh, don't start acting hurt. You know I'm just talking. You heard me when I said I think I love you."

"You were at least somewhere in the ballpark."

She grimaced. "I meant…" She wiped her eyes once again. She said, "Okay, let's face it. We're stuck with each other. Let's just… see how it goes day by day."

"Night by night as well. I'm moving into the guest room."

She stood up in the Jacuzzi. She stood naked before him. She said, "Like hell you are, Martin."

TWO

A good hunter follows trails. He leaves none of his own. That is how the Greek had already found three Saudi women who were runaways. He found two in Spain. He found the other in Italy. Two had been returned to pay for their crimes. Handed over to their families, they did not long survive.

The one in Italy lost heart when she happened upon the body of the woman who had been sheltering her. She locked herself in a bathroom and opened her veins. He took pictures. He gave them to her brothers.

In recognition of his work, or so he had assumed, he was given this important new assignment. This one took him all the way to America.

How important? A princess. Born of Royal Saudi blood. Still a mere child, only fifteen and a virgin, but that wouldn't save her. Nor would her rank. She did much that cannot be forgiven.

And yet he'd been instructed that he mustn't harm her. She was only to be found and kept under surveillance until others came to take her and question her. He had brooded upon this. It was almost insulting. He was the Greek. He was not some sniffing dog. He could take her by himself. He could make her talk. By the time he was through, she would be begging to talk. About what, though? No one would tell him.

His true name was Mulazim. It was Arabic for "tenacious." A most appropriate name for a hunter. They called him "The Greek" because, unlike most Saudis, he looked like the statues of Greeks in museums. Perhaps not so well muscled, perhaps not so handsome, but he was light-skinned and beardless and he had a straight nose. His eyes were brown, but of a lighter shade than most and his hair was more curly as well. This is not so uncommon in places like Cairo where many still have some Greek blood in their veins from the days when the Greeks ruled all of Egypt. It was rare, however, in the land of the Saudis because there, Arab blood had stayed pure. The Greeks must have seen nothing worth conquering.

When he was a boy, other boys would make fun of him. They would tell him that he is no Saudi. They would say crueler things. That he must be a bastard. That he must have been sired by some European who came here to pump out the oil. Worse, by some American. Worse than that, by some Texan. Because of this he had a great many fights as a boy. Many rocks were thrown at him and by him.

But no more. No more rocks, no more teasing. Now they feared him. When he grew to adulthood with no skills to find a job, he applied for a post where no skills were required. With the Mutawain, the Saudi Religious Police. No one teases a member of the Mutawain. However, even the Mutawain had rejected him at first. It was mostly because of his appearance. He could grow a beard of sorts, but it was so thin. In the Mutawain, they like substantial beards. But then a certain old sheik took notice of him and decided that his looks could be useful. He was assigned to a unit called the Hasheem. In Arabic the name means "Crusher of Evil." The Hasheem hunts apostates and heretics.

How were his looks useful? He could go anywhere. He could board any airplane without raising eyebrows. There would be no facial hair. He would be dressed in western clothing. His passport would say that he is Greek. He already knew some Greek, but not enough to fool anyone. To learn more, he was sent to a mosque in Piraeus where he also worked on his English. He got training in computers, in the art of the hunt and in various interrogation techniques.

Less useful were the once-a-week slide presentations showing enemies of Islam the world over. Most were Muslims themselves, but not the right kind of Muslims. There were Shiites and Sufis and Hanafi Muslims and even a few Saudi Muslims. What they weren't, were Wahhabi, the only true Muslims, and had voiced a denial of its primacy. Not useful because it could take ten whole lifetimes to make even a dent in such numbers.

Many, however, were not Muslim at all. There were Christians and Jews, mostly men, but some women, on whom fatwas had been issued condemning them. On some there were big cash rewards. The idea was two-fold. First, know the enemy. The second was that he should keep his eyes open. You never know when you might spot one.

Six months in Piraeus. Much memorization. After that, more travel on minor assignments until he was judged to be ready.

He went on to prove himself. Three times already. Within only one year he was known by those who mattered as the hunter who always found his prey. He was Mulazim, the Greek. He bore the name proudly. One day he would have sons who would move up in the world because their father was Mulazim, the Greek.

This newest assignment, the one that took him to America, would earn him more praise than all the others combined. A Saudi prince had lost his daughter. She was his only child. He must not have been very attentive. But she hadn't just run off. She had been spirited away. This young girl had been smuggled out of Riyadh by the women of the Nasreen Society. Who are they? Muslim feminists. That is what they call themselves. A bunch of lesbian whores is more like it. Worse, they are destroyers of families. They encourage young women to flee their homelands to pursue their own selfish ambitions. Young women who want to drive cars or some such. By fleeing, they humiliate their fathers and brothers. Every one of them ought to be stoned with small rocks. Big rocks to the head are too merciful.

The girl in question had been gone for more than three months before her father came to his senses. He said he was trying to keep the thing quiet, so he didn't even report her disappearance to the Saudi Security Police. Instead, he'd asked the help of Rajib Sadik.

Who is Rajib Sadik? He is not even Saudi. Depending who you talk to, he is not even Arab. What he is though, is a big shot with Palestine's Hamas. He's on the council of their political wing but he mostly heads up their social services. He is also said to be a little too friendly with the man who heads up the Israeli Mossad. Even now. Even after the Israelis flattened Gaza. How can this be? He must be playing both sides. This Sadik is said to have all kinds of such connections including, some say, with the Nasreens. This must make him too useful to be killed.

Sadik told the prince, "We are not a milk carton." Mulazim was not so sure what that meant; only that it was a refusal. Sadik also, it seemed, didn't think much of the prince. He'd remarked that the prince would be driving a taxi were it not for the accident of his birth. But this should not have been a factor where honor was at stake. This Sadik can't be a very good Muslim.

The prince then put a cousin in charge of the search, but the cousin was as floundering as he was. The cousin had tried to track her down through the Internet and would log all possible sightings. This is keeping it quiet? This is a hunt? Some of these sightings, by anonymous tipsters, were, almost certainly, laying false trails. They were probably placed by the Nasreens.

Why, one might ask, did the father of this girl not come to the Hasheem in the first place? It was because he was embarrassed. He was mortally embarrassed. It turns out that his daughter, this fifteen year-old princess, had been promised in marriage to – this is the best part – promised in marriage to a certain old sheik who was now the head man of the Hasheem.

Yes, that same sheik. The one who saw the potential of the young Mulazim and took him under his wing. True, he is old. He could be her grandfather. True, his face is not much to look at. A big part of one cheek was lost to cancer. Even so, no excuse. The daughter should have felt honored. She also should have obeyed.

Mulazim was glad to get this assignment because otherwise he might have been sent on a hunt for someone who doesn't exist. The Hasheem had been asked to track down some prophecy that was causing unrest throughout the region. It says the Prophet's wife, Aisha, has been reborn. She's come back to raise up the women of Islam and to knock the men off their high horses. Who says so? The Internet. It's all over the Internet. She is to make her appearance very soon, any day now, an avenging flame-haired angel at her side. For this, Hasheem hunters have been sent to Iran, charged with finding and silencing the source. This was thought to have begun in Iran.

A ridiculous waste, in Mulazim's opinion. All it was, was gossip. Internet gossip. Blaspheming schoolgirls having their fun. There was no more substance to it than that.

His sheik knew where the daughter had probably gone first. Most likely north to Jordan where the borders are porous and from there to France, to the city of Toulon, where the Nasreens have long kept a safe house.

He'd asked the sheik, "We've known this? And we haven't destroyed it?"

"It is deep within a warren of old buildings," came the answer. "There is only one way in. Very hard to get close. Besides, those buildings are all joined together. Many ways to escape over rooftops and through cellars. Even if we could destroy it, they'd just move to another. They have dozens in Europe and elsewhere."

"Kept under surveillance?"

"Those we're sure about, yes. We try to photograph who comes and who goes, but the Nasreens keep their eyes and ears open as well. Some of the spies that we've posted have been beaten. Their cameras have been smashed. Sometimes their heads."

The sheik held up a hand. He said, "I know your next question. You want to know if they managed to photograph the girl." He drew an envelope from his desk drawer. "Nothing useful from Toulon, but we have one from her father." He drew it out and showed it to Mulazim. "This is Princess Rasha," he said.

The photo showed her face clearly, but not much else because she was dressed in full hijab. It was a face that might be called pretty were it not for a sullenness about it.

"We think we know," said the sheik, "where she has probably gone next. She had spoken to some of her friends in school of her dream to live in America one day. Also the girl speaks American English. Her mother once taught English, having learned it in that accent. She is probably in South Carolina."

Mulazim raised an eyebrow. "You could narrow it down so?"

"In this envelope," said the sheik, "there are maps that you will need. They show a place called Hilton Head Island. Rich Americans move there to play golf until they die. On that island, there is also a big tennis school where young people are enrolled from all over the world. The Nasreens have long kept a facility there."

"Also known to us? Also never attacked?"

"Mulazim... it's an island. Just as difficult as Toulon. Again, only one way on or off."

These Nasreens seem to know what they're doing, thought Mulazim. Many students coming there from many countries to learn tennis? Easy to hide a few young Muslim girls. "This girl will be there?" he asked.

"She at least will have been there. Of that, we feel certain. This facility serves as a relocation center. Nasreen clients stay there, sometimes for months, before being placed in their new circumstances. Almost always they are placed with Muslim families."

"Not good Muslim families. Not if they do this."

The old sheik waved a hand. He said, "Don't jump ahead. This girl might still be at this interim location or she might have moved on. For you, though, it is the best place to start. But should you manage to trace her, you are not to approach her. You are only to report where she is and stay near. Others will be sent to retrieve her."

Mulazim's face had shown his surprise. This girl had disgraced both her father and the sheik. Could the sheik still want her to warm him in his bed? Surely he knows that she can't give him sons. The pills he takes for his cancer took his manhood.

The old sheik knew his thoughts. "Don't be stupid, Mulazim. This girl has far more value than you can imagine. She has taken something with her that we must recover. It can do far more harm than you can possibly grasp. You don't need to know any more than that. Find her. We will take it from there."

"This girl is so important, but you send only me?"

He had asked this question expecting a compliment. Why you? You are the best. But the sheik didn't say that. He said, "This needs someone who will not stand out. Others have not been able to get close. But they are ready to move in should you succeed."

So, thought Mulazim, he was not the first choice. Nor are the others all out chasing that prophecy. But the sheik is only just using him now? As an afterthought? He is so far down the list? Never mind, thought Mulazim. He would rise above the insult. What's important is that these others had failed. That would make his success in this hunt all the sweeter. No one's ever bested Mulazim, the Greek.

Here, once again, the old sheik knew his thoughts. He said, "Mulazim… yes, you are tenacious indeed and, yes, you have had a few modest successes. But you've killed when there was no need to have killed. We don't need hunters becoming the hunted."

"I have only killed enemies of God."

"Mulazim… shut up and listen to me. You think God guides your hand and that may be so. But don't count on it, Mulazim. You must still use your head. Don't let it get too full of your own high opinion. Pride stands in the way of good judgment."

The old sheik was wise, but not so good at motivation. Shut up and listen? Try using your head? Even so, Mulazim thanked him for his advice. He promised obedience. He promised humility.

But Mulazim would show him.

A few modest successes?

There will be nothing modest about this one.

And so, two days later, he was in South Carolina. A tedious flight, five stops in four countries. The last stop was the city of Savannah in Georgia. No trouble with Customs at any of these airports. His papers stood up well to every scrutiny. He'd brought four cell phones with which to report. Use each only once and then discard it. No weapons, of course, but five thousand in cash. Enough to buy anything he needs.

He'd entered with his false Greek passport and visa, but had brought, as a back-up, his real Saudi passport. If caught, at worst he'd be quietly deported. They try not to make waves with the Saudis.

He took the airport taxi to Hilton Head Island. It was only an hour to the north. Using the maps that the sheik had provided, he had the taxi take him to this school for tennis where he found that he could walk about freely. Within an hour he learned, to his surprise and then confusion, what the sheik should have known, but did not.

Muslim girls at this school? Not so. They were gone. The Nasreens took them elsewhere more than three months ago. Why? Because someone had murdered the two Nasreens who ran it. Slashed one's neck with a knife, stopped the blood to her brain. And abducted the other who was found miles away. The other had been smothered to death.

Murdered by whom, though? Abducted by whom? Clearly not by anyone sent by the sheik. By other hunters, perhaps, who came from other countries? Looking for runaway women of their own? The Iranians, maybe. Or some other Shiite country. The sheik would not have known because they would not have told him. The Shiites, after all, are heretics themselves and therefore have no love for the Hasheem. Especially for those who they've caught inside their borders. Either dead now or rotting in their prisons.

Nor did this happen on the grounds of this school. It happened elsewhere on the island at the house of a woman who often came here to teach tennis. That woman was lucky to have been somewhere else or she, too, would have been killed or taken. Mulazim learned these bits and pieces by asking other students. He pretended to be greatly saddened and shocked, all the better to conceal his disappointment.

The police had nothing. No suspects, only theories. A burglary that had gone badly, perhaps. No one was supposed to be home. The American woman who owned this house was believed to have plenty of money. Whatever had happened, the police had concluded that it wasn't related to their being Nasreens or even to their being Muslims. Why? Who knows what their reasoning was? If it wasn't a car bomb it can't involve Muslims? Or maybe they were sweeping this under a rug lest it be labeled a terrorist attack and the rich might then go elsewhere for their golf. On the other hand, they could just as well have been right. The killings could have been a coincidence.

All the same, this was most inconvenient. He'd spent a day and a half on the grounds of this tennis school. He had asked several students where the Muslim girls had gone. He pretended that he had grown to know some of them, but had been back in Greece these past months.

He'd been friendly, he said, with one in particular. He showed several a photo that he said she had given him. In this photo, the princess wore an abaya. Only her face and half her forehead could be seen. He had hoped to get one in which she was bareheaded, but this was the best that her father could provide. Most of those he asked shook their heads; they didn't know her, but at last he found two girls who did.

One said to the other, "Isn't that little Rasha?"

The other looked more closely. She said, "Oh, sure. She was one of the new ones. Nice kid."

Mulazim blinked in surprise. Here she used her real name? She must have felt very safe indeed.

The first asked Mulazim, "But what's with the abaya? None of them dressed Muslim while they were here."

"Old photo," he told her. "She had nothing more recent."

The other said to the first, "She still covered up. She'd only play tennis in a full warm-up suit. She wasn't ready for a T-shirt and shorts. Girls don't show much skin where they came from."

"But she was into it. She worked at it," added the second. "Only a beginner, but she could be good. Especially if Elizabeth's still teaching her."

"Still?" asked Mulazim.

"She took Rasha with her."

Elizabeth must be the American woman. "These cowardly murders took place in her house?"

"I guess that's why she didn't want to stay there," said one. "She and Aisha came and got Rasha."

"Aisha, too?" asked Mulazim, as if he had met her.

"Oh, sure," said the girl. "Elizabeth wouldn't go without Aisha."

Another Aisha, thought Mulazim. There's already one too many. So much effort being wasted on that stupid prophecy. Good luck finding a particular young woman named Aisha. There must be millions of Muslim girls with that name. He waved it off. "So this Elizabeth took both?"

"And the other two new ones. The two sisters who got out of Iran."

Mulazim raised an eyebrow. "Those two as well?" He asked this, once again, as if he had known them.

"The Darvi sisters," said the second girl, nodding.

"Niki and… let me think. Oh, yeah. Shahla," said the other. "Aisha wouldn't go without them either."

Mulazim made a mental note of the names. Shahla, fairly common. An upper-class Persian name. But Niki? What Muslim girl is called Niki?

He asked if they knew where Elizabeth had taken them. One answered that Elizabeth had friends up north someplace, but was unable to be more specific.

He asked, "You haven't heard from them? No postcards or letters?"

"Umm… a couple of the kids here got emails, I heard. From Niki, She's the younger Darvi sister."

"Recent emails?"

"I guess so. A week or two, maybe."

He brightened. "Which kids? Might I speak to these kids? News of Rasha would ease my heart greatly."

These two conferred briefly. They were trying to remember. In the end, they could not recall who. They had only, one said, heard of this through the grapevine. He took this to mean indirectly.

"But what of the content of these emails?" he asked them. "Niki must have had some news to pass on."

"Let's see," said one, musing. "They're planning a party. For Aisha. Her birthday's coming up."

Not helpful.

The other asked the first, "And they moved again, right? They moved in with some man."

"Some old friend of Elizabeth's. An old boyfriend, I think. Niki said he bought Rasha a puppy."

The other shook her head. "No, she said a kitten. Saudi Muslims think dogs are unclean."

Mulazim wanted to scream. Kittens, birthdays, no relevance. He calmed himself, asking, "Moved again? From where to where?"

They didn't know.

"This man they moved in with. Did she say this man's name?"

The two looked at each other. More shakes of their heads. "If she did, we never heard it," said one.

But the other, seeing his great disappointment, suggested that he speak to a woman named Bernice. This woman, she told him, worked at the front office. She assumed that Bernice would be forwarding any mail that might come for any of those girls. She might also know who this man is.

The girl said, "You can catch her if you go up there now. Or else you'll have to wait until Monday."

He understood. This was Friday afternoon. In the West comes two days off after Friday. He said "Thank you and God bless you," to these two.

He would speak to this Bernice, but not at the office. Unlike these two young students of tennis, she would probably not answer the questions of a stranger, no matter what story he concocted. And she would likely report that this foreigner had asked questions.

A good hunter would not take that chance.

THREE

He waited for Bernice until she quit for the day. She was a black woman, in her forties, and big. Bigger, maybe stronger, than he was. Mulazim followed her to her car as if he were strolling toward his own. She took a remote key out of her purse and clicked it, unlocking all four of her doors. When she climbed in, he leaped in alongside her.

He said, "I have a gun, but I have no wish to harm you. I need only to get off this island."

She looked him in the eye. She said, "Let's see the gun."

Part of his training in dealing with women was how to take advantage of their feminine nature. How it's easy to play on their sympathies. So he made a show of seeming to sag and making his chin and lips quiver. He drew his hand from his pocket. He showed both empty palms. At this, he pretended to break down and weep.

Women always soften when they see a man weeping. Not all are sympathetic, but all are less afraid. He brought his hands to his face as if he were ashamed. He said, with a sob, "All I wanted was to work and send money to my family. Now they will arrest me and deport me."

"Go on."

He told her that he was in this country illegally. Last night, men came to get him in the food store where he worked. Men in suits and dark glasses. He did good honest work, but someone had betrayed him. He ran. He didn't know what else to do.

This was a gamble, but it seemed one worth taking. This was a woman who'd helped shelter so many Muslim girls. This woman, who might even be a Nasreen herself, knew a thing or two about illegals. He thought it unlikely that she'd turn him in. The question was would she be willing to help him? This would be so much easier if she were.

She asked him, "Last night? What have you been doing since?"

"Hiding. No sleep. I am so tired."

"Have you eaten?"

"Not today. My stomach is all knots."

She shook her head as if having a debate with herself. But she started her car. She backed it out of her space. She said, "Okay, we'll get some food into you. After that, I might know someone who can help you."

Her house was on the other end of the island. There were no rich peoples homes where she lived. They'd passed clusters of old

26

trailers, most on dirt roads. On her street, however, there were mostly real houses, all small, all older, but neatly kept up. All her neighbors seemed to be black people as well. Here the streets were paved. Young children played on them.

He was relieved to find that Bernice lived alone even though her house had four rooms. He had confirmed this by looking through her medicine cabinet. Prescription bottles showed only her name. All her toiletries suggested only one user. He saw no products for men in her bathroom, no clothing for men in her closets. The only evidence of family was in framed photographs on the bookshelves of her living room. Nor was she Muslim. On her shelves he saw a bible. Also he found bacon in her icebox. A small nook in her kitchen housed a laptop computer. He touched a key. It blinked on. Many people leave them on. Not such a good idea, but good for him.

Before all this, of course, he drove a fist into her kidney as she was fixing him a sandwich and heating noodle soup. It took more than a fist. It also took two good kicks. This was a formidable woman. But he was able to bind her to a stout chair with arms and stuff a dish cloth into her mouth.

The chair was in her kitchen. A rack of knives sat on the counter. He chose a thin filet knife for his work.

For twenty minutes he inflicted great pain on this Bernice, prying at the joints of her knees with this knife. Even gagged, they beg to know why this is happening to them. They ask with their eyes and the sounds that they make and with a frenzied shaking of their heads. Even gagged, they beg to give you whatever you want if only you will stop hurting them. Stop too soon and some will curse you. You'd have to start over. It's best to get them well softened up.

At the end of twenty minutes, he said to this Bernice that he would now ask her where the Muslim girls had gone. He would pull out the dish cloth, but he'd shove it back in if she should feel disinclined to answer. He removed it and waited while she gagged and she retched.

He jabbed her. "Kindly answer my question."

"Gone. Just gone, you miserable cock su…"

She stopped herself short. Calling names was not prudent. But little by little, in response some encouragement, she answered the question more fully. There were nineteen in all. Mostly girls in their teens. Older women had come and packed them all up. Gone where? All over. Some as far as California. Mail? They had no mail. They never got mail. Or if they did, it never came through the office.

Perhaps not. But what of emails? He told her that he knew that other students got emails. This seemed news to this Bernice. He saw that in her eyes.

He gestured toward her computer. "Emails to you?"

She shook her head. She said, "Never."

Well, thought Mulazim, we shall see about that. He showed her the photo of the princess named Rasha. He watched her eyes. He saw that she knew her. She looked away. He stuck her. He said, "Speak or more pain."

She blurted, "New England. Some place in New England."

At this she made a deep growling sound. It seemed to him that she was berating herself. For telling him this. For being so taken in. He felt himself wanting to offer her comfort. He wanted to tell her she should not be ashamed because this was his talent. He was Mulazim, the Greek. He'd have defeated her one way or the other.

He knew of New England. It was close to New York. But this could still be a lie. At best it was vague. "To another Nasreen safe house? There is one in New England?"

She blinked. She made an involuntary shrug. His sense was that she did not know of a safe house. He was about to ask her what city or town, but he thought it better to test her first by asking a question whose answer he knew.

"You said they have gone north. They means who?" He asked this while tracing a line with the knife along an uninjured part of her thigh.

She swallowed before speaking. She glanced toward the photograph. "Rasha was one. And two other new girls."

"The Iranian sisters. Niki and Shahla. Don't make me squeeze such details out of you. You get one chance to tell me who else."

She gritted her teeth. She knew that he knew. "Those three," she said softly. "Aisha went with them."

"Taken by?"

"Aisha's… friend."

"Named Elizabeth," he told her. " Do not dawdle. This provokes me. Who is this Aisha? Another Nasreen?"

"No. Just a girl." She said this with force. It seemed an attempt to be protective of her. Bernice added, more softly, "She's… sort of a counselor. She was helping the new ones get settled."

"Helping them to turn from God? And from their families?"

"Not from their religion. No one here would do that."

Doesn't matter, thought Mulazim. They are already lost to God. He asked, "Where in New England? What address?"

She answered, "I don't know. Nobody here knows. They went there to meet someone. I don't think they planned to stay."

Aha, thought Mulazim. This agrees with what those two girls had told him. He said, "I know they met a man who was a friend to Elizabeth. I know that he stayed with them when they moved someplace else. And I know that you know where that is."

"I do not. No one knows." She fairly shouted these words. "That's the whole point. To be gone. To not be found. To live in peace."

Bernice said this so firmly, looking into his eyes, that he thought it could well be the truth. All nineteen were fugitives from Islamic justice. Yes, probably the one called Aisha as well. Fugitives don't leave forwarding addresses.

He shrugged. He said, "Very well. I believe you. You have saved yourself more pain. You have spared me the need to inflict it."

He stood up and laid the knife on her kitchen counter. He tasted the soup and ate half of the sandwich. Peanut butter. Very good. With grape jelly. This was also to give her more time to be grateful. They talk even more when they are grateful.

He went to her icebox to find something to drink. He saw something there called CranApple juice. He drank from the bottle. Very tasty. Her icebox was the new kind. It spits ice through the door. He found a box of plastic bags in a drawer by the sink. He took two bags and filled them with ice. These he wrapped in two other dish towels. He placed them on the knees of this Bernice as proof that he regretted her discomfort. Although she did not acknowledge this kindness, she gave a small sigh of relief.

He said, "No address, and yet they told you New England. Why would they tell you even that?"

She took a moment to rock in her chair as if she were considering her reply. She said, "They didn't tell me. I overheard. They were waiting in the lobby with their bags and their prayer rugs."

Prayer rugs, thought Mulazim. At least they still pray. But useless. Their prayers are not heard.

He said, "Go on. What did you overhear?"

"Aisha was telling the other three girls about a man who was meeting them there. For all I know, it could have been an airport, not a town. But it sounded as if this man intended to take them somewhere else where they'd be safe."

"I will ask you again where that place might be. Keep in mind that I already know a great deal. I even know about Rasha's kitten."

Her eyes showed confusion. "What kitten?"

He could see that Bernice had no knowledge of the gift. Not good. She was not so up-to-date after all. But she still might know where they went next.

"Someplace safe, you say. Someplace far away? What?"

"Some place where they won't be easy to find."

He heard defiance in her tone. This was also disrespectful. He reached to remove the two ice packs. But she realized her mistake. She said quickly, "All I meant is… a place where they would fit in."

"A place with many young Muslims?"

"No. Well… I don't know. I think it's more that they'd go to a place where new faces don't attract much attention."

Mulazim grunted. This was sensible of them. Not helpful, but certainly sensible.

He asked her, "Who is this man they were meeting?"

"I don't know."

He reached again. Again she spoke quickly. "He's someone Aisha knew… and who Elizabeth knew… but Elizabeth had believed this man to be dead. Aisha, I guess, had just learned that he wasn't. She was very excited about seeing him again. But she was telling the others that she'd known it all along. Her mother told her in her dreams that he was alive. So she knew he'd come back to them one day."

Mulazim wondered whether he had heard this correctly. "Her mother speaks to her in dreams? Where is her mother?"

"With God. She's dead. Both her parents were murdered."

She said this accusingly as if to suggest that they were murdered by people like him. But he brushed that thought aside. He found himself staring blankly. A man back from the dead? Information from dreams? This intelligence seemed less than reliable. Unless, of course, this man they were meeting was named. It would make them somewhat easier to find.

He asked, "And the name of this man who was thought to be dead?"

"I only heard Martin. "

"First name or last?"

"Aisha wouldn't have called him by his last name."

Mulazim supposed not. That would be impolite. Nice to hear that good manners aren't totally forgotten after being exposed to the West. He adjusted an ice pack that was sliding off her knee. He mouthed the name Martin. Not much, but it was something.

He said, "A few more questions and then I will leave you. Tell me about this Elizabeth."

"I... really didn't know her that well."

"She's a teacher of tennis? She's the one who taught Rasha?"

The woman paused to reflect on how she might reply. "No, she's not an instructor. I mean... she's not on staff. She's just a friend. A friend of the Nasreens. She and Aisha were especially close."

"Such a friend that she would give up her home on this island for the sake of four Muslim girls?"

"She... didn't want to live in that house anymore. It's where Jasmine was killed. It's up for sale."

Jasmine. The name of the murdered Nasreen. Small pieces were coming together. "This Elizabeth," he asked. "Is she a Nasreen? Even with a name like Elizabeth?"

The woman paused again. Reflecting again. She said, "No. Not a Muslim. Not a Nasreen. I think she knew some Nasreens from a long time ago. From over there somewhere. From the Mideast."

"This Elizabeth lived there?"

"In Israel, I think."

"A Jew?"

"Not a Jew. She just… worked there."

Mulazim felt a chill at the back of his neck. Elizabeth… Martin. Elizabeth… Martin. These names seemed to ring a distant bell. He asked, "This Elizabeth. What is her full name?"

She took a deep breath and let it out slowly. She asked, "Are you going to kill me?"

"In this I am forbidden. On this I can swear. However, when I go, I must leave you tied up. In how much comfort depends on what you tell me."

"Are you going to hurt Rasha?"

He gasped at the suggestion. "Touch the daughter of a prince? He would chop both my hands off. All he lives for is to see his daughter again. I am instructed to look but never touch."

"Then her last name is Stride. It's Elizabeth Stride." This Bernice's voice was stronger as she spoke it.

Mulazim's mouth fell open. He felt thunderstruck. Those slide shows in Piraeus. All those enemies of Islam, hundreds of slides, but of these only three or four were women. These were not so boring. To these he paid attention. The worst of the lot was named Elizabeth Stride. Worse, far worse, than most of the men. Her fatwa carried one of the biggest rewards. One million in gold for her head.

Could this possibly be that Elizabeth Stride? The one who was an assassin? In the pay of the Israelis? Sent to kill Muslim men on an Israeli death list? The one who the Israelis called the Black Angel?

And she had a lover. Equally dangerous. A German. An adventurer. The name might have been Martin. He couldn't remember. This mention of her lover had been incidental. This man, too, had been known to work with the Israelis and with other intelligence services before that. Equally dangerous. That's what it said. And yet this man was not on the list of most wanted. Why not, though? Perhaps because they thought he was dead? Like the Martin this Aisha had spoke of?

Slow down, thought Mulazim. Slow down and think. This must be a different Elizabeth Stride. Otherwise, would she use her real name? He would not have thought so, but then there's the princess. She kept her real name although hunted.

So what do we have here? A friend to the Nasreens. One who's known them from the Mideast. How many women named Elizabeth Stride would be such a friend to Muslim women? How could she have become a friend in the first place after killing Muslim men for the Israelis? Hmmph! Foolish question. That might even be the reason. And if it's her, she's worth a million for proof of her death. What proof, though? Her head? Showing up with both her hands? No good photographs of her have ever been found. They probably have no fingerprints either.

The slide show had one photo, but it was next to useless. For one thing it was taken from too much of a distance. Even worse it was only believed to be Stride because of certain people who were in the photo with her. Besides, this woman was dressed in an abaya so all you could see was from chin to mid-forehead and only a little more than half of her face.

Why would this Elizabeth be dressed in an abaya? It's because full hijab was a tool of her trade. It was how she managed to get close to her victims. Close enough to use another one of her tools, the curved Moroccan knife that she favored. And then she could melt away into the crowd, looking just like a thousand other women.

Oh, and there's more. It was slowly coming back to him. There were descriptions of scars on her body from wounds she is known to have suffered. Bullet wounds to her abdomen. They alone should have killed her. And a scar up high on her forehead.

He touched this Bernice's knee with the knife. "Describe this Elizabeth. I will know if you lie. I have had this discussion with others."

"White woman. Middle thirties. Maybe five nine or ten."

"This describes many. Say more."

"She is... very attractive. An elegant woman. Blond hair. Reddish blond. She wears it short."

"Blue eyes or brown? I ask this to test you."

"Not blue. Not brown. More like amber. Like a cat."

One more test. He touched his chin. "She has a big mole right here?"

The woman shook her head. "There's no mole."

Correct. No mole. She was telling the truth. "But she has other markings on her face, does she not?"

Bernice wet her lips. "You sure you're not going to kill me?"

"I have told you. I am forbidden."

She swallowed. "There's a scar on her forehead."

Mulazim was thrilled. He tried not to show it. "Here? At her hairline?" He touched himself again. "This scar goes straight across side to side?"

"She wears her hair to cover it. But, yes, I've seen the scar."

Mulazim felt transported. He was in another place. Other than the unusual color of her eyes, it was the one detail of the Black Angel's description that most accounts of her agreed on. A wound from a knife fight. Some say a straight razor. Some say a bounty hunter was about to take her scalp when she managed to rip him crotch to chest. Which is true? Doesn't matter. The scar is the main thing. It's her. He had no doubt. She's Elizabeth Stride, the Black Angel.

But what now, though? What's first? Think this out.

The proof would be the scars. A pair of hands would not suffice. Nor would even her head because some might dispute it. They might say, "Not enough. Not worth the whole million. A few thousand maybe. Don't complain." But delivered alive? Forget the one million. They would gladly pay twice that and more. And only he, Mulazim, knows where she has gone or at least where she went from this island. She's gone north to New England with four Muslim runaways, one of whom is none other than the princess.

Mulazim rubbed his hands. This gets better and better. And we haven't even gotten to the best part. It's this thing the princess took that makes her so important. The sheik wouldn't say what, but it could do great harm. "More harm than you could possibly imagine," he said. One assumes that she still has it, but look who has her. It's the woman at the top of the most wanted list. A woman who would gladly do great harm.

Should he use one of his cell phones to make a report? The Americans claim that they monitor such calls, but in truth they intercept maybe one in five hundred and they translate maybe one in five thousand. Fewer still for calls made to Saudi Arabia. The Saudis always get kid glove treatment.

No, he would wait until he knew more. Even then, he won't say anything about the Black Angel. If he did, the sheik might send many fighters, each one claiming a share of the bounty on her. Well, to hell with them. Finders-keepers.

He was envisioning the Stride woman tied up like this one, him causing her more pain than she'd ever known. One cut for each of her victims, but none fatal. Him delivering the young princess in the bargain. Her and whatever she took.

In this other place where his mind had gone, he was barely aware of what his hands were now doing. From behind, they had seized this Bernice by the throat. Her chair was bouncing. She was bucking and kicking. Ice cubes clattered on the floor. She was trying to suck air, but it had no place to go. Before long she was quiet. She went limp.

Too late, he realized that he should have waited. He'd forgotten about her laptop computer. He might need her help with its workings. He put his fingers to her throat. He felt no pulse. She was finished.

He sat before the screen. He saw the icon for documents. Among them was her address list. He spent twenty minutes browsing through these. There was not a single name that he recognized. Friends and family, probably, almost all from this area. Also some doctors and a dentist. He spent another twenty minutes on her other documents. He did a word search in each for Nasreens and then for Stride. He also tried Rasha, even Martin.

No results. Nothing. Not even a mention of the tennis school. Her office computer might contain something useful, but she'd probably been cautioned against taking files home. Near the bottom of the screen he saw the icon for the internet. He took a deep breath, not daring to hope that she had told it to remember her password. But she had. God is great. The screen came alive with long lists of emails that this woman had sent and received. Even recent emails that she had deleted were still listed under "Deleted." He scanned down the names of the senders of these emails hoping for a name that he recognized.

Again, no luck. At least not for the moment. Most email addresses are cryptic. Most offer no clue as to their owner. He would read every message, but no time for that now. He would take this laptop with him when he left here.

He was about to shut it down when a heading caught his eye. The heading was called "Favorite Places." It referred to those websites most frequently visited by the person who owned the computer. He clicked on the heading and a long list appeared. There were sites for getting Internet news, a few about cooking and some black history sites. There were also quite a few involving Islam. Of these there were some that spoke of the Nasreens and five or six websites that showed the name Aisha.

His hopes rose, but were dashed. They referred not to Aisha, the girl who went with Stride, but only to this blasphemous prophecy. That Aisha was known as "The Lady of the Camel" because of some battle in which she led an army, giving orders from the back of a camel. He opened one of these sites. It gave the whole text. It also told of the flame-haired angel named Qaila who will send men to hell if they don't change their ways or if the try to hurt Aisha. Down below there were comments, dozens of comments, by women, it seemed, from all over the world.

"Bring her on," wrote one. "What took her so long?" Another woman wrote that she lived in Damascus and hoped that Damascus would be her first stop. Someone wrote back, "Never fear. She is coming. Her words will soon ride the lightning."

Even this angel had a website about her. Its first comment to this angel was, "We're with you, Qaila. When do we start kicking ass?"

Stupid women.

He was about to slam the laptop shut when his eye caught the user name of person who answered the woman from Damascus. The user name was Nikram102. This name seemed familiar. Where else had he seen it? Ah, yes. Among the emails that were sent to Bernice. He rolled the mouse and returned to that list. No, not there. Try the ones that she'd meant to delete.

And there it was. Nikram102 at a server called Hotmail. When he opened it, Mulazim squealed aloud with delight. It read:

Oh, please don't. Elizabeth would kill me. I only emailed that one girl at the school. She'd been nice to me. She was helping me lose weight. I promised that I'd let her know how I was doing. I told her and I said that we're all still together. Yes, I mentioned Aisha's birthday and Rasha's new kitten and that Elizabeth is back with Martin again, but only because these are happy things to say and I couldn't see how it could hurt. I did not say where we are or anything like of that. I promise I won't email her again.

She'd signed it "Niki"

Niki. Short for Nikram. He should have guessed it. Nikram, like Shahla, is a proper Persian name. He scrolled down and saw that beneath this message was the one from Bernice to which Nikram had responded. Bernice had written:

You were told no contact except through me. That meant NO CONTACT EXCEPT THROUGH ME. If you do this again, I WILL tell Elizabeth. The least that will happen is you'll get your butt kicked and she'll take away your computer. More likely, she'll conclude that you can't be trusted and have the Nasreens come and get you. I have a good mind to tell her anyway.

God is great, thought Mulazim. This is gold. True, it's only an email address. Hard to trace to a source, but there might be no need. He can email her from Bernice's machine. He can think of some reason to ask for her address. She will think it is Bernice who is asking.

He slapped his head. Aisha's birthday. Of course. This Bernice would want to send her a card of birthday greetings. Possibly even a gift.

Mulazim could barely contain his excitement. He stood up from the laptop and stepped to Bernice. Leaning close, he shouted into her ear. "Liar," he snapped. "I wish you were still living. I'd show you what you get for lying to me. But see? You didn't fool me. I am Mulazim the Greek. No woman fools Mulazim the Greek."

Bernice dead, however, presents problems.

First things first. What to do with her body? With luck, she won't be missed until Monday morning when she fails to arrive at her desk.

She had one closet that was large enough to accommodate her and the chair. He could drag her. When eventually found, it would be clear that she'd been tortured. By whom? By thieves. Maybe looking for drugs. From what he had heard about the blacks in America, the police, when one is murdered, always think in terms of drugs. He would spend a little time ransacking her house. He would take whatever jewels and money she had and whatever else a robber would take.

And of course her car because he needs a car, but also so it looks like she's away. Wait for dark, get off this island, put some distance between us. Her car was a small SUV painted silver. Made by Ford, it was called a Ford Escape. He'd seen others much like it. It was probably quite common. There would be no urgent need to find another.

Along the way, he would stop at some large shopping center that has many cars in its lot. There, he would steal a new license plate and scrape the tennis school's sticker from her windshield. He would shop for new clothing, American clothing, after noting what other men who shopped there were wearing. Also for binoculars and, of course, for a weapon. A more suitable weapon than is found in a kitchen. Then he would find a motel for the night where he could go through her laptop at his leisure.

Mulazim felt sure that he would find what he needed. He was doing God's work; God would help him. His sheik had said, "You must also use your head." Well he has. Look what he's found. In just one afternoon. And once again, he will be leaving no trail.

But first he would finish his sandwich.

FOUR

The Saudi, Mulazim, had not been alone in dismissing the talk of this prophecy. Most Muslims, men and women, shrugged it off at first hearing. Abbas Mansur, a senior mullah in Iran, had certainly been among them. Now what, he'd wondered? An Islamic Joan of Arc? And she's supposed to show up any day now?

Yes, a young woman. More than that, a quite beautiful and radiant young woman. They never seem to be homely, thought Mansur. But that aside, what is her purpose? Why is she coming? Is she to be the promised Mahdi who'll bring peace to the world by converting all its people to Islam? No, her mission is considerably more specific.

But first, the best part. Who is she, exactly? It's seems that it's none other than Aisha herself. It's the Prophet's favorite wife, his warrior wife, the one who went into battle at his side. The one who led an army, well after his death, against the break-away Shiites. She led it while dressed in white head to toe and perched high on the back of a camel. Called "The Lady of the Camel" ever since.

And now she's back. Reborn. Flesh and blood, or so we're told. And with a whole new agenda. It isn't just Sunni versus Shiite this time. Nor is it merely to correct any other departures from the teachings that Allah made known through her husband. No, it seems that she's gone feminist on us. Aggressively feminist. According to the bloggers who've been spreading the word, she intends to box the ears of all Muslim men who have failed to give our women their due.

Well, if so, she'll have her hands full, thought the mullah.

And coming where? Right here. To the Republic of Iran. Specifically, to its capital, Tehran. Or at least that seemed to be the consensus as to where she planned to make her first stop. But she's definitely coming, says the Internet buzz. Well if so, she certainly took her time getting round to it. The original prophecy that foretold her return is more than nine hundred years old.

Not only old, but obscure in the extreme. He, a scholar of no small repute, could not recall reading or hearing about it even in terms of apocrypha. He'd had to ask an assistant to research it. He'd expected the assistant to come back and report that nine hundred hours was more like it.

But there really was such a prophecy.

The original still existed, written in Berber, or rather in one of that language's dialects no longer in use in written form. It is on a vellum scroll that is stored in the vaults of the old Hassan Mosque in Morocco. Rarely seen, of little interest to historians or scholars. No record of anyone examining the text since Morocco was under French Colonial rule. The only other references that

Mansur could find were by some Sufi mystics a few decades later. These said that she will come when all hope seems lost that Islam will ever regain its old vigor. She will bring a new dawn. She will show the way back. She will do so by raising up Islam's women. Woe to anyone who gets in their way.

But nothing from them since. Not from anyone else either. And yet here it is. And it's everywhere. Worldwide. Wherever there is access to the Internet.

Why, he'd wondered, would a prophecy so long ignored suddenly be a topic in chat rooms? His assistant could think of only one reason. His guess was that someone was researching its author, found a reference to it on Google or wherever and saw that it seemed to foretell, not just Aisha, but also the invention of the internet.

"Look at the language," said his assistant. "She will speak to all nations with words writ on wind. Her words will ride the lightning. They will be as shooting stars.' Whoever found it couldn't help but be struck by the fact that these words fit the internet very nicely."

"Too good not to pass on?"

"But anonymously. This is playing with fire."

Mansur rubbed his chin. "So... we're to believe that Aisha sat back for nine hundred years waiting for technology to make her job easier?"

His assistant could only spread his hands.

He'd asked the assistant, "She's still coming here first?"

"To Tehran? Some still think so, but now most are not sure. It was only that so much of the original traffic seemed to come from one Internet café here."

"The one at Jaam-e Jam Mall? Where our young people congregate?"

The assistant nodded. "In the food court there, yes."

The food court, thought the mullah. With its pizza and burger stalls. Where young singles are allowed to intermingle unmolested. Not legal, strictly speaking, but winked at until lately. And Aisha, according to the language of the prophecy, will be making her move when she reaches full womanhood. What's full womanhood these days? Sixteen or so? Eighteen? That's about the average age of those young singles.

He asked the assistant, "So this started with the mall rats?"

His man blinked. "Excuse me?"

"An American expression. Girls who hang out at malls. Do we now have a patron saint of mall rats?"

The question troubled his assistant. "You would, of course, know better than me... that in Islam we do not have saints."

The mullah made a calming gesture. "It's a joke, my young friend. Just a figure of speech. Another one would be, 'Let us lighten up a little.' I ask you again. That's where this started?"

The assistant shook his head. "Not started at. Spread from. It popped up one day on several screens at that café. Where from? No way to tell. It's untraceable."

"Like most urban legends," said the mullah.

"Not many urban legends cause this much excitement. Young people all over our region these days are arguing about where she ought to come first. They discuss what regimes have held women back the most. The Saudis seem to be the primary target, but some think she'll hit us all at once."

"Good," said the mullah. "Let her knock herself out. Let's not waste any more of our time on this."

Abbas Mansur was no doctrinaire zealot. He was known to have an open and inquisitive mind, respected even by the reformists. A former diplomat, a scholar, widely traveled and an athlete. He coached soccer and basketball, he skied and he fenced. His eyes, blue and piercing, were his dominant feature. They suggested wry wit and intelligence. But for all his intelligence, he had grossly underrated the impact that this prophecy would have.

What began as a trickle some three months before had turned into a flood, a tsunami. It had not only swept across all of Iran, it now seemed the talk of the whole Muslim world. Women, all over, were spreading the word that the day of "Hislam" was coming to an end and having a grand old time doing so. The Council of Guardians, which he currently chaired, was demanding that action be taken.

He'd asked, "What sort of action? We need only to debunk it. It's a spurious prophecy. No one's coming."

"And yet it keeps spreading. It must be stopped."

"Stopped how? Mass arrests? Let's try not to go crazy. It will stop soon enough when she fails to appear. It's a fad. A passing fancy. Nothing more."

First Danish cartoons and now this, thought Mansur. An under-reaction would be nice for a change. So would a president of Iran, for a change, who doesn't antagonize the whole western world every time he steps up to a microphone. Calm down. Give this time to blow over.

But the fancy didn't seem to be passing. If anything, it was picking up momentum every day and not only among the young and restless. Groups of women, all ages, gathering in public. Not really demonstrating. Simply waiting and praying. In doing so, defying their husbands and fathers. Enduring taunts from the crowds that they attract. All those women risking being pelted or worse. Crowds egged on, in some cases, by demagogue clerics, but most often by reporters with video cameras. Reporters start more riots than clerics.

He'd placed a call to Colonel Aram Jalil inviting him over to shoot a few baskets in the schoolyard down the street from his office. Jalil was with Savama, the secret police, but a fair man, a thoughtful man, not a zealot like some. The colonel knew that when Mansur said, "Let's go shoot some hoops," it really meant "Let's talk in private." Both knew that it was almost impossible to eavesdrop past the sound of a ball being dribbled.

Mansur got there first, wearing sneakers and sweats with the ball that he kept in his office. Four young men were using the opposite court. They nodded their respect, but kept their distance. Jalil arrived wearing street clothes, a gym bag in hand. Mansur dribbled as the colonel laced up his sneakers. He asked him, "This prophecy. How serious?"

"The coming of Aisha?" Jalil let out a breath. "It's grown far beyond what I'd thought possible," he answered. "I would say it's very serious indeed."

"And they're actually starting to believe that she is coming?"

"Not starting," said Jalil. "Tens of thousands already. And not coming; they think that's she's already come. They believe that the prophecy has been fulfilled. Some, through anonymous postings on the web, have claimed that they have seen her, spoken to her, described her and now have flocked to her banner."

The mullah grunted. "One-upmanship. That's how stories grow. There's always someone who's ready to embellish them."

"All the same, some believe them," said Jalil.

"Some always do, but what of the rest? Are they actually convinced that she's reborn as their champion? Or do they only wish it to be so?"

"If you ask how many wish it," said the colonel from Savama, "the number must be tens of millions. I judge this from the hits on all those internet sites and the comments that many of them post. Not just here. It is everywhere. Name almost any country. And it isn't only Muslim women either."

Mansur arched an eyebrow. "Oh? And who else?" He arched the ball toward the basket. It missed.

Jalil took the rebound and dribbled in turn. "Well, of course, all the feminists. The usual activists. But the bulk of them seem to be ordinary women. They give their names and their ages. They are mostly young women. And many of them write, 'I am not a Muslim, but… ' They say if it's not true, it ought to be true. They have seen what's happening here on TV. They are cheering our women on."

The mullah had seen the TV coverage himself. Programs beamed down by satellite, impossible to jam. Groups of women, sometimes scores of them, holding candlelight vigils. They gather at the Jaam-e Jam Food Court where the word of her coming first appeared. They gather hoping that she'll turn up there in the flesh. They stand, their lips moving in silent prayer. Others stand chanting her name.

Many, especially the youngest among them, brazenly baring their heads. Doing so to show off an unusual hairdo that's lately become all the rage. Hair cut short at the nape and shaped like a helmet. Shaped like, well... a female warrior's helmet, the hair flanging out at its base. Some of them being beaten for refusing to disperse. Some of them being dragged off.

Dragged off by whom? Sometimes by male relatives. By fathers and brothers who are against what they're doing or are at least fearful of their safety. Beaten by whom? The Basij Militia. The same ones who show up at every student demonstration and start, as they put it, "giving moral advice," by smashing heads and knees left and right. Always easy to pick out with their green and yellow headbands. And otherwise referred to on those satellite broadcasts as "Iran's version of the Hitler Youth."

Not entirely fair, thought Mansur, but close enough. He'd been trying for a year to get that bunch disbanded. It was high on his list of priorities.

But here again something different is happening as well. Here and there we see some of them facing off against each other. Some seem, if not in sympathy, at least more reluctant to club defenseless women and their daughters. A few have even prevented some of Colonel Jalil's men from taking down names and addresses.

Jalil faked past Mansur and drove to the basket. His layup went in off the backboard. He passed the ball to Mansur.

Mansur said to the colonel, "You have a wife and a daughter. What do they say about this?"

"To me? Not much. They are mindful of my office. But they certainly speak to each other. Only yesterday, I heard them at my daughter's computer. My daughter was surfing the prophecy sites. New ones appear every day. I heard her marvel at how big this was growing."

"With pleasure?"

"With… concern."

"Please speak freely," said the mullah.

The colonel wet his lips. "She's enjoying it, yes. It's my wife who is concerned. I heard my daughter say, 'This is really getting good.' My wife replied, 'No, this is already trouble. It's going to get some girls your age killed.'"

The mullah frowned. He shot from several feet beyond the key. The ball went through the net cleanly. Then came polite applause from the opposite court. Mansur acknowledged it with a grin and a wave. He asked Jalil, "Has that happened?"

The colonel sighed. While dribbling, he answered, "We don't know, but I would think so. Some might have been killed by their husbands or their fathers. Honor killings happen. They are seldom reported. As you've seen, however, there are many who've been beaten. Dozens arrested in this city alone. Hundreds more have gone into hiding or they've fled across the border into Kurdish Iraq. Other women, sympathizers, are helping them to flee."

"What other women? The Nasreen Society?"

"That bunch? Not this time. Surely not on this scale. The Nasreens couldn't handle such numbers."

Perhaps not, thought the mullah. But they, too, must be enjoying it. They've been helping Muslim women flee to the west for at least ten years, maybe longer.

The colonel had fed the ball back to Mansur. He said, "Let's see you hit two in a row." Mansur tried. It hit the rim, bounced twice and dropped in.

"Luck," the colonel muttered. "That's why no applause." He added, "But no, this doesn't seem organized. It's just women at random protecting each other. I say 'just women,' but I should include men. Many fathers have sent their daughters away in order to keep them out of trouble."

"And what of them?" asked Mansur. "I mean, men in general. What has been their reaction to the prophecy?"

"Some scoff. Most are patient. They think, as you thought, that this will soon run its course without lasting harm being done. But some call it heresy and, as my wife fears, they are demanding the deaths of all who spread it."

The senior mullah smiled wearily. "Including some on the Council. They are always demanding somebody's death. Mostly, it falls on deaf ears."

The colonel hit with a fade-away jumper. He answered, "True. But only mostly."

Mansur asked, "And you? What do you believe?"

"Our faith does not teach that the dead can return. On the day of judgment, yes, but not before."

"Nice dodge," said the mullah. "Now please speak your mind."

The colonel paused for a moment, choosing his words, all the time dribbling the ball. "Once, in America, I dined at the home of a friend who left Iran when the Shah was deposed. He'd settled in Los Angeles, got married, had children. Nice woman, good Muslim, old Persian family. On the wall of her kitchen, I saw a little sign. It read, 'If Mama Ain't Happy, Ain't Nobody Happy.' There, it was a joke. Here, it isn't. Not now."

Mansur gestured for the ball. He said, "Go on."

"Any society is made up of families. I think this prophecy could well turn ours upside down if we don't find its source and discredit it."

"But we know its source. It's twelfth century Berber. And the Berbers were Sunni; that's what make this so strange. Why should Shiites believe an obscure Sunni prophecy about a female messiah?"

"Because they have one and we don't?"

"I'm serious, Aram."

"Well, then, Shiite or Sunni, she would still be sent by God."

Mansur took another long shot and missed. He said, "If so, yes. That would blur the distinction. Still, it's so old. Forgotten even by the Sunnis."

"Until someone rekindled it," said the colonel. "Who and why?"

Mansur repeated his assistant's opinion. Someone with a computer. Time on his or her hands. An avalanche starts with a snowflake. But the colonel was doubtful. He stood shaking his head.

Mansur asked, "You think it's more? Part of some larger scheme?"

"If it is, I think it's brilliant. Utterly brilliant. No troops. No invasions. Just sit back and wait. Help our women to decide that they 'ain't happy' either. Give them a leader to rally behind. If that leader is a ghost who can't be found, so much the better. I'm surprised no one's thought of this before."

"And who are these conspirators?" asked the mullah. "The Americans?"

The colonel rocked one hand. "There are those who suspect so. The prophecy says that she will come from the west. All that's west of Morocco is America."

"But you're not so sure?"

"Too subtle for them. This is not shock and awe. This would be someone very clever, very patient."

"Some other government?" asked Mansur.

"Or some company," Jalil answered. "Don't rule out Big Oil. All those companies are governments unto themselves."

"Their objective being…?"

"Money, of course. In the end, it's always profit. Money and the power that comes with it. But they can be patient the way vultures are patient. First, lay the groundwork. Create unrest. Create distraction. Someone always takes advantage of distraction."

Mansur nodded. He said thoughtfully, "Confusion to thine enemies."

"Beg pardon?"

"Jewish bible. It's just full of good advice."

"So now you think it's Jews?"

Mansur winced. He said, "That's the last place I'd look. Why? Because once we start blaming Jews, our minds tend to slam shut. Let's keep them open."

"Fine, but you're right about confusion," said Jalil. "We're so busy keeping an eye on these women that we don't have time for much else. Bear in mind that our leaders all have wives and daughters. What authority will they have if they start being smirked at? You know what it's like? A fifth column."

The mullah demurred. "Let's not go overboard. That phrase refers to an enemy within. I really don't think we're quite there yet."

"Your own wife. Is she so docile? Mine isn't. Not of late. Women nag. They cajole. It has always been so. On the whole, however, they accept male authority. But this is new. You've seen their defiance. These smirks, if not stopped, become open contempt and contempt leads to open rebellion. Already, on the internet, some are promising vengeance against men who have treated them badly."

"Not waiting for Aisha?"

"They feel sure she won't mind."

"Have any acted?" asked the mullah.

"A few that we know of. And a few is all it takes. As it is, many men who've mistreated their women are learning to sleep with one eye open."

"Such men should," said Mansur. "They should reap what they sow. But I hear you. It's a much wider problem."

"One that you're now charged with stopping," said the colonel.

"Stopping? But how? By breaking more heads? That makes them hope that she's coming even more."

"We could try shutting down all those Internet cafes. That is where many first learned of the prophecy. That is where they discuss it and spread it."

The mullah raised the ball on one finger and spun it. "It's not just the cafes. Like it or not, the whole world is wired. One can't shut down orbiting satellites. In any case, the damage has already been done if so many hope that the prophecy is true. The question now is how best to contain it."

He let the ball drop. He caught it on his instep. He launched toward the backboard. Once again, it dropped through the hoop. More applause from the opposite court.

"You're beginning to annoy me," said Jalil

Mansur laughed. He said, "Sorry. Pure chance. First time ever."

He retrieved the ball and stood dribbling it thoughtfully. He said, "The best way to contain it is to prove that it's a fraud. This female messiah or mahdi... whatever... didn't come when the

Berber said she would come and she isn't coming now either. So let's… What's wrong? Your hand is rocking again."

"Nor did Jesus," said the colonel, "but the Christians still expect him. And it's been two thousand years, not nine hundred."

A valid point, thought Mansur, but not quite the same thing. Jesus wasn't known to have a feminist agenda. On the other hand, his mother seems to keep turning up. Her face appears in stains coming through cement walls and on grilled cheese sandwiches sold on E-Bay. And if his mother, why not Mary Magdalene? If, as some claim, she was married to Jesus, maybe she'll show up flashing her ring. At the very least, she might have something to say about being called a harlot all these years.

Jesus' mother, Mary Magdalene and now Islam's Aisha. Interesting that they're all women.

Jalil gestured toward his gym bag. "I brought two beers. Still cold. One for you, one for me."

This phrasing told Mansur that his was non-alcoholic. It said Jalil's might be as well, but don't ask. Mansur said, "You go ahead. I'd best wait."

As colonel Jalil popped his can, Mansur said, "Very well, Aram. Let's go with your premise. Let's assume a larger scheme, a conspiracy. Let's say some western entity resurrected this prophecy and saw it as a way to destabilize our region at no cost to itself should it fail. If so, let's track them down, flush them out in the open."

"And make the women with their candles feel foolish," said the colonel.

"Do the Christians feel foolish? Let's tread carefully on that one. Unless we want to sleep with one eye open as well. Ridicule is never forgiven."

"Ah, yes. And if Mama ain't happy…"

"Get to work. Find the source. It had to start somewhere. Contact all the Islamic intelligence services. They'll be just as keen to track this as we are."

"Some even more so," said Colonel Jalil. "The Saudi Hasheem is already on the case. They blame us, by the way, for letting this spread to them. Some even think it was deliberate."

Mansur sniffed. "The Hasheem? The crushers of evil? One could not call that bunch an intelligence service. Misfits. Fanatics. Otherwise unemployable."

"No less dangerous however. They hate everyone."

"Have any shown up here?"

"At least two. We have them," said Colonel Jalil. "We're not treating them gently. If there are more, we'll soon know. Do I have a free hand in this matter?"

Mansur shook his head. "Only with the Hasheem. Beyond them, again, let's try not to go crazy. All I want is some detective work for now. While you're at it, I'll do a little digging of my own. I think I'll call my old friend, Sadik."

"Sadik? Which Sadik? You mean Rajib Sadik?"

"Of Hamas. I take it you know of him."

"Yes, of course," said the colonel, "but why should he help? Hamas has been no friend of ours."

"Not ours," said the mullah, "but maybe still mine. This prophecy business must have touched him as well. I'd bet that Sadik, who seems to know almost everyone, has already begun looking into it. He'd have started with the Nasreens."

"He knows them?"

"As I've said..."

"He knows everyone. I heard you. May I ask... how is it that you know Sadik?"

"I knew him before I became what I am and before he became what he is."

"You mean before he became so big in Hamas?"

"I knew him before he was even Sadik." The mullah paused. "You say we've put dozens in prison?"

"Mostly those from that Internet café at the Food Court. We think some of them know a lot more than they're saying about how this whole business started. We think they know who sent those first prophecy messages."

"You mean originally? Or someone who simply passed them on."

"The latter, mostly likely," said Colonel Jalil. "Not the ultimate source. But perhaps, just perhaps, a link to that source. A name. A location. One more piece of the puzzle."

"They're not talking?" asked the mullah.

"They will," said the colonel.

"But why haven't they already? They would only have to say, 'You can't blame us for this. We can't help what shows up on our screens. We didn't believe it; we were just talking about it. No one thought that it would get us in trouble.'"

"They can't tell us," said the colonel, "that they don't believe it when they've been telling others that it's true. Anyway, it's already much too late in the game. I've just finished saying how far this has spread. But what other lead do we have?"

The mullah pondered for a moment. "These are all young women?"

"College age. Some younger."

"Sadik has a soft spot for women in trouble. Perhaps I can entice him to fly in for a visit. Let him question a few of them. See what he can learn."

"If you say so," said the colonel, "but why should they talk to him?"

"People do. People trust him. Including the Nasreens. And they, as you'd imagine, would be crazy to trust any other Muslim male that I can think of."

"So?" The colonel shrugged. "What's so special about Sadik?"

"A great many things."

"I meant to the Nasreens."

"I suppose because Sadik's wife is one of them."

FIVE

On a Saturday evening, fully half a world away, Charles Haskell rose to add a log to the fire that crackled on the shore of a shimmering lake. The shimmer came from the light of a hundred such fires that burned along its quarter-mile length. A circle of men sat at each of those fires. Up to a dozen at some. Only three or four at others.

Haskell could hear the soft hum of their voices, broken sometimes by laughter, sometimes by song. He stood for a moment absorbing it all, a smile of satisfaction on his face. "We really do run the world," he mused aloud to the others. "I mean, think of it. Just us. Just the men at all these fires. It still boggles my mind, but it's a fact."

There were five at the fire that Haskell was tending. Those in his group were younger than most. All five were in their late forties, early fifties. All were dressed casually, windbreakers and slacks. All sat barefoot. All but one were bareheaded. Only Haskell himself had the toned and rugged look of a man who spent much time outdoors. Two of the men were not members of the club. They had come as guests. They had arrived that afternoon.

"The whole world?" asked Howard Leland, one of the two guests. "I'd have to call that a bit of a stretch."

"Oh, would you? Look around you. Look at all those fires," said the chairman of Trans-Global Oil & Gas. "That's the greatest concentration of power and wealth that has ever, I mean ever, been seen in one place. Especially now, with world markets imploding. No government on earth has more influence."

"Ours included?" asked Leland, who was senior in that government. A cabinet officer. Secretary of State.

"Ours especially," said Haskell. "Who put it in office? It serves at our pleasure, for our purposes."

The third man in their group was a banker. He was British. He could see that Leland had taken offense. He said to Leland, "The first day at this gathering is always a bit heady. But you'll find that it settles quite nicely after that." He said to Haskell, "Charles, you really must mind your words. Howard Leland has never been anyone's puppet. I'm sure that you were not suggesting otherwise."

"Of course not," said Haskell. "He's one of us. Or he will be. My apologies, Howard. Want a beer?"

Leland declined. He said, "Later, perhaps." He'd begun to regret having come.

"And, okay," said Haskell. "Maybe not the whole world. But you'll see before you leave that I'm not so far off. Leave out China for the moment. We'll get to them later. The Mideast and its oil is a work in progress, but well underway. And leave out all the countries that have nothing we want. I should have said we run the world that matters."

Leland made himself smile. "That clears it up. Thank you."

"Yes, lighten up, Charles," said the fourth man at their fire. He said to Leland, "We're not really so full of ourselves. Give it time and I think you'll be pleasantly surprised. You'll see former presidents letting their hair down, behaving as they did in their frat house days. Senators, statesmen, all doing the same. I'd imagine you already know many of them. Do you?"

The man who asked that question was the media mogul. He owned more than a hundred newspapers worldwide and some seventy-five TV stations. Leland answered dryly, "I'd imagine."

"Of course you do," said the mogul. "Those in government, surely. But one can never have too many friends in high places. We'll see if we can't broaden your reach."

The fifth man at their fire was a Saudi. A prince. Unlike the others who were tall, clean-shaven and lean, he was squat and he was fleshy with a beard in need of trimming. He formed a lump where he sat. The image was enhanced by the bath towel he'd brought which he wore draped over his head and his shoulders. He was staring at the fire. He sat rocking back and forth and he'd not said a word. He had acknowledged Leland's presence with a nod.

Haskell had taken Leland aside. He said, "Don't mind him. He's in a bit of a funk. Some problem involving his daughter back home. He won't discuss it. Be thankful."

"I assume he's in oil?"

"What Saudi prince isn't?"

"How high up, though? A minister?"

"Oh, something much better."

"Higher?"

"Way lower. But that's what makes him useful. He hates all the princes who have more than he has. And he knows where a lot of them keep it."

The banker overheard. He said, "Charles, that can wait. For now, let's enjoy this lovely evening."

The proper name of the place was The Bohemian Grove. More commonly, and by custom, it was simply called, 'The Camp." In terms of ambience, however, and in terms of creature comforts, it was no more a camp than Camp David. But the surroundings were unspoiled. Dense forests. Pristine lakes. California's Russian River ran through it. The Grove covered almost three thousand acres some forty miles north of Sacramento.

Its expanse was well patrolled; its gates aggressively guarded. The odd paparazzo had managed to slip in, but was quickly discovered and rudely ejected after watching his equipment being smashed. Members were forbidden to discuss what took place here. No interviews given, no questions answered, not even concerning the most ordinary activities. Guests of members were required to pledge silence as well.

All contact with the outside world was limited during one's stay at the Grove. Members and guests were allowed to receive mail, but no phone calls, barring genuine emergencies. Cell phones were forbidden, surrendered upon entering. Certainly no cameras or recording devices. No TV in the guest rooms. Not even radios. These were seen as frivolous distractions. Books could not be brought in, but books were available. These, however, were limited to the business of the club, its history and its traditions. Laptop computers were allowed for some reason, but only if their internet access was disabled. One assumes that if aliens were to invade, an announcement would be posted on the bulletin board. Otherwise, it might go unnoticed.

No bodyguards either, no personal security, or at least not within the camp proper. Guards who normally traveled with members and guests were housed in special quarters outside the main gate. Among them were the two who had accompanied Leland, armed officers of the Diplomatic Security Service. Reduced to sitting and waiting until he emerged and having his car at the ready.

The occasion was the annual two-week retreat of the members of the Bohemian Club. It was held every year in late July starting on the third Sunday of the month. This year, more than twenty-two hundred had gathered. The members converged from all over the nation and from some fifteen other countries. Members of at least five years' standing were permitted to bring one guest each. Guests could mix freely in social activities, but could not attend certain private sessions. Few guests felt deprived by this limitation. It was thought an honor just to be on grounds in the company of the great and the powerful.

Howard Leland had considerably more stature than many. He'd been a career diplomat who'd risen through the ranks in embassies throughout Western Europe. He'd been named as Acting Secretary of State when the woman who'd held that office had a stroke that left her with minimal brain function. He would probably never be confirmed in full. Careerists seldom were. They were rarely party loyalists. That was why he'd been more than a little surprised to be asked to attend as Haskell's guest. He was a lame duck. His influence was limited. How did Haskell hope to profit by inviting him?

Haskell was indeed a major player in oil. His control of Trans-Global was absolute. Infamous even by the standards of that industry, Leland thought him to be a man without conscience and had already said as much to his face. Far from being offended, Haskell seemed pleased to hear that he was known to stand out from the pack.

Leland, being curious as to Charles Haskell's motives, and more so about the Bohemians at large, accepted, although not without misgivings. He'd cleared his schedule, but only through Wednesday, not for the full two-week session.

Haskell had told him that the media mogul would be one of their "bunk-mates" as he'd put it. "Can't hurt," he'd said, "to have this guy as a friend. You sure as hell don't want to be on his shit list." The British banker would also be a part of their circle. His bank had branches throughout the Mideast and it had funded Trans-Global's rise to prominence. "The guy is a walking ATM," said Haskell. "Except, trust me, he spits out more than twenties."

The Saudi prince was there as the guest of the banker. "He's a dimwit," said Haskell, "but that's okay; he's our dimwit. Or he will be by the time this session's over."

"And me?"

"And you, what?"

"Am I to be… yours?"

"Howard, we're Bohemians. One for all. All for one. Relax. There's no way for you to lose by having come here."

The media mogul said, "I'll take one of those beers. The letting down of hair begins now." He opened their cooler and passed cans of Heineken to Leland, to the banker and to Haskell. Leland saw that none had been offered to the Saudi. He thought he understood why. An observant Muslim. But not even an iced tea or a cola?

Haskell read Leland's mind; he said, "We're not being rude. We just don't indulge his pretence of abstinence. The Prince's drink of choice is bourbon, straight up. He'll catch up in private, never fear."

The Saudi had to have heard this, but he barely reacted. He let out a sigh and kept rocking.

The mogul said to the banker, "Here we are, away at camp, and we're sitting round a fire. Shouldn't someone be telling ghost stories?"

"No ghosts here," said the banker. "Can't get in unless invited. But we could summon Satan if you like."

The mogul smiled. He said to Leland, "I assume you've heard the rumors. Devil-worship and such. I never cease to be amazed at what people think goes on here. The damnedest thing is that some of these stories have appeared in my own publications."

"Then they must be true," said the banker with a nod. "We all know how unbiased your editors are."

"I'd have a talk with a few of them were it not for the rules. I'm forbidden to correct them. I can't tell them a thing."

The banker said, "More's the pity. I think people should know. Not all of it, of course. Not all that we do. But it might be a comfort to them to know that their world is in capable hands."

Leland thought to himself, Here we go again.

Haskell said, "What he means, although he's too polite to say it, is that unlike the mass of our elected civil servants, we don't have our heads up our asses."

"I liked the polite version better," said Leland.

"Oh, he didn't mean you," the British banker said quickly. "Nor were you elected. You were appointed on merit. You are nonetheless part of a political system that limits, even thwarts, your effectiveness. But perhaps we might help you to focus your energies where they will do the most good."

"For whom, sir?"

"For the world, sir. And indeed for ourselves. Truth be told, we do run it. Or we run a great deal of it. We run it better and more profitably than it's ever been run by anyone since…"

"The robber barons?" asked Leland.

"I was going to say the Romans. They brought law. They brought order. But you say 'robber barons' as if it were a pejorative. I think you know your own history better than that. The robber barons, as you call them, were the men who built your country. It certainly wasn't the government. It was they who built the railroads and the steel mills and all else. They amassed great wealth, but they used it well. They endowed universities, hospitals, libraries. All considered, they gave better than they got."

The media mogul added, "As do most of us, Howard. And none of us set out to have this sort of power. Once achieved, however, it's a burden we've accepted. We regard it as a trust. A sacred trust."

"Precisely," said the Saudi, nodding under his towel. This was the first word he had spoken. He added "It is sacred because God has willed it."

Charles Haskell rolled his eyes. He told the Saudi, "Not here."

The Saudi looked at him, blinking. He did not understand.

Haskell said to the Saudi, "That will of God business. Do not say that here. Someone might think you actually mean it."

"But, I do," said the Saudi. "All that happens is God's will."

"And that's a handy excuse for not making things happen. That's what we're here for. Try to keep that in mind. The only will that matters in this place is our own. Save that crap for the rag-heads back home."

The Saudi's eyes turned cold for the briefest of instants, but he forced them to brighten. He grinned. He said to Howard Leland who was visibly ill at ease, "You see that I am smiling? These men are my friends. What is friendship without a little pulling of the leg?"

Haskell said to Howard Leland, "We, of course, applaud his piety. He's been known, however, to leave it behind when his aircraft departs Saudi soil."

"He leaves his taste in women along with it," said the banker. He nudged the Saudi with his elbow. "Scandinavians, correct?"

"I am not undemocratic. English girls are good too."

"As long as they're not much older than twelve," said Haskell while winking at the media mogul.

"No, I think you mean his bourbon," said the media mogul. "It's his bourbon that has to be older than twelve. A lowly Dutch beer is beneath him."

The Saudi said to Howard Leland, "More pulling of my leg. A good Muslim does not drink either beverage."

"Except when no one's looking," added Charles Haskell. "Drop by his room, you'll find a case of Jack Daniels. I should know. I had his bar stocked with it."

The Saudi shrugged. "You have a saying. When in Rome. For me, this is Rome. I might take an occasional sip." He said to Leland, "But I will not deny that I chafe at the policy that requires all here to be celibate. We are men in full vigor. Our needs are our needs. Did you know that no women are provided?"

"I... don't recall that it came up," Leland answered.

"Too late now," said the Saudi. "We are both out of luck. The only women who have ever been allowed on these grounds are the cooks and the housemaids, none younger than fifty. I have sacrificed much to be here with good friends."

Haskell gave Leland a look that said, "Perhaps you now see what I meant." To the Saudi, he said, "I'll have a sheep sent to your room. Beyond that, your friends will make your sacrifice worthwhile. You're going to be glad that you came."

A cell phone chirped. Its sound was muffled. It chirped again. All heads turned to the Saudi. The sound came from somewhere on his person. Haskell looked at him, glaring. "Did you bring a phone?"

"Do not worry," said the prince as he cupped both hands over it. "I have been careful to keep it concealed."

"Concealed? The damned thing's ringing. Shut it off."

"Yes, at once."

The Saudi fumbled for the phone that he'd secreted in his jacket. He silenced it and he peered at the read-out. He chewed his lip. He was visibly nervous. "It is one of my cousins. This must be an urgent matter. He knows not to call me unless it is urgent." He started to tap out a number.

Haskell said, "Stop right there."

"You are right. I will wait."

"No, what you'll do is walk down to the shore and throw that thing into the lake. You will try to do so in a casual manner. Try to look as if you're skipping a stone."

The Saudi drew a breath. His color rose.

The banker said, "Better yet, throw it into the fire."

Haskell said, "No, because the battery might explode and, if not, its remnants would be found in the morning." He asked the Saudi, "What else have you brought? What else that I told you not to bring?"

"Only this."

"After you've tossed it, why not take a little swim? Take off all your clothes. It's called skinny-dipping. That's another of this club's traditions."

The Saudi's face went blank. "I… do not understand."

"You've forgotten one rule. Another might have eluded you. A recording device comes to mind."

"You accuse me?" asked the Saudi.

"No, I alert you. Because if you had 'forgotten' that you'd brought such a thing, you'd be out on your ear and me with you."

The banker rose to his feet and unzipped his own jacket. He said to the Saudi, "I could do with a dip. I'd be honored if you'd let me accompany you."

The Saudi stiffened. "To watch me undress?"

"Not at all. It is our custom. It is called the buddy system. We'll wade in together and I'll turn my back. You'll have ample time to make any adjustment that might add to your comfort and ours."

The Saudi hesitated. "I have no such device."

"I believe you," said the banker, "but let's do it all the same. After that, we needn't ever speak of this again. We will continue to nurture the level of trust that I feel is now growing between us."

The Saudi said to Haskell, "This man has good manners."

"He's a beacon to us all. Enjoy your swim."

SIX

Howard Leland watched them go. "A bit hard on him, weren't you?"

"I'm going to take a walk. Care to join me?"

"Saudi men don't undress before other men. And this one's a prince. You've insulted a prince."

"Saudi princes, as you know, are as common as houseflies. There are what, six thousand?"

"Something like that."

"And they have a pecking order. This one's near the bottom. He's been sucking hind tit all his life."

"Even so..."

"And I didn't insult the damned fool," said Haskell. "His honor, such as it is, is intact. One can only offend the honor of an Arab if another Arab is present to hear it. We're all infidels here. By his lights, we don't matter. The insult, therefore, never happened."

"If you say so," said Leland.

"The point is, so would he."

"Still, you seem to have nothing but contempt for this man. Just him? Or toward Saudis on the whole."

Haskell shook his head. "I have no such prejudice. I respect competence wherever I find it. I admire courage in whatever culture. This particular Saudi is possessed of neither virtue. He'd be a dickhead wherever he came from."

"Then what use is he to you? Hind tit and all that."

"That's easy. He knows how to get at the front ones. Did I mention that he is a banker of sorts?"

"I... gathered that money is involved."

"Oh, indeed," said Haskell. "About ten billion dollars, most of it skimmed. It's money that was meant for certain Islamic charities."

"That instead goes to militants? Hamas and the like?"

"Oh, some of it, yes. Far less than you'd think. I'll give you one guess where the bulk of it goes."

"Off-shore banks?"

Haskell nodded. "Numbered accounts."

"Flight money?"

"You betcha. For hundreds of Saudis. It's not just the lesser royals who are stealing and stashing. It's almost anyone who's prospered by sucking up to them. They're all building considerable nest eggs for themselves against the day when that regime is overthrown. The house of Saud has been circling the drain for some time. We could hear a great slurp any time now."

"Are you telling me that this one has access to those funds? And that you now have access through him?"

"Not as we speak, but we're working on that. As to his access, it was all a happy accident. Unlike most of the princes, this one actually has a job. He'd never had one, didn't want one, but they cut his allowance. The top princes get two or three million a month. This one got less than a hundred thousand, but they cut that in half when the Saudi treasury turned out to be a leaking bucket."

"The Saudi treasury? Short of cash?"

"Oil revenues are down, but that's not the half of it. There are all kinds of hands in that till. You'd be surprised. Anyway, to a Saudi prince, anything under a hundred K a month is a burger joint minimum wage. So of course he started wheedling and whining. He got the support of a powerful cleric by offering his tasty young daughter in return. This cleric persuaded the royals to relent. They did so, but only up to a point. They said, 'Okay, he goes back up to the original figure, but in return we want him kept out of our hair.' They gave him a job at Saudi Overseas Charities. They gave him an office and a meaningless title and told him that he had to show up every day. First in every morning, last out every night and don't call us again, we'll call you."

Leland wasn't sure that he understood. "You say he's not very bright."

"Your average poodle is smarter."

"And yet the Saudis trust him with ten billion dollars?"

Haskell smiled. He said, "I'm sure it never crossed their minds. They gave him what amounts to a clerical job. His tasks are insultingly trivial. They gave him a computer for routine correspondence. Some kid had to show him how it works. He hates them for this and he wants to stick it to them. He'd have liked to skim the skimmers, but he didn't know how. He's learning, however. We've provided a tutor. That's his tutor down there splashing with him now."

"The banker?"

"Good cop," said Haskell. "He plays off my bad cop. He's stroking the prince's bruised ego as we speak. He's reminding him of the day, not far off, when all those other princes can't seem to find their stashes and will be coming to him on their knees. But, of course, he won't have it. We will."

"I see. You plan to steal ten billion dollars."

"Howard, most of that money has been stolen to begin with. It's just languishing now in off-shore accounts. I intend to employ it more usefully. But we won't be piggish. Some, we'll even give back, but only in trade for certain services."

"You… do have a labyrinthine mind, don't you, Charles?"

"It's called negotiating from strength. You're familiar with the concept. Come on. Let's go stretch our legs."

SEVEN

Mulazim had driven up the coast for two hours, arriving at the city of Charleston. On its outskirts was a big shopping center. Many stores, many cars in the lot. In the glove compartment of the Ford Escape he'd found a device called a Swiss Army knife that contained several tools folded up. Among these were two different screwdrivers.

Thus equipped, and making sure there were no shoppers nearby, he removed the license plate of the Ford Escape and replaced it with one of a similar design that he took from a neighboring car. The owner of that car had backed into its space and might therefore not notice that his plate was missing before the next morning at the earliest. Mulazim knew better than to simply swap plates. True, a different plate was less likely to be noticed than a space where a plate should have been. But if noticed and reported it would have been easily traced and Bernice might be found inconveniently soon.

He was eager to find a quiet motel so that he could get to work on the laptop. But the stores were right here. He had some shopping to do.

He entered a very large store called a Wal-Mart. There he took some time to observe what sort of clothing men his age wore. On the whole, they seemed to favor short pants and T-shirts and shoes for either running or for boating. No hats except the kind meant for baseball. Some wore jackets intended for golf.

He found everything he needed at this Wal-Mart. He bought pants both short and long; he bought something called gym shoes; he chose shirts with plain colors that wouldn't stand out and that didn't have some stupid design printed on them. He bought a golf jacket the color of sand and another that he couldn't resist because its color was called Hunter Green. He bought a blue cotton sweatshirt that came with a hood and sweatpants of an almost matching color. He had seen other men who were wearing such garments. Loose-fitting, baggy, but baggy was good. Baggy conceals a great deal. Also two baseball caps, one red, one blue, with the emblems, apparently, of popular sports teams. He'd seen people glance at men wearing such caps, but only at the emblem, not so much at the face. Attracting such glances didn't seem a good idea, but the caps might make him seem more American.

Next, still in the Wal-Mart, he bought a video camera. Very small, pocket sized, it also took photos. In the sporting goods section, he bought another knife. The Swiss Army knife was good for some things, but it was unwieldy to open. The one he bought was very flat, no sharp edges, just a point. This knife was intended for throwing. Mulazim had no such skill, but its flatness made it ideal for concealment. No bulges when taped to an arm or a leg.

He would grind a cutting edge later. He bought a whetstone and a pair of binoculars and two different kinds of sunglasses.

He had hoped to buy a shotgun that he could cut down, but the clerk said that the Wal-Mart no longer sells firearms. Another customer, standing near, said to him, "Damn shame," and advised him to go up to Virginia where "our God-given rights still mean something." He rubbed his fingers adding, "And that's where money talks. There's always a gun show somewhere in Virginia. No damned waiting period. Still America up there."

Mulazim understood his meaning. Very well. No shotgun. He would look at a map to see how far is Virginia. But for now he at least had his knives.

He left with his purchases and drove to a motel that he'd passed a mile or two back. He checked in for one night paying cash in advance. No ID was asked for. He made up a name. It's no wonder that so many come here illegally. This country makes it almost too easy.

In his room, the door locked, he opened his laptop. He spent another hour going through Bernice's files, hoping to find something else that might be useful. He found nothing that he recognized as such. He was actually stalling. He realized that. The one thing he had was the email address of this girl from Iran known as Niki. Incidental to this was the knowledge that one of them had a birthday that was fast approaching. He'd been rehearsing in his mind how best to phrase a message asking Niki where a gift could be sent.

But wouldn't Bernice already know that address? The request would be suspicious. It could put them on their guard. They might have some friend back on Hilton Head Island go and verify with Bernice directly.

But it was all he had. He would have to trust in God. He typed in Nikram102 at Hotmail and went about composing a message.

He wrote: "Niki, I pray that this finds that all of you are well. I wish to send birthday wishes to Aisha. Remind me of your address."

He cursed himself. Idiot. This sounds nothing like Bernice. He said a silent prayer before trying again.

He wrote: "Is there any SPECIAL address to which I should send Aisha a gift for her birthday?" He wrote the one word using upper case letters because Bernice liked to do so for emphasis. He signed it "Bernice" and, holding his breath, he clicked the "Send" button and sat back. All he could do now is wait and hope. However not even two minutes went by before the laptop announced a reply.

It read: "No, same address. Just write Aisha, no last name, care of Harrison Whistler, P.O. Box 2625, Belle Haven, VA 23307. If you mail it tomorrow it should get here by Wednesday. We're giving her a sweet sixteen party at a little Italian restaurant we like. And thank you for not telling Elizabeth."

Mulazim's spirits fell. A box number only? In the name, not of this Martin who they were to join, but of someone named Harrison Whistler. He couldn't very well ask her who this man is. But Bernice must have had this address all along. The name would not be unknown to her.

With clenched teeth he wrote, "Is Mr. Whistler there WITH you?"

The answer came promptly. "No, Mr. Whistler is back in Geneva. He came over to help us move into his house. He only uses it when he has business in Washington. You should have seen the two bodyguards that came over with him. But you wouldn't. Not together. Only one at a time. But you never know which one is which because they're twins. They are funny little men. They don't look at all scary. Martin, however, says we shouldn't let that fool us. He says they're very good at their job."

Bodyguards, thought Mulazim? Who is this man if two bodyguards are needed. No matter, however. They are gone.

Mulazim asked her, "But Martin is still with you?" There seemed no more need for upper case.

"Mr. Kessler? Oh, yes. He is more than still with us. Elizabeth won't let him out of her sight. She doesn't like to sit in bars, but he does so she does. She says it is only to make sure he behaves."

Kessler. Martin Kessler. He remembered the name now. The German. An adventurer, known to be reckless. But equally as dangerous as the Black Angel. Make sure he behaves? This does suggest reckless. Like her, he had also worked with the Israelis. The dossier had said the Israelis "among others." These others must include this man, Whistler.

Mulazim sorely wished that he could ask Niki the full address of this house. Would Bernice have asked? It didn't seem likely. Not if all she was given was a Post Office Box. Even so, it seemed reasonable that she would inquire as to its physical description.

He wrote, "Room for six plus three from Geneva? It must be a very big house."

She replied, "Big, but not as big as some in Belle Haven. Some have their own tennis courts. But all four of us have our own rooms and computers so that we can work on our studies. There is also a separate apartment for guests. No tennis, but we do have a beautiful pool. It has a warm waterfall that comes down over rocks and a hot tub for when it gets colder. Mr. Whistler seems to have houses all over. One is a ski lodge in the French Alps. Mr. Kessler says he owns half a mountain. Mr. Kessler has skied there. So, I think, has Elizabeth. Mr. Whistler invited us all to come visit. He says there is snow at the top even now, but Mr. Kessler says we'll wait until there's more."

Enough about skiing. Enough about this Whistler. Mulazim tried to think what else Bernice would ask. Ah, he remembered. "Are you still losing weight?" This was only to keep the talk going.

She answered. "I am trying. Elizabeth thinks I spend too much time at my computer. She wants me to go out and play tennis with them. But they are all too good. Even Rasha can beat me and she is so small. They all try to be nice. They give me easy shots to hit. But I don't think such playing can be much fun for them. For exercise I swim every day."

Tennis, thought Mulazim. A more useful subject. If this house has no tennis court, where do they play?

"Are there tennis courts close by?"

"Several," came the answer. "And they are lit up at night. The closest are over in Marcey Park. Elizabeth prefers to play under the lights because it's cooler and not always so crowded." She added, "Bernice, I must sign off now. I have much to do on my computer before dinner."

Much to do, thought Mulazim? "Not more emails to friends here."

"No, I kept my promise. Only with strangers who don't know where we are. It helps me to work on my English."

"Good night, then. All is well here."

Mulazim used Google to locate Belle Haven. It was part of Alexandria, south of Washington, D.C. He typed in the zip code that Niki had provided. A page of demographics appeared on the screen plus a section describing the community. Very wealthy, it said, but he'd gathered that much. Several senators and congressmen live there. More interesting to him was the number of foreigners. Many diplomats and their families from all over the world. Many foreign businessmen as well. Google says that the number that are foreign born is thought to be one out of four.

So, thought Mulazim, this is why it was chosen. Easy not to stand out if you speak with an accent. Many would surely be from Muslim countries. All the easier not to stand out.

He brought up from Google a map of Belle Haven looking for the place called Marcey Park. He added "tennis" to his search and it popped up at once. Yes, Marcey Park. Courts lit up at night. The little park was described as being off by itself, no houses close by, only woodlands. Good.

That is where he would look for them.

Tomorrow, thought Mulazim, he would drive to Virginia. Tomorrow evening he would be at this Marcey Park watching for who comes to play tennis.

It is good that his journey takes him to Virginia. He remembered what the man at the Wal-Mart had told him. Virginia is the place to buy guns.

Also he would find a new license plate that shows he is no stranger to Virginia.

EIGHT

The media mogul had asked if he might join Haskell and Leland on their walk. "The prince," he said to Haskell, "is about to be undraped. That vision will haunt me if I sit here alone."

As if for emphasis, he shielded his eyes with his hand as they walked past the prince and the banker. There was a dock nearby from which members could fish. A few canoes and a kayak were tied up to it. At the top of its ramp stood a rack of light fly rods.

Haskell led Leland onto the dock. He asked him, "Ever do any fishing?"

"Some. Deep sea. I've hooked a few Marlin."

Haskell sneered. "That's not fishing. That's baiting and waiting. Fly fishing is an art. It takes patience and practice"

"And learning to reel them in slowly," said Leland. "Is this where I learn how you hope to use me?"

"Use you? Not at all. But I will ask a favor. It concerns the activities of someone you know who has done me great harm in the past."

"Um... who?"

"Kessler. Martin Kessler. He's back in this country. I need to know what he's up to."

"Charles... Kessler's dead. He's been dead for more than two years."

"Well, we know better, don't we. He's been in Angola. While there, he thwarted an attempt by my... consortium... to get our fair share of their offshore oil."

"You don't say."

"Reserves at least equal to those of Kuwait. And diamonds. Top quality. Alluvial diamonds. You don't even have to dig. They're on the surface."

"And fought over in a brutal fifteen-year civil war," Leland added. "Which is finally over. They've learned to share among themselves. Thanks in no small part to Martin Kessler."

"And thanks to Kessler... in no small part is it?... our people were expelled from Angola. Some were shipped home in coffins. Some only their heads. I think you know this full well."

Howard Leland shrugged. "You give him too much credit. It seems to me the Israelis had a hand in your misfortune. The Israelis have their own interests in the region, advanced by Yitzhak Netanya's Mossad."

"Quite so. In the diamonds. Less so in the oil. Martin Kessler was Netanya's top dog in Angola. Well, not really. Kessler ran his own show. And guess who got to broker the offshore drilling rights. Kessler's old friend, Harry Whistler."

"My, my," said Leland. "Kessler did get around. You ought to be relieved that he's dead."

Haskell curled his lip. "Don't play games with me, Howard. He's been back in this country for at least three months. I'm told he's reunited with Elizabeth Stride. I have made you aware of my interest in the Saudis. Stride, who has also worked for the Israelis, has killed almost as many Saudis as the clap. I need to know what they're planning."

"You think they're planning to thwart you again? Charles, the word paranoia comes to mind."

Leland, out of the corner of his eye, saw the media mogul make a gesture with his hand. He'd moved his fingers in an up and down motion. He was urging Charles Haskell to go slowly.

Haskell saw the gesture. He chose to ignore it. "They are gathering speakers of Arabic."

"Speakers of Arabic?"

"I'm reliably informed."

"To… get you expelled from the Mideast as well? And then what? Take over? Rule the world?"

Haskell reddened. "This is no joking matter. This country's interests and mine are inseparably related. Are you willing to help me or not?"

"Help you find him and kill him? Is that what you're asking? Over some old grudge and some crackpot suspicion that he sees you as unfinished business?"

Leland saw in Haskell's eyes that that's exactly what he's thinking. He thought he'd best try to defuse this.

He said, "Very well, Charles. I'll tell you what I've heard. Yes, Kessler and Stride are together again, but by all accounts they'd like nothing more than to settle down and try to live in peace."

"Well, it's not as if they've bought a Bed & Breakfast in Vermont. They've..." Haskell caught himself. He quickly switched gears. He asked, "Why the speakers of Arabic?"

"That part makes no sense. Stride herself is fluent in Arabic. If you're asking are they plotting some grand scheme against the Saudis, I think I can assure you that they'd have no interest. Kessler avoids that part of the world and Stride has had quite enough of it."

"Well, Kessler's plotting something. What else could it be?"

"Not your death. You'd already be dead."

"What about Roger Clew, your Director of Intelligence?"

"What about him, Charles?"

"Has he been in touch with Kessler?"

"Charles... I'd have no way of knowing."

"You wouldn't? Clew reports to you, does he not?"

"He does. When I need to know something."

"Need? Or choose?"

"Well, that would depend. But now that we're clear on what I do and don't know, what else can I do for you, Charles?"

Haskell felt his jaw tightening. He made an effort to control it. He said, "We can do a great deal for each other. Especially if you became a member of this club. I assume that you appreciate the many benefits thereof."

Leland raised an eyebrow. "Are you offering to propose me?"

"I've been thinking about it."

"I'm speechless. No, I'm not. I do have a question. I probably know at least three hundred members. Explain to me why I need you."

"To apply? You don't. To be accepted? You do."

"You're… saying, I take it, that you could have me blackballed. What a warm, cozy feeling that gives me."

The media mogul spoke. "If I might butt in…"

Leland said to him, "Thank you, but I think I've got the picture." He said, "Charles, I don't often use indelicate language, but I think you should finish our walk by yourself. Find a nice quiet spot and go fuck yourself."

Haskell's head had turned before Leland finished speaking. He said, distractedly, "Wait. Hold that thought."

His attention had been drawn to the edge of the lake. He'd heard the voice of the banker. "Put that away, damn it." Haskell saw that both men had stripped down to their briefs, but that the prince had kept that stupid towel on his head. The banker had already waded in to his waist. The prince had held back, in only to his knees, and he had one hand under the towel. Haskell realized that the prince must be using his cell phone. He was probably returning that earlier call after being forbidden to do so.

Whatever the subject, it was clearly upsetting. The prince's voice and his manner were anguished. The prince waved the banker off and turned back toward dry land with the banker now sloshing in pursuit. The prince's voice rose in pitch; he was shouting in Arabic. Several heads at other fires were turning.

Haskell strode from the jetty toward the two men. He hissed to the banker, "Shut him up. Grab that phone." The banker reached the prince and snatched the towel away. The prince lost his footing and fell backward. The banker pried the phone from his hand and turned to wade into deeper water. The prince splashed after him, but he was too late. The banker gave the cell phone a Frisbee-like toss and it plunked some fifty feet out. The prince, distraught, began wailing, but in English. He seemed to be trying to persuade the banker why he must have that now sunken phone. With one hand, he was stabbing at the eastern horizon, in the approximate direction of his homeland. With the other, he was tearing at his hair.

The banker got him to lower his voice, but the prince was no less distraught. The banker left him in the water and waded ashore where he bent to snatch up his clothing. Haskell called to him, "Well? What was that all about?"

The banker replied, while stepping into his trousers, "Family problems. Bad news from home."

Haskell motioned the banker back up toward their fire. Howard Leland and the mogul joined him there.

"It's his daughter," said the banker, still dressing. "I knew that she'd run off. That was more than three months ago. Last he'd heard she'd got to France, safely out of the country. He's had people looking for her ever since."

Haskell asked, "That's it? His cousin called him here for that? Run off how? You mean as in eloped?"

"On the contrary. She'd run off to avoid a forced marriage."

Haskell nodded. Then to Leland, "To that cleric I mentioned."

"The cousin," said the banker, "is in charge of the search. He had enlisted the cleric and his heretic hunters. Are you familiar with the Hasheem? Well, apparently, the daughter's now been traced to this country and she's learned, don't ask me how, that they're hot on her trail. She'd already warned them against coming after her. She'd backed up the warning with some kind of threat. The prince has just learned that she's made good on the threat. As you've seen, it got quite a reaction."

"He didn't say what is?"

"Only that he wishes he'd killed her at birth."

"Young runaway Muslims," said the media mogul. "There seems to be more and more of that lately. It's on all the Islamic news wires. And not just daughters either. Wives as well. There's some sort of prophecy making the rounds that's emboldened them to kick up their heels."

"A prophecy about what?"

"About Mohammed's favorite wife. His warrior wife. It says that she will be, or has been, reborn. It says she's coming back with a fiery sword to right the wrongs that have been done to Muslim women."

"Actually," said the mogul, "it's not her with the sword. A female angel's coming with her to protect her."

Haskell tossed a hand. Fairy tales didn't interest him. He could have done without the distraction. "This girl," he asked, "how could she have gotten out? Saudi women can't even leave their homes unescorted. How could this one have made it to France, let alone get into this country?"

Howard Leland answered, "They've been getting smuggled out. And it isn't just lately; it's been going on for years. There's a sort of underground railroad that does it."

The media mogul asked, "Is that the Nasreen Society?"

Leland nodded. "You know of it?"

"I'm in the news business."

Leland said to Haskell, "The Nasreens are a Muslim feminist group. Not just advocates; they're more like a spy ring. They provide safe houses, new identity papers to women who seek their assistance. Based in France, at first, but now they're all over. They've resettled, I don't know, perhaps a thousand young women. Most simply want the freedom to make their own lives, but quite a few have opted to join the Nasreens. I think we're going to see a lot more of it."

"All Saudis?" asked Haskell.

"By no means," said the mogul, "although they top the list. Iran's a close second. Pakistan's next. Quite a few of them come from prosperous families. They must pay up the nose to get out."

Leland shook his head. He said, "They needn't be rich. The Nasreens pick and choose; they look for talent and ambition. Girls from wealthier families simply tend to be more restless. They're better educated; some have traveled abroad and they've seen firsthand the opportunities elsewhere that have been denied them at home."

"Not this one," said the banker. "She's never been anywhere. Except through whatever books she might have managed to get hold of. She'd be beaten if her father caught her reading them."

"You've met her?" asked Leland.

"As a rule, one doesn't meet Saudi women, but yes, I've seen her at his home. She and her mother would scurry from the room, covering their faces as I entered. From the way I've seen him treat them; I'd have thought they were servants. I've seen him slap them both. Some minor housekeeping matter. He'd shame his wife in my presence for not giving him a son and his daughter for not being that son."

Haskell shrugged. "Then one would think he'd be glad to be rid of her. It's not as if they place much value on girls."

"True, but this one," said the banker, "has considerable value. She's a minor princess, but a princess all the same. Any Saudi who isn't a prince would pay dearly for the chance to marry into royal blood even if she's as ugly as sin."

"Is she?" asked Haskell.

"I've only glimpsed her face, but no, not at all. One might even call her... cute... if she ever smiled. Tiny little thing. Expressive eyes even when she kept them lowered. And she's only fifteen. Her name is Rasha, by the way. That's Arabic for gazelle. An apt name for a runaway, don't you think?"

Haskell didn't answer. He didn't care what her name was. "It wasn't the prince who backed out of the marriage. He'll still keep his job, will he not?"

"Let's just say he'd damned well better find her."

The Saudi prince, while dressing, was still whimpering and whining. Haskell asked the banker, "What is he saying now?"

The banker cupped his hand to his ear. "Still cursing her mostly. He says that she's ruined him."

"Ruined what? His family honor by taking a powder?"

"That, too," said the banker, "but I think more than that. He was calling her a thief because she took some things with her. She would certainly have taken any jewelry she owned plus whatever cash she'd been able to save up. But if that were all she took, he wouldn't be this upset. I'm only catching a word here and there, but it sounds as if she's been at his computer."

"Insurance," said Leland. "Business records and the like. Shady dealings in particular. She'd have copied them onto a disk."

"You know this?" asked Haskell. He seemed suddenly alarmed.

"No, but I'd bet on it. All Nasreen clients are encouraged to do so, especially those whose fathers would harm them if found. Once out of the country, they would email their fathers. The message would say something like, 'Here's what I have. If you leave me in peace, no one else is going to see it. If you try to have me kidnapped or killed, the whole world will see it posted on the web.'"

Haskell frowned. He said, "So this kid knows computers."

"Not surprising," Leland told him. "Many thousands of them do. That's how most of them have learned that there is another world and other more progressive schools of Islam. It's also how they've learned about the Nasreens. It's how they apply to be spirited out. It's how the arrangements are made."

"By e-mail?" asked Haskell. "Can't the Saudis read their e-mail?"

Leland shook his head. He said, "Needle in a haystack. Besides, they use proxy servers, high speed multiple servers and such e-mails are encrypted in transit."

"Wait a minute," said Haskell. He turned to the banker. "You told me that the prince didn't have one at home."

"A computer? He doesn't. Just the one on his desk at Saudi Charities."

"Then where would the daughter learn to use a computer?"

"In school and... oh, dear." The banker seemed stricken. "It's his daughter who taught him how to use it in the first place. He would often bring Rasha to his office in Riyadh. He had her do all of his clerical work. She might know about those off-shore accounts."

Haskell closed his eyes. "Go find out."

The banker hurried down the shore to the Saudi. The Saudi stood rocking, his arms tightly folded. His whimpering had turned into wailing. Haskell watched as the banker tried to get him to speak. The Saudi managed a few fragmented sentences. Haskell saw the banker seize the Saudi by his shoulders and shake him to get him to spill it all out. Haskell knew that the problem must be serious indeed. One doesn't put one's hands on a Saudi prince even when no other Saudi is present.

The banker returned. His expression had paled. He said to Haskell, "Mr. Leland's quite right. She did copy those files to a disk before she left. Her father did get one of those emails days later. He was afraid to tell us at the time."

"His kid has what we have been trying to get?"

"All of it. The whole list of accounts. It must have been the daughter who found it in the first place. I'd always wondered how the prince with his… limited abilities… was able to get access to such files."

Haskell made a fist. He pounded his palm. He asked Leland, "What will she do with it?"

"Nothing. I've told you. If he lets her go quietly."

"But as you've heard," said the banker, "she was still being hunted. And so – here's the worst part – she got back in again. She went back in only this morning."

"Back in to Saudi Charities? From where?"

"She got in remotely from wherever she is now. Remember, she'd have to have found all the passwords in order to get at them in the first place. Her father never changed them, not that he'd have known how. So now she's changed those passwords. No one else can get in. Those accounts are effectively frozen."

Haskell blinked. "No one else. You mean no one else but her?"

"As of this morning. It would seem so."

"You're telling me that this kid, this fifteen-year-old kid, can now help herself to ten billion dollars?"

"Very possibly, I'm afraid. As we speak."

Leland said, "But she won't. I can almost guarantee it. The Nasreens would not allow it. They don't steal."

"Not even from thieves?"

"They're funded by donations, but not of this sort. They don't want to be seen as extortionists."

Haskell rubbed his chin. "You say it's strictly insurance?"

"Insurance against honor killings and such. It's also meant to protect any family or friends who may have abetted their departure."

"So that money is safe? Those accounts are intact?"

"I'm not saying they wouldn't be tempted," said Leland. "Many of the Nasreens are Saudi women themselves. If they've seen the stashes of these larcenous princes and realize that they're stolen from legitimate charities… in their place, I'd want to see justice done. I'd start by going public with the names of the thieves."

Haskell leaned toward him. "But you're not in their place. Would the Nasreens drop a dime on them or not?"

Leland considered letting Charles Haskell dangle. But he answered, "They would not. They're honor bound."

"You're asking us to bet…"

"I'm not asking you a thing. You wanted my opinion. I gave it."

The mogul touched Haskell's arm. "And I'm inclined to accept it. If the Nasreens have had that disk for three months, Howard's right; they would have gone public by now."

The banker said, "We have a much more immediate problem. Those Saudis will be swarming all over that office when they learn that their accounts have been blocked."

"But you say she only did that this morning?"

"So we're told."

"And it's the weekend. The office would be closed."

The banker shook his head. "The Saudi work week starts on Sunday. But anyone who's tried to log in today would assume that it's merely a malfunction. They'll try again later. That's when they'll start to wonder. The real swarming wouldn't start for several days."

Haskell nodded. "Okay, that gives us a window. If you flew back tonight, could you fix this?"

A shrug. "Perhaps. If I could get at that computer. I have an excellent technician at my branch in Riyadh. Altered passwords are not insurmountable. But his daughter probably knows that as well. The Nasreens would have coached her. Getting in won't be easy."

"You won't know until you try. Leave tonight."

"But we'd need the prince to get us into the building."

"Of course, you will," said Haskell. "Take him with you."

"But… why would he let us get into those files? He's dim, Charles, but he isn't entirely witless. He'd know that we'd no longer need him."

The mogul cleared his throat. "What we need is the daughter."

Haskell said, "Yeah, I know. But one thing at a time."

"Well," said Leland, who was looking at his watch. "If you gentlemen will excuse me, I think I'll retire. I'm sure you'll want to sort this out in private."

Haskell held up a hand. He said to Leland, "Please wait." He turned to the banker. "You say the prince doesn't know how to use a computer?"

"My grandchildren know more than he does."

"Then he still needs you. You're his only hope. He's a dead man once word gets out about this. Tell him, 'Trust us or we hang you out to dry.'"

The banker agreed. "My plane's in Sacramento. It's kept fueled and ready. We can be in Riyadh tomorrow afternoon, their time. My technician will meet us; we can get right to work. But as I've said…"

"I heard you," said Haskell. "Keep him scared. He'll fold. We'll see what we can do on this end."

"While you're there," said the mogul, "get a photo of the daughter. Full face, if you can find one. No headscarf."

With a nod, the banker turned and walked toward the shore. The prince saw him coming. He dropped to his knees. Hands clasped, he was begging the banker to help him. Haskell said to Leland, "Good start."

Haskell saw the banker pull the prince to his feet. He was trying to calm him. To reassure him. Haskell muttered, "Wrong. Let him grovel."

The banker realized that Haskell was watching. He sharpened his tone. Whatever he was saying made the prince shake his head. He squealed, "They will arrest me. I cannot." The banker replied, "You have one chance. One day. You won't do it? Very well. Then we're finished with you." He started up the path toward their cabin. The prince looked up at Haskell, his hands clasped as before. Haskell made a show of turning his back. Leland watched as the prince began to stagger about, looking this way and that as if for help. Finding none, he ran after the banker.

"I believe he's reconsidered," said Leland to Haskell. Haskell turned once again to observe. They couldn't hear what the prince was saying to the banker, but the banker flashed a brief thumbs-up signal at Haskell. Haskell replied by rotating his fist. The gesture meant, "Keep twisting that knife."

Leland said, "Well... best of luck to you all. Now if you don't mind..."

"Sorry. Let's get to why I asked you to stay."

"Oh, I wouldn't have missed it," said Leland with a yawn. "This was better than The Jerry Springer Show."

"Kidding aside, this girl, can you find her?"

"I doubt it. On the other hand, why should I?"

"You seem to know so much about these Nasreens. You must have some way of contacting them."

"I might. Indirectly," said Leland.

Haskell's eyes narrowed. "Through Elizabeth Stride? Wasn't she involved with that group at one time?"

"She's known some of its founders. But she's not a Nasreen."

"Even so," said Haskell, "she'd know who to ask."

"Not for you, she wouldn't. And not for me either. In any case, I've never met her."

"Okay, then," said Haskell. "Through your man, Roger Clew."

"Through whomever, Charles, but what if I did? They certainly wouldn't surrender the girl."

Haskell shook his head. "Not the girl, that disk and that new set of passwords. They're welcome to keep the prince's daughter. In return, I guarantee that he'll leave her alone. I'll put up a cash bond if that will help."

"You didn't answer my question. Why should I?"

"Because," said Haskell, "I'd then owe you a favor. You didn't let me finish on that membership business. Blackballed? Not a chance. You're too highly regarded. There is, however, a waiting list of almost two thousand who'd give anything to join. Most are just as well-regarded as you are. My friends and I can vault you to the top of the list. Once in, you'll be able to accomplish many things that you can't in your current position. No more rivalries with Defense, Homeland Security and Justice. No more taking stupid orders from the president's minions. No more taking positions with foreign leaders that you know they can never accept. You'll be able to do what ought to be done and you'll have our total support."

"Because Bohemians run the world," Leland answered. "I got that."

"I regret that exchange. I know it sounded overbearing. But it really isn't far from the truth."

Leland asked, "My contribution would be…?

"Your integrity. Your knowledge. And your contacts, of course. We also deal in favors. We scratch each others' backs. You'd be free to say no to any request. All we'd ask is that you hear us out."

Leland paused. He said, "This business with Kessler…"

"Fair enough. I drop it. Forget that I asked."

"The world will rest easier. Thank you."

Haskell watched as Leland bent to pick up his loafers. He said, "Howard, I'm asking you, humbly, as a friend, to help me with some damage control."

Leland smiled. "Now we're friends? Charles, I don't even like you."

"Fine," said Haskell. "Let's skip all the bullshit. What will it take for you to help?"

"I'd need to know what you intended to do. What were your plans with the Saudis?"

"Pretty much what his daughter is doing to this one. We intend to blackmail certain key Saudis to make sure they play ball with Trans-Global. Yes, it's extortion; don't wince at the word. They've been doing it to us since the seventies. We'll benefit, sure, but so will this country. So will every driver who stops to pump gas. On that, I can give you my word."

Leland chewed his lip. "These key Saudis. Who are they?"

"I'm not going to give you any names just yet. For one thing, I only have a small sampling because that's all the prince would let us see."

"As a tease?"

"Exactly," said Haskell. "Until we've made a deal. That's why he's here. To make the deal."

"And you recognized these names?"

"Every one of them, sure. The prince also dangled their current cash balances, some in the hundreds of millions. But no account numbers or access codes. The disk would have those numbers and codes. Without them, we can't get at the money."

Leland asked, "They're all in oil?"

"One way or another."

"You say you've seen a sampling. How many in total?"

"More than twelve hundred," Haskell answered. "The prince says that half the oil ministry is listed. That's a couple of hundred right there. Also on the take are top security officials, a few hundred assorted colonels and generals, plus – and I trust this won't come as a shock – four of their most rabid Wahhabi clerics, including his daughter's intended."

"I see."

"If our friend, the banker, can get into that system, end of story; we don't need the daughter. If he can't, however, we must have that disk. Wherever she is, she has the mother lode with her. There has to be a deal we can make."

"You understand, don't you, that if I should retrieve it..."

"You'll want something in return. Name your price."

Leland's eyes hardened. "I don't want their damned money."

"Of course you don't, Howard. You're an honorable man. What you'd want is to have a few aces up your sleeve the next time the Saudis try to jerk you around."

Leland folded his arms. He said, "Go on."

"Tell you what. We'll share. I'll give you some and they'll be biggies. There are only about a hundred that I need for my purposes and those I will keep; you can't have them. You can put the squeeze on yours for any purpose you like. In return, you must agree to sit on them for a while. No sharing them with anyone else until you get the green light from me."

"Charles, I did take an oath. It wasn't to you."

"You swore to uphold. You want something to uphold? If we don't keep this quiet, that flight money's frozen and they'll hang the prince by his nuts. Keep in mind, these are thieves. That money should have gone to charity. Tell you what. Most still will. It's not the money that's important. It's knowing who stashed it and blocking their access and blowing the whistle if they don't play ball. Either way, they're not getting it all back."

Leland thought for a moment. "Which charities? Do you know?"

"No, but that kid would. One more reason to find her."

Leland was still thinking. "Some will be legitimate. Food and medicine and such. But some will be a cover. Some always are. Who would get to decide where that money goes?"

"Would you like to? You got it. Build a hospital. Build ten. The Howard Leland Pavilion in Gaza."

Leland hesitated. He was rubbing his chin.

"Howard, I can put the hammer to some of these bastards in a way that you can't as long as you're in that job. We both know that they have it coming."

"I will sleep on it," said Leland. "Goodnight, Charles."

NINE

"The Howard Leland Pavilion?" asked the media mogul as he watched Leland climb toward the cabin they shared. "If that doesn't seduce him, what will?"

"Don't be smart."

"And in Gaza, no less. Want a better way to help all those poor Palestinians? Myself, I'd use the money to build them a few casinos. Look how our Native Americans have prospered. Right now, most of Gaza is inhospitable desert, but so, of course, was Las Vegas. See that? In a stroke, I have solved the Mideast conflict. No more fighting because they're too busy getting rich. Instead of tanks, we'll have busloads of blue-haired old ladies coming in to play the fifty-cent slots."

Haskell closed one eye. "Are you through?"

"By the way, you said 'humbly.' You were asking him 'humbly.' I'm surprised you know the meaning of the word."

"I did overstep. I had to back off a little."

"The word 'humble,' by the way, would also apply to your description of our intentions. Extortion? Re-embezzling? Giving some of it back? And where's the grandeur in picking a few Saudi pockets? This is the Bohemian Club, after all. We're expected to reach for the stars."

"Well, I had to say something. We were caught off guard. Anyway, it was the truth. Those are our intentions. Are you saying that I should have laid out the whole plan? He'd be on the horn to the White House right now. By tomorrow, we'd find ourselves dragged off to Leavenworth for planning to control Saudi Oil."

"Not controlling," said the mogul. "I prefer the word 'managing.' Western governments won't do it, so we must. Leland needs to be brought around to our way of thinking. However, Leland said it himself. It's always best to reel them in slowly."

"That's what I was doing. Until that damned phone call."

"No, until then you were fixated on this Martin Kessler fellow. You'll recall that I've urged you to get over it."

"He's in this. He's part of it. I can feel it."

"Because he knows this woman, Stride? And Stride knows some Nasreens? You see this as a 'gathering' of Arabic-speakers? Leland's right. You're grasping at straws."

Haskell moistened his lips. He said nothing.

"And there you were with Leland, making a hash of it. You thought you knew all the right buttons to push. Let me try. We'll meet for breakfast. Just the two of us."

"Why might you do any better?" asked Haskell.

"Because I speak his language," said the media mogul. "Leland's from an old family. So am I. You are not. It's not a language that one learns in just one generation."

"Good breeding?"

"Don't knock it. All you know is raw power. Social standing is quite something else."

Haskell snorted. "I'm not in the mood."

"I know. You've told me. You've no patience with nuance. But that's because you still don't understand it, you see. May I offer you a couple of examples?"

Haskell shook his head. "Some other time, please. Right now I need to go take a leak."

"I'll be brief," said the mogul. "You've had people killed who need not have been killed. Subtlety is not your long suit. Would it surprise you to learn that I've destroyed a few myself just by scratching their names off a guest list? In my circle a snub can be worse than a bullet. Not inviting them to an important event tells the world that they no longer matter."

"Do any of the people in your circle have bladders? Please. You can educate me later."

"Another weapon of choice – and it's a dandy – is ridicule. That's where the media come into play. I could make a man like Leland look like a fool if he should decide to go against us. Or a liar, or a puppet, or a sleaze ball; you name it. I could fatally damage the man's credibility."

Haskell had started to turn away. He stopped. He said thoughtfully, "And not only Leland's."

"Um… don't tell me. Are we now back on Kessler?"

"Of course not. You couldn't hurt Kessler that way."

The mogul yawned. "Okay, what's left? The State of Israel? Been tried. Yitzhak what's-his-name, the head of the Mossad? He'd probably frame it and hang it on his wall. Oh, I know. Harry Whistler, correct?"

"Say it is," said Haskell. "What could you do to him?"

The mogul winced. "Will you forget about Whistler? You've been burned. Take your lumps. You're letting these people become an obsession, and obsessions almost always turn inward."

"Don't worry about me. I'm on top of it."

"Are you? I'm hearing troubling whispers about you. I hear you have the hots for Elizabeth Stride."

Haskell bridled. "Who the hell told you that?"

"A little bird. We all have our little birds," said the mogul. "You're enamored of a woman who you've never laid eyes on. You've heard that she's a knockout and very much a lady except when she's slicing people up into bait. The sort of woman who belongs on Charles Haskell's arm and not in the bed of some German who bested you. Sometimes I fear for your sanity."

Haskell's color had risen. "Look, wherever this came from…"

"You've researched her. Exhaustively."

"I research all opponents."

"Friends as well. Never hurts. But this woman especially. Every tidbit you could find. Adopted by a family that worked for Aramco. Family moved back to Texas where she grew up. Returned after college to find her birth parents. Disappeared into a Saudi prison where she was probably raped within an inch of her life. Rescued then recruited by the Mossad. I forget how and why she hooked up with Kessler, but I bet you've got it all charted."

Haskell's eyes had grown cold. He said, "Enough."

"Birth parents were athletes. Romanian, I think. Northern Romanian. Good Aryan stock. That's where she got it. Name a sport, she's good at it. I bet you have a list of every trophy she's won and…"

"Hey," snapped Haskell. "Did you hear me? Get off it."

The mogul paused for a beat. He softened his voice. "I was hoping to hear a denial."

"You wouldn't understand. So shut up about it. Back to Whistler. Indulge me. What could you do to him?"

The mogul sighed. "Well, you know what they say. Bright light is the best disinfectant."

"They also say he's untouchable. No one wants to take him on. Everybody I've asked says he's too well connected."

"Untouchable by whom? The authorities, correct? Not by a relentless free press. He's a man who lives large, almost riotously, as well known for his charity as his wealth, unsuspected by most of all the blood on his hands. Shine a bright enough light on the right kind of scandal… kidnapping young boys for sex, for example…"

"He does that?"

"Of course not," said the mogul, "but you get the idea. True or not, the whispers would be with him forever. Those with whom he does business will distance themselves. Certainly a straight arrow like Leland."

"An interesting idea."

"You see? You can learn."

Haskell's eyes took a shine. "When can you start?"

"Alas, there are one or two flaws in that plan. Harry Whistler has resources. He'd track it down. A libel suit would be the very least of our worries if we should make him an enemy."

"He's already…"

"An enemy? No, he isn't. Or at least he's not mine. Which brings me to the most grievous flaw in that plan. I would then have an enemy I needn't have had, one who has a very long reach. I would soon be awakened in the middle of the night by a shadowy figure standing over my bed. To keep my throat from being cut, I would of course rat you out. I would say that Charles Haskell made me do it. Shall I tell you what his… or her… first question would be?"

"It wouldn't be why. He'd know why."

The mogul shook his head. He said, "I can hear the words even now. I'd be asked, 'Charles Haskell? Who the hell is Charles Haskell?'"

"He… knows very well who I am."

"He might. He might not. The question is, does he care? Your world and his don't intersect often. Would he even recognize you if you passed him on the street?"

Haskell darkened. He made no reply.

"Get over it, Charles. We have enough on our plates. Let's deal with that damned Saudi princess."

TEN

Haskell's bladder didn't make it to nearest relief. He decided that a shrub would serve his purpose. That media mogul. Talk about arrogance. Haskell should have whizzed on his shoes.

His own apparent smugness had put off Howard Leland, but he hadn't meant it quite the way it came out. What he'd felt when he made that "we run the world" remark was more a sense of wonder at how far he had come. Talk about breeding. He had breeding in spades. And none of it cost anyone a dime.

His father had been a chauffeur for the rich after failing to succeed as a boxer. That experience in the prize ring, such as it was, became an asset; he could double as a bodyguard. And he'd earn extra money giving boxing lessons to the sons of his employers and their friends. He saved his most useful lessons for his own son. Not so much how to box as how to fight.

Haskell's inner voice said, "No, how to win."

Well, yes, of course. Why else would you fight? It was street-fighting, really. No gloves. No referee. And never use a closed fist. Skulls are hard. Knuckles break. Use the heel of your hand. Or your thumb for soft tissue. The eyes are the softest. Use the heel of your shoe if they try to get up. Not the toe. Toes break, too. Use the heel.

"Charles, he was no thug. You make him sound like a thug."

Sorry. Didn't mean to. No, he was no bully. Tough when he had to be. Easy-going on the whole. But he knew what he knew and he taught what he knew. He'd tell his son, "Don't you ever pick a fight. But if you're faced with one that you can't walk away from, hit fast and hard, no talk, no warning. If someone has to get hurt, make sure it's him and get it done within ten seconds, max."

The other reason for the ten second rule was that when it happens fast, no-one's sure of what they saw. Let them hear you asking, "Oh my gosh, are you all right?" This does two things, said his father. One of them is, you don't get a reputation. Your skills remain a surprise. The other one is that if the cops are called, you're a little less likely to be cuffed.

"Now you're making it sound..."

As if he'd had a fight a week. He didn't. Just a few. Enough to practice what he'd learned. But the lessons still applied to later situations such as those he would encounter while building his career. Lull them into thinking you're no imminent threat. Then hit fast and hard. Good advice.

His mother, however, saw his father as a loser. She'd always thought that she was the one who should have had a chauffeur and limo. If not as the wife of a champion fighter, then in her own right as a movie star. His mother had dreamt of an acting career, probably since she was in grade school. She finally walked out when he was only fourteen. She'd decided to give it a shot.

Actually, she wasn't all that unrealistic. She wasn't looking for stardom. Not at her age. But getting steady work as a character actress seemed an achievable goal. She'd had characters and roles by the dozen in her head as far back as he could remember.

She'd been diagnosed as having a non-existent illness. Multiple Personality Disorder. It was a fad diagnosis, now deservedly discredited, but he knew it was crap even then. She wasn't like Eve in The Three Faces Of Eve. She hadn't invented alternate selves as a shield against some blocked-out abuse in her childhood. Did she alternate? Yes. But between movie roles. Her multiples were all movie roles. Did she talk to herself? So what? So did he. More people should have a good long talk with themselves. It would help them cut through their own bullshit.

She did manage to be cast in some minor stage productions. Mostly she worked as a waitress. But she was never the same waitress two days in a row. She'd be Katherine Hepburn one day, Bette Davis the next. She'd also done the same thing at home. And she was good. She could even cross over and be Orson Welles. She could do Brando; she could do Charlton Heston. She'd memorized speeches from their movies.

Disappointed, and probably clinically depressed, she finally snapped and ended up institutionalized. He'd never gone to see her. There seemed little point. On any given day, she would be someone else. She would therefore, understandably, not know who he was because he didn't have a role in the movie. When she died, his father went to make the arrangements. He was told that she had carried herself with great dignity during her final hours on earth. He was told a number of things that she'd said. He recognized most of them. He'd heard them before. They were lines from a movie called, Lilies of the Field. She was Sidney Poitier when she died.

His father's later years were considerably more balanced. He'd come to like working as a chauffeur, never finding it demeaning in the least. And he'd tell his son stories of the rich and the famous. Most were amusing. A few were disillusioning. But all were in some way instructive. Through these stories and a few first-hand glimpses of his own, Haskell began to develop a taste for the sort of lives these people lived. Chauffeured limos, private jets, stately homes, important friends. He'd seen the sort of deference with which they were treated whether they'd earned it or not. He'd seen the presumption that they were superior. He'd seen how people stepped out of their way. He wanted that kind of respect.

"Respect?"

Well, no. That wasn't the word. He wanted the power that went with real wealth. Not just access to power. The power itself. As a boy, raised sort of Catholic, he had actually knelt and prayed. He prayed to Saint Jude as his mother often had. Saint Jude, she'd told him, was the go-to guy when faced with a difficult quest. A fat lot of good he'd done her.

But this was then, so he gave it a try. He swore that he would always use his influence wisely and for the greater good of mankind. He later liked to tell the story of how Jude responded. The good saint had said to him, "You're shitting me, right? I'm putting you on hold while I redirect your call. The devil has a better sense of humor."

It's hard to hustle a saint. Over time, they've heard it all. Jude saw right through his professed altruism. Jude knew that he knew, even at that tender age, that he might have to leave a few bodies in his wake if they should stand in his way.

"Um…"

Okay, that's not true. He didn't think that way then. Stepping over people, maybe, but not whacking them wholesale. That would come later after life taught him that half measures seemed to take twice the effort.

His mother might have always been a bit of a loon, but that didn't mean he couldn't learn from her. She was forever acting; forever in a role, and he would often be her sole audience. He'd come to know most of her speeches by heart and would often recite them himself, and in character. The difference was that Haskell knew he was acting. His mother, for the most part, did not. From her, he'd learned to be a chameleon. He could seem to be whatever he needed to be. All it took was some study and rehearsal. Add in a little identity theft, a few forged documents, a well-thought out plan and, voila, here he was, Charles Barrington Haskell, with nowhere to go but straight up.

Barrington, thought Haskell. That was a nice touch. He'd found the name on a street map of Chicago.

From the outset, he'd decided to build his career where the money and the fun was. Big Oil. He'd considered Wall Street, but it held no appeal. Sure, one could get rich in the financial game. Obscenely rich. As his banker friend had. Even richer when so many others went under. Bottom-feeding on their scraps while taking government largesse. Some investment bankers found finance exciting, but all they really did was move money around while raking off as much as they could. A criminal mind was certainly an asset, but theirs was a risk-averse criminal mind. That smacked of cowardice to his way of thinking. He felt sure that he'd soon die of boredom.

Big oil, however, was inherently criminal. Unabashedly so. Almost gleefully so. Rough and ready. Bare knuckles. Nor was he being cynical. God had seen fit, in his infinite irony, to put most of the world's oil in the hands of thugs and despots. The Middle East certainly. No exceptions in that region. Ditto Russia, Venezuela, Nigeria, Angola, and especially Iran and the Caucasus. Every oil company, therefore, needed thugs of its own who were ready to "downsize" those who wouldn't stay bought. Or to "educate" any who resisted being bought. But we don't call them thugs. We used to call them contractors. That term, however, had fallen from favor after all those unpleasant episodes in Iraq. Now we call them mediators. They reconcile disputes. It has a much better ring to it. Something like marriage counseling. Except that these often end in something more than divorce.

Nor, for that matter, are their actions really criminal. Well, technically they are. There are laws on the books. But none of the industry's more aggressive undertakings has ever even led to an arrest that he knew of, let alone a criminal conviction. Why? We need that oil. We need all we can get. An adequate and uninterrupted supply is vital to our national security. And no two words in the history of any country had covered a greater multitude of sins than those two. National Security.

He had risen to the top while still in his late thirties. CEO of Trans-Global Oil & Gas and its many "independent" subsidiaries. One of these, called Scorpion Systems, was an oil field security firm. The mogul found it for him. Got it to sell out to him. The mogul had, and still has, something on its founder that would have destroyed him if published. Wouldn't say what it is. That would stay between them. The mogul likes to keep a few cards up his sleeve. Fine. Just don't forget who you're playing with.

"Suffice it to say," the mogul had told him, "that this flawed, but exceptionally talented man will stay at the nominal helm of the firm and will do whatever is required of him."

"Answering to whom?"

"Why, to you, of course, Charles. I merely hold the leash to keep him from straying. Perhaps a little tug now and then."

Scorpion Systems was a gold mine, not to mix metaphors. An oil ministry - Saudi or Kuwaiti, for example - would hire the firm to assess how vulnerable its facilities were to attack. The primary focus was on terrorist attacks, but sabotage by competing oil interests was always a danger as well.

To find likely weak points, Scorpion Systems would, of necessity, be given unlimited access. It would know those installations inside out from well head, whether on land or off-shore, to refinery to the storage tanks at dockside. All of it computerized every step of the way, so his firm had access to those systems as well. It would recommend and implement protective measures against all conceivable threats. But it would also know how to defeat those same measures if and when doing so would benefit Trans-Global.

Beautiful. Couldn't lose. He had it both ways. They'd be paying for protection from everyone but him, never dreaming that he'd planted a few bugs of his own, especially in their computers. He could shut a field down for a month with one phone call and then he, the mogul and their good friend, the banker, would make a few million off the spike that it would cause in the spot market price of crude oil.

Great fun, but there always seemed to be something missing. It took him a while to realize what it was. After a day of high-stakes machinations, he'd go home to one of his big empty houses and the place would feel like a tomb. No one to talk to. No one to tell. Sure, there were women. The kind attracted by power. Easy pickings. Use and discard. But nothing that could be called a relationship. Or even, for that matter, a friendship. So he'd shopped for a wife of a different sort. Or rather he'd hired a search team to find one. It found several likely candidates and he wooed and married two of them, but neither had worked out all that well.

The first was the socialite. Family fortune in timber. She taught him how to entertain properly and she was, of course, endorsed by the mogul. But a dullard otherwise. Sent her packing three years later. Then the concert pianist. A touch of class there and much better in the sack. Low maintenance, too, because she practiced for hours. That meant fewer demands on his time. No excitement, however. Aside from the sex, she was more of a pet. More like one of his holdings than a wife. He found himself yearning for the type of woman who could match him in daring, in adventurousness, who could challenge him, stand up to him, be a true partner, a woman who could cover his back. Was there such a woman out there? He knew of only one. And that was one more reason to detest Martin Kessler. He has her. He has Elizabeth Stride. And worse, he comes and goes. Why does she take him back? Well, he won't be coming back from where Charles Haskell sends him. Then maybe she'll come to her senses.

Where were we? Ah, his holdings. Aside from Trans-Global Oil & Gas, he had interests in several other companies as well, all of which had relevance to national security and therefore basked in that same protection. He was big, but he could have been bigger.

He'd formed a partnership with Artemus Bourne. Bourne was a giant. He was bigger than Trans-Global. A dozen senators in his pocket. Several foreign heads of state. The deal was struck on this very spot. Sitting around a fire. Done with a handshake. Bourne was, of course, a Bohemian. It was a deal that would have been worth tens of millions to himself and to several other members of this club. It would have given them control of Angola. America would have benefited as well. It would have had a substantial guaranteed source. Not a cheaper source, perhaps. This was no freebie. But this country would no longer have the need to pretend that the Saudis are allies and friends.

But Bourne, without consulting yours truly, decided that he wanted the diamond trade as well. This put him into conflict with the Israelis, which is to say Kessler, not to mention with Harry Whistler. Start with Kessler, Bourne decided. Neutralize him. Not kill him, use him. Against the Israelis. How? Very simple. What does Kessler value most? The answer? Elizabeth Stride.

Stride thought him dead. Kessler had let her think so. Why? Nobody seems to know. But she was alive and Bourne's people found her. She was living, quite openly, on Hilton Head Island. Quite brazenly, considering the price on her head. Maybe she continued to use her real name so that Kessler, on the chance that he was still alive, would be able to find her one day. Or maybe she had a death wish herself. Whatever her reason, Bourne wouldn't have cared. He certainly didn't care about the reward. All he did care about was having her as a hostage to make Martin Kessler play ball.

And he blew it. Or his thugs did. They went to her home, found two women there, snatched the one they believed to be Stride and left the other woman with her throat cut. They got her off the island bound and gagged. Too well bound. Too well gagged. The woman suffocated. Long story short, the world collapsed on Bourne's head. Bourne, himself, was dead two days later, his house burned down around him, his empire in tatters. By whom? Kessler surely. And Elizabeth Stride. Aided by, one assumes, the Israeli Mossad and by Harry Whistler with his storied long reach.

There was more to the story. Actually much more. But to think those outside forces could do so much damage… and then slink away… as Stride has since done… probably plotting further revenge… answering to no one for what they had done. The injustice of it. The disproportionateness of it. Don't we live in a nation of laws?

"Say, what?"

Okay, thought Haskell, some hypocrisy there. But the rest of us know that there can be a price. Kessler and his gang seem totally immune. And it's not over, is it? How could anyone think it is? They surely intend additional mischief because one simply doesn't do what they've done without a longer range purpose in mind. And yet they're left alone. It's insane, but there it is. Because of them, here we are, back working with the Saudis, reduced to subverting this moronic minor prince who can't even control his own family.

Well, perhaps not much longer. He would rather have that disk. With the disk, the banker's right, they'd have no need of the prince. The fly in the ointment, however, is Leland. Will he help or will he not? Or will Leland decide to grab that disk for himself? Let me sleep on it, he says. And he will. He'll consider it. He'll also consider the power he'd have if all those Saudi princes had to kiss his ass every time they need to make a withdrawal.

We'll need a new plan. Plan A was a washout. Invite Leland here, say we'll sponsor him for membership, ask a few simple favors of him in return – that Kessler business being just one - and assume that he'd be thrilled to comply. It had actually been the banker's idea. Haskell had not been so sure.

He'd asked the banker, "What makes you think that he'll go for it?"

"Of course he will. Do you know anyone who wouldn't? He'd stand among the most powerful men in the world."

"Um… he kind of does already, don't you think?"

"Acting Secretary, Charles. The man is a temp. An appointed position at the pleasure of the White House."

"Even so," Haskell answered, "he's no empty suit. Howard Leland has earned every stripe."

"And he's in a job that he'll no longer have beyond the next election at the latest. He'll join the lecture circuit for a year or two or be given a red sash and shipped off to some embassy. He'll never have bonded the way we do here. He'll never have awakened with the first rays of dawn realizing that he is the rarest of men. Realizing that he is a Bohemian."

Haskell smiled. "I feel like bursting into song."

"And with good reason," said the banker. "This is no mere conceit. No club in the world is more exclusive than this one. No membership, anywhere, is more desperately sought."

"Okay," said Haskell. "I suppose it's worth a shot."

"Believe me," said the banker, "he'll jump at the chance. You couldn't buy this sort of influence, this sort of prestige, if you had all the money in the world."

Brilliant man, thought Haskell, but a bit of a twit. He makes his own kids, now full grown; call him "Sir." You can't touch him, however, when it comes to knowing how to build a fortune using other people's money. Especially when they don't know he's doing it.

He's right, however, about the club's roster. Name a top CEO or any global financier and chances are he's a member. Name an important federal government official and he's either a member or he's on the waiting list. And the wait for those willing to wait their turn has been averaging more than eight years. At least seven former presidents have been members as well, one of whom was holding court just two campfires away. Haskell avoided ex-presidents and such. They're inclined to be bores, still living in the past, too long out of the loop to have any real influence.

Truth is told, except for the networking aspect, this whole two-week retreat was a bore. "Weaving spiders come not here," said a sign at the entrance. It meant that wheeling and dealing are discouraged. Of course it is widely ignored. So, to some extent, was the no-cell-phone rule, but you mustn't be seen with one at your ear. Very bad form. You'd be asked to leave at once. And God help you if it were to start ringing during one of the rituals or lectures.

There were several scheduled lectures; they were called "lakeside talks." They were given by prominent members and guests. They were almost never worth hearing. By the time the speakers spoke, what they said was old news to members who had even better sources. Some spoke of the future. Almost always upbeat. Our institutions will prevail. A new dawning for mankind. These were speakers who lived in guarded estates behind razor ribbon-topped walls. The only mankind most of them ever saw were men like his father, driving their cars, or women like his mother bringing their meals.

During the day it resembled a summer camp where rich old white men played at being boys again. Except that nobody slept in a tent or a lean-to. The so-called cabins, though rustic, were more like country inns. All were named for distinguished former members and guests. Theirs was named for Teddy Roosevelt. He'd been a member. He'd slept there. Each had a breakfast room on the first floor that doubled as a reading room or card room. Several, like his own, had a cozy little bar whose walls were covered with assorted old photos, some dating back more than a century. And the head of an elk and the pelt of a cougar, both shot by Teddy himself.

Most cabins had eight or ten bedrooms or suites and all were equipped with every comfort. Most had their own wet bars. Most bathrooms had Jacuzzis. The rooms had phones, but they were room-to-room phones. No outside calls made or taken. No locks on the doors either. Not on any of the rooms. Not even a latch on the door to one's bathroom. The founders felt that locks were inimical to good fellowship. A little framed sign on the desk downstairs said so. Haskell had never felt especially chummy while taking a dump at six o'clock in the morning, but at least the bathrooms had doors.

There were lots of silly rituals, recitations of oaths, and another old custom involving bodily functions. They would gather around this huge statue of an owl that stood about twenty feet high. Some elder would recite some gem about wisdom and, on his signal, they'd all pull out their peckers and, in unison, piss. The urination was symbolic. You were purging your cares. The only members who actually partook in this, however, were those few who were able to produce a decent stream. Most couldn't. Aging kidneys. They pissed in Morse code. They kept their cares to themselves.

On other nights, they'd put on plays. Men would dress up in drag. There were amateur nights and sing-along sessions and guided nature walks through the redwoods. Richard Nixon came once. He wasn't impressed. Nor is Nixon fondly remembered after going back home and famously calling it, "The most faggy goddamned thing you could imagine."

Good old Dick. A great man. Damn those tapes.

There was tennis and canoeing and fly fishing contests. There was an archery range and skeet and trap shooting, but they'd put an end to all wildlife shooting lest a member should take an errant bullet in the head. The attitude was, one can't be too careful. This is, after all, the Bohemian Club. The rumor mill, almost surely, would assume that it was murder. The conspiracy theorists would not lose a moment. We'd hear that the victim had declined to play ball with one power-broker or another. An investigation, however impartial, would soon be labeled a cover-up. It's all nonsense, of course. But it's the price one pays. Secrecy always gives rise to gossip and this is, most assuredly, a secret society.

There was one death two years ago, but it wasn't a member. It was one of the many maintenance workers, not a titan who would be missed. He was up on the roof of one of the cabins blowing pine needles out of the gutters. He slipped and got tangled in the cord of his blower. It looped around his neck as he slid off the eaves. The other end was snagged around a chimney. A senior member saw him up dangling, called the maintenance chief and said, "Could you clean that up quietly?"

And that was it. He was buried somewhere far out in the woods. Payroll records showed that he'd quit the week before and had said that he was going back to Mexico. It was the banker who'd told Haskell this story. He told it to illustrate the club's preferred method of dealing with such inconveniences. When Haskell expressed doubt as to whether it was true, the banker said, "Believe it. We won't mention any names. But the member who saw it is no stranger to us." He then cocked his head toward the mogul.

He later asked the mogul why they'd bother with a cover-up for what was clearly an on-the-job accident. The mogul answered that it might have been perceived as something else. The gossip mill and all that. Besides, he was a Mexican, in the country illegally. It's best treated as a housekeeping matter.

Haskell did enjoy some of the more colorful rumors. Tales of dark, cultish rituals worshiping Satan. Babies snatched from their cradles, burned alive as an offering. And orgies, off course, with smuggled-in whores who are, after use, ceremonially strangled, weighted down and dumped in the lake. What, you don't believe it? How terribly naïve. Do you really think that such powerful men could go for two weeks without sexual release? Testosterone levels that high need an outlet. That must be why no women are allowed to be members. They'd be gang-raped before the first week was out and, well, you know women. They tattle.

Haskell chuckled to himself. He'd yet to meet anyone in this whole club who could overpower any woman he knew. Let alone someone like... well... someone like Stride. We'd see who ends up in the lake.

He'd reached the cabin. He glanced down toward his fire. The last log that he'd added had collapsed into embers. A fitting punctuation for the evening's events. For now, though, thought Haskell, he could do with a scotch. A good single malt in a big brandy glass to sip and sniff as he pondered his next move.

ELEVEN

At the bar, he scanned the faces of the others in the room. A few looked up and raised their glasses to salute him. Others kept their heads down, avoiding eye contact with him. He'd bonded with them all in one way or another. And there are all manner of bonds.

Yes, the banker was right about the value of membership. He was wrong though about what you can and can't buy and with considerably less than all the money in the world. But even for Haskell, with all his connections, this club was no easy nut to crack. You couldn't charm your way in. You couldn't bribe your way in. You could, however, extort your way in if you were able to dig up the right kind of dirt on the members whom you needed to propose you. Not so hard. Or at least he'd thought so at the time. Not in a club with almost three thousand members. And as someone once wrote – it was Balzac, thought Haskell – behind every great fortune there lies a great crime. There should have been lots of crimes here to choose from. He'd put a team of researchers to work.

There were crimes, but most were old because the money was old. Far from embarrassing the eventual beneficiaries, they were proud of great-grandpa's predations. New money, fortunes made through securities fraud, wasn't a whole lot more fruitful. Anyone who'd cooked his company's books only had to place calls to one or two other members and, presto, indictments were quashed. A dead end there. So much for crime.

There was a time, not long ago, when the threat to reveal drug use was enough to get the druggie's attention. Now it's no big deal. Found out, they go to rehab. Closet gays no longer seem to fear being outed. On the contrary, they're encouraged, even admired. It's fashionable, these days, to be supportive of gays as long as they don't bring Armageddon upon us by trying to legally marry. Nor does the revelation of adulterous trysts earn anyone a scarlet letter anymore. The biggest factor there is probably Viagra. The older they are, the prouder they are to have bullets back in their guns.

All that was left in that quickly drying well was sexual deviance with children. That was and always will be a no-no. Kiddy porn, for example, found on their computers. Or chicken hawks trolling internet sites looking for a minor, same sex or otherwise, who'd be willing to meet them and gratify their needs in exchange for the price of a Sony Play Station or perhaps a shiny new mountain bike. Haskell never understood why anyone would do that. Making blind dates? On the internet? With children? The "child" was just as likely an FBI agent trying to get them to cross a state line.

His researchers were considerably more successful in this instance. They only found one member – a biggie - who'd actually made such a date, but they found a few more who'd trolled those sites as often as ten times a week. His associate, the mogul, took it from there. He'd tell some story about an informer who was out to discredit the member in question. Wanted it published. Had the evidence. All those logs. Not to worry, however. They've been safely locked away. Pending their final destruction, of course. And his good friend, Charles Haskell, at the mogul's request, had encouraged the informer, now deceased, by the way, to purge his computer of any trace…

"Beg pardon? Deceased?" the member would ask.

"Suffice it to say that Charles Haskell is thorough. Just the sort of man we need in this club."

"And these logs," said the member. "You say that you've kept them?"

"Not me. Haskell has."

"To what purpose?" asked the member.

"Oh, believe me, you have nothing to fear. He'll destroy them once he's in and is bound by our oath. Would you care to be one of his sponsors?"

His researchers had served him well on the whole. As they damned well should have for what they had cost him. Both of them had worked for the CIA. Not officially, though. As an alternative to prison. It seems that they'd hacked the CIA itself and gotten into the bowels of its more sensitive files. The CIA had them hacking almost everyone else including the Department of Defense. They'd hacked the FBI, but that was no great achievement. Any Boy Scout who'd earned a merit badge in computing could probably have done the same thing.

Their indenture ended with the proviso that they never go near a computer again. That's like telling a bulimic to stop throwing up. He'd hired them and he gave them an unlimited budget to equip an electronic Disneyland. He ensconced them in a townhouse in Seattle. They almost never left the townhouse because they had no wish to. Compulsives are like that. They need no other lives. They sit at their keyboard 18 hours a day amassing data they care nothing about. The thrill is in the hack, not the use of it.

Haskell knew how to use it. Well, some of it anyway. A lot was in code or in some foreign language. He had linguists on his staff, but the volume was such that he'd have needed a hundred times their number. Even then, most of what they'd translate would be crap. Routine correspondence, inane chit-chat and such. Even jokes. Every culture, even the Muslims, told jokes. That shouldn't have surprised him, but it did.

The only useful information that he got out of them came when he gave them specific instructions to hack a particular individual or competitor. They succeeded during his quest for sponsors and for members who might have blackballed him. They succeeded quite brilliantly in giving him the means to sabotage those Mideast production facilities. They'd failed, however, to penetrate the system of Saudi Overseas Charities. Hence the need to romance this ridiculous prince.

And they'd failed to get more than a foot in the door of the intricate system employed by the Mossad, or that of its stepchild, Harry Whistler's.

It was one of them, probably, who'd told the mogul, that he seemed to have a"thing" for Elizabeth Stride. He'd wanted everything about her, no detail too small. Well, it isn't a "thing." It's more like respect. He would pick that bone with them later.

He'd flown to Seattle only three days before the start of the Bohemian Club's gathering. It would be his last chance to meet with his hackers. He'd wanted a progress report. Their reports, on the whole, were a mixture of bragging of their technical brilliance and a litany of their limitations.

One had said, "Look, you have to understand. We can get into the Whistler system. We can even get into Mossad. But those systems know we're there within maybe five seconds and they turn on you and bite you in the ass."

"Bite you how?" asked Haskell.

"They send a worm of their own. It penetrates us. The worm screws up our systems like you wouldn't believe. We've never seen anything like it."

"Does it tell them who you are? Where you are?" Haskell asked.

"I doubt it. We don't leave many bread crumbs."

"Well? Where are we? Can you crack them or not?"

"There's gotta be a way. There always is."

"You've been at this now for almost three months and you've given me nothing to show for it."

"Not true," said the hacker. "This should brighten your day. We might know where Kessler and Stride are."

"Go on."

"We were digging into Whistler through open sources. We got a list of all the companies he controls – or at least the ones that show his name on their reports – and a list of houses and apartments he owns. One of them is in a suburb of Washington, D.C. We know that Whistler's not there. We know that he's in Geneva. But someone's using that house."

"Someone?" he'd asked. "Why Kessler and Stride?"

"They needed a place. Harry Whistler had a place." The hacker raised a hand before Haskell could respond. "Yeah, I know. That's pretty thin. But whoever's there, they're sending out a lot of internet traffic. It goes out all over the Mideast."

Haskell's eyes narrowed. "Where Trans-Global does business?"

The hacker answered, "Well, yeah, but to other countries, too. Like Iran. You don't do business in Iran. Like Turkmenistan, Uzbekistan, that whole Caspian area."

"All oil-producing countries. So it is about oil."

The hacker shook his head. "No, you can't really say that. Jordan, too, for example. There's no oil in Jordan. Egypt and Turkey. Not much oil there either."

The hacker's partner said, "Looks like some kind of slogan." He had not turned his face from his screen. "Three words. Same three words every time."

The first hacker said, "At least that's what it look like. They're encrypted in transit, but the codes look the same. Three words. We think English. Can't be sure."

"A slogan?" asked Haskell. "Or might it be a signal?"

"Too random for a signal. No pattern to who's getting it. It seems to go to almost anyone, anywhere in that region, who sits down and boots up a computer. For all we know, it could even be a prayer."

Haskell, with effort, held on to his temper. "A three-word prayer from Kessler's Arabic speakers? What would make you think it's a prayer?"

"Because Muslims send things like 'God is great' all the time. They're supposed to pray to Allah five times a day. I bet a lot of them count that as a prayer. I know you think this must be more than that. But remember. It's random. Think spam. There's no more a discernable pattern to this than to the junk mail we see every day."

Haskell stared at his man. "It isn't junk mail."

"If you say so."

"If it's coming from Kessler, it isn't spam either. Unless he's selling penile enlargements on-line, trust me; those three words are important."

Another shrug. The hacker reached for a piece of note paper. "Here's the address of that house that it comes from. Alexandria, Virginia. A section called Belle Haven. Big houses, big money, high security. I also wrote down the two email addresses that are sending almost all of these messages."

"I traced those," said the second hacker with pride. "Want to know how? It was really neat. First you have to..."

"Later," said Haskell. He didn't care how. He was looking at the Belle Haven address. He knew Belle Haven. Been there several times. A number of Bohemians kept homes there as well. He knew that the streets were heavily patrolled by local police and by private security. Harry Whistler would likely have considerable clout there. Good choice for a base. If it's Kessler.

He saw the email addresses. One was Nikram102 using Hotmail as its server. The other was Handmaiden1 using Gmail.

He asked, "No identities? No names to go with these?"

"Nope. They're blocked. It's a hell of a system. If we tried to go in hard, like to bug it or cripple it..."

"They'd hit back in five seconds. I heard you."

Handmaiden, thought Haskell? Could that be Stride? No, not likely. Handmaidens are submissive. Stride is anything but. He asked, "Nikram. A word? Or is that someone's name?"

"Girl's name. Shiite name. I looked it up. There's your Arabic speaker, but that name's mostly Iranian."

"Looked it up? Why not ask her? You have these addresses. Why not try to get a friendly chat going?"

"We're not stupid, Mr. Haskell. We tried that."

"And?"

"Failure notice every time if they don't know the sender. It protects against penetration."

"And that's just one way," said his partner. "They got lots." The first hacker said. "But we're writing some code that we think might sneak in. It's like what we did for those Saudi fields we bugged. But how deep can we get? Look, I've gotta be honest. What we need is someone there to make a mistake."

"Of what sort?"

"There's this lockout code they use, rotating numbers and characters, with five billion possible combinations. Oh, and their server…"

"Bottom line, if you please. Keep it simple."

"It's a code they punch in before they go on line. If they forget, they're wide open until they go on again. Someone has to forget to enter that code."

"How likely?" asked Haskell, drumming his fingers.

"They're human. It could be an emergency. Or it could be someone new who's not familiar with the system."

"You're telling me," said Haskell, "that I shouldn't hold my breath."

I'm telling you were good, but so is the Mossad, and they've been at this a lot longer. We'll keep at it. We'll get in. You just have to be patient."

"That is not among my virtues. Get it done. I've got to know what Kessler is up to."

The hacker said, "Look, this is none of our business, but if this guy is such a problem, you've got goons by the truckload. Send them down to this house in Belle Haven. If Kessler and his broad are there, pull their plugs."

"Don't call Stride a broad. She's a remarkable woman. Don't use that sort of language when you speak of her."

"Um… sorry." The two hackers exchanged a what's-with-him glance.

"Never mind," said Haskell. He gathered himself. "One doesn't go blasting in a place like Belle Haven. It upsets the neighbors and the media would notice." Not to mention it leading to an all out war against Harry Whistler and his allies. "Whatever's done must be done quietly."

"Okay, so send someone to at least take a look. Whoever's there doesn't stay in that house all day long."

"My thought exactly," said Haskell.

Control yourself, Charles, he'd thought after that discussion. That "broad" thing was dumb. Unprofessional. Undetached. It's one thing to have a private feeling about someone. It's another to let it blurt out.

The mogul thinks he's obsessed. Intrigued is more like it. She's become like the tune one can't get out of one's head. She plays tennis, they say, at a near-champion level. Well, he plays a pretty strong game himself. Although he'd never admit it to the mogul or the banker, he'd envisioned himself playing singles with her. On his own court. At one of his homes. The one in Palm Beach should impress her.

Hell, for her he'd rent Wimbledon Stadium, center court. Play a set or two before breaking for lunch. He'd have it catered and served in the royal box. What woman could say no to that?

Well, she could. And would. She'd have to know him a lot better. Given time, she would like him. She really would. Or at least she would like whatever version of himself seemed to appeal to her the most.

"Charles…"

Right. Don't do that. Not with her. Be yourself. A little gentler, perhaps, with a touch of Sidney Poitier. Every woman has a past. But every woman has a yearning. Most don't know what for until the right man comes along. From then on, past is past. All that matters is the future. Dreams come true. The spirit soars.

And don't say it.

I know.

This is horseshit. Won't happen.

We both know that, but one is entitled to one's fantasies. As long as we keep our thoughts to ourselves. Until Kessler is out of the way.

And it's not just Stride. Let's be clear about that. It's also about retribution for Angola. Can anyone think we'd fold our tents and go quietly? A loss on that scale, if gone unavenged, is seen as a weakness. It emboldens other enemies.

And whatever Kessler is scheming at the moment, it probably has to do with retribution as well. For the ill-fated attempt to snatch Stride. For forcing her to give up her home and her friends and the quiet life she was trying to lead. If Kessler is unfinished business to us, we are surely unfinished business to him.

Well, we'll see who finishes whom.

Within an hour of his meeting with his two hackers, he'd chosen the man who he would send to Belle Haven. By the next day, he had his man in place. His man's charge, for the moment, was strictly surveillance. Who's who, who does what, who goes where; that sort of thing.

His man, Gilhooley, tried to balk at the job. Too dull. Not what he's best at. Not what he's used to. What he's best at is blowing things up from a distance. What he's used to is living exceedingly well in between and even during his assignments. In Belle Haven, however, the best way to avoid notice is to masquerade as a handyman. They're seen all the time driving ratty old pick-ups. He'd have to find a cheap room on the fringes of Belle Haven and take all his meals in local taverns or diners. A working stiff. That would be his cover.

Beneath him? Well, tough. It served this man right. On his most recent job, he'd been sent to London on mission that he botched up entirely. No explosives this time, just one troublesome journalist. He got the right address, a townhouse in Kensington, but he managed to get the wrong people. The intended target and his wife had gone off to the country. They'd swapped houses via one of those internet sites with a couple who wanted a week in the city. Gilhooley, unaware of this recent development, stole into the house in the dead of night. He put a bullet in each of their heads while they slept. Only then did he shine a light on the two and see that it was not his best work.

One would think that at least he'd have got away clean. But he was pulled over not two blocks away for, of all things, a malfunctioning tail light. The policemen who stopped him asked for his license. He felt that even if he'd been let off with a warning, this was too close for comfort to the scene. When the two dead house-swappers were eventually found, he would surely be remembered as a possible suspect, not having resided in that area. Add two London Bobbies to his tally.

There was hell to pay, of course. A nationwide manhunt by an outraged Scotland Yard. More nasty reportage by the journalist.

Ordinarily, he would have disposed of Gilhooley. But in fairness Gilhooley had been given a task that was not within his primary expertise as developed during his IRA years. Gilhooley worked from a distance, not so up close and personal. He blew up cars and trucks, sometimes yachts, not sleeping heads. He never went anywhere without ready access to a few pounds of Semtex and the means to ignite them. Haskell, instead, put him on probation and gave him a task that he couldn't screw up. Be a bar-fly-on-the-wall, so to speak, in Belle Haven. And don't be caught with a weapon.

Haskell told him who he'd be watching for. It turned out that he knew Kessler, but by reputation only. And of course he knew of the owner of that house. Everyone had heard of Harry Whistler. But he'd never heard of Elizabeth Stride and Haskell chose not to enlighten him. His thoughts might have turned to that price on her head. At the very least, it might color his judgment, make him less objective. Haskell wanted objective reporting.

Gilhooley had called in his first report as Haskell was preparing to leave for the Grove. He'd confirmed that indeed there were several people living in the Belle Haven house. He'd seen a woman who has to be Stride according to Gilhooley's description of her. He'd seen her cutting lilacs in the front yard accompanied by a young dark-haired girl who was holding a kitten in her arms. He'd seen a man who must have been Kessler doing most of the driving to and fro. He'd seen Kessler in a restaurant with two other girls. The bartender knew them. He'd called both girls by name. One was called Nicky. The other had a name that sounded like Eye-sha. Haskell assumed that the name must be Aisha. A common Muslim name. Not so with Nicky. Must be the short form of something else.

Gilhooley took pictures wherever he could. Haskell told him to FedEx them all to the Grove along with a written report.

"Take plenty of photos of all who come and go. Those who live there and anyone you see visiting. Especially get some good photos of the woman. Good clear photos of her face and some full body shots. Take note of everything about her. I want it all, no matter how trivial. What she's wearing, how she seems, what sort of person do you make her. I'll be the judge of what's important."

Gilhooley didn't try to hide his annoyance.

"That's what this is about? It's for one of your doxies?"

Haskell's voice turned hard. "Watch your mouth."

TWELVE

Mulazim reached Belle Haven in the late afternoon. The first thing he did was to look in a phone book. He found nothing for a Harrison Whistler. He tried Information. He was told that the number was not listed.

Phone number not listed, post office box address. Must be a man who doesn't like to be bothered when he comes to stay in this house.

He spent the remaining hours of daylight driving the winding streets to get to know them. He drove looking at houses that were of a size that seemed to fit this Niki's description. There were too many. That was no help.

While driving, he would watch for young girls, especially those with dark hair. He did see two who might be Arab or Persian, but the first was ten years old at the most and the other, the right age, but with a ring on her lip and on a skateboard and half naked. Most unlikely.

When darkness approached, he made his way to the tennis courts that Niki had told him about. It was where he was mostly likely to spot them. The easiest to spot would probably be Rasha if she still played her tennis in long pants and long sleeves. Especially if she played with Elizabeth Stride who would not be so hard to spot either.

This place, Marcey Park, had three lighted courts. Only two could be easily seen from his car, so he had to get out and walk around them on foot. There were several benches where he could sit and watch through the pair of binoculars he'd bought. He went dressed for comfort, also for anonymity, in the sweatshirt with a hood and the sweat pants from the Wal-Mart. He also wore a pair of yellow-tinted sunglasses of the type that wraps around the sides of one's eyes.

There were very few men. They were mostly young women either playing or waiting to play. He saw some of them marking a list that was posted. There was apparently a limit of one hour for each group. Some played in tennis dresses that could almost be called modest. Most, however, were utterly shameless. Some played with legs bared all the way to the hip. Some played with bare shoulders in a garment called a tank top and some with even bare bellies. With most, you could see their breasts bouncing as they played. One in particular enjoyed being watched. She and her partner looked to be in their late twenties, bearing no resemblance to any he sought. She looked over at him and cupped both her breasts as if asking if he liked what he saw. Such a slut.

Those he did seek, however, were not there the first night. He was not dismayed. A good hunter is patient. He would choose a new motel and then he'd go out for his first good meal since he got to this country. On Bernice's laptop, he searched for a restaurant

144

that served the sort of food that would not give him gas. He was pleased to find several boasting Mideast cuisine, most of them within a short drive. Most had the word "kabob" in their names. He chose the one nearest. It was in a shopping center.

After dinner he would choose a new license plate.

The next day, more driving, more looking around. Except that he knew the streets well by now, it was not a productive use of his time. As the hour approached to go back and watch tennis, he was suddenly struck by a thought. Last night, instead of searching for Mideast cuisine, he should have been looking for Italian. Niki had written that Aisha's party was planned in "a small Italian restaurant that we like."

He'd wondered at the time why Italian was chosen. So much garlic, so much sauce. Why not food that they knew? But she had also said that Martin likes going to bars. Italian restaurants have bars. Mideast restaurants, not so much. He had probably influenced the choice.

Once again, he plugged in Bernice's computer and did a search for Italian. There were many. Too many. The list went on for pages. More than two hundred fifty in this part of Virginia. Of these, more than forty were not far from Belle Haven. Three of these, however, were described as being "intimate." If one of these was the restaurant that Niki said "we like," it follows that they all must have eaten there before, perhaps often enough to be remembered. Mulazim wrote down the names. He would visit all three. Success comes to the hunter who is thorough.

That day, however, did not end so well. He was forced to kill a policeman.

He'd been aware that he'd been noticed by some tennis players when he was the only spectator. But mostly only glances. On the whole, he was ignored, seen only as a man who liked to watch tennis and this was, after all, a public place. Anyway, his dark hooded sweatshirt from the Wal-Mart helped him to blend into the shadows.

But the slut was back again, dressed much as before, playing with the same other woman as before. The partner wasn't so bad. A loose T-shirt and shorts. Also skinny, not so much to show off. The sluttish one deserved to be caned. On her, fully half of her breasts were revealed. He could see the line where they'd been partly tanned. Her body glistened with a sheen of sweat the way wanton women glow after sex. And she had a tattoo at the base of her spine. He raised his binoculars to see what it was. Hard to tell. Maybe some kind of bird.

Watching her caused a stirring in his lower region, but the sin was not on him; it was on her. A stiffness followed. It would not go away. He was tempted to go into the restroom near his bench and relieve what had become a protrusion.

Those two had reached the end of their hour. Both were on the far side of the court. They were gathering their equipment and toweling off. The slut was making a call on her cell phone. He would not have thought the call had any relevance because she did not look in his direction. But not three minutes later, she was pointing at him. She was pointing him out to a uniformed policeman, an older man perhaps in his fifties.

The policeman approached. He asked, "Well? What's the story?"

"Story? No story. I am here watching tennis."

146

The slut with the cell phone had also approached. She said to the policeman, "That's not what he's watching. He never even looks where the ball is going. All he looks at are asses and tits."

Mulazim reddened. "This is not so."

"Easy, young lady," said the policeman. "We don't need that kind of language."

"Well, I'm sorry," she answered, "but we don't need creeps either. And why would he need a pair of binocs to watch tennis from fifty feet away?"

The policeman asked the girl, "Only looking, you say? Has he bothered you otherwise? Has he said anything?"

"Heavy breathing was enough. We could hear it from the court."

He said, "Sir, let's take a walk to my car."

"No, no," said Mulazim. "You both misunderstand." He took care to keep his eyes from this one's breasts. "I am looking, yes, but I am looking for my niece. She ran away from the school that she attends in New York along with one of her classmates. Her mother is afraid for her. She asked me to help find her. When last heard from she was here because her classmate comes from here. Her mother says that these two play tennis all the time. I come here in the hope that they come here."

The policeman said, "That accent. Where are you from, sir?"

"I am Hungarian. From very near Budapest." He wasn't sure what led him to say that. But his answer seemed to satisfy the policeman. He nodded. He said, "So you're new in this country."

"New, yes, but my sister is not. I came over to visit. It is five years since I saw her. Until I got to her house only three days ago, I did not know that my niece had run off."

"You don't know her on sight? You need binoculars to find her?"

Mulazim was no stranger to police asking questions. He had found that he has a good mind for it. He said, "I have not seen her since she came here from Hungary. She was only this high." He held a hand at hip level. "She is now fifteen years old, but still not very tall. I have with me a photo that my sister gave me. It was taken, she told me, this past year at her school. May I show you this photo of my niece?"

The policeman nodded. "And some ID."

Mulazim reached into the pocket of his sweatshirt. He drew out the photo that he always kept with him. He said to the slut, "To you, my apologies. You will see why I need to look closely."

The slut looked at the photo. "What is she? A nun?"

Mulazim smiled within himself. A nun? Good idea. "No, no, it is a costume. This is for a school play. But all it shows of her face is from her chin to mid-forehead. Is it possible that you might have seen her?"

The slut, now less impudent, said, "No. Not off hand."

"When she was little, she was burned with hot oil. She knocked a pan off a stove. Bad burns scarred her legs and one of her arms. That is why I was looking at legs in case she no longer covers them up even though my sister says she does."

The slut winced. She said, "Ouch. How bad are the scars?"

"She is marked for life. Very sad."

"She covers them with what? With a warm-up suit?"

"A warm-up suit, yes. That is the term my sister used." It was what that girl at the tennis school called it.

"A lot of people wear them, but on cool mornings mostly." She studied the photo. "What color's her hair?"

"Dark brown," said Mulazim. "Much darker than mine. And long, although she might have cut it.

The slut narrowed her eyes as if trying to remember. She said, "Yeah, I've seen a group that comes in here some nights. Mostly dark-haired, or at least the kids are. Come to think of it, one of them does play in warm-ups. And yeah, I guess she's pretty small."

Mulazim's hand went to his mouth, such was his excitement. "You say kids? How many? Is there also an adult? A parent, perhaps, of the classmate?"

Her eyes again narrowed. "Three girls. No, wait. Four. There was one who only watched. And a couple of adults. A woman, mostly, but also a man. But they didn't look like parents. They were both lighter skinned. Instructors, maybe. They were coaching the girls. I've seen them playing each other while the girls watched. They go at it. They're both pretty good."

Mulazim asked, "Please. Could you describe this man and woman. This might help me to find my little niece."

She squinted. "Let's see. The woman's blond, fairly tall, I guess about thirty five. And she's hot. Stays in very good shape."

"And the man?"

"A little older. Rugged-looking. Curly brown hair. More laid-back than she is. Kids around with the girls."

"What of names," asked Mulazim. "Did you hear any used?"

"Look, I really wasn't paying that much attention. We come here to play our own game."

Mulazim understood. Nor did he need any names. The description of Stride was enough. "But they did not come here last night or tonight. Is there another place where they might play?"

She replied, "I don't know. Maybe they switched to mornings." She said to the policeman, "My friend's waiting. I'm her ride."

The policeman said, "Sure. Go ahead."

Mulazim's head was spinning as he watched her cross the court to where her tennis partner was waiting. Even the way this one walked was immodest. Deliberately so. To invite sinful thoughts. Her friend, not so brazen, but sitting, legs spread. He would like to teach both of them a lesson.

But the policeman said, "Let's still take that walk. I'd still like to see some ID."

"Yes, of course," said Mulazim. "You must do your duty." He gestured toward the restroom. It was in the same direction as the parked cars. "Do you mind? I am in some discomfort."

The policeman nodded. He said, "Yeah. Me too." They entered the one marked for men. Mulazim stood at his urinal only pretending, while he reached up his sleeve for the flat throwing knife that he'd fastened to his arm using bandages. The policeman had taken the urinal adjacent. Mulazim waited until he was fully engaged, his head tilted forward, looking down. He freed his knife and plunged it down hard where the policeman's spinal column joined his skull.

It was very efficient. No outcry. No sound. The policeman went rigid before he went soft. Mulazim left the knife where it had entered in order to prevent a gushing of blood that he would have to waste time cleaning up. He embraced the policeman before he could fall. With great effort, he managed to drag him backward and into the nearest toilet stall. He sat the dead policeman on the toilet. Only then did Mulazim reclaim his knife. There was blood this time, but only a trickle because now the man's heart had stopped pumping. And yet he kept peeing in several short squirts. This surprised Mulazim. Every day you learn something. He wiped the blade clean with toilet tissue.

Mulazim took the policeman's Glock pistol and the extra clip of bullets from his belt. Also his handcuffs. They might come in handy. Also his taser. Same reason. He took the squawky little radio from his lapel. He arranged the policeman in a natural position and pulled his pants down to his ankles. The little radio would tell him when his dispatcher started calling this policeman to ask where he is. Getting no answer, more police would come looking. Not a problem. Mulazim had plenty of time. It would probably be thirty minutes or more before any would think to look in this restroom.

He thought of latching the stall door and then climbing over, but that seemed unnecessarily strenuous. It was enough to jam some toilet paper into the latch plate. It would keep the stall door from swinging open. With this housekeeping done, he stepped out of the restroom. No one was approaching. No one was near.

No sound except the whop of tennis balls being struck and a single car's engine being started.

Those women. Those two women. He could see them in their car. It was a white convertible, top down. The sluttish one was backing it out of its space. He started to run, to try to catch them, to stop them, but he knew it was useless, twenty seconds too late. By the time he could get to where the Ford Escape was parked, they would be more than a mile ahead of him.

At least he knew their car. Another Ford. A Ford Mustang. Its Virginia license plate had five letters, no numbers. The license plate read "IMAIO" He puzzled for a moment. Is that a word? Did it have meaning?

Ah, yes. What it meant was "I am a 10." He had heard of such things. They're called vanity plates. More than mere vanity, this was a boast. It claimed the highest ranking of physical attractiveness. Why would this slut have such a thing on her car and yet take offense at her breasts being watched? She was not only wanton, but a hypocrite.

But never mind that now. He'd left a witness alive. True, a good hunter never leaves a trail, but sometimes a good hunter has his hands full. Tonight or early tomorrow at the latest, those two would learn of the dead policeman and they would surely come forward. They would describe the man who they'd left with the policeman within minutes of the time of his death. Unless he could find those two before that, there would be a big manhunt for him in particular instead of one for an unknown assailant. The slut would describe this "niece" he said he sought. She would tell the police that he'd asked for a description of the man and the woman who were teaching tennis to three or four girls with dark hair. Might the police make a public appeal for anyone who might know of such people? If so, Stride would hear of it. They might run again. Maybe. Maybe not. But this wasn't good. The best thing was to silence those two women.

Where to look for that Ford Mustang? Perhaps outside bars. Those two look like the type that goes to bars. They will probably first shower and put on other clothing before going out for more flaunting of themselves. God willing, he will spot the white Mustang at one of the bars in this town.

He realized that the more sensible course would be to get away before the manhunt begins. Call in a full report. Let others take over. Negotiate first for his portion of the bounty if they should take Elizabeth Stride and the Saudi princess named Rasha. It still would not be fair. He would always feel cheated. Look at all that he'd learned, all that he had accomplished. Right this minute he might be within a few streets of them.

All of them.

Including these last two.

THIRTEEN

Roger Clew was at home in his Georgetown apartment watching a night baseball game. Yankees versus Red Sox. Red Sox leading in the eighth. Last game of a three-game series at Fenway. He had taken a pill to help him sleep without tossing, washed down with the second of two vodka tonics. The pill hadn't yet taken effect.

Top of the ninth. Yankees batting. Two out. Then, as always seemed to happen at climactic moments, one of his cell phones started buzzing. It was a phone whose number wasn't generally known. He glanced at the read-out. It was Howard Leland. Clew was mildly surprised. He knew the no-phone rule. Leland had told him that, barring an emergency, he'd be out of reach through this Wednesday.

He used his remote to mute the TV. He picked up the phone. "Good evening, sir."

"Hello, Roger. Do you have a few minutes?"

"Of course, sir. Is there a problem?"

"Roger, that attempted grab of Angola's oil. Beyond a few indictments that are pending at Justice, is that done with as far as you're concerned?"

"Yes, it is."

"Is it done with as far as Martin Kessler is concerned?"

"Uh… sir, are you calling from Bohemian Grove?"

"No, I took a little ride with my security detail. This conversation is private if that's your concern. I'm well outside the gate as we speak."

"Sir, I take it that this subject has come up at the camp. Who's asking? Charles Haskell? Is this why he's playing host? To get you to keep Justice off his back?"

"His primary concern seems to be Martin Kessler." A pause. "Please answer my question."

"Okay, yes," said Clew. "I think I can assure you. Kessler never had any interest in Haskell. I don't think he even cared who got the oil."

"Yes. It was the diamonds. I remember."

"The Israelis had a deal. Haskell's group tried to queer it. They got hammered for it. End of story."

"Is it the end as far as the Mossad is concerned?"

"Their only interest was helping their country secure the Angolan diamond concession. The Angolans, for a change, didn't end up getting screwed. As far as they're concerned, that case is closed."

"You discussed this, have you, with their senior people?"

"With Yitzhak Netanya. He's as senior as they get. He and I talk all the time."

"Then what about as far as Harry Whistler is concerned?"

A sigh. "Sir, this might be hard for Haskell's ego to take, but Harry couldn't give a flying fuck about him and that goes double for Kessler. They've moved on. So should Haskell. So should you, by the way. I don't think you're in very good company."

Leland's voice became cool. "Please don't lecture me, Roger."

Clew grunted. "You're right. I'm sure you know what you're doing."

"It's called keeping one's ear to the ground," said Leland. "I'd be in better company at a church picnic, but I doubt that I'd learn very much that is useful beyond how to frost a cake properly."

"Point taken. My apologies, sir."

"Ear to the ground, just as yours always is through all those back-channel contacts of yours and your many off-the-books operations. You don't hear me offering gratuitous judgments about their morality, do you?"

"Sir…"

"Don't get me wrong, Roger. They do get results. But there's really no getting away from the fact that most are essentially criminal."

"Criminal?" asked Clew.

"As in lawless," said Leland. "They're no Eagle Scouts, Roger. People like Kessler and Whistler and their ilk live by their own set of rules."

"Sir, they have one rule. They take care of each other. That's what all of us should do, but we usually don't. And I'll remind that our government, our nation of laws, has been known to bend a few on occasion."

"Not our government," said Leland. "Rogue elements usually."

"Sir..."

"I know. I know. There are always rogue elements. I guess all of us work outside the law when we must."

"No, sir, you don't because I do it for you. And I get people to do it for me. But mine don't take orders. What we do is swap favors. And if I ever asked them to do something shabby, they'd not only tell me to shove it and decline, they'd block it from happening at all."

"What of Kessler's current project? No shabbiness there?"

"Um... what project is that, sir?"

"The one involving the Mideast, which usually means oil. He's been gathering people who are native to that region and who are, of course, fluent in Arabic."

Clew had sipped from his drink. He spit half of it back. Grinning, he said, "Sorry. Went down the wrong way."

"Did I say something funny?"

"This is coming from Haskell? And you're buying into it? Sir, that is so far off the mark."

157

"You're saying it does not involve oil?"

"It involves being back with Elizabeth Stride. It involves taking care of some young Muslim girls after their Nasreen guardians got killed."

"Runaways?" asked Leland. He sounded surprised. "Do you happen to know any of their names?"

"I've met Aisha. She's been here four or five years. She's practically a daughter to Kessler and Stride. The others are recent. I don't know who they are. Why are you asking, Mr. Leland?"

"Oh, just curious. I'm sure it's… not important."

"Sir, I need a few minutes. Let me call you right back."

"Go ahead. Ask him. I'll wait."

Ask him. Oh, right. Leland thinks he's calling Kessler. Well, he's not. He wants to see if Boston blows it.

Clew broke the connection. He wiped the spray of vodka tonic from his shirt, picked up his remote and turned the sound back on. The Yankees had scored while he was talking to Leland. They'd tied the game, then flied out to right field. The Red Sox were now batting, bottom of the ninth, one out with a runner on second. Other than wanting to see if they'd score, Clew needed a few quiet moments to decide how much Leland was entitled to know. Especially when his reason for wanting to know was to ease the mind of his new buddy, Haskell. What's Kessler up to? Not a damned thing. On the other hand, here were the Boston Red Sox one base hit away from a sweep of the Yankees and into solo first place. One must keep one's priorities straight.

Yes!! A bloop single dropped into short left. The ball's bobbled, late throw, the runner scores standing up. Crowd at Fenway goes nuts. There is justice in the world. This is worth another vodka and tonic.

As Clew mixed it, he returned to the subject at hand. Kessler gathering speakers of Arabic. Why? What's he up to? Must involve Mideast oil. Take it one step further and it must involve some sort of plot against Trans-Global Oil. Leland must have had a reason for asking the names of the four Muslim girls Stride took in. Clew was sorry that he even named Aisha. It's those two vodka tonics. Loosened lips. Never good. Aisha's had enough trouble for a lifetime already. Mother and father murdered in Egypt when she was... how old? Not yet twelve. Some uncle was behind it, Clew seemed to recall. Oh, yeah. He needed the family money for some weapons deal he'd put together. He could get it under Egyptian law, especially if he knew the right judge. But their only heir, Aisha, would have to go too. The Nasreens blew that for him. Got her over here. The uncle didn't live very long after that. Clew never heard how, but it wouldn't surprise him if Stride, herself, had paid him a visit. No reason to think so. It just wouldn't surprise him.

He'd met Aisha once. Terrific kid. A beautiful kid. She's how old now? Sixteen? Yeah, just about. It seemed to him she's got a birthday coming up.

Oops, thought Clew. He was starting to feel the pill that he took. Better call Leland back while his brain was still working. And he thought he'd better tape the conversation, this time. He picked up the cell phone, jacked it into his recorder and tapped the read-out that showed Leland's number.

Leland answered on the first ring. He asked, "Well? What did he have to say?"

Clew had almost forgotten. "Kessler sends his regards. He thinks of you fondly. Stride yelled hello from the kitchen."

An impatient sigh. "About those girls, Roger."

"Your so-called linguists? Yes, of course they speak Arabic. They grew up over there. There's nothing more to it than that."

"Which girls? Did he tell you? Other than Aisha?"

"No, he didn't. You told me this wasn't important."

"From what countries?" asked Leland, ignoring the reminder. "Do you know their nationalities at least?"

Clew didn't. Oh, wait. He remembered. "Two of them are sisters. They got out of Iran. Harry mentioned them in passing a few weeks ago."

"Harry Whistler?"

"Uh-huh. He was over for a visit. With them. Not with me. But he came back through D.C. and we went out to dinner." Clew was tempted to bust Leland's balls by saying that Yitzhak Netanya had joined them. Yitzhak hadn't, of course. One criminal was enough. This phone call didn't need more complications.

"Iranians, you say. They speak Farsi, not Arabic."

"Sir…"

"Sorry. Quite right. Farsi's written in Arabic. They'd probably know classic Arabic as well."

"And some Kurdish, some Turkish, to say nothing of English. You hear all five and more in Tehran."

"Tehran? That's where the sisters are from?"

"I believe so," said Clew. "That was my understanding."

"Might the fourth girl be a Saudi? More than that, a Saudi princess?"

"Sir… what is this? What's going on?"

Haskell again. He's here with that girl's father. She disappeared from Riyadh within this same time frame. For reasons that I'd rather not go into just yet, it's put something of a crimp in Haskell's plans."

"Which are?"

"He wasn't about to lay them all out for me. I only have bits and pieces. But if this princess is with Kessler, a long shot, I grant you, I think he'd do almost anything to get her."

A crimp in Haskell's plans? Wouldn't that be too bad. Clew said, "Howard, I don't know, but I very much doubt it. If Harry thought to mention the two from Iran, he sure as hell would have mentioned a princess."

"Unless he chose to keep it from you?"

"Howard, why would he? He knows all I'd have to do is hop into my car and…" Shit, thought Clew. Damn that pill.

Leland paused for a beat. "They're so near?"

"Not so very," he lied. "A few hours."

"Call again and ask. Just for my satisfaction. And as for Harry Whistler, he's in oil, is he not?"

"Harry's in almost everything, Howard."

"Oil included."

He's brokered drilling rights, tankers and drilling equipment and, I think, pumping stations for pipelines. But none of his business is with Arab states. By now, he's even out of Angola. Almost all of its with the former Soviet republics developing the Caspian oilfields."

Leland said, "Hmmm. He won't work the Mideast?"

"Howard, it isn't a won't; it's a can't. Or doesn't need to. He's got all he can handle in the Caspian."

"So it follows that he's not in competition with Trans-Global."

Clew groaned. "You mean with Haskell. No, he is not. Trans-Global doesn't work the Caspian either. They've tried but they've been shut out."

"By Harry?"

"Not at all. Don't tell me he thinks so."

"He hasn't said that. At least not to me. I'm just trying to get a grip on the dynamics here."

"Sir, Haskell's paranoid. That's the dynamic. He's also mistrusted. That's why he's shut out. Harry Whistler is neither. That's why he's in. Does this sum it up for you, sir?"

Another long silence on Leland's end. Clew could almost hear counting to ten in an effort to keep his temper in check. Clew said, "Sir, I apologize. It's late and I'm tired."

"Hold on just a minute," said Leland.

Clew heard the sound of a powerful car. It approached, speeding by, its tires spraying gravel. He heard a few sharp slaps that almost sounded like gunshots. He heard a voice, not Leland's, shout "Hey, watch it. Slow down." It was probably one of Leland's two bodyguards. He heard Leland say, "They didn't waste any time," in a tone that seemed almost amused.

Clew asked. "What was that? What just happened out there?"

"It's that Saudi prince and one of Haskell's associates. Trouble at home. They're rushing back to Riyadh. Kicked up a few stones as they passed. Where was I?"

"Going nowhere with your line of questioning, sir."

All this talk was beginning to swim in Clew's head. He was glad that he recorded it. He stifled a yawn. He said, "Sir, I've taken a sleeping pill."

"I'll let you go. Just one more thing. I need to find that Saudi princess and soon. Find out for me where the Nasreens have sent her. If she isn't with Kessler, he need not be involved. But once you learn where she's gone, I'll need you to…"

"Back up, sir," said Clew. "Involved in what?"

"I told you. This business with Haskell,"

Clew grimaced. He said, "Sir, I need to end this discussion. It's starting to go around in circles."

"Roger, I need to know. By tomorrow if possible. I'm sure that Elizabeth Stride can find out through her close ties with the Nasreens. Then, I'm going to ask you to set up a meeting…"

"Sir... sir, the answer is no. There's no way I'm going to touch this."

"You're refusing?"

Sir, here's a better idea. I don't know what's cooking between you and Haskell. I'm sure that you mean well. I'm sure Haskell doesn't. Can you still see the tail lights of that Saudi prince's car? Follow them. Get out of there tonight."

"He's planning something, Roger. Believe me, it's big. And this little Saudi princess is his key to moving forward. We need to find her before he does."

"This girl, I take it, didn't run off empty-handed. She dipped into her father's private papers?"

"Something like that. She copied some sensitive material onto disks."

"Like what?"

"Roger, for the moment, I'd rather not say. But it's more than sensitive. It's political dynamite. It could devastate the Saudi regime."

Clew nodded. "Uh-huh. And you want to see it. Mr. Leland, that's not going to happen."

"Roger, need I remind you..."

"Remind me of what? That I work for you? I do and I don't. I think we both understand that. Either way, I think you're missing the point. The Nasreens would never give up that... whatever. It would be useless as insurance if they did."

"They can keep it. Roger. I just want to review it."

"That of just this one girl?"

"Just the Saudi."

You said Haskell would do almost anything to get it. Might that include snatching the princess?"

"First he'll try to recover the material at its source. That's why those two are flying back to Riyadh. Failing that, he hopes to get it through Stride. You do know where she is, do you not?"

"You know that I do. But don't ask."

"Well, I've got the feeling that Haskell might know. He at least knows they're not in Vermont. If he does, he'll set up some sort of surveillance. He may even have done so already. Unless Stride's girls are being kept out of sight, he might be tempted to take the first one he can get at and use her to bargain with Stride. By the way, I heard him ask for a photo of the Saudi. He might have one within the next day or two."

"Okay," said Clew wearily. "Tell Haskell we talked. Tell him that as soon as I got off the phone, I called Kessler and told him to blow town tonight. Tell Haskell that even if he knows where they are, they won't still be there in the morning. Tell him that Kessler will stash his four girls and then he and Stride will come looking for him. Then get on a plane and come home."

"Roger, I'd like to find her for my reasons, not his. As I've said, she's the key...

"To some grand scheme of Haskell's. Yes, I heard you," said Clew. "There are always grand schemes where oil is concerned. Can you think of one that ever went as planned?"

Roger, yes or no. Will you try to locate her?"

I wouldn't mind, thought Clew, seeing what she has myself. He might make a phone call. Not tonight, though. Tomorrow. "Let me give it some thought. I'll do what I can. But right now I must get to bed."

"Very well. Get your rest. Just one other thing. Are you aware of that new Muslim prophecy that seems to be all over the internet?"

"The female messiah?" "A Joan of Arc type. It seems to be causing quite a stir in their world. Muslim women are embracing it, especially the young. They're passing it on to other young women and some have been arrested for doing so."

"Sir, that prophecy's not new. It's centuries years old."

"But revived by whom?"

"I'd have no idea."

"Can it be traced to its more recent source?"

"Not a chance," said Clew. "It's way beyond tracing. By now it's passed through a few million computers to say nothing of faxes and word of mouth and it's probably in half the world's languages."

Leland asked, "We trace viruses, don't we?"

"This is no virus. A virus is a code. It's an entity in itself. It has only one version at a time in most cases. This is more like a rumor whose versions keep changing. Who's to say which one kicked this off?"

"I'd have thought with our technology…"

"Only in the movies."

Leland was silent for a long moment. Clew could hear him drumming his fingers, probably on the hood of his Lincoln. "This wife of Mohammed, his warrior wife... are you aware that her name was Aisha?"

"Oh, for Pete's sake," said Clew. "It's a common Muslim name."

"Food for thought, though. Is it not?"

"Not to me."

"As for who revived it, Muslim feminists seem most likely. One would be inclined to suspect the Nasreens. However, another odd thought has just struck me. It only re-emerged less than three months ago. That's when Kessler came back from the dead."

"Mr. Leland. On my life. No connection."

"Very well. I accept that. But there's one more coincidence. It began soon after those Hilton Head killings. It refers to an angel accompanying Aisha. A flame-haired angel bearing a sword. Who does that sound like to you?"

"Angel. Black Angel. So it must be Stride? I think you must be as groggy as I am."

"I'm getting there," said Leland. "But you see how it looks. And if that Saudi princess should happen to be with them..."

"Uh-huh," said Clew drippingly. "Makes it clear as a bell. Stride and Kessler found out that this princess's father had some kind of a deal with Charles Haskell. Kessler saw a chance to not only screw Haskell, but to what? You just said it. Dump the Saudi royal family. Harry Whistler is in it with him. So, while we're at it, is Yitzhak Netanya. Suddenly they're in control of half the world's oil. Hey, you can't say that Kessler thinks small."

"Roger..."

"No, wait. It gets better. Think even bigger. Not just Arabs. He decides to destabilize the whole Muslim world by passing off one of these runaway girls as some resurrected feminist warrior. How convenient that he's even got an Aisha on hand who seems to be just the right age."

"I can do without the sarcasm, Roger."

"My apologies, but yes, I do see how it looks. At least to a schizo like Haskell."

"All the same..."

"Sir, listen to me. So far this isn't serious. It will be if Haskell does something dumb in response to a threat that doesn't exist. You're in a position to keep that from happening by persuading him that Kessler has zero involvement. You're there. Use your time there. Find out what you can. If it's criminal, and it will be, call justice, let them handle it, but for God's sake, keep the rest of us out of it."

"Now you're asking me to stay?"

"Ear to the ground, sir. I guess it can't hurt."

"I think I'll have him believe that I've spoken with Stride."

"Directly?"

"Very well. Through you. You routed the call. I'll say that she's agreed to contact the Nasreens and recover whatever the princess took. She said it might take a few days."

Clew squinted. He asked. "She's agreed to this... why?"

"In return for his assurance that he'll leave Stride in peace if Stride and Kessler will leave him in peace. And that no harm would come to the princess."

"Uh-huh. And you think that Haskell will buy this."

"It should at least keep him dangling for a few days. In the meantime, you'll contact Stride yourself and get her to get you a look at that disk. If you can and its contents are what Haskell says they are, we'll have beaten him at his own game."

"Good plan," said Clew who was twisting his lip. Sir, I'm out on my feet."

"You can reach me through my security detail. You'll let me know soonest?"

"Goodnight, sir."

Clew kicked off his shoes. He unbuttoned his shirt. He was more than just tired. He was tired of this shit. See this? This is how. This is how it always starts. Wrong conclusions drawn from unrelated events. Lives end up getting wrecked. People end up getting killed.

Arabic speakers being gathered by Kessler. Wrong. No such thing. They're only young girls who Stride's taking care of until the Nasreens can find them good homes. Except for Aisha, of course. She's a keeper. Could Stride and Kessler have the princess? They might. If they don't, sure, they could find out who does. Either way, though, the princess would no longer have that disk. The Nasreens would and there are none in Belle Haven. Where are they? All over. They have a half dozen chapters in this country alone. Where is that disk? It's locked away somewhere. It would be held for a year or two, three at the most. When the princess is deemed to be safe, they'd destroy it. It would probably never be opened.

Oh, and now there's that prophecy. Gee, look at the timing. It only started making the rounds at about the same time Stride took those girls. Mohammed's take-no-shit wife is coming back and she's pissed. All you Muslim men out there, guess what; the party's over. No more burkas and abayas. We want Donna Karan. We want to drive our own cars and go out on dates and get laid without being stoned to death for it. And by the way, get up off your asses. From now on you're going to give us some help around the house. You can start by picking up after yourselves. Take the garbage out. Dry the dishes.

And here's the clincher. Are you ready for this? What's the name of Mohammed's young warrior wife? Aisha, right? Give that man a cigar. And what's the name of the girl who Stride is protecting? It's Aisha. What more proof do you need?

And who else is behind this? Must be Harry Whistler. And/or Yitzhak Netanya. To say the least, Yitzhak's no fan of the Saudis. But neither are most other Arab states. Anyway, what's their game? What are they up to? Not a damn thing, you say? Then how do you explain this weird timing?

Round and round she goes. Where she stops, God only knows. It's the dumbest thing Clew had ever heard.

He finished undressing and climbed into bed. As heavy as his eyelids had become, he now wasn't sure that he'd be able to sleep. Too many thoughts, names and faces were colliding in his head. Should he alert Kessler or would that be crying wolf?

Maybe this will all quiet down by itself if Leland is convinced that it's all smoke and mirrors and is able to mollify Haskell. But is Leland convinced? He seemed to be, yes. Clew had trouble remembering all that had been said. He'd replay the recording in the morning.

Time enough to think about it then.

FOURTEEN

Mulazim was ready to begin his search for those women in the little white convertible. How would he find them? He would rely on God's guidance. God would want them just as badly as he did. He would want them found and punished for immodesty.

The first thing he'd done was return to his motel, slipping in without being seen. Having changed into his clothing from the Wal-Mart, Mulazim studied himself in the mirror of the bathroom. A new man. He looked typically American. He tucked the Glock pistol that he took from the policeman into his belt at the small of his back. He checked in the mirror to see if it bulged. It did not because such jackets are designed to fit loosely in order to make a good golf swing. He switched the policeman's little radio off and slid it into the pocket of his trousers. He'd had it on while he was changing, listening to calls between several policemen and their dispatcher. They had not found the missing policeman.

Thus equipped, he would now hunt the Mustang's driver especially, the slut who had caused all this trouble. He was sure that she could no longer identify him except, of course, by the sound of his voice. Even so, she'd seen his photo of Rasha and she'd heard his explanation for watching so much tennis. She'd seen his response to what she had said about the man and the woman who played with her there. She knew far too much. She must be silenced.

He had parked his car directly outside his door. He stepped out to it carrying the bag meant for laundry which he squeezed down behind his front seat. Next, he reentered his room and went out again through the door that led to the corridor. He walked down to the lobby's front desk. There was a woman on duty. He asked her to recommend a good tavern or bar. Someplace lively, he said. Not a restaurant for families. Someplace young that is suitable for unmarried people where he might find laughter and fellowship. The woman at the desk knew of several such places. She said she would be happy to show them on a map.

She produced not a street map, more a map of cartoons. It showed oversized drawings of restaurants and bars and a few other places such as book stores. She said, "They're all on a stretch of about a quarter mile where Glebe Road crosses Old Dominion." His eye caught a drawing of a place called Mangiamo. He touched a finger to the name.

"Italian?" he asked her. "Small restaurant?"

She nodded. "Mangiamo. That's Italian for 'Let's eat.' Fairly small, but very popular. It does have a bar, but the crowd isn't really what you'd call young."

Still worth looking into, but first things come first. He said, "I would like to meet people my age. The span is middle twenties to not much over thirty."

"Gotcha. That would be these." She circled three. She said, "It's Sunday, so I don't know how active they'll be, but all three of them fit that description."

Mulazim thanked her and said, "Oh, I must make a complaint. I was taking a long nap and left a call to be awaked. There was no call. I might have missed my evening out."

She said, "Sorry about that, sir. I'll look into it."

Mulazim dismissed it. "Forget that I spoke. I must have needed a three-hour nap."

"Well, sir, have a good evening all the same."

It might be useful, thought Mulazim, one never knows, to have this desk clerk convinced that he'd been in his room at the time that policeman was last heard from. As for these bars, he knew where they were. He'd seen them all during his driving.

Back in his car, he turned on the police radio. He was pleased to learn that they still hadn't found him. But the voices did not seem very concerned. One joked that he had probably picked up some… hottie?… it being past the end of his shift. Foul play didn't seem to be even considered. Instead, one got the feeling that this was a safe town where not much very bad ever happened. Even so, shouldn't they think to look in the rest rooms? Suppose he got sick and wished to stay near a toilet. This seemed very careless of them.

Mulazim drove north on Old Dominion Road to where it intersects the Grebe Road of the map. Along the way, he saw a house that was under renovation. In front, a large container for construction debris. It was there that he disposed of his laundry. He continued on to the first of these bars. He turned into its lot and drove slowly through it.

There were not so many cars. Perhaps a dozen or so. None was the Ford Mustang that he sought. He did the same when he reached the next bar. He could see through the window many big televisions, all of them on and showing baseball. A few young people were standing outside smoking cigarettes. He drove in. It was an old building with alleys and byways. Cars were parked in a chaotic fashion, easy to get blocked in by others. Very inefficient if they ever got busy. But again, not so many. And no Mustang.

He proceeded to the third bar that was circled. A sign promised live music and two-dollar long necks. He didn't know what a long neck was, but regardless, the offer seemed not enough to lure more than a handful of customers.

Inefficient? Chaotic? Well, so was this search. He knew perfectly well that success was unlikely unless God were to answer his prayers. Those two girls might have gone to any number of places. Another restaurant, to a movie, or they might have stayed home. But this was better than driving to all possible such places. It was also early. It was only nine o'clock. It had only just gotten fully dark out. Those two girls, if they were coming to either of these, would have taken much more time than he took to get ready. They would have painted themselves while deciding what to wear. It would probably be another hour at least before they got to any of these places.

In the meantime, he hadn't eaten.

He proceeded to the restaurant that was called Mangiamo. No parking lot at this one. Only parking on the street. Not a young clientele, the motel clerk had said. But just to make sure, he drove once around the block. He saw cars of all types, but, as expected, no Mustang. He parked a little ways up the street and went in to pass some time having dinner.

A good Muslim, of course, does not go to bars. But here there are no restaurants that do not have bars unless one wants to live on hamburgers and fries. One good thing about bars is that a man by himself is not likely to attract undue notice.

The bar itself was to his left as he entered. Five men and one woman were sitting along it. Sunday night. It was another sparse crowd. To the right were small tables that were known as cocktail tables. Such tables were higher than the kind meant for meals and some could hold only two persons. For meals there was a dining room in the back that was entered through an archway decorated with vines. It was otherwise hidden behind a wall that showed a big mural of what he assumed was some old village in Italy. There was no one in the back taking meals.

Mulazim was forced to take a seat at the bar. Otherwise, he would have stood out. Even so, he chose a spot that was close to the entrance where the bar took a curve toward the wall. His seat was also a good place of vantage for watching the TV at the opposite end even though it was only showing baseball.

This clientele seemed a mixture of various stations, some in nice clothing, some not so nice. The woman, not young, middle forties perhaps, sat doing a crossword puzzle. The man next to her seemed to be helping. That man, same age, had the look of a worker, all dressed in denim that was faded and frayed and in his ear he wore a big hearing aid. He was also the only one who glanced up when Mulazim came through the door. Other than, of course, the bartender. Mulazim asked if he might see a menu.

The bartender was a very large man who had, thought Mulazim, a certain fearsomeness to him, yet his greeting was entirely amiable. Mulazim ordered a veal chop that came with spaghetti and a salad with tomatoes and olives. Meanwhile, he asked for a Pepsi.

The big man asked, "How do you want your chop?"

"Oh, how cooked? I prefer it well done."

"We don't do well done here. This is Mangiamo. Even cooking it medium louses up a good chop. You want at least medium rare."

This seemed more a command than friendly advice. Very well, though. "It will be as you suggest."

Where he comes from, meat is always well cooked if you don't want to get the shits and the vomits, but perhaps here the meat is not so old. The one waitress on duty brought his plate from the kitchen. When it came, he cut into it. It was pink. Almost bleeding. Even so, the taste was delicious.

The big man watched him chew. He said, "Well?"

"You are right," said Mulazim. "So much better."

"First time here? New in town?"

"Yes. First time. I came to visit a friend. But sadly, I appear to have missed him." Mulazim didn't know what made him say that. Sometimes an inner voice whispered to him. Not God, because the voice is sometimes stupid.

The bartender asked, "Who's your friend? Does he come in here?"

"It was him who spoke of the food in this restaurant, but not of this excellent veal chop."

"No kidding. What's his name? I probably know him."

"His name is Mr. Harrison Whistler."

"Harry?" The bartender boomed out the name. The woman at the puzzle looked up and smiled. The man who was helping her reacted as well, but his look seemed more one of surprise. "Sure, I know Harry. High-stepping Harry. He says he flies over every chance he gets to get his fix of our Lobster Tortellini."

"Lobster Tortellini. Ah, yes," said Mulazim. Crustaceans. Unclean. Disgusting.

"Yeah, Harry was in just a few weeks ago. He came in with a whole... Just a second."

The bar phone had rung. Such terrible timing. A whole what? A whole group? All young dark-haired girls? In the company of Elizabeth Stride? Be patient, Mulazim. Be calm.

The big man answered the phone. He said, "Mangiamo. This is Sam." He listened with a deepening frown to whatever was being said to him. He said, "Yeah, she's here. Hold on, Dave." He raised a hand toward the rear of the bar. He was waving at the woman who'd been doing the puzzle, motioning her to come forward. She came, a wearied look on her face. She said, "Damn it, Sam. I'm off duty."

He told her, "Eddie Fitch. They just found him. He's dead. Someone left him propped up on a Marcey Park toilet. Sergeant Ragland's been trying to reach you."

She took the phone from him. "Dave? It's Karen." She said nothing more for a full thirty seconds. She stood nodding gravely as she listened. She said to the bartender, "Clean kill with a knife." She touched a finger to the base of her skull. "Took his gun. His radio, too." She listened further, eyes narrowed, more nodding. She told the bartender, "They might have a witness. It's a woman who made the 911 call that brought Eddie down there in the first place. They have her name and her cell. They're trying to locate her." She told the caller, "I'll be right in."

Mulazim didn't need to pretend that he wasn't listening closely. The others at the bar were hearing as much. They were murmuring with each other. "Eddie Fitch. Someone killed him. Eddie Fitch? You mean the cop? Yeah, he comes in here a lot with his wife. Oh, God, I wonder if she knows yet. Damn. He's like a year from putting in his papers. They were planning to buy an RV, tour the country."

Mulazim had no trouble showing equal concern, but for very different reasons than these others. They have the name of this girl and the number of her cell phone? Of course they would. How could he not have known? All such calls to the police are recorded. If they have a name, they have an address. They're trying to locate her? That must mean she's not home or has turned off her phone. And that means that he might still be able to find her before she can tell what he knows.

The woman handed the phone back to Sam. She said, "State cops, too. They'll be setting up roadblocks. It's going to be a long night." She turned to leave. Sam said, "Let me know." She nodded. They held each other's eyes for a moment. She nodded again and went out.

This exchange that was largely unspoken seemed odd. A bartender telling the police to report? But Mulazim did not dwell on it. Perhaps it meant nothing. Mulazim saw this Karen get into her car. She placed a red flashing light on its roof and lost no time speeding off. He could also hear distant sirens. The bartender told him, now unnecessarily, "Karen's a cop. Friend of Eddie's."

Mulazim wanted to leave, but he wanted to stay. He wanted to hear what else was said. He wanted to resume his discussion with Sam about those who came here with this High-stepping Harry. He wanted to ask which house, what address, but he couldn't. A friend of Harry Whistler would already know. All this was very frustrating.

Very frustrating and also unnerving. But one thing was certain. God had guided him here. How could that be doubted? All he'd wanted was to pass some time having dinner before starting his search for that white car in earnest. But look at all that's been laid at his feet. Such things do not happen by chance. Maybe God even caused the slut of the Mustang to go out again leaving her cell phone behind. Very possible, thought Mulazim. God wouldn't want the police finding her before he can find her himself.

What to do now, though? Resume his search? Not with all these sirens. Not with roadblocks springing up. Certainly not with a knife on his arms and a dead policeman's pistol in his belt. Did he dare to go back to his motel room? Even if he got there without misadventure, he'd be sitting there in ignorance of all that is happening. In his part of the world, when a suspect is sought, dozens, even hundreds, would be rounded up. Could that happen in Belle Haven? A late knock on his door? A questioning of all new faces?

Better to stay where God sent him to begin with. Better to stay where he is known to have been dining when that policeman's body was found. Better to stay where he is likely to hear all of the latest developments. Better to get into conversations with the others. If they know this Harry Whistler, they would very likely know Elizabeth Stride. In conversation, where she's living could easily come up. Yes, better and smarter. He would stay.

"Hello there," came a voice approaching behind him. He turned to see the man dressed in denim pull out the stool nearest him. "Friend of Harry's, are you? Let me buy to a beer."

He offered his hand. "Name's Gilhooley."

FIFTEEN

Roger Clew replayed Leland's call the next morning. He did so in the "Quiet Room" near his office at State. He realized that he had been less than respectful in response to some of Leland's speculations. Leland, on the other hand, had been deliberately vague about what he knew of Haskell's plans.

Why so? Because they're huge? Earth-shaking? Life-altering? Or is it because he likes being in the game and not looking on from the sidelines. Perhaps he's tired of knowing only what he's been told by people who are closer to the action. Clew couldn't say that he blamed him. So, Clew decided, let him have his fun. Let him, as he suggested, string Haskell along by saying that he's got Stride on the case.

Clew considered downloading the recording and emailing it to Kessler with a little background added. Kessler would respond. He'd say keep me informed while probably shaking his head in... disgust? Disgust or amusement. More than likely, some of both.

Amusement when he got to the part about Elizabeth being a prophesied angel. To say nothing of Aisha. Changing the world. Clew, in his place, would say "We don't need this. Let's get those girls to the nearest Nasreen safe house. This is nuts, but let's not take any chances." Kessler wouldn't, however. Kessler thrives on taking chances.

Elizabeth is the one with the much shorter fuse. She would say, "What, for this? You'd uproot them again for this? Stride would say, "Tell you what. Where's this Haskell right now. I'll go and do some uprooting of my own."

That sounds like Stride. Or at least the old Stride. She'd surely want to put an end to this quickly. But she might also want to put an end to old Roger for upsetting them all with this nonsense.

Clew extracted his recording of last night's conversation. He slid his chair to a nearby computer. He hadn't paid much attention to the prophecy before this. He typed in a code that accessed State's data base. The data it contained was up to the minute, fed constantly by literally millions of items from sources all over the world. Only a fraction were intelligence reports. The bulk were, for example, almost every news item printed or broadcast by all the world's media. There were also reams of NSA intercepts of wireless traffic by phone or computer, much of it in code or in some foreign language, but usually not decoded or translated because there was simply too much of it.

As with any computer one could narrow one's search by entering a keyword or two. These might be the name of a person of interest or, in anything related to Muslims, a long list of words that had been known to appear in traffic related to hostile intentions. Clew entered "Aisha" and "Prophecy" separately. He clicked on a box that said "Summarize."

Clew let out a whistle. There were thousands of entries. He'd need to narrow it down to… well, a real summary, but first he wanted to scan a few items in which names that he recognized appeared. One was that of Colonel Aram Jalil, heads up part of Savama, Iran's Secret Police. Jalil had been trolling other Muslim nations' services asking whether they could shed any light on the source of what he called "this bit of mischief." He said he'd been so tasked by Abbas Mansur. He'd been at it for a couple of weeks now.

Abbas Mansur? The name seemed familiar. Clew entered the name and his bio came up. Oh, sure. A senior mullah. Currently chairing the Guardian Council. As Clew recalled, the mullahs rotate into the chair. Helps explain its wild swings from one year to the next in how hard they crack down on their citizenry. And Mansur's a good one by most accounts. Thought to be the most open-minded of the twelve. Intelligent, urbane, educated in the West, known to be fluent in three or four languages and passably conversant with some others.

Under the bio were several sub-headings. One concerned an NSA intercept of a telephone call that was placed by Mansur to Rajib Sadik of Hamas. There was no transcript. Clew would have to request it. But it did contain the key words he'd entered. Mansur must be trying to track it on his own. Clew knew of Sadik. He knew that his bio would be similar to Mansur's. Multilingual and highly intelligent. Except Sadik was a doctor. Trained as a surgeon, also somewhere in the West. Now based in Hebron on Palestine's West Bank. Believed to have chosen Hebron as opposed to Gaza to distance his Social Services wing from the extremists. Good thinking. Israel doesn't bomb Hebron. Not much more is known of Sadik's prior life before he turned up over there a few years ago and quickly rose in Hamas.

But why would Mansur be calling Sadik? Iran was far from a supporter of Hamas. They supported Hezbollah and other Jihadists. Hamas, itself, was not really jihadist except where the Israelis are concerned. And yet… wait a minute. Rajib Sadik. He's known to have semi-regular contact with Yitzhak Netanya of Israel's Mossad. Not surprising in itself. We all need our back channels. And Yitzhak is a friend of both Kessler and Whistler.

The world is suddenly getting much smaller.

Clew typed in his request for the transcript of that phone call and more on both Mansur and Sadik. He also wanted a charting of all media items that mentioned the prophecy, pro or con. In other words, a summary of a summary. He also wanted to see more detail on the sort of responses Colonel Aram Jalil was getting from the other Muslim states. The report said that these were all over the lot, some seeing it as a major concern and others brushing it off. It said some were actually blaming Iran for permitting the existence of Internet Cafes. They said Iran could have nipped this in the bud. What does this mean? That it started in Iran? He'd have to wait for the translated text.

For now he'd see what's available on the web to anyone who with access to a PC. Let's see how real people are reacting. He brought up Google. He typed "Aisha Prophecy" Again the screen exploded with thousands of hits. Most were written in Arabic, several dialects thereof. He scrolled down until he found a site that translated the prophecy's text into English.

It read:

"The Lady of the Camel will come, born again, to show men that they have fallen into error. She comes to raise up the women of Islam. She comes to teach and she comes to bring justice. It is not revealed when, but she will come. She will be of the East, but turn your eyes to the West because that is where her banner will unfurl. She will have grown up among you, dressed in white, pure of heart, until the day when she reaches full womanhood. The flame-haired angel, Qaila, sent to guide her and protect her, will, on that day, reveal to her that she is the Lady of the Camel reborn. She will know that it is true and she will come. She will speak to all nations with words writ on wind. Her words will ride the lightning. They will be as shooting stars. And the angel, Qaila, will be with her, sword in hand. Woe to those who would deny the truth of her words. Woe to those who would silence her. Woe to those who would slay her. The angel, Qaila, will send them to hell."

The prophet, it says, was a 12th century Berber named Muhammad Ibn-Tumart. A major figure in his day, led the Almohad clan. Their turf covered more than half of Morocco including the whole Atlas Mountain range and another good chunk of Moorish Spain. A reformer who, among other things, stopped the practice of kidnapping Christian women and shipping them east through his territory to be sold in what is now Saudi Arabia as concubines and slaves. So it seems his interest in raising up women went beyond just the women of Islam.

Clew had expected that he'd be some wandering ascetic. Obscure. But not so. This guy was an emir, a spiritual leader and a military leader, never defeated in battle. As for the Lady of the Camel, no doubt about her. The Lady of the Camel was Aisha for sure. Wonder why he didn't come right out and say so.

Clew found a dozen or so other sites that were written in English or translated into English. Most translations of the prophecy were essentially identical although he found several variations here and there. Some of them added to the scope of Aisha's mission. They tacked on some additional "Woe to…" threats that condemned, not so much the suicide bombers, but the "slinking rats" who recruited and encouraged them, especially the "ignorant clerics."

Most, however, stuck to Aisha's feminist agenda, arguing mostly pro, but sometimes con. He spent an hour browsing through them, curious to see how Muslim women reacted in various parts of the world. Quite a few of the entries rejected the suggestion that Muslim women needed raising up. Were they posted by men pretending to be women? Clew thought not. Muslim men tend to rant. These sentiments seemed genuine. They thought that their way of life was just fine. They felt valued and respected in their roles as wives and mothers. They were deferential, more or less, toward the men in their lives, but that, they wrote, was the way it should be and the way it has been throughout human history. They said that they did not feel oppressed.

Well and good, thought Clew. Southern Baptists feel the same. But those cons were in the minority. For every Muslim woman who took that view, he'd count five who thought it high time for a change. And not just for their own sakes. For the sake of Islam. It had been the most progressive society on earth while Europe was still in the dark ages. First in scholarship, science, the arts, you name it. Now all of that had been lost. New ideas were shouted down. And women had been "put in their place." It was wasting the potential of half its population out of, as one Egyptian feminist had put it, "a blind adherence to the encrusted thoughts of old and incurious men."

Some entries were flippant. "I love it. Bring her on." One wrote, "I'm a Catholic. We could use her at the Vatican. They're just as anti-women as the Muslims." But most were more articulate and more deeply felt. Most thought that the prophecy was a breath of fresh air whether they believed it or not. Quite a few of the hits used only three words. The words were "She is coming." A mantra. Sounds like it. Curious about it, Clew did a broader search. A prompt came on the screen. It asked, "English only?" Clew shrugged. What the hell. He opened a drop-down list of his choices. He clicked on the one that said "All."

The result almost pushed him back in his chair. He saw that there seemed to be tens of thousands. "She is coming." Only that. In many hundreds of languages. Unspoken, apparently, were the words, "Pass it on." This thing now seemed to have a life of its own. It's no wonder that Tehran is hot to track it.

Leland had asked him who's reviving this prophecy. Who could it be? No idea, was his answer. He'd just wanted to get off the phone. But if he had to guess, he'd say the CIA. Or any of the western intelligence services. Why? Because they do this sort of thing all the time. They monitor all the Islamic websites, especially the radical sites. And they don't just observe. They participate. They use those sites to spread all kinds of rumors meant to keep the jihadists off balance. Rumors that cause argument, disunity, confusion.

Sometimes they'll pretend to be moderate Muslims and will troll the sites of those urging violence which are always under a pseudonym. They'll have cyber-discussions that might last for weeks, pretending to gradually come around to a much more extreme point of view. They'll ask, "What can I do? How can I strike a blow?" Then there'll be a suggestion that they meet somewhere for coffee. Voila, they now have a name and a face. It's not unlike on-line dating.

Or they might pretend to be angry jihadists themselves, spewing venom against Jews and Christians alike in the hope of being recruited. One might claim, for example, to be a technician working at some nuclear power plant. He'll say he can cause an American Chernobyl if only he had the right help and some funding. Or he's a chemist and he's made a big batch of Sarin. What's the best way to use it that will kill the most Jews. The New York subways? Holland Tunnel? Help me out here. Anyone who bites gets whisked off to Gitmo or wherever they're being warehoused these days.

The problem is that anyone can log onto these sites. Time and again, they think they've been recruited and the person recruiting them turns out to be some nerd who's just been amusing himself. No jihadist with a brain in his head would try to recruit on the internet. They'll recruit through local mosques where they can see what they're getting and where they can bring the recruit along slowly. Even better than the mosques, they'll recruit in our state prisons where most, yes, most, Muslim chaplains are Wahhabis. Saudi Wahhabis, not a moderate among them, and all of them on the state's payroll.

He had to give the Saudis credit. They pulled it off. They got some hack at the Bureau of Prisons to believe that moral guidance for poor black convicts can only be a good thing. Why not chaplains who represent the full range of Islam? Because theirs, they say, is the only true Islam. All other variations are heresies. A couple of respected Muslim organizations have finally caught on and have filed suit to change it. They know that the Wahhabis have an agenda that goes way beyond moral guidance.

You want converts to Islam? Fundamentalist Islam? That's where you'll make them. In prisons. You want angry black men who hate the white world? You've certainly come to the right place. Who put you in prison? Who keeps you down? White cops and Jew judges, that's who. Some convicts convert because they want to believe. Some have never had anything to believe in before. But many convert or pretend to convert because there is safety in numbers. Those numbers protect them from the skinhead gangs that are found in every prison in the country. Not to mention, of course, racist guards.

And that's okay, Clew supposed, as far as it goes. The law protects a convict's right to have access to a chaplain of his faith. But so many Wahhabis when they're such a minority? So many Wahabbis when much of what they teach is an active hatred of Christians and Jews and of all other Muslims who aren't Wahhabi.

Wait, thought Clew.

We're getting too far off the track here. It's nice to see that the Aisha prophecy is starting to wake people up. Getting millions of Muslims to take a hard look at the more extreme forms of Islam. It's not just the violence. It's the willful ignorance. The denial of one's right to think for one's self. Keeping Islam from being the force for enlightenment that it once was and could be again.

But sadly, nothing much is likely to come of it. It'll probably blow over in another month or two when Aisha fails to turn up. A more immediate question is what ought to be done about Haskell's obsession with Kessler. Maybe nothing, thought Clew. That might also blow over. Leland's there. He's with Haskell. Let him keep a lid on it. He's got through Wednesday to calm Haskell down and keep Kessler and Stride the hell out of this.

Except... except... for that Saudi princess and whatever she's got on that disk Haskell wants. Political dynamite is what Leland called it. It could devastate the Saudi regime. Clew couldn't imagine what it might be, but if it even begins to have that sort of potential, they sure as hell can't let Haskell get it. And except... except... maybe Kessler and Stride are deeply into this after all. Maybe they have the princess. Maybe they have the disk. Maybe Stride already got it from the Nasreens. Maybe the Nasreens never had it. If anyone has a motive to "devastate" a few Saudis, you'd have to put Stride pretty high on the list.

Clew was tempted to buzz down to Belle Haven. Drop in unannounced. See who's there. Say to Kessler and Stride, "I'm asking straight out. Are you out of the game, as you've told me you are, or do you have plans for that disk?" They'd know that he knows. That would be a start. On the other hand, though, if they don't know a thing, him asking might pull them back into the game whether they like it or not. So slow down. First things first. Do they have that Saudi princess? Harry Whistler would know. He spent several days with them. Ask Harry straight out. Do they have this missing princess? If his response is either, "Why are you asking?" or "I think you might want to stay out of this, Roger," then he'll know that Harry is in this as well and might have his own plans for the disk. And maybe Netanya. Maybe Rajib Sadik.

Oh, Roger... shut up.

Are you listening to yourself?

You're sitting here developing a conspiracy theory and it's dumb, really dumb in so many ways. If Harry was part of this... if he even had a clue... he would not have parked Kessler and Stride in Belle Haven. He'd have jetted them all off to his base in Geneva or more likely to his ski lodge in the French Alps that's more like a fortress than a lodge.

So he's not part of anything. He's just been a friend.

But he'd know whether Stride had that princess.

SIXTEEN

Mulazim had risen early on Monday, eager to see what was in the newspapers. He had not slept well and woke up feeling poorly. The cause was those three beers that he drank last night.

A good Muslim doesn't drink, but he'd had little choice. It didn't seem a good idea to be a Muslim just now. Better to be Greek as is shown on his passport. He knew from his time of study in Piraeus that a Greek will drink anything put in front of him.

This man, Gilhooley, had bought him the first one. After that, another. Then came a third. The last one came unrequested by Gilhooley. Sam the bartender brought it. He said, "On the house."

Gilhooley had overheard his exchange with Sam about Harry Whistler and his taste for crustaceans. Gilhooley also knew of this man. Gilhooley asked him, "How do you know Harry?"

The question seemed asked in a friendly manner. Mulazim, thinking quickly, said, "He comes to Piraeus. My business is shipping. He uses our ships. We have dined together on many occasions both in Piraeus and in Geneva because sometimes our business took me there."

Gilhooley, "So you're Greek. And in shipping. Like Onassis."

"Not so big as Onassis," he answered.

"Did Harry have a favorite restaurant in Piraeus?"

This seemed an odd question. Was it a test? There is one called Vassilenas, very popular, many courses. Mulazim had eaten there himself. He said, "His first choice was Vassilenas most times. But I could name others that he liked just as well. There are many seafood restaurants in Piraeus." Mulazim had eaten in several.

Gilhooley nodded. "Vassilenas. A good one. They know how to cook a fish. By the way, I don't think I caught your name."

Mulazim was not eager to say too much, but again, he wasn't left with a choice. "My name is Polykarpos. I am Zenobias Polykarpos." It was the name that appeared on his passport. An instructor had told him that Greek names are good because those who are not Greek don't remember them so good.

This was true of Gilhooley who said, "That's a mouthful." He asked, "What do your friends call you? Let me guess. They call you Zeke?"

Zeke, thought Mulazim. Also non-Muslim. He said, "A good guess. They call me Zeke." The bartender heard this. He said, "Zeke the Greek." He said this as he drew two more beers from the tap which he placed before them on the bar. Gilhooley must have gestured for more beer.

Gilhooley said, "So I bet you know Elizabeth Stride."

This was too much. He didn't know how to answer. Was this second beer intended to loosen his tongue? Gilhooley saw what he thought must be ignorance of her. He said, "She's staying in Harry's house. Her and some others. Haven't you been up there?"

He wanted to ask where? Where is there? Which house? But he couldn't, so he said, "I called and I was told he is in Europe."

"By a woman?"

"A woman, yes, but I did not ask her name." Mulazim took a long sip of his beer in order to have a moment to think.

The bar phone rang again. It was a reprieve. Sam picked it up and held a finger aloft as if saying he was getting some news. He listened for a minute or two. He said, "Thanks, Karen. You'll get him." He hung up.

He addressed all who were still at the bar. He said, "They found the witness. She saw that the cops tried to call her on her cell. Seems she was in the shower, didn't hear it. They're bringing her down to the station now where they've got a sketch artist waiting for her. They already have a description. Guy's a foreigner. He's Hungarian, she says. They want to get that sketch to the papers tonight. They have to get it in before eleven."

A man at the bar asked, "So this guy killed Eddie?"

"They're not sure. They just know he was talking to Eddie when this girl and her friend finished playing and left. The girl did say that this guy seemed creepy."

So much, thought Mulazim, for his search for the slut. This could be bad. Very bad. And a drawing in the papers? What next?

"Hungarians," said Gilhooley. "Gloomy by nature. Highest suicide rate in all of Europe."

Mulazim wondered, who is this Gilhooley? How is it that a man who is dressed as a laborer seems to know something of restaurants in Piraeus and also of Hungarian temperament? It is not surprising that he knows Harry Whistler if Harry Whistler comes to this place. The same can be said of Elizabeth Stride who might well have accompanied this Whistler.

He said, "Maybe Hungarians. Not so with Greeks. We know how to have good times and enjoy." With this he let out an involuntary belch. He had swallowed his beer much too quickly. It was also having other effects. Among these was a growing discomfort from his bladder. This was on top of the discomfort he felt that was caused by this man, Gilhooley. There was too much about him that seemed not quite right. Also his eyes. His eyes never stopped moving. This, thought Mulazim, was the look of a hunter. For right now, though, he had need of the rest room.

He excused himself, and walked toward the back. He found the one marked for men and went in for relief. He took his time. He washed his hands and wet his face. He took water from the tap and rinsed his mouth with it, hoping to reduce the effects of the beer. It did little to help. He dried himself.

When he came back out, Gilhooley was gone. He could see Gilhooley through the front window, just now climbing into an old pick-up truck. He watched as Gilhooley pulled away from the curb. Mulazim was far from displeased to see him go. Even so, why this sudden departure? This whole business was very unnerving.

He wanted to leave. He needed to think. Perhaps he should get into his own car and go. Keep driving until he is out of Virginia. Call his sheik. Report. Let others take over. He was heading toward the door, that course of action in mind, when the bartender stopped him. He said, "Zeke, you have a tab."

Of course. His veal chop. He's almost forgotten. He reached into his pocket to pull out some cash. That was when the bartender produced his third beer with the words, "This one's on the house."

Mulazim thanked him. He sipped it. He did more than sip. This one tasted better than the two that went before. That's probably what is so pernicious about alcohol. It did seem, however, to be easing his anxiety. A voice inside him said, "No, it is dulling your edge. Go back to your motel. Sleep it off. Wake refreshed. Don't make snap decisions after drinking."

God speaking. Must be. He obeyed.

He took his change and left a good tip of five dollars. He wished Sam a good evening and went out to his car. He clicked on the key that unlocked it from a distance. The front and rear lights all flash when he does this. He saw, this time, that one tail light was broken. It wasn't broken when he locked it. He felt sure of that. Who could have done this? Gilhooley perhaps? He'd been parked just beyond Gilhooley's pick-up.

Sometimes this is done, he remembered from his training, to make a car easier to follow at night or to make it stand out even during the day from other cars that are too similar. But if so, why didn't Gilhooley just wait?

Never mind. Just go. He drove back to his motel. He reminded himself that the clerk at his motel was part of his alibi, as were those at the restaurant. So calm down. All will be well if you don't panic. Along the way, a police car drove past him slowly. The policeman driving was looking him over. Mulazim gave him a wave with his fingers. The policeman waved back. He moved on.

You see? Nobody suspects you.

The next morning early, the newspaper came. There was the drawing, right on the front page. But it would be little help to the police.

It was a face within the hood of his sweatshirt from the Wal-Mart, eyes hidden behind tinted glasses with sides. They covered fully a third of his face. Eyes could be seen through them, but they were not his eyes. His eyes were not so close together. Otherwise, as far as his face was concerned, there was not a single recognizable feature except perhaps for the shape of his hairline.

This, he suspected, was often the case when suspects are sketched from a description. Those describing the suspect are probably inclined to describe him in unflattering terms. This one showed his mouth with what looked like a leer. Well, perhaps this was the case while the slut was flouncing, but that was not his normal expression. Was it? No, it wasn't. But just in case it was, he would conceal that as well. He would try to wear a smile from now on. That, and he'd keep his red baseball cap on, its visor pulled down on his forehead.

The caption spoke of this man as a possible witness, the last person seen with the dead policeman. The authorities wished to interview him as to who else he'd seen in that vicinity.

Witness? Not a suspect? This must be a ruse. Clearly intended to put him off guard and not feel the need to flee Belle Haven. The only other thing the description got right was that this possible witness spoke with an accent and was heard to say he was Hungarian. There was no mention of his claim that he was looking for his niece and had shown a snapshot of her dressed as a nun. The police often choose to withhold such details. They like to know more than they're saying.

He did speak with an accent; that couldn't be helped, but his accent was a mix of Northern Saudi, some Egyptian and quite a bit of Greek from his time in Piraeus. Such accents are sometimes called Mediterranean for want of a better narrowing down. He didn't think he'd ever heard a Hungarian accent, but it didn't seem likely to be similar.

He went out to his car and fished out the radio that he'd hidden underneath his spare tire. Also there was the dead policeman's pistol along with his handcuffs and taser. Not easily accessible, but not easily detectable in any but a diligent search should he be stopped.

He switched the radio on, changed his mind, switched it off. The police knew that he had taken it. They would assume that he'd be listening. They would be making false broadcasts in order to mislead him, to try to put him off guard. False broadcasts preceded by some prearranged code word. Two, however, could play at that game. Maybe he would drive a hundred miles away, wipe it clean and drop it into a mailbox, leaving a false trail of his own. For now, though, he would stay, perhaps try again to sleep, perhaps take a fizz pill to settle his stomach. After that he would go where information is reliable. He would go back to Mangiamo for lunch.

The restaurant was far more busy for lunch than it was on the preceding night. The same bartender was working again, but he saw no one else who looked familiar. It was a mix of men and women dressed for business. Three waitresses this time. Several tables in use. There was no sign of Gilhooley.

Only two empty bar stools. He took the one nearest. In other places, the bar was two-deep. Men stood in the aisle talking sports, from the sound of it, with those who were seated on stools. All of them had beers in their hands. Further back, near the tables, he saw another cluster that looked like a meeting of the staff. One was a waitress, another wore chef's apron. The third was a woman with a pen in one hand and what looked like a notepad in the other. They were going over some sort of checklist.

Mulazim told Sam he'd like some sweetened iced tea and… let's see… what is light?

"Try the Eggplant Parmagiane."

This didn't sound so light, but he knew not to argue. The bartender put in his order. The front door opened and a man stepped through it. He stood by the front window peering at faces, craning his neck to see better. At least twice his eyes had paused to linger on Mulazim. This began to cause tightening of his stomach. This man signaled to Sam as Sam came back down the bar. He leaned over, whispered something. Now it was Sam who turned to look at him.

But Sam smiled as he turned back to this man. Sam said to him, "Zeke the Greek? He's a friend of Harry Whistler's. He's okay. Anyway, he was right here last night."

The man seemed more than satisfied. It seems he, too, knew Harry Whistler. He said to Sam, "Well, keep your eyes open."

"Always," Sam answered. The man left.

Sam stopped by his stool. "That was Dave Ragland. Sergeant Dave Ragland. He's the guy who called last night with the news about Eddie."

"Ah, yes. I remember that you spoke his name. He expects to find the killer having lunch at Mangiamo?"

"Could be anyone, anywhere. Cops always look for strangers."

Sam looked up toward the rear of the bar. He said to a woman who was approaching, "You all set? You got everything you need?"

She replied, "We're looking good. I just gave them the menu. I'm bringing the cake and the decorations. See you Wednesday afternoon if not before."

"Any time, Elizabeth. Have a good day."

Mulazim's stomach completely turned over. He spun to see the woman now just walking out the door. Tall, short blond hair, almost red when sunlight hit it. Without looking at Sam he managed, "Who... who...?"

"Yeah, I know," said Sam. "She's a real head-turner."

Mulazim struggled to control his breathing. "This woman is... what? A supplier for this restaurant?"

He smiled. "Oh, no. She's more or less regular. Just now she's setting up for a party Wednesday night. Birthday party. She reserved the back room."

Mulazim barely heard this above his own heartbeat. This could only be Elizabeth Stride.

"By the way," Sam told him, now with a smile, "She thinks Harry Whistler will be back for it."

This, Mulazim heard. He said, "Wonderful. Good news."

"The party's private, but the bar will be open. Come in then and you'll catch him. If not before."

"Excellent," said Mulazim. "I will be here."

Mulazim was still watching as she crossed the street. She got to her car. It was a green SUV. She paused to reach into her purse for her compact. She raised it as if to examine her right eye. Perhaps she was doing so. Perhaps she was not. He suspected that she was being watchful. She put it away. Now she reached in for her keys.

Mulazim so wanted to ask her last name, but the question became stuck in his throat. No matter. He knew it. There could be no doubt. Elizabeth Stride, worth one million in gold, had just now passed within inches of him. He wanted to leap up and run out the door. He wanted to follow her to where she lives, but this was impossible; Sam would see what he was doing.

Calm yourself, Mulazim. Breathe deeply. Breathe slowly. At least now you know where she will be on Wednesday. And the birthday party? A sweet-sixteen party. Niki told him they were planning it. For Aisha.

Still, he couldn't take his eyes off her as she eased the green Subaru into traffic. He couldn't read her plate, but its design was familiar. Like Bernice's, it was from South Carolina.

Bernice. This was Monday. When will she be found? Will news of her death reach Belle Haven? He didn't know. There was no way to know. He knew about Wednesday. That was enough. He knew that Stride, surely Kessler, and all four of the girls would be all in one place Wednesday evening. The guest list is growing? Who else besides this Harry? Must be the bodyguards Niki mentioned.

Still looking out the window he saw Gilhooley's pick-up. It was coming left to right, slowly picking up speed. Gilhooley, not much question, was following the Subaru.

But why, though?

Gilhooley, last night, had brought up her name. Gilhooley indicated that he knew Harry Whistler and therefore he knew which house was his. Another bodyguard, perhaps? Employed to watch over Elizabeth Stride? Does he sit in bars keeping an eye out for strangers who might possibly be Muslim hunters? Mulazim thought that unlikely. Muslims don't go to bars. Not unless they are exceptional hunters. Even so, this Gilhooley needed watching.

Should he call the sheik now? Have him send more Hasheem? They could be here by Wednesday. Some others sooner. The sheik had said that there were others who wouldn't be far, but Mulazim knew who he meant when he said it. He meant former convicts who converted to Islam while they were in American prisons.

Not just any converts. Blacks known to hate whites. But unless they showed up in good cars dressed like African diplomats, they would set off alarms in Belle Haven.

Same thing with the Hasheem. They would come, but then what? You saw Sergeant Ragland. They look at every new face. The hunters from Hasheem would surely shave off their beards, but that would leave a paleness on their chins and on their necks. They would be stopped and searched, their papers examined. Stride would be alerted. She would vanish again.

No, Mulazim would wait. Be patient. Bide his time.

He'd see who comes to this party Wednesday night.

He would be there with his video camera.

SEVENTEEN

On that same Monday morning three time zones to the West, Charles Haskell was about to attend a scheduled lecture. It was entitled, "Oil. The Coming Crisis. Some Solutions."

Haskell snorted when he read it on the calendar of activities. Coming crisis, indeed. It's already here. And he damned well had solutions of his own. But he'd go and he'd listen to the usual pap, if only to make sure that he, as always, was still at least two moves ahead of them.

He hadn't heard from the banker and the prince. He assumed that they're probably still in Riyadh trying to undo the daughter's damage. Perhaps they're already on their way back. Two moves ahead? If they were successful, make that at least three. He'd have hundreds of powerful Saudis by the balls. Arrogant bastards. He'll show them.

The mogul, speaking of arrogant bastards, had scheduled an activity of his own. Much smaller in scale, it was his breakfast with Leland. It was the mogul's I-speak-his-language attempt to elicit Leland's assistance. Fine, thought Haskell. Let them out-snob each other. Haskell was ahead of that as well.

He'd knocked on Leland's door while Leland was shaving. Leland came to the door in the green terry robe that every guest found in his bathroom. The club's insignia was embroidered on its breast.

Haskell said "Well? You told me you'd sleep on it."

"A civil 'good morning' would be nice, Charles."

"Sorry," said Haskell, "but I'm off to a lecture. Your room was on the way. I seized the moment."

Leland wasn't cheery, but he did have good news. He said that he'd done more than sleep on it. He said he'd spoken to Elizabeth Stride. He'd said he'd reached her by way of Roger Clew.

Haskell felt his pulse pick up a few beats. He found himself imagining the sound of her voice. Low and sexy? No. But cool and confident, surely. Not overly cordial toward a man she'd never met. But respectful of his rank. She would be courteous.

"Charles…"

He shook it off. He asked Leland, "You called her from here?"

"Not from the Grove. From outside the gate. No cell phones, remember? I'd have had to take a swim."

"Very wise. Rules are rules. Where is she these days?"

"I don't know," Leland told him. "Clew routed the call. He spoke to her first and then he put me though."

Fair enough, thought Haskell. Clew probably declined to say where she is. A part of Haskell wanted to say, "Well, I know. She's at Harry Whistler's house in Belle Haven, Virginia." But that would have been showing off. "What did she say?"

Leland said that she confirmed that three young Muslim women were in fact staying with her and with Kessler. Two were sisters, Iranian, not Saudi. The third was young Aisha who was born in Egypt, but who has been here since she was twelve. Ms. Stride knew nothing of a Saudi princess, but agreed to make inquiries of the Nasreens. She said she would seek to recover that disk. She said she owed Roger that favor.

Haskell must have blinked. "You told her what was on them?"

"No, I did not. And she didn't ask. She assumed that they contained nothing of interest to anyone other than the family in question. I assured her that the girl had no need of insurance because I intend to see to it personally that her father will not be coming after her."

Haskell asked, "And she trusts you?"

"She trusts Roger Clew."

"And?" asked Haskell. "When will you hear from her?"

"She's to call me on Thursday when I'm back at my desk."

Three days, thought Haskell. "Not before then?"

"She might, but I didn't think I should push. Perhaps if I'd told her that it's you who's asking, she would have leaped into action."

Smart-ass, thought Haskell. "Good thinking."

Haskell thanked Howard Leland and left for his meeting, still seeing Elizabeth Stride in his mind. His was a breakfast meeting as well, held at one of the conference facilities. The attendees were mostly senior oil executives. Two experts had been scheduled to speak. Both of their topics dealt with the likelihood of a catastrophic drop in world oil supply due largely to Islamic "insurgencies."

Insurgencies, thought Haskell, were the least of our problems. They hate us, sure. They hate each other even more. Although no one liked to say it out loud, the entire gulf region, our "allies" included, was pretty sure it had us buy the balls.

The first speaker was more comfortable blaming the jihadists. He stressed the vulnerability of the pipelines and refineries of the Saudis, Kuwaitis and Iraqis. They were, between them, the world's largest exporters and would be until the Russians catch up. Sabotage of their facilities was occurring almost weekly. Although the Saudis did their best to keep that quiet, production was down by almost thirty percent and the price of raw crude had quadrupled. That combination could well, if sustained, cripple most of the developed world's economies.

Well, then we mustn't let happen, thought Haskell to himself. But the only solution that the first speaker offered had to do with new drilling on rich offshore fields that were, by their nature, more immune to attack.

True enough, thought Haskell. But off-shore is expensive. More than double the cost of extracting on land. They'll drill for it anyway because it is there, but he'd be damned if he'd be pushed into it. He'd show them an attack they won't forget.

The second topic was even more alarming than the first. It was also one closer to his heart. It had to do with the likelihood that the Shiites of Iran and those of Iraq would combine with those of Eastern Saudi Arabia to form what would amount to a whole new cartel. A Shiite cartel. Much more powerful than OPEC. That cartel would control a full two thirds of the world's known oil reserves.

It was more than likelihood. It was inevitable, thought Haskell. Or at least the attempt was inevitable. Iran and Iraq have plenty of oil. Iran and Southern Iraq are both Shiite. But the Saudis are Sunni. More than that, they're Wahhabi. And Wahhabis feel only contempt toward the Shiites. How, therefore, one might ask, could they ever unite? They've been at each others' throats now for centuries.

Aha, but not all the Saudis are Sunni. A small minority, maybe five percent, are Shiite. And where does one find this Shiite minority? In easternmost Saudi Arabia. They are concentrated along a four hundred mile strip that is flush against the Persian Gulf due south of Iraq and Kuwait. They feel cultural ties to Iran and Iraq and zero to the Saudi regime. How are they treated? They are barely tolerated. Even the best and brightest of them are reduced to second class citizenship. They go through their lives being sneered at as heretics by the Wahhabi majority.

The strip is called the Hasa by the Shiites who live there. It's called the Eastern Province by the Saudis. It gets its name from the Hasa Oasis which happens to be the world's largest. Less than two percent of the country is arable and most of that two percent is there. Fertile enough to be self-sufficient, even without all its oil. Endless acres that grow dates, watermelons and grapes. There are wheat fields as big as some in Kansas.

"Kansas?"

Well, okay, not that big, but for that region? They're huge. Who'd have thought that the Saudis not only grow wheat, but so much of it that they can export it?

Above all, however, this Hasa strip holds nearly all the Saudi oil reserves. It's the region that Saddam intended to invade after securing Kuwait. He'd have let the Saudi royals keep all the rest of their country. He would have let them keep all the sand.

Saddam thought, with good reason, that he would be welcomed. Hitler, after all, was welcomed most warmly when his troops reclaimed the Sudetenland. It's people had always been German, not Czech. As Czechs, they were a powerless minority. They felt liberated when Hitler marched in. Why would not the Hasa Shiites feel the same?

They would not have, of course, for a number of reasons. First among them was that Saddam was, at least nominally, Sunni. As importantly, they knew how Saddam operated. They'd be trading one oppressor for a sociopath who'd do more than sneer at them; he'd kill them en masse and replace them with the Baath Party faithful.

Now, however, it's a whole new ballgame. Whether Iraq stays in one piece or not, there is going to be a Shiite Iraq. To those who take a long view of history, a union of those two Shiite peoples would seem natural. Existing borders would mean less than nothing. Those borders were imposed on them anyway.

So they'd say, this is wonderful, let's at last be together. They'd say, but we don't mean under one flag. They would form a commonwealth of independent states; Iran, Southern Iraq and the Hasa. Kuwait and the Emirates would join up or strike a deal.

Their own Shiites would soon force the issue. As would Bahrain with all its natural gas and a populace that's three quarters Shiite. They'd say, "Have you noticed? The whole thing forms a crescent. If that's not a sign from Allah, what is?"

Iran would try to be dominant because of its size. Seventy million. Too big to push around. An educated middle class. Women vote and hold office. It has, like Turkey, but unlike all the others, a functioning governmental system. Iran may or may not ever have the bomb, but will allow it to be thought that it might have the bomb, having learned to play that game from North Korea.

But Iran still won't dominate. Not for long anyway. For one thing, Iran's mullah management is unraveling. Iran's younger generation has had quite enough of them. For another, the Iranians are Persians, not Arabs. A shared adherence To e Islam notwithstanding, those two cultures are still a world apart. Ask a Persian what he thinks of Arab culture and he'll tell you that there's no such thing. Persia was a world power for a thousand years before any Arab even took his first bath. The printing press had been invented for three hundred years before the first Arab country permitted its use and only to print the Koran. Oil to an Arab was some foul-smelling goop before the Brits came along and said they'd take it off their hands. Ask an Arab what he thinks about Persian culture and he won't even know what you're talking about. The only culture worth mentioning is his own brand of Islam. He certainly won't tell you to go read a book. Most Arabs still think there's only one.

Even so, they'll unite. Or they'll certainly try. If they succeed, they'll have formed a political union that is richer and more powerful than any on earth. At least until corruption sets in and religion gets a nice pat on the head. And at least until the oil runs out or until theirs is no longer needed.

But it is needed now. It will be needed tomorrow. We can't have those people controlling so much of it. And he, Charles Haskell, would see to it that they don't. He intends to persuade them to let him control it. A good part of it anyway. The whole Hasa region. He'll show them how easily it could be set ablaze if they should fail to name Trans-Global as their final arbiter on production and pricing. Not just a few wells. Entire fields burning. Production down for a year. The oil field security firm that he owned had prepared a compelling demonstration in the Hasa. Nearly all was in place. It was now just a matter of picking the right time and having the right people where he needs them to be. Especially certain Saudis. Certain names on the list. Certain Saudis who will then either do as they're told or face utter ruin and disgrace.

You want to see a world power? I'll show you a world power. His name is Charles Barrington Haskell.

Haskell left the breakfast meeting. It was half past ten. It was time to go check his mail. The desk clerk at his cabin had received several pieces, all of which came by Federal Express. All save one were from Trans-Global Oil. He glanced at their contents. All routine reports. None required his immediate attention.

The one he saved for last, the one not to be rushed, was the one sent by Desmond Gilhooley. Sent yesterday. Sunday. Wonderful service. From Belle Haven to the boondocks overnight. Haskell opened the envelope and looked inside. There were photographs. A stack of them. And with the photos some handwritten pages containing whatever he'd learned since last Friday.

"Is everything all right, sir?" The desk clerk was asking. He must have heard Haskell suck in his breath at his first sight of the contents.

Haskell smiled. He said to him, "Better than ever."

Haskell wanted to dump the photos out then and there. But these deserved to be savored in private where he needn't pretend to conceal his excitement. He tucked the several FedExes under his arm and climbed the stairs to his room.

Good man, Gilhooley, his last outing notwithstanding. His cover, however, was Haskell's idea. An itinerant handyman, worked at odd jobs. A little carpentry, light plumbing, brush-clearing and such. This explained his popping up all over town in a dented and rusty old pickup. He wears a clunky old-fashioned hearing aid in one ear, the better to pick up and record conversations. The older models never seem to be suspected of being anything else. But that might not be true of his camera cell phone. A useful tool for spying. No question about that. It does seem, however, a bit too hi-tech for a man who pretends to live hand-to-mouth. But Gilhooley says no. All the high school kids have them. Half the town drives around with one at their ear. He remarked that landlines are becoming extinct. Anyway, he's clearly got another good camera, equipped with a telephoto lens.

Haskell shut his door, sat down on his rocker, and poured the collection onto his lap. He sifted through them looking first for the photos of Stride. And there she was, in the shot Gilhooley mentioned, in Whistler's front yard cutting lilacs. A young girl watching, chatting with her, an orange-colored kitten held in one arm and a basket for the cuttings on the other. It showed Stride stretching to cut a high branch. Up on her toes, not showing strain. Languidly graceful. Like watching ballet. Except no ballerina would have curves such as Stride's. See the way her chest thrusts as she reaches.

There were others, a good dozen, of her playing tennis. Some playing against Kessler, no doubt beating him handily. In others, the two of them are playing mixed doubles with two dark-haired girls, perhaps the sisters from Iran. One looked older. He'd guess that she was nineteen or twenty. The other was a strikingly beautiful girl. A lot younger. He'd guess mid teens. The tennis they were playing seemed far less intense than in the singles where Kessler and Stride were going at it. Intense or not, look at her. Moves like a cat. You could see it even in a still photo. In another, one of the girls only sat and watched. On the chubby side, that one. She could use some hard play.

Enough about tennis. Let's see Whistler's house. Gilhooley had taken some wide angle shots, probably standing in the bed of his pick-up. He'd have had to in order to see over the wall. The wall wasn't all that high, perhaps it came to chest level, but it surrounded a good bit of the property. The only entrance was through a wrought iron gate that was doubtless electrically driven. The rear of the property was enclosed by thick hedges that had been planted along a green wire fence. The lot was two acres at least.

The house itself was a split-timbered Tudor. Three stories, not counting the basement and attic. There was a matching three-car garage, detached, that had a second floor of its own. Servant quarters? Guest apartment? Whatever. Both were faced with tan-colored stone down below and with aged brick up above. The bricks had been laid in the old Tudor fashion that leaves the mortar sort of squeezed out between them instead of wiped off in clean lines. Haskell had always admired that look. His first wife, the timber heiress, had a similar house. He'd sometimes regretted not buying that house. Maybe Whistler would consider selling this one.

"Not likely."

Oh, I know. He's probably put a lot into it. Other than décor, good art, some nice murals, his security system would be second to none. Cameras all over. All kinds of sensors. And, as Haskell's hackers had found, a communication system that was almost uncrackable. Men like Whistler don't scrimp on such things.

"Semtex."

What? Gilhooley's stash of it? It wouldn't be enough to bring that house down even if he could get in there and plant it. Besides, that would be criminal. Such a beautiful house. It's not the house's fault that Whistler owns it.

There were photos of the cars that they'd been seen driving. One was a green Subaru SUV. Probably Stride's. If so, disappointing. He'd rather see her at the wheel of something more fiery. But then, she'd have needed an SUV to haul her three girls and all their gear.

"Charles…"

Never mind. Gilhooley's notes would say. Another was a black Mercedes sedan. S-class. Not quite the top of the line. Whistler's, most likely. Keeps it there for his use. He must have told them to feel free. A third was another SUV, a Ford Escape. Silver. That one didn't look quite right for some reason. Down market? That's not it. Same bracket as the Subaru. He saw it now. A lot of road grime on that one. That's probably what made it stand out.

He picked up Gilhooley's handwritten notes. Ah, there it is. The Ford Escape isn't theirs. It belongs to some character Gilhooley had noticed driving up and down the streets of Belle Haven in what seemed an aimless fashion. This was when? Oh, yesterday. Sunday. That's the first Gilhooley noticed of him. But the driver, he writes, paid no particular attention to Whistler's house or the other two cars or any of the occupants thereof. This is just Gilhooley demonstrating his vigilance. The driver was probably checking out real estate. Or maybe a burglar, looking for easy pickings. Cars left unlocked. That sort of thing.

Gilhooley had added some photos of a restaurant called Mangiamo. One taken from outside, several more of the interior. Bar area in front, dining room in the rear. An assortment of patrons, one bartender on duty, none of them circled or highlighted. Haskell took that to mean that none were of interest. The bartender looked more like a bouncer.

Haskell had put these aside, not knowing their significance, but here it is in the notes. The restaurant, it seems, is their favorite in Bella Haven. He says he's learned that it's also a favorite of Whistler's whenever Whistler blows into town. Which explains it. Whistler must have recommended it. They like it so much that they've reserved the back room for a party they're throwing this Wednesday night for Stride's Aisha who's turning sixteen.

"Charles…"

I know. Something's bothering me, too. Can't quite put a finger… Oh, wait. Let me see. He went back to the photos. He'd been paying so much attention to Stride that he didn't see what was right there in front of him. Leland had said there were only three girls. There were four dark-haired girls in these photos.

216

Here's the older one playing with pretty one. Here's the one with the kitten who plays wearing warm-ups. Here's the girl who was shown looking on. She and the older one look something alike, or at least much more so than the other two. The chub and the older one must be the sisters. The pretty one would have to be Aisha. Why? Because, as noted, she's a beautiful young lady. There's simply no way that she got those looks from a camel-faced sloven like the prince. That leaves the one with the kitten. The mogul had described the prince's daughter as "cute." What else had he said? He said, "A tiny little thing." If that's her, the prince's genes must have skipped a generation. Either that, or she got them from her mother.

Does this prove that Stride has the princess after all? Not conclusively, perhaps, but it seems the way to bet. The least it means is that Leland had lied. Either that, or Stride had lied to Leland.

Here's an even better answer. He never spoke to Stride. He spoke to Clew. They discussed the princess. They discussed that disk. If Clew didn't know about either before that, his interest has certainly been piqued.

Shit.

Shit, double shit and for shame, Howard Leland.

You've not only lied, but you've broken your word. And with all that good breeding. Tut-tut. Isn't done.

One does not break one's word to Charles Haskell.

EIGHTEEN

On Monday, Clew had called Harry Whistler. He reached him at his home in Geneva. He told Harry to look for an email he'd sent. He'd attached the recording of his long talk with Leland after Leland's first day at Bohemian Grove. He asked Harry to call back when he'd heard it.

Harry did. They exchanged a few pleasantries. Harry asked about his Red Sox. Clew asked about the family.

Clew had met Harry's wife, the former Kate Geller, and his son, Adam, by his first wife, long deceased. Also Adam's young lady, the remarkable Claudia, who happened to be the daughter of Kate Geller. Son Adam had gone his own way for a time. Felt a need, Clew supposed, to make his own mark. He'd done so in spades, meeting Claudia and Kate along the way. How they all got together... you could write a book about it. Hell, you could write one on Claudia alone. But what counts is they're together. Working together. He has family that he knows he can trust with his life. As does Kessler. Clew envied them both.

Harry said, "As for Haskell, you're right on the money. Neither I nor Kessler care squat about him. My hope would be to keep it that way. As for Aisha and Elizabeth being Aisha and Qaila, I don't know when I've heard anything dumber. I agree, however, that Howard has a point. I can see how it might look to some."

"Harry… the princess. Does Stride have her?"

"Yes, Roger, she does. But trust me on this. Neither Stride nor Kessler know a thing about that disk. If they did, guaranteed, they would have told me."

"Especially when they're living in your house," said Clew.

"That's the least of the reasons," Harry told him.

"Well, they need to be alerted to what's going on here. Howard thinks that Haskell might know where they are. This could easily get very ugly."

"You say you don't know what might be on that disk?"

"You heard the tape. I don't. Howard does. You heard him say that it could devastate the Saudi regime. Howard's never been one to exaggerate."

Harry was silent for a long moment. "You're right. They must be told. And it's a damned shame. These three months may have been the best months of their lives. They're a family. I know how that feels."

"I… know that you know," Clew replied.

"Wait for me," said Harry. "We'll tell them together. I'll need tomorrow to sort out a few things from here, and then I'll fly to

D.C. Wednesday morning. When I know the flight plan, I'll give you a call. You'll meet me at Reagan. Bring a limo."

"Are you bringing… any family?"

"If you're thinking Claudia, certainly not. You know her. She's otherworldly already. She doesn't need to hear about a Muslim Joan of Arc."

"Yes, I know her," said Clew. Talks to animals. They talk back.

"I'll just bring the twins. We might not need them for this. But barring trouble, they'd enjoy another visit with the girls."

"In time for Aisha's birthday. I think it's this week."

"It is. It's on Wednesday at a restaurant called Mangiamo." Harry added, "By the way, do you remember Sam Foote?"

"The guy they called Bigfoot? Solved a few problems for us?"

In Italy, yes. Well, he now owns Mangiamo. He got a nice bonus when he gave up the life. That's part of what he did with his bonus. As for the party, I'd told Elizabeth that I'd try to make it if I could. I'll call her now and tell her we'll be there. You as well."

"Will the Beasley twins be armed?"

"Of course they will, Roger. That's why you'll be on the tarmac when my Gulfstream touches down. You'll see that we're not held up, won't you?"

"I'll wait for your call. Goodnight, Harry."

NINETEEN

The banker had returned to Bohemian Grove. He'd been gone for less than thirty-six hours. He'd come back unannounced. He'd brought the Saudi prince with him. The prince knew that if he had stayed in Riyadh, he'd have electrodes attached to his genitals by now. The trip had been a disaster.

After their hasty departure from Riyadh, his plane had stopped in Lisbon to refuel. Until then, the prince had been near-catatonic. Once there, he seemed to have recovered sufficiently to ask if he might get some air. He deplaned, walked off, then broke into a run. No direction in mind. He just wanted to hide. It took airport security four hours to find him. It took another two hours to convince the authorities that this wild-eyed Saudi was no terrorist.

In the end, thought the banker, it was just as well. They would have got back in the middle of the night were it not for that confusion in Lisbon. This way they arrived at a more civilized hour, touching down in Sacramento at seven, Tuesday morning. By nine, they'd reached the gates of the Grove.

The banker had led the prince to his quarters. "Stay here," he told the prince. "Do not leave this room. Don't open your door for anyone but us. We need time to decide how to deal with this."

The prince nodded vaguely. He'd gone straight to his wet bar. With trembling hands, he poured a Jack Daniels from one of the bottles that Haskell had provided. He took a sip, then a swallow and then drained the glass. He reached to fill it again.

The banker asked, "Did you hear me? Say that you understood me."

The prince answered, "I must speak to Mr. Leland."

"Howard Leland? What for? Surely not about this."

"I cannot go home. How can I go home? Mr. Leland must help me to stay in this country. Where is he? Is he in his room?"

"Um… no. He has a full schedule of meetings. But, you're right. You need protection. Except let us handle it. We'll attend to it quickly and quietly."

The prince took another swallow. He choked on it. He heaved.

The banker picked up his room phone, he called the front desk. He said, "The prince is feeling poorly. He is not to be disturbed. Please hold any calls that might come in." Especially from Leland, thought the banker.

The receptionist answered, "As you wish, sir."

He lowered his voice. "Where is Mr. Leland now, do you know?"

"Gone canoeing, sir. On the Russian River. It's one of today's scheduled activities."

"Can he be reached?"

"Yes, sir, If need be. But unless it's an emergency..."

"When will he be back?"

"Not before early evening. A picnic is included."

The banker covered the mouthpiece. He said to the prince, "As I thought, he's tied up. Can't be reached."

He said to the receptionist, "Please locate Charles Haskell. Tell him I've returned. I'll be waiting for him on the fishing dock." The dock was the only place he could think of where they wouldn't risk being overheard.

"Sir, he's off playing tennis. There's a tournament."

"Send for him, please. Do it now."

After breaking the connection, he removed the jack from the rear of the room-to-room phone. Using his thumb nail, he snapped off its plastic clip so that it could not be reinserted. He picked up a desk chair. He said to the prince, "Prop this under the doorknob after I've gone. Don't open it for anyone other than us. Lie down; get some rest and leave this in my hands. Don't worry. We're going to take care of you."

Haskell arrived. The mogul was with him; they'd been partners at doubles. They were both in sweat-dampened tennis attire and both had their racquets in their hands. The mogul saw the look on the banker's face. He said, "I gather that the news isn't good."

The banker opened the laptop that he had brought with him. He said, "The prince and I stopped first at his villa before going downtown to the office. He needed to change into Saudi attire. He was trying not to be noticed."

Haskell nodded. "What have you got?"

"I scanned this in while the prince was dressing." He moved the mouse of the laptop and clicked on a file. A snapshot appeared. Some large family gathering. The prince, his cousin, their wives and their offspring. He touched a finger to the face of a somber young girl who looked as thought she'd rather be elsewhere.

He said, "Here's the daughter. This is all the prince had. I couldn't find one in which her head isn't covered. This cousin who's been hunting her had taken all the others. It seems he gave them to the Saudi religious police. Have you ever heard of the Hasheem?"

"What about them?"

"Special unit of the Mutawain. Think Spanish Inquisition. Headed by that cleric who was left at the altar. He has men hunting the girl, but not for that reason. I suspect that he might know what she took. That said, Hasheem's hunters are notoriously inept. A much bigger concern is Hamas."

"Hamas?" asked Haskell. "What do they have to do with this?"

"Until yesterday, nothing. Until the prince shot off his mouth. I let him out of my sight for just a few minutes. How was I to know who'd be waiting outside when…"

"Hold it. Hamas? The terrorist group?"

"They… see themselves differently. I'll get to that shortly."

"No, now," said Haskell. "How is Hamas involved?"

"We got to the office. Saudi Overseas Charities. Doctor Rajib Sadik, who's very senior in Hamas, had flown in to find out why his funding had been stopped. He'd been counting on a transfer of two million dollars out of one of the legitimate charities. He'd tried to access the fund from his office in Hebron. All he got were three words that came up on his screen."

Haskell remembered what his hacker had told him. "Three words? What were those three words?"

"They were, 'She is… ' Wait. Let me do this in sequence."

"Just tell me," said Haskell. "What were the words?"

"Please," said the banker. "Let's first understand their context. Let's start where we got to that computer."

The mogul said to Haskell, "Let him tell it his way."

"Then get to it," said Haskell. "Do you know where these words came from?"

"For heaven's sake, Charles. Let him talk."

The banker explained that he'd persuaded the prince to let his technician try to open the files whose passwords the daughter had changed. The prince told the other staffers that the two men he'd brought with him were merely computer repairmen. He said that he'd mistakenly punched the wrong key and had lost a list of telephone numbers. They knew his lack of skill; they had no doubt that he had done so. The prince locked the door of the office they were in. He stood over the shoulders of the technician, ready to stop him, if he should succeed, before any of the files could be read.

The technician turned it on. He played with it for while. Suddenly a message box appeared on the screen. Not up in one corner. It filled the whole screen. The banker touched the mouse of his laptop again. He turned it for Haskell and the mogul to see. The message read:

HELLO.

LET US SAVE YOU LONG EFFORTS.

THE ONLY PASSWORD YOU WILL NEED IS 'SHE IS COMING'

"She is coming," said Haskell. "Were those the three words?"

"That Sadik got? Yes. But bear with me."

"And sent in English?" asked the mogul. "Why not Arabic?"

"Stilted English, but yes. Why not Arabic? I don't know. Perhaps they used English to disguise who they are. In Arabic, one can narrow down the dialect."

"Whatever," said Haskell, snapping his fingers. "It says they're a password. Did you try it?"

"Not right away. We were fearful of a trap. My technician set to work looking for another way. A new message popped on. Here's the next one."

The banker tapped a key. The second message appeared. It read:

SUCH A COWARD. STOP WASTING TIME.

WE PROMISE THAT IT WILL NOT BLOW UP IN YOUR FACE.

WE PROMISE NO MORE HARM TO YOUR FILES.

"And this was coming in remotely?" asked Haskell. "Real time?"

"Precisely. They knew that we had logged on. They'd rigged it to alert them the moment we did. My technician was very impressed."

"From the sound of it, they could hardly wait," said the mogul. "They were having their fun. They were taunting you."

"Not me," said the banker. "They'd know nothing of me. They meant this for anyone who tried to get in. They would have been expecting a Saudi."

Haskell slapped his racquet against his thigh. "You keep saying 'they.' Who the hell are they? We're not talking just this kid, this little princess, am I right?"

"That was my question. I asked them, 'Who are you?'" The banker tapped another key. "Here's your answer."

WE ARE THE HANDMAIDENS OF SHE WHO IS COMING.

GO AHEAD. TYPE IT IN. WE'RE FEELING BOREDOM.

The banker said, "I asked the prince, does this sound like his daughter? He said it does not. He said her English is excellent. Her mother used to teach it. Nor would she ever speak in such an insolent tone. To make sure, I typed in a response of my own. I wrote, 'Rasha, you know me. I've been to your home. Your mother is worried. Are you safe? Are you well?'" Another tap. "Here's the answer that came:"

LAST CHANCE FOR YOU TO TYPE IN THE PASSWORD

WE DO NOT HAVE ALL MORNING.

WE ARE MISSING GOOD BREAKFAST.

ON THE MENU IS RIPE OLIVE PANCAKES AND EGGS.

EGGS ARE SCRAMBLED. DO YOU LIKE SCRAMBLED?

Haskell stared. He asked, "What's all that about?"

The banker said, "I don't know who mixes olives with pancakes, but I do know you won't enjoy scrambled." He added, "By the way, I suspect that her mother assisted her in making her plans to run off. Her mother, I've learned, detested the cleric to whom her husband had promised their daughter. With that in mind, I think it unlikely that her daughter would have ignored her concern, even though it was I who expressed it."

"Meaning?"

"It's not Rasha."

"You just said that," said Haskell. His patience had been stretched. He said, "Cut to the chase. Did you get into the system or not?"

"We did," said the banker, "while holding our breath. If not a crash, I expected, at a minimum, more teasing, or perhaps the full text of the prophecy. Which I've downloaded, by the way. I have it in English. But we did use that password and got in without incident. There appeared on the screen a list of all the accounts. Thirty per page. Forty pages in all. Do the math; that's roughly twelve hundred accounts. Most balances range between three and thirty million. The top ten are in the hundreds of millions."

Haskell asked, "Still ten billion in total?"

"Actually, more. I'm told it's mostly in Euros."

"Whatever," said Haskell. "Was it still intact?"

"Well, let me show you." He clicked on his mouse. The first of those pages appeared on the screen. It showed three columns of figures.

"The short answer is yes. The money's all there. At this point the prince was greatly relieved. He reached to shut it down, but he stopped when he realized that something was missing. He saw that there should have been a fourth column. He realized that there were no names."

The banker touched a blank space on the screen. He said, "Here is where the names should have been. Not only the names of the Saudis who've been stashing it, but also the names of the legitimate charities from which their flight money has apparently been skimmed. They're gone. They've all been deleted."

"But so what?" asked Haskell. "These are numbered accounts. I'm looking at the numbers. They're still there."

"The account numbers, yes, each ten digits in length, but those numbers are useless by themselves. Each needs to be used with an access code. The second column here shows those codes." The banker touched his finger to the laptop's screen. "As you see, these codes are more complex, a combination of numerals and letters. The last column shows each account's balance as of the most recent deposit. About half of them contain twenty million or more. I'd be willing to bet that those with much less are mostly the legitimate charities."

Haskell had little interest in those. He wanted the names of the skimmers. "So we don't have the names. What does that do to us?"

"Oh, we'd know the biggest names soon enough," said the banker. "They'll raise a stink all over the banking world. They'll want my bank's help in getting at their money."

"Isn't that what we want?"

"If only life were so simple. I'm afraid that's the least of our problems."

The banker clicked on his mouse. The screen scrolled through thirty pages. He said, "Here's what appeared at the end."

The message read:

SO MANY THIEVES. MORE THAN ONE THOUSAND THIEVES.

HYPOCRITES WHO HAVE STOLEN FROM THE POOR AND THE SICK.

SHE WILL BEGIN BY TAKING BACK ALL THESE MONIES.

AFTER THAT, THEY WILL FEEL QAILA'S SWORD.

"Qaila?" asked Haskell.

"A guardian angel. Has a flaming sword. The prophecy says she'll send them to hell."

"Never mind that shit," said Haskell. "So they do want this money."

"Charles, let's hear the rest of it," said the mogul.

The banker told them, "This is where the prince fell apart. He starts wailing, 'I am dead; they will kill me; I am dead,' referring to the Saudis, not the angel. It's when he turned and ran out of the room. It's when he ran into the official from Hamas, who, I told you, had turned up outside and…"

Haskell said, "No, stay with this. Future tense?"

"The 'she will begin' part?"

"Yes. Does that mean they haven't yet?"

"It doesn't seem as though they have, but they might as well have. We tried to get into a few of these accounts by entering their numbers and their access codes. Each time, the computer said the entry was invalid. My technician fooled with it for another twenty minutes before another instant message appeared." He tapped the key. "I guess they did take a quick break for breakfast."

The message read:

WE ARE BACK NOW.

HOW DO YOU LIKE YOUR EGGS?

WE DON'T THINK THAT YOU LIKE THEM SCRAMBLED.

Haskell said, "Scrambled eggs again. What the hell does that mean?"

"It's their little joke. They mean nest eggs," said the banker. "They've scrambled all the numbers and codes in each of the three

231

remaining columns. The account numbers, codes and the current cash balances are no longer in sequence; they're scrambled."

"Can't they be reconstructed?"

"Perhaps. Over time. By trial and error. But it wouldn't do us any good. Each access code consists of six digits and letters plus another code, a four-digit suffix. The suffix identifies the specific off-shore bank of which, as you know, there are hundreds. They've deleted the suffix that shows where the money is. Without that suffix, we have nothing to go on."

Haskell still wasn't sure that he understood. "Say I've banked fifty million on Grand Cayman or wherever. I know my account number. I know my access code. Why can't I get at my own money?"

"Because you don't know that your money's in Grand Cayman. It could be, as I've said, in one of hundreds of banks, laundered and relaundered through a half dozen others. The Saudi or Saudis who first organized the skim, had set the system up in this way to make sure that no one can bail out prematurely. If discovered, that could ruin it for everyone else. Take my word; you'd have to go through this system."

"Except now I can't."

"I don't see how," said the banker, "but these 'handmaidens' can. The only unscrambled list in existence is now on the disk that Rasha made before she ran. But I still don't think it's Rasha who's doing this."

"Kessler," muttered Haskell.

"Oh, please," said the mogul. "It not even the work of an adult."

"Because it sounds adolescent? That can be faked."

"Yes, it can," said the mogul, "but why would he bother? To mislead? He wouldn't have to. None of this would point to him. He's never had any truck with the Saudis."

"Except through the Nasreens. A lot of them are Saudi women."

"Not them either," said the mogul. "From what I've heard, Leland's right. This sort of thing is not at all like them."

"Which reminds me," said the banker, "is he going to help? I know that he made a call Sunday night. I saw him talking on a cell phone outside the gate as the prince and I drove out past him."

Haskell's eyes turned hard. "I wouldn't count on it."

The mogul said to the banker, "I met with him this morning. That call was to Elizabeth Stride. She's agreed to track down that disk for him."

"Uh-huh," said Haskell. "He told me the same thing. But he lied. He only spoke to Roger Clew."

The mogul was startled. He asked, "How could you know that?"

"As you've said, we all have our little birds."

"You have someone at State?"

"I have someone almost everywhere."

The mogul said, "Let me try another way. Is this someone who knows that Stride is unreachable?"

"She's entirely reachable. I know where she is."

"I leap to the conclusion that you have someone there. For this purpose, or to peep? Which is it, Charles?"

"If I were you, I'd be careful," said Haskell.

The banker could see that a raw nerve was touched. He asked both men, "Who's Elizabeth Stride?"

"Lovely woman. An angel," said the mogul.

"Anyway," said Haskell, "She's not doing this. This handmaiden crap isn't like her at all. She doesn't play games. It's not her."

The banker said to the mogul, "Who the devil is this woman? Will someone please explain…"

The mogul touched the banker's leg with his racquet, a signal that he'd best drop the subject. His eyes fell to the laptop. They narrowed. "I'd like a few moments to study these, please. My sixth sense says there's something we're missing."

He took the laptop from the banker and exchanged his racquet for it. He walked with it to the farthest end of the dock. He placed the laptop on a table that was meant for cleaning fish. He stood, fingers drumming, deep in thought.

"His sixth sense?" asked the banker.

"He thinks he has the gift. Let him have his psychic moment. Now, what happened with this rag-head from Hamas?"

"Don't dismiss him with that term. As it happened, he was dressed in a business suit and tie. He looks more European than Arab."

"Whatever."

"His name is Rajib Sadik. Ever heard of him?"

"No."

"One of their top fund-raisers. No fanatic. Well respected. He's a doctor, educated, I believe, in western Europe. Beyond that, we don't know much about him. The story is that he gave up a lucrative practice to return to his roots and help to build a new country. I'm telling you this to help you understand why the prince would spill his guts to the man."

Haskell closed his eyes. "How much did he tell him?"

"Too much," said the banker, "but he put his own spin on it. It's all the Nasreens. They kidnapped his daughter. First they forced her to copy those files by threatening to assassinate him if she didn't. She agreed, so great was her love for him. But she scrambled them first so that they couldn't use them. She realized that nobody else could either, but she intended to restore them as soon as she got out. The Nasreens, however, found out what she'd done and have tortured her to get her to fix them. She refused and bravely went to her death. Ergo, the money is safe for now. Access to it will soon be restored."

"Sadik knows it's ten billion?"

"He didn't. He does now. And that most of it's been stolen. He knows that charities don't use numbered accounts unless someone doesn't want them to be audited."

"What about the Nasreens? Was he buying that story?"

"Of course not," said the banker. "It was clearly absurd. His own account was accessible until three days ago. The prince's daughter's been gone for three months. And he knows the Nasreens. He knows they'd do no such thing. Incidentally, he

235

knew that they'd got Rasha out. The prince had tried to enlist Hamas, among others, to find her and capture her or kill her."

"Why Hamas?"

"Because Hamas has supporters wherever there are Arabs. There are Arab communities all over western Europe and all over the United States as well. All the same, Sadik refused him. He knew why she ran. Still, he might have tracked her down if he'd known about the disk. But, back then, the prince didn't dare tell a soul that his daughter had copied those files."

"Then why, God damn it, did that schmuck tell him now?"

"He didn't have much choice. Here's this foreigner, me, playing with this computer at Saudi Overseas Charities. The prince proceeded to explain what I was doing there. He told Sadik that I, too, am a banker and that I, along with other men of great wealth are such friends of the prince that we rushed to his aid. And you, by the way, are his best friend."

"He named me?"

"Oh, yes," said the banker. "And he didn't stop there. He claimed that Howard Leland is an ally in this matter and so, therefore, is your government. Even better, so is The Bohemian Club of which the prince claimed to be a member. He told Sadik that we'd just flown in from the Grove, dispatched to either restore these accounts or cover any losses ourselves. He told Sadik that we'll now fly back to the Grove where you and Leland are awaiting our report."

"We'd cover their losses?"

"I amended that. Not those of the thieves. I said those of the legitimate charities. I thought he'd buy that more easily, but he didn't. I said we'd begin with his own two million. Charles, I think we'd be wise to let him have it."

Haskell raised a hand. He said, "Not so fast. Had Sadik ever heard of the Bohemian Club?"

"Charles, he's no hick. He's a cultivated man. He asked the prince whether we still sacrifice babies and dispose of dead whores in the lake."

"No hick, but he believes that?"

"Oh, he wasn't serious. He was needling the prince. Sadik would know that those stories are nonsense. He also knew that there was no way in hell that the prince would be considered for membership. But regardless, yes, he's quite aware that it exists. He's also heard of you and, of course, Trans-Global Oil. And he certainly knows who Howard Leland is."

"Wait a minute," said Haskell. "Those two were outside. How could you know what they were saying?"

"Because Sadik pushed past him. He came into the office. He's no dummy; he wanted to see for himself and he wanted to hear it from me. While the prince was standing there wetting his pants, he repeated all that the prince had just told him. However, I was obviously less than prepared. The girl's death by torture was news to me. Sadik could see that on my face."

"And then?"

"He gave the prince a look. The look, I thought, said, 'You're right. You're a dead man.' He turned to me and said, 'Men like you don't have friends. Men like you have only accomplices.' I swore up and down that we weren't there to steal, that we really only wanted the names. Sadik understands blackmail, so that he believed. More than believed, I think he approved. He said, "They deserve that and more."

Haskell raised an eyebrow. "So you think this guy's straight?"

"I do. He's Hamas. They're not like the PLO. Hamas doesn't tolerate corruption."

"Go on."

"I said that some of what the prince told him was true. I said whether the daughter is dead or alive, somebody, somewhere, got hold of that disk and we're trying to track down who is doing this. He said, 'Show me these messages.' So I did."

"Because?"

"The prince had described them. How could I not? All Sadik had to do was pick up the phone and have Saudi Security drag us off to a cell. But Sadik seemed more interested in the messages themselves. He, too, thought the language didn't sound like the daughter."

"He'd met her?" asked Haskell.

"There at the office. This was not his first visit. Anyway, he then sat down at the keyboard and read through that series of messages. He cleared the screen and brought up the search engine. After turning the monitor so that we couldn't see it, he typed in a code and sat reading what came up. He said, 'Same three words. Wherever we look. She seems to be coming to a great many places. Everywhere there are Muslims. Not just Iran. But the Saudis seem to have first priority.'"

Haskell didn't understand. "Now he's sharing this with you?"

"Not really," said the banker. "More like thinking out loud. He hit a few more keys. What came up made him smile. He shook his head and muttered, 'Bad girls.'"

"Meaning what?" asked Haskell. "He knows who is doing this?"

"I asked. He ignored me. But I had that impression. I think he'd just realized who might be behind it. Not just Rasha. Bad girls. He used the plural."

"The plural," said Haskell. "So what? So would I. Handmaidens is a pretty good clue."

The banker's chin came up. "Would you rather not hear this?"

"Keep talking. What happened next?"

"I'm telling you that something had clicked in his head. From that moment, he showed no further interest in us. Whatever he was thinking, he put it aside. He asked, 'When all these Saudis come looking for their money, will they see this series of messages?' I said, 'No, it's off line now, but when they try, I think they'll probably still get She is coming.' Then that smile again. He said, 'So will they be.'"

"Meaning?"

"My impression? He meant that they won't sit and wait. They'll move heaven and to track down those behind this. Sadik is fully aware of that prophecy. You should read it. Here's a copy. There's some interesting wording."

Haskell took it. He said, "Later." He asked, "How was this left?"

"I don't think you've quite grasped the point of his remark. It won't be just us who'll be hunting down that disk. Nor will it be only the disk that they're hunting. They'll be hunting down the source of the prophecy, Charles. The source seems to be one and the same."

It damned well is, thought Haskell, and that source is Kessler. Score one for his hackers. Those three words. They were right. Three words beamed from Belle Haven to the whole Muslim world. He said, "So we're now in a race."

"A race? It might be more like a cavalry charge. Most other Islamic regimes loathe the Saudis, especially the Shiite regimes. Sadik mentioned Iran. Good example. They'd love to get hold of this flight money list. And publish it. Embarrass them. Maybe start an uprising. For the Saudi Shiites, the eastern province Saudi Shiites, that list could be the last straw. It could make them all the more willing and eager to cast their lot with Iran and Iraq and form that Shiite crescent you've envisioned."

Haskell shrugged. He said, "Good. We're well positioned for that."

"Maybe, but not for the totally unexpected. By that, I mean this prophecy. It could open the floodgates. Every Muslim regime will want to see it proved false as more of their women hear that 'She' is on the way. It's very much in their interest to quash this thing before they find themselves facing their own revolution by a few hundred million Muslim women."

Haskell sighed. "Okay. Is that all of it?"

"We left the building, made a dash for the airport. We got out while the getting was good."

"Sadik didn't try to stop you?"

"We thought he was about to. He did pull out his phone. I froze, but he wasn't calling Saudi security. Too many digits. An overseas call. He asked to be put through to someone named Mansur who apparently wasn't available. He said, 'Tell Mansur it's Rajib Sadik and ask him if he still has those girls.' This wasn't in Arabic. He was speaking in Farsi. He must have been calling Iran."

"About this?"

"No, the weather," snapped the banker. "Of course, about this. What's more, although Mansur is a common enough name, there's an Abbas Mansur who chairs the Guardian Council. He's one of the most popular clerics in Iran and likely, I think, to be its next president if they ever hold an honest election. If it's him…"

"Skip the guesswork. What else did you hear?"

"He waited until a voice came back on. He listened and seemed shocked by whatever he was hearing. He asked, 'What girl? One of those who were arrested? And they're torturing her? Does he know about this?' He listened. He didn't like what he was hearing. He said, 'Find Mansur. Tell him I'm on my way. In the meantime, stop it. Do nothing further. Get her to a hospital now.'"

"Get who?"

"I don't know. A girl. All he said was a girl. One who seems to be in need of his attention. And whoever he was talking to was giving him an argument. Sadik started cursing this person out. Really furious. Blindly furious. He no longer seemed to care that we were still in the office. It seemed a good time to slip away."

"Iran, huh?" said Haskell. His expression had gone distant.

"What are you thinking?" asked the banker.

"Kessler has two girls who are sisters from Iran."

"Sadik said girl, not girls. This time it was singular. And he was speaking of someone still there."

"Someone he wants to talk to."

"He'd be doing so by now. If she's still able."

"Some friend of those two sisters? Maybe someone who's heard from them?"

"No idea," said the banker. "But it's obviously related. If not to the sisters, surely to this damned prophecy. And we can safely assume that he's joining the hunt for the missing ten billion dollars."

"Joining it? He'd be leading it. He's way out in front. No one else knew about any of this until that shithead prince..." Haskell paused. He asked, "Where is the prince now?"

"Quarantined in his room with his good friend, Jack Daniels. I've left word that he's not to be disturbed. You are... probably wondering why I brought him back."

"You couldn't leave him in Lisbon. I know that."

"He's asked to see Howard Leland. He wants to defect. Happily, Leland's..."

"Off canoeing. All day."

"Leland would have had him out of here in ten minutes. Whisked off to some army base. Exhaustively debriefed. The prince has become a liability, Charles."

"So it seems."

"If there are... adjustments that ought to be made, that sort of thing seems more up your alley."

Haskell nodded. He said, "I'll take care of it."

The mogul approached, the laptop open in his hands. He spoke to the banker, his head cocked to one side. He said, "The language certainly seems adolescent. But that could be a ruse in itself. The strangled syntax as well."

"We've discussed that," said the banker. "We're not sure it's a ruse."

"These so-called handmaidens. This exchange you had with them. What time of the day would that have been?"

"In Riyadh? Late afternoon. It was about four o'clock."

"So let's see. That would be eight in the morning in Washington. Roger Clew is in Washington. And it's breakfast time there."

Haskell folded his arms. "You're point being?"

"This handmaiden. She said it. She wanted her breakfast. You don't want to believe that it's Stride who's behind this. We're told that the Nasreens don't do such things either."

"Speed it up. Tell us something we don't know."

"I don't like to say it, but you might be right. If it isn't Stride, it could still be Kessler. And Kessler could be working with Clew."

Haskell curled his lip. "This is your big epiphany?"

"I'm trying to agree with you. You said it yourself."

"I said I could feel it. You said I'm deluded. But here's the reality. They're all that we have. There's no other place to start looking."

"Leland swore that Stride and Kessler do not have the disk. He swore, Charles. I think he believes it."

"He's playing us."

"Not Leland. He wouldn't swear lightly."

"Okay, then his man, Roger Clew, is playing him. Clew wants that disk for himself."

The mogul nodded. "No doubt. And so will almost anyone else who happens to learn of its existence."

"You think so?" asked Haskell. "You don't know the half of it." He said to the banker, "Fill him in about Sadik. Me, I'm going to take a shower. We'll talk later."

The banker said, "I will. But this is getting beyond us. Perhaps we should…"

"No. We're not backing off."

"I was going to suggest a more wait and see posture."

"And leave that disk to Sadik? Or to God knows who else? We've got too much invested and the payoff will be huge. Not again. Not twice. I will not let that happen."

"Twice?" asked the banker. He was looking at the mogul.

The mogul didn't answer. He said to Haskell. "Take your shower."

Haskell hesitated. He cocked his head to one side. He had the look of a man who'd just had an idea and who wondered why he hadn't thought of it before. The mogul saw it. He said, "A revelation? Care to share it?"

Haskell answered, "I'm thinking. Maybe we don't need the disk. Maybe there's another way to do this."

"Do what, exactly, Charles?"

"Two birds with one stone."

"The second bird being Kessler? I'm not sure I want to hear this. But let's have it. What do you have in mind?"

"Later," said Haskell. "I need time to think it through." He turned and slowly walked off the jetty, rhythmically tapping the face of his racquet against the side of one leg. The mogul saw his head nodding as if in agreement with a voice that only Charles Haskell could hear. The mogul groaned within himself as he watched.

He heard the banker ask again, "What's this twice?"

"Kessler again, thwarting Haskell, or he thinks so. The first, of course, was that business in Angola. You and I lost some skin on that one as well. You and I have moved on. Charles Haskell has not. It's become a psychosis with him."

"And another seems to be with... what was that name?"

"Elizabeth Stride. I'll fill you in later. Suffice it to say that she's sinned against Haskell by not realizing that she is intended for him."

"How many psychoses are we dealing with here?"

"With Charles? Hard to say. Charles Haskell is more than one person, you know. It's hereditary, probably. Gets it from his mother. Did you know she ended up in an asylum?"

The banker raised an eyebrow. "I did not."

"Lost all touch with herself. She became other people. Charles does the same thing every now and again, depending, it seems, on who he thinks he needs to be. He says it's deliberate, but I'm not so sure. Nor am I sure that he's always aware of it."

The banker didn't understand. "Who does he become?"

"Oh, various film actors and characters from books. He was Fred Astaire when he wooed his first wife. Took a course in ballroom dancing and tap. Hard to picture, I know, but it's true."

"That… hardly suggests mental illness," said the banker.

"For the next one, the pianist, he was Tom Hanks, I think. He felt the need to seem engagingly vulnerable. But you're right. It's role-playing. Not troubling in itself. But let's hope that he's never seen The Silence of the Lambs. Someone might end up as his dinner."

The banker smiled at what he thought was a joke.

The mogul asked, "Ever talk to yourself?"

"I suppose we all think aloud on occasion."

"We do, but Charles has discussions with himself. Perhaps they're with his better nature, if he has one. Or perhaps an evil twin. I'm never sure."

The banker frowned. He asked the mogul, "Why are you saying this?"

"So that you'll understand him. Forewarned is forearmed. No, I wouldn't go so far as to say he's unbalanced. But he has a touch of madness and you know the old saying. Nothing great has ever been accomplished without it. The man's certainly driven. Takes the bit in his teeth. I've yet to see anyone else best him."

"Other than this Kessler, you mean."

The mogul rocked a hand. He said, "Well, not really. If I were to bother pinning the blame, I'd look more to Harry Whistler and to the Mossad. But they don't have Stride. Martin Kessler has Stride. That is the long and the short of it."

As the mogul spoke, he was still watching Haskell. Haskell, still nodding, had quickened his pace.

"Harry Whistler's an American, is he not?" asked the banker.

"When it suits him. Why do you ask?"

"A citizen, but your government seems to take a blind eye…"

"To his activities? Yes, they leave him alone. It's in their interest. He helps keep the oil flowing. No surprise. Look at Haskell. They leave him alone. And he's indictable a hundred times over."

Yes, look at him, thought the mogul. See that purposeful stride? The mogul paused to smile at his unintended pun. "Do you suppose he's on his way to kill the prince?"

The banker stiffened. "You mean now?"

"Uh-huh. As we speak. He certainly can't let him get to Leland." Haskell was climbing the steps of their cabin, taking them two at a time. "As I've said, he takes the bit in his teeth."

"Kill him here at the Grove? He wouldn't think of it, would he?"

"Perhaps not. But never mind. And that's a sensible 'never mind.' We'd have nothing to do with it, would we?"

The banker's hands went to his cheeks. "Surely not."

"We'd have nothing to do with any of this. If it should go badly. And unless it goes well. We are both prudent men, are we not?"

"To a fault."

"Now tell me. What about this Sadik?"

TWENTY

Tuesday morning. Qasr Prison. In the center of Tehran.

Sadik had rushed to Riyadh's King Khalid airport where he grabbed the first flight to Tehran. As he'd feared, he was already too late. The young woman had been sentenced to eight hundred lashes to be meted out one hundred at a time. She would not survive eight hundred. No one ever had. Her name was Farah. She was nineteen years old. In her language, Farah meant joy.

She had barely survived the first two sets of one hundred. They had been spaced only three days apart. Her body was in shock, wracked by chills and convulsions. One more session. Sadik knew, and her mind would be gone, even if her heart went on beating.

The guard, a sergeant, who carried out the sentence had plenty of experience in these matters. He knew that this would be her last chance to talk. If she didn't, or couldn't, it was much the same to him. She was only getting what she deserved.

This was justice, thought the sergeant, because her mind had been poisoned. Too smart for her own good. Too many books. This one, he'd been told, was in her second year of college. She was learning about business and the use of computers. College for women? Look where it got her. She would never again see the sun.

The charge had been heresy and the spreading of that heresy. She'd been caught at one of those Internet cafes that the mullahs should have closed long ago. She'd been confronted with a message that she'd passed to many others. It began with the words, "She is coming." Its source was believed to be a close friend of this one, a friend who had sneaked off to America. The friend spoke of the prophecy and swore to its truth. The friend said that she was with the one who was coming. She said the Lady of the Camel is reborn, flesh and blood, and soon the whole world will know it. This one, therefore, knows where the heresy had come from and where the false prophet whom it spoke of could be found.

Moreover, she'd been seen to take pleasure in her crime. A witness had testified that he saw her smiling as she typed words that had been forbidden. And she was giggling and whispering with other young women who were seated at other machines. All of those had been arrested and imprisoned as well. They'd been put in a pen a few steps down the hall from the room where the sentence was being carried out. This was so that they could listen to her sobs and her screams and know what they, too, might have in store for them.

The old mullah who judged her had tried to be merciful. He had given her the chance to recant and confess. She was told that if she did, her sentence might be suspended after only fifty lashes with a strap. The strap would be the soft one, made of wool, although with knots. It would not be the one that they showed her, made of wires. In return for that mercy, she must tell all she knows. Who first told her of the prophecy? Who did she tell in turn? She was to name every person to whom she had sent this, and not only those within the borders of Iran. Also those in America. Especially those. The ones she wrote to were thought to be as many as eight hundred. Give their names or the sentence would be one lash for each.

But this women had been obstinate. She was frightened. She wept. Even so, she said, "I will not betray my friend."

So the lashes were administered one hundred at a time using the electrical cable. The first hundred were followed by three days of semi-healing, time to reflect on her error. She was then brought down again for one hundred more. For these, she was allowed to remain fully covered because the mullah who judged her had wished to be present. The old mullah had expected that she would relent within the first dozen or so strokes. But she did not, nor would she scream for the others to hear. When the first one hundred ended, she had gasped through gritted teeth, "It is true. It is true. She is coming."

The sergeant who lashed her, in his long plastic apron, shook his head and pretended to be saddened. He had said to the mullah, "You have said it yourself. Too much learning ruins women. Give them books and they're soon lost to God."

The beaten woman cleared her throat. She rasped the words, "It is you."

The mullah wasn't sure what she'd said. He leaned closer.

She then raised her voice with effort. She croaked, "It is you. It is you who are lost. The angel Qaila will send you to hell."

That earned her a caning on the soles of her feet. These blows were extra, not counted toward her sentence. She didn't have so much to say after that. This morning, back on schedule, she would get her next one hundred. He sent two guards to fetch her. She was conscious, but barely. The guards strapped her, face down, to a long wooden bench. The sergeant dismissed them, closed the steel door behind them and slid its heavy bolt into place.

Her chador was torn, her clothing clotted with blood. Parts of her smelled like apples, a sign of gangrene. Her only words this time were like animal sounds. The old mullah had chosen not to attend. He said he saw no purpose in wasting his time if she is unlikely or unable to recant. In the mullah's absence, the sergeant had decided that her modesty need no longer be considered. Left to him, all prisoners would always be naked. Naked prisoners are always more frightened.

And some you could have sex with if the mullahs weren't watching. The sergeant would have liked a few minutes with this one before the first session began. She had a fine young body. Not so fine anymore. But he had no regrets because she had this coming. Heresy or not, she deserved what she was getting for being so full of herself with her schooling. All his life, her kind had turned their noses up at him. She was also too tall. Being tall makes women proud. Women shouldn't be taller than men.

He tore off what remained of her chador and its cowl. Long brown hair, now matted, tumbled over her cheeks. He next peeled off two more blood-stiffened garments until her thighs and her buttocks were bared. She was heard to whimper softly as he did so. This is good, he thought. She still feels.

He raised the cable and was about to strike when there came a loud knock on the door. A familiar voice called, "Open up." He threw back the bolt and to the sergeant's dismay, the old mullah had returned, and with a visitor. The mullah saw her nakedness. He averted his eyes, but the visitor did not. The visitor made a hissing sound through his teeth. His look was not one of approval.

"This man has come," said the mullah, his eyes still cast downward, "to question the heretic and those others. He is a guest of the Guardian Council."

A guest of the Council? Not some minister; the Council. This man must be important indeed, thought the sergeant. Unlike the old mullah, he was dressed in western clothing. His dark suit fit him well and it didn't look cheap. Middle aged, maybe fifty, but no middle aged belly. Eyes gray. Like his hair. Hair cut by a barber. Not Iranian probably. Not with a necktie. Here, you don't see many neckties.

The mullah spoke as if reading his mind. "This is Doctor Sadik. He is a leader of Hamas. He is helping to stamp out the heresy."

Hamas, thought the sergeant? Why should this concern Hamas? Their business should be killing Jews.

The man hadn't taken his eyes off the woman. He asked, "Did Mansur know that this was being done?"

A high mullah, thought the sergeant, called by his last name? Does this man have so little respect? The old mullah answered, "He was not to be burdened. This is a small matter. Besides, he's been away at a conference in Tabriz. He is not to return until tonight."

"Still, I'd asked that no further injury be done. I didn't come here to question a corpse. I had asked that she get medical attention."

The mullah answered, "She is not here to be healed." He asked the sergeant, "But why is she exposed?"

The sergeant quickly draped the torn chador over her. "It was only for a moment," he said to the mullah. "It was to see if any of the cuts are too deep. She shouldn't die from loss of blood before confessing."

The Hamas man muttered an expression of doubt. It was in reference to the excrement of cows. The sergeant knew that his word was being impugned, but worse, that his skills had been doubted. He felt the need to show this man from Hamas that the use of the lash was an art. He reached to pull up the hem of her chador, revealing a portion of her lower back that remained almost free of cuts and of welts. He stepped back while flexing the cable.

"This whip is heavy," he said to the visitor. "If you're a doctor, you should know that it could crush the liver and also maybe rupture the spleen. This could cause much bleeding that is hidden. This is why," he said, pointing, "I am careful where I strike. Upper back, her legs, the soles of her feet. These won't kill her so quickly, but they are no less painful. Believe me, if they know, they will talk."

Sadik could hear the voices of the others down the hall. They were weeping and praying for the one to be lashed. Some were calling her name, saying, "Farah, be brave." Others were cursing and insulting her torturer, telling him that he is shit on a shoe.

Such insults caused this runt of a sergeant to smile. He knew he'd change their tune soon enough.

Sadik stepped closer to the girl on the bench. Except for a slight rise and fall of her chest, she hadn't stirred since he entered the chamber. The wire whip, he saw, had done far more damage than this imbecile jailor had supposed. True enough he'd focused on her upper back, but it had shattered several ribs and crushed her scapula. The flesh around those wounds was necrotic. So was the flesh of her buttocks and thighs. He wondered whether her mind was still capable of even understanding his words.

Sadik asked the Mullah, "That's the question. Does she know?"

The mullah was dismissive. "She knows gossip. She knows lies. But when lies become heresy, hell awaits all who..."

Sadik raised a hand. "Let's try a simple yes or no. This young woman believes that the wife of the Prophet is reborn and will come from the West, does she not?"

The mullah's hands went to his ears. "This is heresy."

"Well... yes. We all know that. Aisha's not coming back, but..."

The mullah turned away, his hands still at his ears. He said, "You must not speak that name."

Sadik closed his eyes. This mullah was a blockhead. It seemed useless to point out that million's of Iran's women were already speaking that name to each other.

He said to the old Mullah, "I must speak it one more time." He gestured toward the young woman named Farah. "I'm told she's been in contact with two girls, two sisters, who have fled your country and have claimed to be with Aisha. Two sisters named Darvi, correct?"

"Both like this one. Lost to God," said the mullah.

"This young woman was their friend from early childhood, was she not? The older sister was her classmate all through school."

"A friend does not lead you to go against God."

"Whatever," said Sadik. "The two sisters ran off some three months ago, correct? They've been keeping in touch by means of the internet. Have they told this one where they are now?"

"They are dead in our eyes," said the mullah.

"Very well. They are dead. But where are they dead?"

"Where means nothing when one is lost to God."

Sadik groaned. In his mind, he threw up his hands. He said, "It is my wish to question her privately. I will ask you both to please wait outside."

The sergeant protested. "I must keep to my schedule."

Sadik said to him, "Go. Leave the whip."

The sergeant misunderstood his intention. "What, you want to use it? That is not how we do things."

The old mullah said again, "He is here from the Council. If he wants to use the whip, it is permitted."

The sergeant was pouting. He said, "At least let me demonstrate. I should show you the best way to do it."

"I know the best way," said the doctor.

He held out his hand and received the whip from the man who took such pleasure is using it. He lashed the air with it as if judging its effect. "Behind schedule for more whippings? Executions? Which is it?"

The sergeant said, "I have two hangings. First my lunch."

Sadik spoke the words, "First his lunch," to the mullah. He spoke them again, this time to himself. His face darkened; his mouth twisted; a growl rose from his throat. As it emerged, he swung the cable at the cheek of the sergeant. It opened his face, ear to chin. The sergeant's scream was as much in surprise as in pain. He staggered backward; he cringed, both arms raised to his head. Sadik swung the heavy cable twice more. This time he struck at the elbows of the sergeant. He heard the dull pop of those bones being crushed. The sergeant, now shrieking, tried to run for the door. He tripped over tangled feet and he fell. Sadik stood over him. He struck again at both knees. The old Mullah, once again, had brought his hands to his ears and his eyes had gone wide in disbelief. Sadik approached him. He backed toward the door. Sadik seized one of his arms by the wrist and pulled it away from his ear.

"You damned fool," he spat. "Do you think this will stop it? Whipping women to death? This is why so many hope that the prophecy is true. Some believe it; most don't, but many hope." He kicked at the legs of the blubbering sergeant. "Get out of here and drag this thing with you."

Even as Sadik threw the bolt on the door, he knew that he'd gone much too far. Important or not, Hamas or not, he was still just a guest in this country. The old mullah would surely be summoning guards as soon as he recovered his wits.

He approached the table and the half naked woman. His first instinct was to feel for a pulse at her throat. There was no need, however. Her eyes, though fluttering, were opened wide. Her expression told him that she had seen and heard everything. She was trembling, but he saw that it was not out of fear. He removed his suit jacket. Very gently, he used it to warm her.

He took a moment to gather himself. He made an effort to soften his features. That done, he lowered himself to his knees and he brought his face close to hers. He waited, before speaking, so that she could see the sadness and the pity in his eyes.

"If I swear before God that I mean her no harm, will you tell me where I can find her?"

The young woman lowered her eyes. She didn't answer.

"I don't mean your classmate. I mean the one who is coming. I'm referring to Aisha herself."

Her eyes took on a shine. "She is coming."

"I know that," said Sadik. "I know there's an Aisha. I know all about her. And I believe that your friends, the Darvi sisters, are now with her. The Darvi sisters were taken to France and from there they were taken to America. They were taken to South Carolina. Did you know that?"

The young woman looked away. He felt sure that she did.

"Another girl, a Saudi, was taken there as well. Same time, same way, first to France and then America. She did arrive safely, did she not? Her name is Rasha."

One eye flickered. She seemed to know that name as well.

"Only tell me this much. They've stayed together?"

The girl hesitated. She gave a slight nod. Sadik let out a breath. He said, "Thank you."

His lowered his voice to a confidential whisper. "They were taken to a safe house run by the Nasreens."

She blinked. He thought he saw a look of surprise that he knew about the Nasreens. He said, "Of course, I know them. My own wife is one of them. My daughter keeps a photograph of their founder on her wall. Myself, I applaud what they do for young women who want only to use the gifts that God gave them. Look into my eyes and believe that."

She did. Her own eyes softened. They hinted at trust. But then her jaw tightened. She closed them.

He said, "But something happened. There was trouble at that safe house. For whatever reason, it was disbanded and its residents and staff were relocated, scattered. Had it been discovered? Had it been attacked?"

Her eyes fluttered. He saw a slight shake of her head. She lips moved as if she were about to reply. She did not, but her manner suggested a denial. Her eyes seemed to say, "No, it wasn't like that."

"No attempt on their lives? The Darvi sisters? Or Aisha? Not that sweet little Saudi girl either?"

Once again, another slight shake of her head. He said, "My daughter will be happy to hear that. She's your age, by the way.

She, too, is in college. She and I have spoken of this prophecy as well."

The young woman finally spoke, her voice a choked whisper. She asked him, "Does she believe?"

He considered lying, if only to comfort her. Instead, he answered, "I think she would like to. You, though. What made you believe?"

She wet her lips. "My friend told me. My friend does not lie."

"Even friends can be mistaken. They can want to believe. We all believe many things because we wish to."

That shine reappeared. "But she came to me."

"Who did?"

"Aisha. She came."

Sadik shook his head. He said, "I don't understand. She came to you how? Through the internet?"

"Here. Dressed all in white. She was so beautiful."

"Yes, but... what is here? Do you mean in this prison?"

Farah nodded. "She came. She touched her hand to my face. After that, the pain was less. And I believed."

Delirium, thought Sadik. Delirium and shock. Thank God for delirium and shock. He said, "I'll tell my daughter. This will please her."

He saw that softening again. Not yet trust, but a beginning. He said, "I say again, I intend them no harm. But you must know that there are others who want them all dead. Especially Aisha.

She's the one they'll want most whether she's the true Aisha of the prophecy or not. My interest is in keeping her alive."

A small shake of the head. "She cannot die."

"But many others can and will. Many others will suffer. Look what's already happening to you."

She winced at the thought of it. Her eyes went toward the door. She said, "You are a man. You are with them."

"I'm with whom? Those two dolts? You saw what I thought of them. I came on my own and my motives are just. If I lie, may I never see paradise."

She started to speak. She paused to bite her lower lip. She said, "If I betray my friend, I won't either."

He heaved a sigh. He reached a hand to touch her cheek. He said, "Oh, you will. I have no doubt of that. You've been loyal and true and firm in your faith. Your name will be honored. I will see to it."

Tears welled in her eyes. She said nothing.

He asked, "When she came to you, did you see her face?"

She said, "I saw her glow. I felt its warmth."

"Did she speak?"

"Not in words. But I heard without words. She said to me, 'Take heart. I am coming.'"

"When, though?" he asked her. "Is it to be soon?"

"Soon. She is almost of age."

261

"So she knows that she is Aisha? That she's Aisha reborn? Or has that not yet been revealed to her?"

Her expression showed confusion. "She must know."

"Because she came. I understand that. But the prophecy says that she must first come of age. You said that she is almost of age."

The young women tried to concentrate. She seemed not to be sure. She said, "I think soon. Very soon."

"Until then, is she safe? Is she well protected?"

A nod. "The angel Qaila protects her."

He smiled. "Yes, I know. I am familiar with the prophecy. The flame-haired angel, Qaila, who has guided her, protected her. But this angel has more than one name, does she not?"

She blinked her eyes uncertainly. The equivalent of a shrug. Disappointing. She did not seem to know.

He could now hear loud voices approaching the door. They were berating the guards who had left him alone with her. The guards were protesting. They were blaming the sergeant. The sergeant was bawling, "Look what he did to me. He broke both my knees. Shoot him. I order you to shoot him."

The old mullah's voice: "He's from the Council. No shooting."

"Smash him," yelled the sergeant. "Cut off both his hands."

"No cutting," said the mullah. "Arrest him."

Sounds of trying the door. Someone's boot kicking at it. Sadik knew that he had little time left with her.

He spoke a name. He said, "Elizabeth Stride."

He watched for some sign that she recognized the name. He couldn't be sure. He tried again.

"I think the angel called Qaila is Elizabeth Stride. If that's so, you're quite right. She's in very good hands. I haven't met her myself, but I know much about her. She is also known as the Black Angel."

He had hoped, he supposed, that saying this would elicit, if not recognition, some additional trust. If not their new location, an email address. The ones found on her computer were untraceable. And now the pounding on the door grew more desperate.

He asked her, "Please. Won't you tell me where they've gone? I need to find them before others do."

Her lips formed a word. She couldn't bring herself to speak it. A tear fell. "You ask me too much."

The pounding took on a sharp crunching sound. A battering ram. A sledge hammer, perhaps. With each blow, clouds of dust flew out from the hinges. Soon the door would give way and they would arrest him. Would they hurt him? No. Only rough him up, maybe. Nothing worse, he felt sure, without leave from Mansur. But they'll likely take it out on this girl and what little life that she has left in her.

He said, "You heard them say that I am a doctor. I do not have my medical bag because they would not let me bring it. I would have given you all the morphine that I have. Do you understand what that would mean?"

"I'll... be with God."

"And no more pain. Your body's poisoned and it's maimed, but not your beautiful soul."

She understood. She almost smiled. "You would release it?"

A snapping sound amidst the pounding. The upper hinge had given way. He said, "I have no morphine, but I have one other thing. Let me show you. Try not to be frightened."

From his pocket he produced a stainless steel pocketknife. It was made for a surgeon. It held several small instruments. He opened a blade that resembled a scalpel. He said, "I can't save you, but I can free you. I will only do so if you wish it."

He waited until her eyes focused on the blade. They showed that she did wish it and that she was ready. He said, "It's very sharp. You'll feel only a tug. Like a necklace that breaks and slides off."

She swallowed. She asked, "The others. Can you help them?" Her head tilted toward the sounds of women praying.

He understood that she meant the other women in the pens. He knew that she didn't mean ending their lives. He said, "I swear that I'll do all I can. And that goes for your friends in America."

"Why?"

"Ask God when you see him. He knows my heart."

She took another breath. She nodded toward the knife. Once again, she almost managed a smile. He leaned forward and kissed the top of her head. Then, with the smallest flick of his fingers, he opened her carotid artery.

She barely flinched. Just a short intake of breath. She could see the pulsing arterial stream. It soaked the hands and shirtsleeves of the man from Hamas. He had made no move to avoid it.

She asked, "What is your name? I could not hear your name."

"Like the angel, Qaila, I have more than one. But God knows me as Rajib Sadik."

She whispered, "I'll remember. I will ask God about you. I will ask him to bless you if you're telling the truth. I will ask him…"

Her expression went blank before she could finish. Her brain, starved of blood, had stopped functioning. Gently, he reached to close both her eyes. Once again, he leaned forward and kissed her.

TWENTY ONE

On Tuesday evening, half a world to the west, Howard Leland had returned from his canoe trip. He was sore and he was sunburned; he'd stretched seldom-used muscles. But he'd also been in more pleasant company.

He'd been with men who'd relished being out on open water, doing what most hadn't done since they were young. They were wealthy, accomplished, but one wouldn't have known it. Nor were they especially deferential to him. To them, he wasn't a cabinet officer. On that day, he was simply Howard to them, one of thirty in all, three in each of the canoes. They'd encouraged each other when they fought against currents. They'd sung songs; they'd told jokes; they reminisced of their school days. It was all very wholesome indeed.

It had been a far cry from yesterday, Monday. That day began with Haskell showing up at his door before he had fully collected his thoughts, Haskell pumping him about Elizabeth Stride. After that came his breakfast with Haskell's associate.

The mogul had questions of his own about Stride. They were personal questions. Unexpectedly so. The mogul had asked what it is about her that might explain the powerful effect she seems to have.

"On whom?" Leland asked him.

"On… men in general."

Powerful effect? What effect was that? His only knowledge of her was through Roger. The mogul seemed to wonder, although he never quite said it, whether she was some sort of enchantress. Stride? An enchantress? Does he think this woman got close to her enemies by batting her eyelashes at them? From what he'd heard, she was far more direct. He had told the mogul the same lie that he'd told to Haskell, to wit, that he spoken to her late Sunday evening and that she'd agreed to do what she could in recovering that disk from the Nasreens. He said he doubted that she would use witchcraft to do it. She would probably just make a few phone calls.

The mogul reddened slightly. Hemming and hawing. "Sorry. Just wondered. No reason for asking. Not important. Let's discuss something else."

The next item on the mogul's breakfast agenda was some neo-Darwinian drivel about the concept of natural selection as it applied to themselves. The mogul was intent on getting him to bear in mind the sort of people with whom he belonged by virtue of his family lineage. It was more of that arrogant we-run-the-world business, but couched, thought the mogul, in more acceptable terms. Something like the divine right of kings.

"It's a genetic imperative, this position we hold. We didn't get to choose. We were chosen."

He'd replied, "You don't suppose we were just lucky, do you? Being born into families of means?"

"Not born into. Bred into," insisted the mogul. "Luck has little to do with genetics."

Leland's eyes became hooded. "There are some who'd disagree. Tell that to all those who've been struck down in their prime due to one lurking gene or another."

The mogul shook his head. "Not us. They're bred out of us. The best and the brightest of us are the strongest. Luck has no bearing. What it is, is preparation."

"For what, though?" asked Leland. "To rule? Or to serve. My parents brought me up to serve."

"One serves by leading. We are needed to lead."

The mogul's views were presented as being self-evident. He hadn't seemed to notice, while growing into manhood, that many of his social peers were dimwits.

He'd said to the mogul, "This is all most enlightening, but we'll have to discuss it some other time. I'm afraid I have another engagement."

It was then that he sought an engagement to have. The posted activities list was the place. The canoe trip was on it, but that wasn't until Tuesday. For Monday, there were a series of lectures. The one about oil seemed worth attending, but Haskell would probably be at that one. He'd opted for a skeet-shooting contest instead. He came away from that event with a second place trophy even though he hadn't shot skeet since Princeton.

He ran into Haskell later that day. The two exchanged greetings, but little more than that. Haskell asked him, "By the way, when you spoke to Stride…" but Haskell never finished the sentence. He'd just said, "Never mind," with an odd little smile. He added, "All in good time," as he looked at his watch. He was probably more anxious to hear from the banker whom he had dispatched to Riyadh.

Even so, that smile. There seemed a smugness to it. Perhaps the banker had called with good news.

Leland had kept his distance for the rest of that day. He sought out other company for dinner. By chance, he fell in with a group of men who were planning to join that canoe trip. He'd signed up as well. It seemed just the thing. It would kill another day until the banker returned with his report on that sabotaged computer. It would kill another day until Clew could ask Stride where the Saudi girl's disk might be found.

Ear to the ground, but be patient.

The canoe trip turned out to be more than a diversion. It had been a delight start to finish. Nor did it end when the flotilla returned. Leland and his fellow paddlers and songsters stayed together through cocktails and dinner. More jokes, more laughter, not an ego in sight. These, he decided, were the real Bohemians. Men like Haskell and the mogul and the stuffy British banker must have gotten in through a side door.

Leland's head was swimming when he got back to his cabin and climbed the steps to his room. His canoe mates had bought a round of nightcaps for the house. They'd ordered Black Russians.

Not a sensible drink. Then the house bought another. His canoe mates bought a third. He'd managed to walk the hundred yards to his cabin in, more or less, a straight line.

He peeled off his shirt and stepped out of his shorts, holding on to his bed post as he did so. He could smell the shirt; it had gotten a bit gamey, but a shower could wait until morning. Those Black Russians, however, could not. He stepped into his bathroom and expelled what remained of them. Can urine smell of alcohol? His certainly seemed to. He hadn't noticed the smell before then. He reached for his mouthwash, took a swig from the bottle, swished it and spat it into the toilet. He washed his hands in the basin, ran a cloth across his face, then turned and happily eased into his bed. He lay on his stomach. The room spun less that way. He was mercifully asleep in two minutes.

It was just as well that he'd foregone a shower. It would have made a bad end to his day. If he'd pulled back the curtain to reach for the tap, he'd have learned the true source of that alcohol smell. He'd have seen the Saudi prince staring back at him.

He'd have seen sightless eyes bulging out from a face that looked like a melon ripe to burst. He'd have seen a tongue protruding from a slackened mouth whose lips, like his ears, had turned purple. He'd have seen the green sash of his own terry robe wrapped twice around his throat and tucked into itself. The other end would be attached to a shower head arm that had been partially torn from the wall by his weight. The body would not have been hanging, exactly. It was more of a sag, its feet splayed across the tub. It was not so much a hanging as a strangling.

He would have seen that the prince was now dressed as a Saudi, not the slacks and windbreaker that he'd worn on the beach. He had on a typical Saudi thobe, a white ankle-length garment that now looked like a shroud. A Saudi head dress, a ghutra, had somehow stayed on his head. It would not have seemed that it could have.

Leland might have noticed the sheet of note paper that was folded and pressed beneath the prince's bearded chin, held in place by a wrap of the sash. He might have seen his own name on the paper's outer fold, written in shaky block letters. He'd have wanted to read it before summoning help, but to do so he'd have needed to lift the whole body in order to loosen the sash.

If he'd read it he might have considered destroying it. Tear it up. Burn it. Flush the ashes down the toilet. Say he moved him to try to resuscitate him. A note? What note? A suicide note? No, he hadn't seen any note.

He might have considered it. But he would not have done it. He would not have so dishonored himself.

But Howard Leland didn't have to deal with these questions because he had gone straight to bed without showering.

There would be time enough in the morning.

TWENTY TWO

Sadik had been arrested, not jailed, but under guard. His passport had been taken; no calls were permitted. He was not to leave his hotel room. The next morning, a Tuesday, silent men came to get him. He was brought before the Guardian Council.

Of the twelve-man Council, only five had been available. The rest, he was told, were still up in Tabriz. He stood before a raised dais at which were seated three turbaned mullahs and two lawyers. The lawyers wore the black robes of judges. Mansur sat at the center, his chair higher than the others. Sadik was relieved that Mansur had returned. But only somewhat relieved. He knew that he was in trouble.

But Mansur was a scholar, an intelligent man, possessed of a more open mind than most. Sadik had known him since they were students together. They had traveled and played sports and, yes, partied together. Still a friend, though? He would soon see.

Two weeks before this, Mansur had called to ask a favor. Find, if you can, the source of this prophecy. Why you? Because you seem to have such wonderful connections. Find, in particular, two Iranian sisters who might, we suspect, be close to that source. Come to Tehran, question those who've been arrested. Why you? People trust you. Women especially. We know that some of those arrested have heard from the sisters. Get them talking and we'll let them go home. You'll be their hero.

Sadik had looked into where the sisters might be. Or rather, he had asked his wife to do so. She'd satisfied herself, no doubt through the Nasreens, that they were well and better off than they would have been if they hadn't fled to the west. She'd added, "Better off than you know."

This last was a tease. Women tease. It's in their nature. He, however, had not risen to the bait. She said, "Suit yourself. I shouldn't even be telling you." He shrugged in response. His wife is often egged on by a shrug. She said, "If you must know, they're no longer staying with the Nasreens. They're staying with Elizabeth Stride."

This came as a bombshell, but even so, at the time he was too busy to think more about it. He had declined Mansur's offer to come to Tehran. He had resisted Mansur's flattery, all that "women trust you" business. Now he wished to God that he'd come when first asked. That poor girl, Farah, would never have been lashed and he wouldn't be in this position. Instead, he'd told Mansur, as he'd told Rasha's father, that he had better things to do with his time than tracking down runaway girls or old prophecies.

But here he is. Before the dock. What happens now?

Two other men were seated against the far wall. He recognized one of them, the one wearing a uniform. Colonel Aram Jalil of the Savama. The colonel met his eyes and, discreetly, raised one finger. He waggled it in a gesture that Sadik took to mean, "Naughty, naughty. Now it's time to pay the piper."

The second man seated against the same wall leaned and whispered something to Jalil. The colonel made a face as if he'd smelled something bad. His only other response was to rise, pick up his chair, and put more distance between himself and the other. It was a gesture of utter contempt.

The second man was dressed in a dark business suit. As was Sadik, but this one's clothing fit poorly. A roll of fat hung over his belt and more flesh spilled over his collar. Balding, about fifty, perspiring, one leg twitching. He, as much as Sadik, had the look of a man who would much prefer to be elsewhere.

Sadik, once more, met Colonel Jalil's eyes. He asked Jalil, without words, "Is this who I think it is?" Jalil answered with sneer, not at Sadik, at the other. His lips mimed, "You guessed it," in Farsi.

Sadik had guessed it because he'd already researched him before he'd arrived in Tehran. A minor merchant until the Shah was deposed, then a flunky to the mullahs who took power. He managed to get rich by denouncing his competitors and being given their seized property as his reward. Now he'd risen to the station of deputy minister, but was lately an embarrassment to the Council.

Sadik asked Mansur, "This is Darvi, correct? He's the man whose two daughters fled Iran?"

Abbas Mansur waved his question aside. He said, "Never mind him for now."

"Was it he who informed on the girl you were torturing? A girl who's been a friend of his daughters since childhood? A girl who must have played in his house?"

The man tried to shrink, to make himself smaller. One of the lawyers replied, "We will get to him later. You are here to account for your behavior."

Sadik ignored the lawyer who'd spoken. Instead, he addressed the senior mullah, Mansur. He said, "My behavior? That prison's a disgrace. I saw what I saw and I did what I did. I eased her pain in the only way I could."

Mansur gestured toward the cuffs of his shirt. "I'm glad to see that you've at least changed your clothing before coming before us this morning. I was afraid you'd show up drenched in blood for the effect. No need. Your displeasure has been noted."

Sadik wanted to say, "At least my stains wash off." But that would have been unwise. He kept silent.

"While doing what you did, you also learned what you learned. Be good enough to share it with us."

"Which part?" asked Sadik. "Where the girls are? Out of reach. The two daughters are now in America."

"Only the dead are out of reach," said Mansur. "But let's talk about this prophecy first. What have you learned as to its source?"

"Not much. I'm still trying to put some pieces together."

The mullah said, "Very well. Then share the pieces that you have."

Sadik spread his hands. "All I have is a hunch. I think that I might know who might be involved. As to why they would do this, I have no idea, but I intend to find out."

The second mullah spoke. "To mock Islam is why. To cause trouble for us. And to try to turn our women from God."

Mansur touched his arm as if to say, "Don't jump the gun." He opened a folder that he had before him. He drew out a thick set of papers, clipped together. He raised a staying hand. He took a minute or so to look through them.

Mansur, like Sadik, had lived and studied in the West. He'd earned a degree in International Relations at the University of Geneva. It was in Geneva where Sadik first met him. They'd spent many an evening in lively conversation, more about sports than the state of the world, but religion often entered their discussions. Later, after the Shah was deposed, Mansur served as an envoy, first to Syria, then France, before plunging back into his Islamic Studies at Iran's holy city of Qom. From then on, he lived for Islam, convinced of its truth, but unlike some he did not walk through life wearing blinders. There were mullahs on the Council who had never read a book other than the Koran and the Sharia codes. Nor had most ever traveled abroad except to visit Mecca for their hajj.

With a nod to the others, Mansur said to Sadik, "I have in my hand, some thirty copies of this prophecy. All different translations from all different web sites. After these, I stopped counting. It's everywhere."

Sadik waited.

"Not to mention," said Mansur, "its other appearances. In women's public toilets taped to the mirrors. In the form of flyers on the windshields of cars. Folded and tucked into prayer books at mosques in the sections designated for women. Slipped into newspapers in several of our cities. Not just those of the dissidents. Our own."

Sadik nodded. "Her handmaidens have been busy."

"Handmaidens?" asked Mansur.

"Their word, not mine. I was not aware that she had so many."

"And not just here," said the mullah. "Not with all these translations. I have English and, of course, I have Farsi. I have Arabic, both classical and in six different dialects. I have Turkic and Russian and Urdu... you name it. Wherever Muslims in any concentration can be found, I have the prophecy here in their language."

Sadik already knew how far it had spread. He knew how far and how quickly.

"Some of these," said Mansur, "have taken a few liberties. Punched it up quite a bit. I'll get to those in a minute. But most are quite faithful to the original, or at least to the first one we've seen." He said, "So that we're all on the same page, so to speak, let me read one aloud. Any preference?"

Sadik gestured toward the others. "Read what's easiest for them."

"Farsi, then," said Mansur. He put on a pair of spectacles. He said, "However apocryphal, however obscure, these are said to be the Berber prophet's words." He paused to raise a hand

277

before the others could object. He said, patiently, "Yes, we know. Mohammed is the final prophet. But that hasn't stopped a long line of others from proclaiming that God speaks through them."

The second mullah bit his lip and, like the old one in the prison, made a show of covering his ears. The third mullah hadn't spoken. He was busy taking notes. Mansur cleared his throat and read aloud.

"The Lady of the Camel will come, born again, to show men that they have fallen into error. She comes to raise up the women of Islam. She comes to teach and she comes to bring justice. It is not revealed when, but she will come. She will be of the East, but turn your eyes to the West because that is where her banner will unfurl. She will have grown up among you, dressed in white, pure of heart, until the day when she reaches full womanhood. The flame-haired angel, Qaila, sent to guide her and protect her, will, on that day, reveal to her that she is the Lady of the Camel reborn. She will know that it is true and she will come. She will speak to all nations with words writ on wind. Her words will ride the lightning. They will be as shooting stars. And the angel, Qaila, will be with her, sword in hand. Woe to those who would deny the truth of her words. Woe to those who would silence her. Woe to those who would slay her. The angel, Qaila, will send them to hell."

He said, "Who'd have guessed that Islam's longed-for messiah would turn out to be a woman with a feminist agenda?" He raised a finger. "But stay with me. She's not stopping there."

He sorted through his papers. He said, "Here's one from an illegal website in Syria. Same text, but this one adds the following:

'And woe to all who do evil in God's name and the hypocrite imams who incite them to evil. They say to those they dupe, who they know to be fools, 'What you do is no sin, for all that happens is God's will. You, therefore, are only doing His will. For you, there is no blame, only praise.' But it is Satan, not God, who puts these words in their mouths. And Satan smiles. He knows that soon he will have them.'"

Mansur said, "One more. This along the same lines. This one turned up in Finland of all places, not known to be a hotbed of Islam."

"'Woe to the fools who expect to see paradise when they die having murdered the innocent. There will be no lush gardens watered by running streams as promised to the righteous in the holy Koran. There will be no soft cushions on which to recline. There will be no garments of fine silk and rich brocade. There will be no dark-eyed houris to give them endless pleasure. For them, there is only the fire.'"

Mansur said to the others, "You get the idea. Her agenda is expanding considerably and it seems to be crossing all borders. Are these only other women putting words in Tumart's mouth? Are they even women? Are they even Muslims? Good questions. And no way to tell."

Mansur paused. He put these others aside. "For now, though, let's stay with the original version. The floor's open. Are there any comments?"

"An obvious forgery," said one of the lawyers.

"I meant useful comments," said Mansur.

The mullah taking notes said, "Some scholars doubt he wrote it."

"Or they've chosen to doubt it. I'm asking what you think."

The mullah answered, "Hard to know. The original still exists at a mosque in Rabat. We're told the style is consistent with his other extant works. But Tumart, like Mohammed, didn't write; he dictated. As with Mohammed on many occasions, it was Tumart's wife who wrote them down."

"So his wife made it up? That seems an easy way out."

"For those who choose to take it. I agree. Others point out that it was written at a time when Tumart was known to be dying. The fever that killed him might have caused him to hallucinate."

"Or dream?" asked Mansur.

The mullah smiled. He said, "Let's be careful with that one."

Mansur answered the smile with one of his own. He said to Sadik, "No one wants to say he dreamt it. Most religions, even Islam, began with a dream. But never mind; let's not go there, as they say."

He said to Sadik, "We know that the Berber is referring to Aisha. The Lady of the Camel and all that."

The "all that" was spoken rather dismissively. Sadik was not offended. These were Shiites; he was Sunni, two distinct points of view on some matters. But it was more than "all that" to Sunni Muslims.

Mohammed's favorite wife, Aisha, was only eighteen at his death. He had left no male heir. A strong successor was needed.

Fulfilling that position, that of Caliph, was messy. Mohammed named Aisha's father to succeed him as caliph, but her father only lived two more years. His death might have been natural or he might have been poisoned. The latter, if true, would have come as no surprise because the next three caliphs had been murdered as well. All three murders were related to struggles for power. Religion had little to do with them.

Those murdered included the 3rd Caliph, Uthman, with whom Aisha had worked to assemble the Koran some ten years after Mohammed's death. She was recognized then – and now by most scholars – as the foremost authority on his teachings. Mohammed had experienced many of his visions while resting his head on her knee. He would relate them to her from a trance-like state and would sometimes not remember them so clearly when he wakened. He depended on Aisha to recite his words back to him. This was why she had great influence in selecting those verses that later became the definitive Koran. She knew which were from his visions – that is to say, direct from God – and which were his personal musings.

Most believed her to be scrupulous in reciting his revelations. Sadik had no reason to doubt that. But, by all accounts, she had a good mind and it was, after all, a woman's mind. She might very well have embellished a few as, perhaps, did the wife of the Berber. Or at least that she put more of a woman-friendly slant on some that he had related to her. Either way, Aisha's versions became part of the Koran.

The 4th Caliph, Ali, son-in-law of Mohammed, might well have had a hand in Uthman's murder. Or so Aisha believed as did many others. Ali was also the first of the break-away Shiites. The Shiites wanted a powerful leader who would also be their foremost religious authority. The majority of Muslims remained Sunni. The Sunnis saw Islam as a personal faith. This was then. Before the Wahhabis. While the Sunnis had no problem with a single strong leader, they said they didn't need caliphs or mullahs or mystics to tell them what God really meant. Or to drag them off to war, not for the faith but for more booty. Ali's Shiites were also chipping away at the newly-won rights of Muslim women. They had long since attempted to discredit Aisha through gossip concerning her virtue.

Aisha'd had enough. Uthman's murder was too much. She raised an army against Ali and his followers. She led that army from the back of a camel in what came to be called the Battle of the Camel. She, of course, was the Lady of the Camel. Her revolt was unsuccessful, her army was defeated, but Ali didn't dare have her killed. She was allowed to live out her days in Medina as long as she kept her ideas to herself. But there were other rebellions. There was no lasting peace. The struggle for power went on unabated. Ali was stabbed to death four years later.

The senior mullah, Mansur, waved the Farsi translation. "The prophecy says she's grown up dressed in white. Your Aisha of the camel wore white, did she not?"

"My Aisha?" Sadik bristled.

"Forgive me. Force of habit. It would seem that she's now our Aisha as well."

Sadik answered, "Yes, she almost always dressed in white."

Mansur said, "Hmmph. Not much white around here. She would certainly stand out if she should turn up in Iran. And if she's going to show up, a flame-haired angel at her side, we shouldn't have much trouble spotting her."

Sadik realized that his old friend was being facetious. All the same, it gave him an opening to ask, "Then why bother arresting all these innocent women?

"The authorities felt the need to make a statement."

The second cleric added, "Nor are they so innocent. Every one of them has broken God's law."

"Broke it how?" asked Sadik. "By having thoughts of their own? Sharing those thoughts with other women who think? Or are some of them charged with the crime of having fun? I don't recall either being high on God's list of offenses worth imprisonment or worse."

The "fun" remark was gratuitous. He shouldn't have said it. The reference was to an unfortunate statement made by the late Ayatollah. During an interview, he'd said, "There is no fun in Islam." It was not what most Iranians wanted to hear, especially that half of Iran's population that was now under twenty years of age.

Mansur said, dryly, "One offense at a time." As he spoke, he touched his finger to the prophecy's text. "It does seem to make reference to the Internet, no? It says she'll speak to all nations with words writ on wind. They will ride the lightning. They will be as shooting stars. It seems this Berber prophet must have foreseen the web. So it wasn't Al Gore after all."

Levity, thought Sadik. Perhaps a good sign. He said, "And as you see, it says 'to all nations.' It doesn't say only to downtown Tehran. Those young women you're holding are a drop in the bucket. Be merciful, I pray you. Let them go."

"Lest Qaila pass among us?"

"No, because it is right."

Abbas Mansur nodded. "They won't be held much longer. For the present, their predicament is a lesson to others. Keep spreading this thing and risk sitting in a jail cell. They might also be better off where they are lest some of them fall into the hands of the Hasheem. But there will be no more lashings; that I can promise. Those authorities I mentioned took that upon themselves. They got the prison's oldest mullah to judge her and sentence her. I'd have stopped it, but I wasn't informed."

"Would you like to stay informed? Log onto Amnesty International. It's there. I checked. I checked before I got here. And when they hear a woman's sentenced to eight hundred lashes, you can't expect very high marks."

"I dare say," said Mansur, glancing at the second cleric. The glance seemed to be one of reproach. The second cleric, thought Sadik, must have known about the sentence and had chosen not to mention it to Mansur.

"Speaking of punishments," Mansur said to Sadik, "I'm told that you didn't react very well to the news that two hangings were scheduled after lunch."

Sadik chewed his lip. "Were they women?"

"No, Rajib, they were men. One a multiple rapist. The police had been hunting him for two years. The other murdered his father to get money for drugs. Now and then, we do punish the guilty."

Sadik lowered his eyes. "My apologies."

"Getting back to these women, what exactly is your interest?"

"Same as yours. It's in tracking down the source."

"And that's all there is to it?"

Sadik shrugged.

"What made you think that these two sisters were involved?"

"That, too, can be found on Amnesty International. It gives the reason for the sentence. She would not betray her friends. Where they got their information, I can only guess, but it names this man's two daughters as her friends. Their names are Shahla, aged nineteen and Nikram, aged fourteen. The site gave their reason for wanting to escape him. It says that he was pimping for both of them."

"Lies," cried the father.

"Be still," said Mansur.

"I gave Shahla in marriage. It was my right."

"Twice," said Mansur. "Each a temporary marriage?"

"And each lawful," said the father. "Was this not lawful?"

He had addressed this question to the second cleric. The cleric answered. "It is lawful. Men may take short term wives. This saves them from the sin of adultery."

Mansur snorted. He said, "He didn't give her. He rented her. He took money or favors from two different men who divorced her after only three days."

"They... found her unresponsive," said the father.

"If we were to question her, would we be told that she willingly entered these unions? Or would we be told that she was less than affectionate because she'd been tied to a bed?"

"She would lie," said the father. "She was always such a liar."

"If we find her I'll ask her, but I think Sadik is right. You were profiting from the bodies of your unwilling daughters. Pimping isn't a strong enough term for it."

"Not true," said the father. "Only Shahla was given." Having spoken, he cupped his hand over his mouth. He had not meant to say, "Only Shahla."

"Forgive me," said the cleric. "Nikram's time hadn't come yet. I suppose that means you're only half of a pig. Do not say another word in these proceedings."

The father shrank back. He made a soft mewing sound. Sadik saw that his face was turning purple.

Mansur said to Sadik, "Let's keep our focus on the prophecy. What else did Amnesty say?"

"Their site, like the others, gives the full text. It said that Farah was condemned for not betraying this man's daughters who were thought to have been spreading the prophecy. It said that you've issued a fatwa against them. It said that you've demanded their deaths."

"Not true," said Mansur. "What is a fatwa? A fatwa is not like some Mafia contract. It is simply a religious opinion."

"With teeth."

The senior mullah rapped his knuckles. "Okay, let's be clear. In this case, it pronounced that the prophecy is heresy. It called for the punishment of anyone spreading it. It did not call for anyone's death."

"Farah's dead."

"Overzealousness," said Mansur. "I was not aware of it. How many times must I say that?"

Sadik said again, "My apologies."

"And mine to her. Also mine to her family. They will be compensated. It won't be enough. It might help just a little when they are told that the money will come from Darvi's pocket."

Sadik heard a sigh from where the father was sitting. He said to the cleric, "Yes, it might."

"Farah, this young women, died believing in the prophecy. We know that people die for all sorts of false beliefs. I wish it were not so, but it is."

The second mullah leaned close to Mansur. He was arguing with him in whispers. No doubt, he was disputing Mansur's last remark, reminding him of martyrdom's glories. Mansur said to him, "Please. Another time."

He said to Sadik, "Yes, all kinds of beliefs. But my colleague has a point; let's stick with ours. What effect has it had among your people?"

"Palestinians? Not so much. We have more on our minds. As do the women of Iraq. Saudi Arabia is a whole different story. Women demanding to be let into mosques and to attend graduations and such. Right now they're not allowed to do either."

"And to drive cars?"

"That's the least of it," said Sadik.

"To vote?"

"To be heard. It all starts with being heard."

"Saudi men aren't heard. They have no real vote either. Don't expect them to join their wives in their protests. Not if they want to stay out of jail."

"The Saudis are horses' asses," said the cleric taking notes. He asked Sadik, "What about elsewhere in your region?"

"Same thing all over. Women, mostly young, asserting themselves. Some more aggressively than others. Algeria, Libya, Yemen, parts of Egypt. Even in the fun-loving Emirates, or at least among their imported workers. Further to the east, demonstrations in Pakistan at the risk of having acid thrown in their faces. And hunger strikes in places like Bangladesh where one would think that they're already hungry."

"You say all over," said Mansur. "In America as well?"

Sadik shook his head. "Not so much in the West."

"More than six million Muslims in America," said Mansur. "Half of them women. Are they all so content?"

"If American Muslim women feel the need of a savior, they'll find plenty in the phone book under Lawyers. It's much the same thing throughout all of Europe. There are now many shelters for abused Muslim women. More abusers are getting arrested."

The second cleric said, "Such arrests are not lawful."

"Actually, they are. Here as well," Mansur told him. To Sadik, he said, "Let's stay with this part of the world. What other effects have you seen?"

"On the whole? It's still mostly a passive resistance, but growing less passive by the day. Women less willing to be told what their role is. Insisting that their bodies and their minds are their own, as distinct from the family's livestock. And more women disappearing, some escaping to the West, many being locked away lest they try to."

Mansur said, "And, I gather, there's a financial cost."

Sadik nodded an acknowledgment. "Donations have suffered. Especially donations from American Muslims, no doubt influenced by their wives and their daughters who want to see some changes made first."

"I meant donations from the Saudis," said Mansur.

"There as well," said Sadik. "Monies have been withheld. The Saudis, more than any, have been under Western pressure to withdraw their support of Hamas."

"From what I hear, that's not all they're having trouble withdrawing. We do have an intelligence service, Rajib. I mention this so that you won't be tempted to dissemble any more than your interests require."

Sadik groaned within himself. *Does he know about the disk?* He said, "The fact remains, we need money."

The second mullah scoffed. He said, "I thought bombs were cheap. Even cheaper than the lives of your suicide bombers."

Sadik glared at the man. "I don't do that."

"Hamas doesn't make bombs? You didn't shoot off all those rockets? It's all Zionist propaganda; is that it?"

Again, the first mullah touched the arm of the second. He said to Sadik, "He knows better. He's baiting you." To the others, he said, "My friend here is not with the militant wing. He doesn't build bombs; he builds clinics. This is why the Israelis haven't marked him for death. Like the Aisha we heard from on that Syrian site, he does not approve of suicide bombings."

"Or the slaughter of innocent civilians," said Sadik. "Or the lashing of beautiful young women to death. Or hunting down and killing those who've fled to the West."

The second cleric persisted. "These are not lawful clinics."

Mansur asked, "Oh? How are they not lawful?"

"They teach Muslim women how not to have babies. Worse, they do operations that turn whores into virgins."

Sadik bristled. "Whores? These are frightened young girls."

Mansur nodded. "Ah, yes. The restoration of hymens." He turned to the second mullah. "Very well. Let's discuss it. Would you rather brides be murdered for failing to bleed? Or for bleeding insufficiently? It happens all the time. Yet you wonder why young women want to leave."

"Only the guilty. They flee from their sins."

"Really?" Mansur asked him. "What was Shahla Darvi's sin? Never mind. You can educate me later. On the subject of the good doctor's clinics, they treat those in need, men and women alike, and have improved a great many lives. They are built by Sadik because no one else builds them. Why not? Why didn't the PLO build them? It's because they're free clinics and because they treat the poor. Corrupt bureaucrats find no profit in the poor.

You want sin? There it is. What could be more unIslamic? I, for one, salute him. Let's proceed."

He glanced through his papers, tapped a finger on one of them. He raised his eyes to Sadik. "While we're on the subject of women who flee, we hear that your Saudis are missing a few. We hear that one in particular has escaped a betrothal to a powerful and feared Wahhabi cleric. We hear that you'd been asked to find her. As with me, you refused. So what happened? They turned off the tap?"

Sadik answered, "It was something like that."

"The daughter of a prince. One of thousands, but a prince. She grew up in comfort, perhaps more or less content, until she was promised to this cancer-scarred fleabag while still a budding flower of fifteen. I can't say that I blame her for running."

Mansur gestured toward the man who'd grown too fat for his suit. "And we hear that she, like this man's two daughters, is quite skilled in the use of computers. We further hear that she's believed to be in the same place where this man's two daughters have gone underground. It's a safe house, run by the Nasreens."

"They have many safe houses," said Sadik.

"This spurned Saudi fleabag heads the Hasheem. Did you know that they're hunting this princess?"

Sadik shrugged. This should not be unexpected.

Mansur turned to the colonel. "And some Hasheem hunters have been sent to America?"

"We're sure of one," Jalil answered. "Sent a few days ago. We know that he was routed to Savannah, state of Georgia. Why there, we don't know. We've lost track of him since."

Mansur asked Sadik, "Might you know why?"

Savannah, thought Sadik. He felt sure that he did. But he only spread his hands in response.

Mansur moved a finger back and forth slowly as if he were attempting to make a connection. The finger slowed. It now tilted toward Darvi.

"This man's daughters, by defecting, have humiliated him. A man who can't control his women is no man at all in the eyes of his neighbors and business associates. Yet this one now takes the attitude; 'Let them go and good riddance.' One suspects that they must have some hold over him that prevents him from doing his duty. Does this Saudi girl have such a hold?"

"Most do."

"Well?" Mansur asked. "Do you know what it is?"

"I know the girl's father. He works for Saudi Charities. The money doesn't always go where it's intended. The daughter seems to know more than she should."

"Is her father so important?"

"Not at all. Lowest rung. He has the brain of a bird. But there are others involved, very powerful Saudis. They are about to find themselves inconvenienced."

Mansur grinned. He clapped his hands. "They can't get at their money?" He said to the others. "The reports are correct." This caused the cleric taking notes to smile broadly as well.

Mansur tossed a salute toward Colonel Jalil who was apparently the source of this intelligence.

Mansur's grin faded. He said to Sadik, "You say this Saudi's a nonentity and not very bright." He cocked his head toward the father of the sisters. "All these daughters seem to have much in common."

The girls' father reddened at these words, but said nothing.

"Here's another good guess," said Mansur to Sadik, "The Saudi girl's been at her father's computer."

Sadik nodded. "More than once. She's done considerable damage. He only learned its full extent a few days ago."

Mansur seemed impressed. "These young girls have such skills?"

"They were considerable already. The rest, they were taught."

"Taught by whom? The Nasreens?"

Sadik nodded again.

"So they're taught how to blackmail."

Sadik shook his head. "No demands are made except to leave them in peace. That's not blackmail as far as I'm concerned."

"Aha. But you see, they're not leaving us in peace. They are spreading this prophecy. You can't log on anywhere in this part of the world without seeing the words, 'She is coming.' They're not only saying that Aisha's reborn; they're saying that they've seen her; they're with her. They have caused great mischief. As you've seen, they've caused pain. The Nasreens would seem to have a new agenda."

"It's not the Nasreens. They would not have allowed this. They help only women who wish to be helped, but even then they are very selective. They help those whom they deem to have a promising future, but whose future is being denied them. They are not out to change the whole world."

"Then who is? Three young girls? They cooked this up among themselves?"

"Not likely," said Sadik. "But not impossible."

"Not likely without help. Or adult supervision. Or should I use the word instigation?"

"I will say it again. It is not the Nasreens."

"Then who?" asked Mansur. "Let me think. Who might it be? Could it be an adult named Elizabeth Stride?"

Sadik was startled. He tried not to show it. The basement chamber of the prison. A room used not just for torture, but for interrogations. He should have known that there would have been a listening device.

He said, "That was... only a shot in the dark. The girl gave no sign that she recognized the name. If I'd had time, I'd have tried several others."

Mansur had already reached into his folder. He held up several pages. He said, "I have here a transcription of your words. You didn't simply ask if the girl knew the name. You asked whether this Stride was in fact the angel Qaila. One assumes that you had reason to ask."

"Elizabeth Stride has been a friend to the Nasreens. She's especially been a friend to a young girl named Aisha. But it truly was not much more than a hunch. Tens of thousands of young Sunni girls have that name."

"And many have been picked up for questioning, did you know that?"

Sadik did. That, too, had been splashed on the internet. Young girls all aged between twelve and twenty in at least a half dozen countries so far. Especially any seen riding a camel who happen to be wearing too much white. "So I've heard."

"And many more Aishas have been hidden by their parents, lest someone should decide to start cutting their throats. Mass targeted murder is not without precedent. Herod tried it to kill Jesus. The pharaoh tried it to kill Moses. They survived, but a great many innocents perished. They didn't have their own angel to protect them."

He raised a hand before Sadik could speak. He said, "Elizabeth Stride. An assassin, is she not? An American who kills for the Israelis?"

"She was," said Sadik. "Not any longer."

"She did her work fully veiled. It was the perfect disguise. Moved about like a ghost, unsuspected, unnoticed. They called her the Black Angel, did they not?"

"Some did."

"So now we have two angels. Or perhaps two in one. But first… how did a woman who killed Muslims for Israel become such a friend of Muslim women?"

Sadik rocked a hand. "When you say she killed Muslims…"

"I know. She was selective. Let's not split hairs. Are you able to answer my question?"

"I am," said Sadik. "Stride had been arrested and imprisoned by the Saudis. By the time they released her, she was very nearly dead. A Muslim woman took her in and restored her to health. That women was a doctor named Nasreen Zayed. She's the woman from whom the Nasreens took their name. The original Nasreen was murdered soon afterward. She was burned alive, not for saving Stride's life, but for daring to teach family planning in her village. Stride avenged her and she didn't stop there."

"Recruited and trained by the Mossad, was she not?"

"They taught her how to channel her… displeasure, as you put it."

"And her weapon of choice was a knife, was it not? A long one? Curved? You could almost say a sword?"

Sadik saw where this was going. "Just a knife."

The mullah asked, "And her hair. What color was her hair?"

"Underneath her hijab? Surely black or dark brown."

"To pass as an Arab. We understand that. What was her natural coloring?"

Sadik hedged. "She's a woman. Who knows?"

"I've seen her file," said Mansur. "No clear photographs of her. And conflicting descriptions, but some speak of her eyes, an unusual color, and also the color of her hair. Some say that it's the color of flame."

"What flame? Yellow flame?" Sadik took a weary breath. "I've only heard it described as being blond. Dark blond, light blond, reddish blond, I can't tell you. There are millions of women who have these same colors. Quite a few of them live right here in Tehran and they get such colors out of a bottle."

The cleric smiled. He said, "More and more every day. There is also a new hair style that is suddenly in vogue. It's shaped rather like a helmet with the added detail of hair flipping out on both sides at the shoulders. Care to guess what they call these little flips of the hair?"

"Angel wings," said Sadik. "Yes, I've heard."

"Most keep it covered when they are in public. But alone with other women, off comes the headscarf. Nothing need be said. The others know what it means. How does Stride wear her hair these days. Do you know?"

"I do not."

"Short, I would think. Low maintenance. Functional. The shape of a helmet comes to mind."

Sadik closed his eyes. He groaned aloud. "I'll tell you this," he said, "and with total conviction. Everything I know about Elizabeth Stride persuades me that she would have no part in this either. All she wants is to live a quiet life."

"Having put aside all thoughts of revenge? Or might she have come up with an even grander vision of how to get even with Muslim men without the need to be so selective?"

"Out of the question," said Sadik.

"And yet you suspect that she's involved at some level."

"Suspect is too strong. A possibility. No more."

"Very well. A possibility. What leads you to wonder?"

Sadik hesitated. He said, "Someone close to her might – I say might – be involved."

"And that someone just happens to bear the name, Aisha. A girl of what? Fifteen or sixteen?"

"Thereabouts."

"A girl born in Cairo, but now living in America." Mansur touched his temple. "That rings a bell somehow."

Cute, thought Sadik. "She will be of the East, but turn your eyes to the West because that is where her banner will unfurl." Sadik responded, "I can tell you this much. If the Aisha you speak of is a party to this – and that is still a very big if – Elizabeth Stride would put a stop to it herself. If it should be happening, but Stride doesn't know it, she would end it within minutes of me talking to her."

"You know her so well?"

"I've never laid eyes."

"And yet you're telling us that you know what's in her heart," said Mansur.

"I have other sources," Sadik answered.

"Would one of these sources be a man named Martin Kessler?"

Once again Sadik was startled and again he should have known. The cleric had very good sources of his own. Sadik answered, "Kessler is one."

"This Kessler was once Stasi, East German Intelligence. No plodder, however. Wild and wooly. An adventurer." Mansur ran a finger down a sheet in his folder. "'A loose cannon,' this one calls him. Another finds him amusing. The phrase here is 'entertainingly reckless.'"

All true, more or less. Mostly more, thought Sadik. But he replied, "An adventurer. Not the rest of it."

"If you say so," said Mansur. His finger moved and stopped. "It says here the East Germans published comic books about him. Propaganda for the masses. Detailing his exploits. One can still find old copies on E-Bay."

Also true, thought Sadik, and to Kessler's chagrin. Those comics were a constant embarrassment to him. Sadik, himself, had teased Kessler about them.

"So what is he?" asked Mansur. "Is he some sort of clown?"

Sadik wanted to answer, "He's anything but. He's a man to take lightly at your peril." But he didn't. He just shrugged. Let them learn that for themselves.

"Have you been in touch lately?"

"I have not. I've lost track of him."

"But you say he's been a source as to Elizabeth Stride."

"He and Stride have been together, on and off, for ten years. They first met when she was, I think, twenty four, but already as notorious as he was. They had their ups and downs. Sometimes he'd cry on my shoulder. Well, not actually cry. That is a figure of speech."

The cleric flicked a hand. "I'd assumed so."

"In any case, that is how I know about Stride. We spoke of her at length many times."

"An adventurer," said Mansur, "often does things for the fun of it. Might this prophecy business come under that heading?"

"As a practical joke? You think that's all this is?"

"You know the man, Rajib. I'm only asking."

"Impossible," said Sadik. "He wouldn't dream of it."

"Are he and Stride now together?"

"As I've said, I've lost track."

"But I think you could find them if you put your mind to it. You have an interesting circle of friends." Mansur held Sadik's eyes as he said this. They both knew that the reference was to certain Israelis. They both knew that it was best not said aloud.

Mansur drummed his fingers. "You need money. How much?"

"Two million for now. And you can make it a loan. I'll pay it back as soon as my funding is restored. In return, I promise to do all I can to prevent further harm from being done."

The second mullah asked the first. "Why should we give him money? He's Hamas and Hamas is a Wahhabi front. The Wahhabis see all other Muslims as apostates. They preach that we all must recant or be killed."

Sadik asked Mansur, "Is he baiting me again?"

"Just a little. Yet, he makes a valid point."

"The Palestinians, my people, preach no such thing. They want what we all want. They want honor and respect. They want to build a society that will give them a future. They want peace;

they want families; they want decent jobs. And they want to stop burying their children."

"Well spoken," said Mansur. "We endorse all those objectives. But I didn't hear you mention Hamas' primary goal. I refer to the destruction of Israel."

"That remains a goal to some."

"Not to you?" asked Mansur. "It is specified in your charter."

He might have said, "I don't live in a fantasy world." But he answered, "Let us see to our own statehood first."

"You also failed to mention the greatest goal of all, to establish an Islamic society."

"It's already Islamic. Not like yours, but Islamic. Beyond that, our goal is progress under competent leadership."

Sadik winced within himself. He should not have said that. But Mansur only smiled. He did not seem offended. He said, "That is indeed to be desired."

Mansur asked, "And yourself. Are you firm in your faith?"

"I consider that I am. I try to be a good Muslim. But I also try not to let it get in the way of..." He stopped. He'd almost done it again.

"I know," came the mullah's surprising reply. "There's too much hard-headedness. Even here on this Council. We're accused of resisting liberalization. What we think we're doing is building a base. Islam is evolving. Not its truth, but its politics. Move too slowly, you're conservative. Move too quickly, you're a radical. There are many outside forces that would like to see us fail so that they – as they have so many times in our history – can come in and suck us dry to their profit."

Sadik said nothing. No response had been invited.

Mansur continued, "So I come to this question. Is this Aisha affair just a hoax, a passing fad, or is it an organized conspiracy? If the latter, who's behind it? Not the hairdressing industry. And what is the motive? Destabilization? If so, that result is well underway. You've said it yourself. Rebellious wives and daughters. A not so passive resistance to all male authority, which includes, not incidentally, male conjugal rights. It's bad enough to have the problem of a Muslim Joan of Arc. We don't need a Lysistrata on top of it."

The second mullah asked, "A Lysis-who?"

"It's an ancient Greek play about the women of Athens. They got tired of war, so they said to their husbands, 'You can have war or sex, but not both.' The movement quickly spread to Sparta and beyond."

The second mullah blinked. His expression became distant. Sadik suspected that his own wife had made excuses lately. But Sadik preferred to stay on the subject at hand. He said, "And there's the drying up of funds."

"Funds don't really dry up. They just move around. You'll see the funding restored, but perhaps from new sources, and no doubt with new conditions attached."

Sadik squinted. "I'm not sure I understand you."

"Benefit of the doubt. Let's say it's a hoax. If so, the hoax is having an effect far beyond what its authors envisioned. Other plotters and schemers have been sure to take notice. They'd be looking for ways to use this to their advantage."

"Any plotters and schemers in particular?" asked Sadik.

"Americans, apparently. That seems to be where this started. It actually sounds more like the British to me. Very Byzantine, the British. Americans, by their nature, are more heavy-handed. Either way, the motive would come down to oil. The Americans need it, not to fuel their SUVs, but to fuel their thirsty tanks and jet aircraft. Any power that needs it will try to control it. Any power that has it cannot let that happen. It's why we're taking steps to…"

Mansur stopped himself. He had almost said too much. Sadik knew, however, what those steps had to be. Iran's ambitions went beyond its own oil wealth. It hoped to lead the creation of a Shiite oil crescent that extended through Iraq to the Saudi Eastern Province. The trick was to do so without being invaded and occupied by the western powers. Sadik knew Iran's intention. Mansur knew that he knew it. Even so, it was better left unsaid.

Mansur clapped his hands to break the brief silence. "It's a pity, incidentally, that you don't have a drop of it. You would not be asking us for a loan of two million. You'd spill more than that every day."

Sadik shrugged.

"But I digress," said the Mansur. "Let's get back to Lysistrata. Our women, as you know, have the vote, as do yours. But yours get to nominate candidates of their choosing. Ours do not. Do you understand why?"

Sadik did, but thought it best to let this come from Mansur.

"If they did, they'd vote secular. Wouldn't you in their place? They'd give Islam a nod, an honored nod, to be sure, but no cleric could hope to get many votes unless he was both liberal and cuddly. More to the point, they'd elect other women. Any candidate named Aisha would breeze into office and appoint other women to positions of authority. The men? Emasculated. Marginalized. Reduced to carrying bags for their wives while they shop at Victoria's Secret."

"I... think you exaggerate," said Sadik.

"Not if this happens too quickly," said Mansur. "All people need time to adapt to change. You saw what happened when the Shah was deposed. You saw what happened when the Taliban took power. Overnight, a massive crackdown. Millions of women draped in hijab when they weren't confined to their homes. All their gains erased, even such as they were. Would you like to see that happen again?"

"I would not."

The senior mullah glanced at his watch. He turned to the others. "We need a few minutes to talk among ourselves." He said to Sadik, "Would you please wait outside?" He tossed a hand toward the fat man. "You, as well."

The first to speak was one of the Council's two lawyers. He said, "This Sadik has murdered one of our women. Why aren't we throwing him in prison?"

"Now she's one of our women? We were killing her."

"Well, he also maimed the jailer. He left him an invalid."

"In my view, an improvement," said Mansur. "Let's move on."

"We should at least detain him and question him further. He's not telling us all that he knows."

Mansur curled his lip. "How astute of you."

The lawyer blanched. He said, "I am astute enough to ask questions that you haven't. How is that this doctor, a leader of Hamas, not only knows so much about the Nasreens, but even seems to be defending their methods? How is that he's also such a friend to this German who's a friend to a killer of Muslims?"

"He wasn't always Hamas. He wasn't even Palestinian. And as I've said, he has an interesting circle of friends."

The lawyer asked, "This circle. Does it include Jews?"

"I would think so. They live right next door."

"And you find this acceptable? Collaboration with Jews?"

Mansur rolled his eyes. "Let me put it to you simply. Sadik talks to people. Sadik, unlike some, also listens to people. Most Islamists, by contrast, only talk to each other because, to them, there is only one way. And there isn't. Not even within Islam."

The mullah who'd been taking notes raised his pen. "You never mentioned these neighbors as possible plotters. You mentioned the British and the Americans. Why not the Mossad? This is their cup of tea."

"What is?"

"Disinformation. Subversion. Causing turmoil among us."

"Granted," said Mansur, "but why? To what purpose? Do you think the Israelis hope to grab a few oil wells?"

"It's not always oil. Sometimes it's just deviltry."

"The Mossad always has a clear set of objectives, all of which involve their continued survival. They have no time to make idle mischief. They're probably wondering who's behind it themselves, although I don't think they'll lose any sleep over it. But they, and all the other more shadowy 'theys,' will be watching to see what opportunities arise. That is why this must not get out of hand."

Mansur paused. He addressed Colonel Aram Jalil. He said, "Colonel, did you know that the girl was being lashed?"

He shook his head. "I only learned of it when you did."

"Have you questioned her friends?"

"You said wait for Sadik."

"And now we have," said Mansur. He turned to the others. "We are, however, not much further along in locating the source of this prophecy. Nor have we been able to locate Darvi's daughters who, it appears, are among these handmaidens. Sadik, right or wrong, thinks he knows where to look. He has people who'll help him, this network of his. We should give him whatever else he needs."

"You heard him swear," said the lawyer, "that he means no harm to this Aisha who's supposed to be coming. You heard him say that he approves of what she's done for Muslim women. You heard him say that he wants her alive."

"Your point?"

"This man has a scheme of his own."

Mansur wanted to say, 'How astute of you' again, but he didn't. He said, "Let's get him back in here."

Sadik entered first. The man named Darvi entered afterward, looking even more disheveled and more frightened than before. He entered holding one hand to his cheek. Mansur guessed that Sadik had had a few words to say to him, very likely punctuated with a slap.

He said to Sadik, "How does four million sound?"

Sadik answered warily, "Twice as good as two million."

Mansur gestured toward the father of the runaway girls.. "This man will be happy to donate that amount. It will be wired in your name by the end of this week, but of course the money comes with conditions."

"I'd no doubt," said Sadik. "Let me hear them."

"Find the source. Find this Aisha. Find out who is behind this."

"And then?"

"Swear now that you will report back to me. Tell me who, tell me where, and tell me what other assistance you will need. We have people in America who are ready to serve in any capacity that's asked of them."

Sadik asked, "Assistance? Assistance for what? Say out loud what sort of capacity."

"Not killing her, certainly. The Hasheem would. We would not because, ethical questions aside, that would make matters worse. If we did, we'd soon read that we got the wrong one and that the real one is angrier than ever. What I want is a confession by everyone involved that this was a joke done in very bad taste. I want to see it broadcast on the media world-wide and especially over the internet. I want an apology for the trouble they've caused. Not to us. To the women of Islam."

Sadik suspected that he wanted a good deal more than that. But he said, "Fair enough. What if it isn't a joke?"

"As opposed to what? You think she's really coming?"

"I... meant if it's part of a larger conspiracy."

"Again, who and where. I want names and locations. For conspiracy, also add why."

Sadik asked, "And then?"

"The gloves come off. You know that they must. And you must decide who your friends are."

TWENTY THREE

Yitzhak Netanya, the head of Mossad, had a closet-full of loud Hawaiian shirts. He seldom wore them in public. He'd stand out too much. In Jerusalem, where he lived and worked, the norm was plain white shirts with open collars.

Even so, Netanya prized his collection because all of the shirts had come as gifts. They were all the same brand. The labels said Big Kahuna. This was actually something of an inside joke because although his title was Director of Mossad, his unofficial title was The Big Memuneh. That word was Hebrew for "the one in charge" and Kahuna in Hawaiian meant much the same thing. The two even rhyme. Hence the joke.

Netanya also liked to relax at the beach, dozing off to the sound of the surf. For this reason, he was always deeply tanned. All this taken together had made it inevitable that friends and family would start buying him these shirts. It became a competition. Who could find the loudest shirt?

It was easier now because of the internet. Type in "Big Kahuna" and there they were. Hundreds. There were several to choose from with semi-nude wahines, their modesty protected only by leis, and even a few with the face of Elvis Presley from when he made the movie, Blue Hawaii. Netanya wore them mostly in the privacy of his apartment. But never an Elvis and no semi-nudes. His wife and children would be less than merciful if they were to catch him in either.

On this day, a Wednesday, he was at home. It was his habit to take Wednesdays off because he often got no rest on the Sabbath. He would bring work home with him, but he'd seldom touch it. Wednesdays were for giving his brain a rest and puttering with things that were not so important. Or at least not a life and death crisis.

He had found himself reflecting on this part of his collection because one of the gaudier shirts he'd received a few years back was an Elvis and it came from Martin Kessler. This was typical of Kessler in more ways than one. It was also most welcome in more ways than one because Kessler, back then, had been believed to be dead for at least the second time that he knew of. The card read, "You shouldn't believe all you hear. Bad pennies always turn up." The next time he was dead was of course in Angola, but Netanya knew better so he didn't get a shirt.

One of the first and most voluptuous of his semi-nude shirts was equally surprising, considering its source. That one came with a card signed by Rajib Sadik. One would think that a Muslim would take a dim view of hard-bodied beach blossoms strutting their stuff, but in those days he wasn't high up in Hamas. Back then, he wasn't even Sadik.

Netanya was reflecting on both of these shirts because of a message that blinked on his machine before he'd even got out of his pajamas. An instant message. Not a regular email. It came from Sadik and he was looking for Kessler. The message also mentioned Elizabeth Stride. It asked if she and Kessler were together again. The tone of it was breezy enough. No special reason for asking, it said. Just wondering how an old friend was doing. How is he? What's he up to? Have you heard from him lately? But the breeziness seemed just a little bit forced. Netanya wasn't sure that he was buying it.

He typed, "Who's asking? The old friend or Hamas?"

The answer came, "Oh, don't start. This is not Hamas business. I've been closer to Kessler and for more years than you. I've lost touch and I miss him. Do you know where he is?"

Netanya did. Or he probably did. The last news he had of Kessler was about three months old from when Kessler reunited with Stride after finishing his work in Angola. They've settled down, living more or less quietly, but the Saudis still have a big price on Stride's head, so one can't say that's not Hamas business.

Netanya cleared his screen and typed in another code. A box appeared and he typed Sadik's name. A file dropped down with its latest entry first. That entry showed that Sadik had flown to Tehran as recently as the night before last. From where? Amman? No, he flew from Riyadh. In Tehran, he checked into the Azadi Hotel. The Azadi? That's a good one. Five stars, gourmet restaurants. Sadik has never been one to live high on the hog. Netanya wondered who picked up the tab.

According to the entry, he'd arrived this past Monday, got in around midnight and went straight to his room. No one greeted him, no minders, just Sadik. The next morning, yesterday, a car picked him up. Again, no escort. Just a driver. No report on where he went or who he met with. Interesting, however, that two hours later, he returned, this time with escorts, and seemed visibly upset. The escorts were Savama, Iran's secret police, almost as feared as the Shah's old Savak. The observer was quite sure that he saw fresh bloodstains on Sadik's hands and on the cuffs of this shirt.

Had he been tortured? Had his fingernails pulled out? No, that didn't seem likely. He was seen to be walking with strength and with purpose. Whose blood, then? A patient's? That didn't seem likely either. If he'd come to Tehran to perform surgery on a patient, he'd have done so wearing a surgical smock and with latex gloves on his hands. So whose blood? And why hadn't he washed up?

The report said he took his meals in his room until early this morning when, again, a car pulled up out front for him. He had minders with him, very serious minders. They'd probably spent the night outside his door. The minders, the Savama, made Sadik sit between them and the car headed off to who knows where. Was he being arrested? It certainly seemed so. But the same day, today, he landed back in Amman, apparently no worse for wear.

Netanya clicked down to the next most recent entry. "Hmmph," said Netanya. "Busy man." On the morning of the day when he flew to Tehran, Sadik had flown to Riyadh. There, he took a taxi to a building downtown. The building housed Saudi Overseas Charities. He was there for less than one hour. This entry was otherwise short on details, probably because the trip seemed routine. Sadik made such trips every three months or so for the purpose of drumming up cash contributions toward another one of his clinics.

The Saudis were by far his primary source. They were good for about two million per quarter. And it didn't come easy. Sadik had to work for it. His competition for that money is Hamas itself, especially its militant wing.

Netanya clicked down again. There's another. Three months ago. But the informant who had reported that visit said its purpose might have been personal in nature. He didn't know for sure. He's just heard some local gossip. It seems that some prince was missing a daughter and was in the Saudi doghouse because of it.

Netanya shrugged. He thought, well, so what? Unless this prince thought his daughter had run off with Sadik, Hamas is no missing persons bureau. They must have met for some other reason.

Netanya closed that window and brought up Sadik's message. He hit Reply and typed in, "How were things in Tehran?"

A few minutes later came Sadik's response. "Must you be such a show-off? It's not Mossad's business either. No, wait. Show off more. Run your file on Kessler if you haven't already and give me a way to make contact."

Netanya had, in fact, already done so. He had Kessler's address and several email addresses. But first he had a few questions. He wrote, "Nothing for nothing. Come on, Rajib, give. First, what were you doing these last two days in Tehran and what's with the bloody white shirt?"

Sadik answered, "I repeat. It is none of your affair. It was strictly a personal matter."

"Like Riyadh?"

This time Sadik didn't answer so quickly. His reply, when it came, ignored Riyadh totally. It said, "Tehran was a mission of mercy, you schnorrer. On my word, this is true. Don't make a big deal. Are you able to help me or not?"

Netanya more or less believed him. He's a surgeon, after all. Sadik would be Netanya's first choice as well if they ever found a lump in his chest. And Sadik knew better than to tell an outright lie. It might close a door that's better kept ajar.

He wrote, "If Kessler and Stride are where I think they are, I shouldn't contact them directly. I can, however, reach them through a friend. I'll tell him of your wish to get in touch. He'll ask me why and I'll tell him that you say it's personal. But I'll also have to tell him that you are Hamas and that, I assure you, will raise a red flag. This man is like me; he likes to know what's going on. He's going to want to know what you say to each other. Failing that, he will not let it happen."

Netanya sat back and waited for a response. The "friend," of course, was Harry Whistler. Sadik also knew Harry. Or at least he knew of him. But from another time, another life. Let's see… when did Kessler and Stride first meet Harry? Ten years ago, maybe? Something like that. Sadik and Kessler go back farther than that. Sadik must not know that they'd hooked up with Whistler or it would have been the first thing he asked.

Sadik proved it. He replied, "Yitzhak, you're full of shit. There isn't any 'friend' unless maybe it's you. Never mind. I'll ask someone else."

Netanya wrote, "You wound me. It happens to be true. I can't and won't go around this man because I get the same courtesy from him. If you cannot accept this, by all means go elsewhere. That's if you have an elsewhere to go to."

Sadik replied promptly. "Let me think."

Netanya would wait. Perhaps it really was personal. Perhaps Sadik's business with Kessler and Stride has nothing to do with this part of the world. That would, incidentally, be just fine with Harry who preferred to stay clear of the Mideast and its problems. True, he'd worked with Mossad on a couple of occasions, but on nothing related to the Palestine question or to its Muslim neighbors in general.

Netanya had told Whistler that he envied him that luxury. "Stick to Europe, America, anyplace northern. You have crazies there as well, but not in such abundance. Stick with countries not devoid of all rational discourse. Here, you try to be progressive and you get shouted down. Not just by the Muslims. We have Jews just as radical. Both of them ask, 'Who knows better, you or God?' Each side says that God says the other must be killed, so stop wasting our time with your peace plans.

Better yet, thought Netanya, stick to Geneva. Better still, to your mountain retreat in Chamonix. Build a wall. Make a fortress. Keep the world out. Which, of course, is what Israel is trying to do, and which is damned near what he's done with his ski lodge.

Netanya had misled Sadik just a little when he implied that Harry might not permit direct contact. Under Harry's hospitality doesn't mean he's Kessler's nanny. Nor would Harry have any real control over Stride. Harry might indeed see a red flag in this, but he'd leave it to Kessler to decide for himself as long as Kessler keeps him informed.

Keeping Harry informed, however, was one thing. Keeping Yitzhak Netanya informed was another. Over here, we always need to know what's going on. What we don't know gets people killed every day. If Sadik needs to contact to Martin Kessler, he may, but he'll do so through Yitzhak Netanya.

Sadik's email popped up. It was not what he'd expected. Sadik wrote, "At least tell me; is Aisha still with them?"

Still with them? Yes, of course. They're all she has left. Good for her that she has them. Maybe not so good for them. People close to her keep getting killed. First her parents and then the two Nasreens who took her in. She's already had more than her share of bad luck. Let's hope that it doesn't come in threes.

It's also good that Stride and Kessler are together again. Let's hope that it's more than just an on-again phase of their on-again-off-again relationship. The most recent off-again lasted two years, the time during which Stride thought he was dead. He wasn't, of course. He was in Angola. Working deep cover. Doing a job for Harry Whistler and yours truly.

Kessler was willing to pretend to be dead because he thought he was, in fact, dying from a dose of radiation to which he'd been exposed during his last misadventure with Stride. And he is, very probably, but not for a while. The doctors thought that he had perhaps two good years in him before certain of his organs start to fail. Time enough to do the job in Angola. Now they say they were wrong. They say he's either much stronger than they thought or the dose was fewer rads than they thought. Even so, say the doctors, he's got five at the most and in the meantime he's both sterile and impotent. The impotence factor was another of the reasons why Kessler was willing to get out of Stride's life. But as he himself said, he's like a bad penny. In any event, he did finish in Angola. Next thing you know, he turns up in the States just as Stride and Aisha were forced to relocate when the Nasreens closed their Hilton Head facility.

Was she glad to see him? She was ready to kill him. No word for two years. He'd caused Stride to cry, to shed actual tears, and Elizabeth Stride doesn't cry. Well, not often.

In any case, Kessler survived their reunion. But Stride isn't one to forgive and forget or to purge her homicidal impulses. Instead, she redirects them. Guess who's the new target. Yours truly is who. It's for that Angola business. It's for convincing Kessler that it's better all around if he let her and Aisha believe that he's dead. It didn't help that he isn't and that he came back. It didn't help that it worked out well in the end. It didn't help that she herself had worked for the Mossad and should have known that we do what we must. Yes, we used Kessler. We'd done the same thing with her. But apparently, to Stride, enough was enough. According to Kessler, she laid down the law. She told him, "I forgive you now that I know your reasons, but I don't forgive Yitzhak Netanya. If I'm ever within reach of that man again, I'll carve him up like a roast."

This Aisha, thought Netanya. Maybe sixteen by now. Kessler says she's just beautiful inside and out. Not a trace of self-pity over her losses because she knows, without a doubt, that her parents are with God, as are the two Nasreens who had sheltered her. How can she be so sure? Her mother told her, that's how.

Her mother comes to young Aisha in her dreams and they chat like any other mother and daughter. Her mother tells her what it's like there, who is up there and who isn't. Aisha, of course, asked her about Kessler when Kessler was thought to be dead. Her mother, apparently, did some checking around and reported back to Aisha that, "Nope, he's not here. And he isn't in the other place either." So Aisha never doubted that he was alive and would turn up sooner or later. Aisha, one assumes, told Elizabeth the good news. But she'd also told Elizabeth that there's tennis in heaven, that her parents still play all the time. So Elizabeth, understandably, did not cling to that hope. But one wonders whether Stride became a believer when Kessler materialized.

He replied to Sadik, "Yes, of course she's still with them. She's a daughter to them. Are you asking because someone is hunting her again?"

Netanya wasn't serious. It was more of a coaxing. It was meant to elicit a reply something like, "It's nothing like that. It's only this."

But Netanya, it seemed, wasn't far off the mark. Sadik answered, "You know this? Tell me what you've heard."

Netanya rocked in his chair. This was serious after all. He could not, of course, read Sadik's tone of voice in the text that appeared on his screen. Even so, the words seemed almost desperate. But Netanya had heard nothing. Nothing at all. He wrote, "You came to me. You go first."

Five minutes went by. Then ten. Then fifteen. Sadik must be composing a very long answer. Either that or he's chosen not to answer at all. Netanya decided to give him a nudge. He wrote, "Since when don't you trust your old friend?"

The reply: "Damn you, Yitzhak. Don't play games with me."

Netanya sighed. "Okay, the truth. I know of no threat. Not to Aisha, not to Stride, not to Kessler. But I am your friend and I will help you if I can. You've got to give me something to work with."

Another five minutes passed. Sadik was deciding.

Sadik wrote, "This, too, is truthful. I don't know for sure either. If you're such a friend, you'll get this question to Kessler. Ask him if the Darvi girls are still with him. Also a young Saudi named Rasha. If the answer is yes, I need to speak to him quickly. If those girls have computers, pull all plugs. If I am correct in what I think is happening, yes, Aisha could well be in danger."

Netanya wrote back, "Come on, give. More details. The Saudi, I assume, is the daughter from Riyadh. The Darvi girls? Who are they? Also runaways? Most importantly, what danger? From whom? Angry families? You can't expect me to jump in and help when you're keeping me out of the loop. I don't want to end up looking stupid."

"I'll tell you what I can, when I can," Sadik answered. "Send the damned message right now."

Netanya looked at his watch. Only ten in the morning. In Virginia it would still be the middle of the night. Okay, thought Netanya, he'd send Kessler an email. He'd keep it low key. He should copy Harry Whistler, but he wouldn't just yet. This could easily turn out as not such a big deal. Nor will he mention Sadik at this point. Kessler might decide to skip the middleman.

Belle Haven used several email addresses. Each had a different purpose. He selected the address that Kessler used for routine correspondence, nothing sensitive. He would send this unencrypted lest it seem not so routine. He typed in a greeting, added some small talk, and then got into the subject at hand.

He wrote: "A mutual friend – no names for now – has contacted me to express a concern. He thinks the Darvi girls and the Saudi named Rasha are involved in something – he won't say what – except that you should keep them away from computers. He says whatever it is could mean trouble for Aisha. Can you shed any light? Let me know what to tell him."

He hit "Send."

He copied the text and sent it to Sadik. He added, to Sadik, "Don't hold your breath waiting. It's still dark out where he is. I'll tell you what he says when he says it."

Sadik answered simply, "I'll be here."

TWENTY FOUR

It was the mogul who heard the first shout from Leland's room. He was on his way down to the breakfast room where he was to join Haskell and the banker. He turned on the stairs to see Leland's door fly open. He saw Leland burst through it, barefoot, in his robe. He saw the green robe fly open as well. He saw that the robe was missing its sash. Howard Leland was naked beneath it.

"My shower," gasped Leland as he covered himself. One hand clutched his robe as the other jabbed the air. He was jabbing it toward the door he'd just come through. His mouth formed those words again, but no sound came out. His chest heaved. He brought a hand to his throat.

"Howard? What's the trouble?" asked the mogul.

"My shower," said Leland, his voice dropping to a whisper.

The mogul saw that Leland's face had been drained of all color, his sunny canoe trip notwithstanding. Seeing that, he assumed that this was no plumbing problem. He asked, "Are you in need of assistance?"

Leland swallowed. "It's your Saudi. He's dead."

The mogul squinted. "In your room?"

"In my shower."

The mogul stood frozen, but his mind was racing. He was thinking, "My God. Haskell's actually done it. But in Howard Leland's bathroom of all places?"

He heard another door opening, somewhere down the hall. He said to Leland, very quietly, "Let's step back into your room." He came up off the stairs and took Leland by the arm while touching a finger to his lips.

Once inside, he closed the door. He said to Leland, "Please show me."

Leland shook his head. "I've seen all I need to. We must call the police."

"Not just yet. First let's see what we have."

He went into Leland's bathroom. Leland stayed back. The mogul could smell it before he could see it. Stale alcohol, stale urine, stale everything else. The prince's bowels had released in his death throes.

He reached to touch one of the prince's hands in order to see whether it was cold. It was. It felt like the film on a pudding. He tugged at the prince's sleeve with two fingers. The arm barely budged. The body seemed in full rigor. If so, he'd been dead for ten or twelve hours. Therefore he'd been here since early last evening, well before Leland returned. Leland must have been in his cups indeed, not to have noticed this stench.

The mogul stared at the prince for another thirty seconds. Why the Saudi garments? Had he dressed for the occasion? Ah, yes, he realized. The banker had mentioned it. The prince had stopped at his home in Riyadh to pick up some less conspicuous clothing. He must have flown back dressed this way.

But speaking of clothing, he called, "Howard? Get dressed please. You want to get out of that robe."

"Dressed. Oh, my God. The reporters."

"There will be no reporters. There will be no police. This is the Bohemian Grove. Please get dressed."

He had almost missed seeing the folded note that was tucked in behind the prince's beard, held in place by the sash that had strangled him. Leaning in, he saw the lettering on the outside. Very shakily written, it was Howard Leland's name. What's this, he wondered? A suicide note? Very likely, yes, but why address it to Leland? Why, for that matter, was this done in Leland's bathroom? Charles? What the devil were you thinking?

He looked for a tool with which to work the note loose. He settled on Howard Leland's toothbrush. He forced its handle down between sash and stiffened skin until he had some air in between. Just then, there came a knock on the door. He heard Howard Leland gasp at the sound. The mogul called, "Not a problem. That would be Haskell. No doubt wondering why I'm not down for breakfast."

He gave the toothbrush a couple of twists. The note was almost free, but not quite. Another knock. Can't be Haskell. He'd have walked in by now. The mogul left the toothbrush where it was and went out to see who it was. He opened the door a few inches.

It wasn't Haskell. Close enough. It was the banker. The banker said to the mogul, "Oh, here you are. Charles asked me to see what was keeping you."

The mogul looked for some sign in his manner that the banker had any idea of what had happened. He saw none. He said, very quietly, so that Leland couldn't hear, "I think Charles has probably doped out why I'm late. Now I want you to get a good grip on yourself. Without reacting, without saying a word, go take a peek in the bathroom."

The banker hesitated. He said, "This can't be good."

"But not unexpected," said the mogul. "Go look."

Howard Leland was pulling on the second of his socks. He froze in that position as the banker came in. He said to the banker, "I don't understand this." The banker walked passed him without giving a response, his eyes being fixed on the moguls. Leland said to the mogul, "There's a note around his neck."

The mogul said, "I know. We will get to that."

Leland asked, "But why would my name be on it? I didn't know the man. I'd only met him that once."

"Yes, but you're who you are and his life was in shambles. He'd planned to beg you for asylum."

"Through a suicide note? One wouldn't think so," said Leland. "I want to know what's going on here."

The banker called to the mogul. "A moment with you, please."

The mogul gave Leland's shoulder a squeeze. "Bear with me," he said. "We'll find out."

He went into the bathroom where he saw that the banker had finished extracting the note. With trembling hands, he was reading it.

"Let me see what he wrote," said the mogul.

The mogul saw that note had been written on a sheet that had been torn from a spiral notebook. He'd seen a spiral notebook of similar size sitting on Leland's writing desk. The note was written in longhand and in English, more or less. It was hard to read, cramped letters, words scrawled, and some of the words were misspelled. Other words had been begun and then abruptly crossed out. The prince's pen had ripped the page in some places. It read:

"I curse you, Howard Leland. You have betrayed me. You and your lackey, Roger Clew. You and Harry Whistler, a great enemy of God who pulls so many strings from Geneva in Switzerland. You and his puppet, the German, Martin Kessler, who mocks Islam from Harry Whistler's house in Belle Haven, Virginia where he hides behind walls that will not be high enough. You and those lesbian whores, the Nasreens. Together you have corrupted my daughter and turned many wives and daughters from God. Together you have stolen ten billions of dollars of charity funds with which I was entrusted. You have tried to distract those who should have these monies by spreading your false prophecy among

Muslim women and causing them to ridicule our manhood. She is not coming. This is your lie. Her handmaidens are more of your sluts. In this lie you are in league with Rajib Sadik who is a false Muslim and a spy for the Zionists who has infiltrated Hamas, Charles Haskell tried to stop you. All honor to him as he honors Islam. He is a friend to all Muslims who follow the true path. God is never deceived. God knows his good heart. My honor demands that I do this."

The note was signed, this time in Arabic, with the prince's full name. Prince bin this and ibn al-that. Seven names all told, the last being Saud. They filled a line and a half.

The mogul stared at the words. "Is this his handwriting?"

The banker nodded. "It is. And that's definitely his signature. But the text was obviously being dictated. How else could Charles Haskell be the good guy?"

"His honor demands that he do this, it says. Do what? End his life? Or write the note?"

The banker made a face. "Well, the latter, I'm sure. He didn't know that he was writing a suicide note. He thought he was composing an indictment."

They heard movement in the bedroom. Sounds of Howard Leland dressing. Leland asked them, his voice weak, "What's all the whispering in there?"

The mogul leaned backward and glanced into the bedroom. He saw that Leland had finished tying his shoes, but seemed loathe to approach any nearer. The mogul said to the banker, "Give me two minutes." He slipped the note into his pocket.

He stepped into the bedroom and gestured to Leland. He was motioning him toward the door to the room. He said, "Howard, let me tell you what must have happened. The prince was blind drunk. He still reeks of Jack Daniels. He crawled up the stairs and blundered into your room thinking that it was his own. The rooms have no locks. They are similarly furnished. It's an easy mistake to have made."

Leland's face showed a glimmer of relief.

The mogul said, "Here is what I want you to do. Go down the hall, go into my room and wait there while I deal with this. You cannot have your name connected with this. You need to distance yourself from this tragedy."

"Distance myself? It's my bathroom."

"Be that as it may, none of this is your fault. We should never have exposed you to this drunken fool. Go now. Leave this to me."

Leland hesitated. He glanced around his bedroom. "My briefcase."

"By all means, take it with you. And your notebook."

The mogul opened the door; he eased Leland through it. He steered him down the hallway, away from the stairs. He said to Leland, "Fifteen minutes. No longer."

He closed the door. The banker stepped from the bathroom. The banker asked cautiously, "Distance him how? If you think I'm going to help you haul the body out of here…"

"Never mind the body. That's the least of our concerns. I needed some time to think this out before Haskell decides to come up here."

"Haskell," said the banker. "He seemed edgy at breakfast. Kept glancing toward the stairs. He must have thought that the prince would be found before this. Haskell must have killed him last evening."

"While Leland was carousing. Yes, he must have."

"He'd have got the prince to open his door and... why not there, though? Why bring him in here?"

"For the shock effect, clearly, on Leland," said the mogul. "He wanted Leland, not some maid, to discover the body. He must have had his ear to his own door all night in order to be Johnny-on-the-spot."

"Well, it's shocking the hell out of me," said the banker. "How dare he do this without consulting with us?"

"Oh, stop it," said the mogul. "You knew this was coming."

"And you said we'd have nothing to do with it."

"I did, but here we are. The hand has been dealt. We'll have to make the best of it, won't we?"

"But how?" asked the banker.

"I'm working on that. Let's me see that note again." He read it once more. He could not help but smile. "No surprise, I suppose, that he doesn't mention Stride. I wonder if he thinks she'll fall into his arms once Harry Whistler's 'puppet' is out of the way. Meanwhile Charles is now a hero to the whole Muslim world, the Saudi part in particular. Not the three of us, mind you; only

Charles. And here's Howard Leland, evil genius that he is, who's been running the show all this time."

"In league with Whistler and Clew. To say nothing of Sadik. Sadik's now an Israeli mole?"

"A pre-emptive strike, I would assume," said the mogul.

"Get him killed before he becomes bothersome?"

"Worth a shot, I suppose." The mogul rubbed his chin. He said, "Whistler and Clew. Were those names ever mentioned in the presence of the prince?"

The banker thought for a moment. "No, they were not. I don't think that Kessler's was either."

"No matter. But that's Charles. He likes to touch all the bases. So Kessler is ensconced in Belle Haven, Virginia. Charles must not have had a street map on hand. He'd have attached it with a bull's eye drawn on the house."

"Let's ponder that some other time," said the banker. "We need to deal with the problem at hand."

"Indeed. Let me think for a moment."

The mogul, in his mind, could see the scene that had unfolded. Haskell telling the prince, "Leland says no asylum. Don't take that lying down. Let's go in and leave the bastard a note."

There's the prince at Leland's writing desk, using Leland's own notebook. Haskell standing behind him, telling him what to write. Haskell stopping him whenever the prince added words that to his besotted mind had seemed relevant. That would explain all the scratch-outs. Perhaps Haskell already had the sash in his hands, but a choke hold would have done just as well. Strangle him, drag him, string him up from the shower head. The prince's headdress, his ghutra, could not have stayed in place. Haskell probably saw that it had fallen to the floor and unthinkingly slapped it back on his head. That seems careless. His mind must have been elsewhere.

But where was elsewhere? What could Haskell have been thinking? Granted, he felt sure that Leland had lied to him, that Leland and/or Clew must want that disk for themselves. But why this? A fit of pique? No, that wouldn't have been it. If Leland won't help him one way, he'd help him in another. Charles would use this note and the threat to make it public as trade goods to get at that disk. Through whom, though? Through Clew? No, why bother with a middle man? He'd get them... how?... directly through Stride? No, more likely through Kessler.

He'd get word to Kessler at this house in Belle Haven. He'd say, "Here are your options. The Prince's daughter, Rasha, copied some files. Those files belong to me. I want them back. Give them to me and all will be well. Refuse and here's what will happen:

Howard Leland will be ruined. Front page news the world over. Guaranteed, by the way. I have a friend in the business. The scandal will also bring down Roger Clew. You'll have lost a most valuable ally. Your name, that of Stride and your sundry Muslim-ettes will be central to all of these stories. You'll be deluged by the media, but that is the least of it. Angry Saudis, desperate Saudis will descend on Belle Haven. Some will do so through the senators and congressmen they own. They in turn will enlist the FBI, the CIA. Others will argue for more direct action. They'll send their own brutish security people to kidnap as hostages anyone you hold dear. But as bad as this could get, they are not your biggest problem because all they want is their money.

Your biggest problem, by far, relates to this prophecy. Are you even aware of it? Possibly no. Possibly it's just mischief by some girls who've passed through via this feminist underground railroad that's run by your friends, the Nasreens. But who will believe that you're innocent of it? Here's the prince's note. It's all they'll need.

And you're in league with Sadik? That's what the note says. That must mean you're in league with the Zionists as well. But Sadik, now blown, can kiss his own ass goodbye. Who'll kill him? Any Muslim. But Hamas has first dibs. And then they'll be coming after you.

Talk about covering all the bases, thought the mogul. All that's lacking in this note is a call to arms addressed to half a billion Muslim men. They won't all come to Belle Haven, of course. Some will want you alive until you give up that money. But then, of course, there's the lunatic fringe. The fanatics who will now know the source of this prophecy. How many? A few thousand? Oh, easily that many. And how many car bombs? At least one a day. So much for local real estate values.

The mogul folded the note. He returned it to his pocket. The banker asked, "What are you going to do with it?"

"We, my friend. We. First comes self-preservation. Is Leland your enemy? Is Clew?"

The banker hesitated. "Not so far."

"Is Kessler your enemy? Is Whistler?"

The banker shook his head. "They are Haskell's. Not mine."

"And I propose to keep it that way." The mogul rubbed his hands. "Okay, here's what you do. Go back down and tell Haskell that I can't come to breakfast. Intestinal distress. I've got to stay near a toilet. Has he asked if you've seen anything of Leland?"

"No."

"He will. I don't think he'll be able to resist. If he does, say you have, that he went out for a jog. If he doesn't, bring up Leland's jog on your own. He'll ask how Leland seemed. Say that he seemed hung over. The idea is to keep Haskell glued to his seat waiting for Leland's return."

"He'll... see that something's happened. I'm not that good an actor."

"Yes, he might," said the mogul. "He's not easily fooled. Are you able to pretend that your stomach is churning?"

"That wouldn't be pretending. It is."

"Then go ahead and squirm as you're sitting with Haskell. Let out a loud fart if you can. Let him see you trying to tighten your sphincter. Say, uh-oh, you think you may have caught the same bug that has me confined to my bathroom."

"That I can do," said the banker.

"Then go."

The mogul waited as the banker descended the stairs. He closed Leland's door and picked up his house phone. He said, "The chief of maintenance, please."

The call was redirected. A voice came on. The mogul gave his name and his membership number. It wasn't needed. The voice said, "I know who you are, sir."

"I need a clean-up, a discrete one, with your usual thoroughness. The Teddy Roosevelt Cabin, Room 3, second floor."

"A member, sir?"

"A transient. He won't be missed. Pack up everything belonging to the guest in Room 3 and bring it to me in Room 7. Pack up everything belonging to the transient, room 5, and see that it's properly disposed of."

"Five minutes. Through the kitchen. Sir, you ought not to be there."

"Understood. You'll need a plumber. And some wall paint. And some plaster."

"Sir…"

"Forgive me."

"We can handle it, sir."

"Bless you. Have a good day."

TWENTY FIVE

Netanya took a break. His wife had made him a sandwich. It would still be several hours before Kessler could respond.

When he does read it, though, he's bound to assume that we know a lot more than we're saying. We don't, but we should. I mean, this is Mossad; we don't fly in the dark. We'd better do a little more homework.

He returned to his computer. He sat cracking his knuckles. But where, he asked himself, do we start? Sadik wanted to know, "Are the Darvi girls with Aisha?" He wouldn't say who they are, so, okay, we'll start there. Netanya tapped a few keys. A search engine dropped down. He typed in the name "Darvi" and hit "Enter."

Dumb, he thought. Much too broad a search. His screen had flooded with Darvis. Too common a name in some parts of the world. There were probably dozens in Israel alone. But okay, use your head. Sadik's visit to Tehran. Perhaps there are fewer in Tehran.

He refined his search to read "Darvi Tehran," but again there were far too many hits. Tehran is a city of six million, after all. More people than are in all of Israel. Take a minute, thought Netanya. Let's think this thing out.

Whatever brought Sadik to Tehran had to have been government sanctioned. That's a mystery in itself because Sadik is Hamas. Iran supports Hezbollah, not Hamas. More to the point, they detest the Wahhabis and Hamas had been a Wahhabi tool. Or at least it was at the beginning.

No, thought Netanya. They wouldn't deal with Hamas. They must have needed Sadik himself, irrespective of him being Hamas. He wasn't sure where this line of reasoning was getting him except to conclude that someone high up had invited him and that something big must have been at stake. But that "someone high up" was not someone named Darvi or the name would have already rung a bell.

Darvi, however, was all that he had. He refined his search further, adding "Doctor." It seemed worth a try. Darvi could well be a doctor. Perhaps Sadik was called in to consult on the surgery of this someone or other high up. But Netanya came up empty. No doctors named Darvi. He deleted "Doctor" and typed "Government Official" even though he considered that unlikely. But, bingo, he hit. The list was now down to five. Five minor officials named Darvi.

Netanya assumed that the five were all relatives. In every bureaucracy throughout the Mideast, there are suck-ups who have jumped aboard the wagon. The first to hit pay dirt brings in brothers and cousins. Family members are more readily trusted or at least they're more easily kept an eye on. The senior Darvi of these five must be this first one, Mustafa Darvi. It says he's a Deputy Minister. The other four all have "assistant" in their titles. So, okay, he's a minister, but a minister of what? This says he's with the Council on Energy Services. What's a Council on Energy Services?

Netanya grunted to himself. It was a vague enough title. It could mean almost anything that was energy-related. Not nuclear, however. Netanya would have heard of him. Probably not oil or natural gas either for much the same reason; his file would be flagged. His responsibilities – if he had any worth mentioning – would probably limited to some ancillary service such as servicing pipelines and oil pumping stations. Maybe running a few of the state-owned gas stations. Quite a number of Iranians were given gas stations in return for some service to the mullahs' revolution. It didn't have to be much of a service. They'd been useful, so the mullahs threw them a bone. But Darvi's seemed a pretty lucrative bone. The file showed a good address in Tehran, a beach house on the Caspian, an apartment in Paris and minority ownership of a time-share in Monaco where he takes a gambling trip once a year.

The Mossad clerk who'd compiled and entered this file must have agreed that he was nobody special. Otherwise, there would be more of a personal history. Mossad doesn't spend much time on flunkies. There were no notes regarding his immediate family except to say that he had two sons. No daughters mentioned, but that's not unusual. Sons are everything to people like Darvi. Daughters are just so much baggage. Or, assuming that the daughters are halfway attractive, they're bartered to arrange an early marriage to a groom from a more important family.

Netanya hit some more keys. Another box opened. He dashed off a note to his Deputy Director who didn't get to take Wednesdays off. It read, "Yoni, do me a personal favor. See what else we have on Mustafa Darvi, a minor oil official in Tehran. Find out if he's missing any daughters. Also a Saudi princess named Rasha. The Saudi ran off about three months ago. Find out what you can about her father."

Sadik said "girls" so there are at least two. They could be cousins, but more likely daughters. What might they and the Saudi have in common? Well, Sadik, of course. And certainly the Nasreens.

Under "Search" he typed "Darvi" and added "Nasreens." Once again, his screen flooded, but with only Nasreens. No cross reference with anyone named Darvi. This was no great surprise. He'd just given it a shot. Missing daughters doesn't necessarily suggest the Nasreens. If you're a daughter and you want to run, the Nasreens are far from the only game in town, but they're certainly the most hated and condemned. Six of the first dozen entries were fatwa's. Calling for their deaths. Big rewards for their capture. All of them called lesbian whores and apostates. He wondered if Sadik, when he fights with his wife, has ever called Maryam a lesbian whore. Sadik wouldn't, of course. Nor would anyone else. Not if he liked his nose where God put it.

He did notice, however, that of these rewards, few seemed to be offered for the return of the women whom the Nasreens had helped to escape. Not even rewards for information as to their current whereabouts. That seemed odd, but it was perhaps understandable. Some might have decided to cut their losses rather than to risk failure and more humiliation. Others might have claimed that their daughters were dead. Not just dead in their eyes. Dead for real. Found and killed. It's a safe enough lie unless their daughters turn up. But few will. They'll have taken new identities while the heat is on, changing back later if they wish. Up to them.

Netanya wondered what Aisha was calling herself now. Aisha Bandari was the name she was born with. Did she keep it or change it? What if Stride and Kessler marry? Aisha Kessler? He hoped not. It falls hard on the ear.

He didn't bother with a search of Elizabeth Stride. He knew what he'd find. Spawn of Satan, God-cursed, a long list of her crimes, and a million dollar price on her head. And he knew that there would be few recent entries because Stride, like Kessler, was thought to be dead. There were several accounts - he'd seen them before this – of groups who had tried to claim the reward by providing proof that they'd killed her. On two occasions, they videotaped her. They had her strapped to a chair; she would recite her confession. On one they slowly sawed off her head. On the other they wanted it to be seen that she suffered so they started by slicing off her ears and then her nose as she shrieked and gagged all the while. At last count, she died at least eight different times and in almost as many locations.

The sad thing was that all of these deaths were real deaths. Some were women who were merely suspected to be Stride and made to confess under torture. Two or three were even women who claimed to be Stride in the hope of being admired or enriched, doing talk shows, maybe writing a book. The real Black Angel, they assumed, would not come forward to dispute them. Well, she didn't. But they dug their own graves.

Aisha, he murmured.

Aisha, Aisha. Aisha, Aisha.

Why does that name set off a spark in his brain?

Netanya knew the answer. All this talk of that prophecy. Type "Aisha" into Google and the other search engines; you'll get something like three million hits. This explosion is new because the rumor is new, but the groundwork was already well in place. Type "Muslim feminist" into any search engine and you get about four million hits. If you narrow it down to Muslim Feminist Websites, you're talking four or five thousand. Tehran all by itself has more than sixty.

The Iranians and the Saudis try to block them, of course. It's hopeless because new ones pop up every day and are often disguised to seem harmless. Netanya recalled one that went under the title, "How to cultivate prize hothouse flowers." It took the censors three months to catch on that the prize hothouse flowers were their daughters.

Netanya smiled. He chuckled. But he felt his smile fading. That spark in his brain was flashing again. He saw his fingers moving, almost unwilled, to type the name "Aisha" on his keyboard. To that name, he added the word, "Prophecy." He clicked on "Search" and his screen seemed to shout at him. There it was, in every language, even Hebrew. It didn't name Aisha specifically, but there was no need. Most Muslims who weren't illiterate would know and half of the rest would have heard of her. The Lady of the Camel was Aisha.

This prophecy was what, almost a thousand years old? And pretty much ignored all that time. But here it is, resurrected, just a few months ago. And it came back to life at about the same time when Stride's Aisha relocated to Virginia.

"She will be of the East but turn your eyes to the West because that is where her banner will unfurl."

Of the East, thought Netanya. Cairo is East. And Bella Haven is definitely West.

"She will have grown up among you, dressed in white, pure of heart."

Among you fits with Cairo. Dressed in white is all that tennis.

No, wait, thought Netanya. Get hold of yourself. Next you'll look at this angel named Qaila and say that she sounds like Elizabeth Stride.

As for Aisha, herself, it says she'll soon be of age. Is sixteen of age? Sure it is. Why not? In some countries, sixteen is a spinster. The original Aisha was a child of six when Mohammed took her as a wife. In fairness, however, he was no pedophile. It was an arrangement, uniting two families. Even popes married children that young. And most were willing to wait a few years before consummating the marriage. So how old was this Aisha when her maidenhood ended? Sixteen? That would sound about right.

Netanya growled at himself. Look at me, he thought. I'm sitting here trying to make pieces fit that are probably in no way connected. All roads do not lead to Belle Haven. But what about Sadik? Has he done the same thing? Has he decided that Stride's Aisha is the Aisha of the prophecy?

Impossible, thought Netanya. Sadik is no boob. He would assume from the get-go that the prophecy was dredged up just to see how much trouble it could cause. He also knows Kessler well enough to be sure that Kessler would never go near this. Nor would Stride. Not in ten million years. They would both know that this could be nothing but trouble if this prophecy were laid at their door.

No, thought Netanya. They're no boobs either. But this part of the world has no shortage of boobs. Have some of them done what he caught himself doing? Have some decided – on the flimsiest of evidence – that these two Aishas are one and the same?

Yes, thought Netanya. Some very well might. Even if they don't believe it, they can't dismiss it because so many women seem to want to believe it. They'll want it ended. They'll want it exposed. Still others – and now we're not just talking Muslims – will see, not some hoax, but a deep, dark conspiracy.

To what end? They don't know, but it must involve oil. Why oil? What else? What else here is worth having? And how do you get it? You either buy it or take it. Take means invade and that makes you unpopular. Unless you're invited, but invited by whom? Muslim wives and Muslim daughters? The whole female population? You shouldn't hold your breath until that happens.

Or unless the invasion… go slow on this… wait. Unless it's thought to be sanctioned by Allah himself. Through the Lady of the Camel. Through Aisha, reborn.

Now there, thought Netanya, is one hell of a conspiracy. He ought to call Kessler. Ask him outright. He'd say, "Hi, Martin, what's new? Any interesting projects? Has anyone hired you to seize the world's oil? Just asking. No reason. How's Elizabeth?"

He leaned back in his chair. He muttered. "Yitzhak, get a grip. Too many years in intelligence work. A cigar is sometimes just a cigar."

If he had to make a bet on what's going on here, he'd go with the hoax option first. A bit of mischief by someone who'd had no idea how fast and how far it would spread. Who started it? Who knows? Maybe those Darvi girls. Or maybe that young Saudi princess if she's with them. All they'd need is too much time on their hands and access to an on-line computer.

Their motive? That's easy. It's payback time. Stick it to all the men whose treatment of women was why they wanted out in the first place. Or maybe it's simpler. They're just having some fun. What's that song his own daughter would burst into when he told her she couldn't stay out after ten? Ah, yes. Cyndi Lauper. He'd even catch himself humming it. The song? Girls Just Want To Have Fun.

The telephone rings in the middle of the night.

My father yells, what you gonna do with your life.

Oh daddy dear, you know you're still number one,

But girls, they want to have fuh-un.

Oh, girls, they want to have fun.

So they do, thought Netanya. So they should, thought Netanya. But fun gets you killed in some places.

If this did start in Belle Haven... and that's still far from certain...it's sure to be seen as a Harry Whistler scheme by some intelligence service or other. Why? Because it's happening in Harry's house. And not just a house, another fortified house that is immune to electronic spyware. What's he up to? They don't know, but it must be big because plots are always presumed to be big and always international in scope.

342

He knew he ought to call Harry. Lay this out for him. Even if there's nothing to it, a heads-up couldn't hurt. But he'd wait to hear what Kessler has to say.

"Appearances," he muttered. "Even where there is no substance."

Netanya, in his mind, could see all the meetings if this prophecy should be traced to Belle Haven. Not only among the intelligence services. Not only among all the Muslim regimes and a hundred or so groups like Islamic Jihad. He saw meetings in Big Oil boardrooms as well. One theory after another being put forward as to Harry's reasons for doing this. Assignments handed out. Task forces put together. Whatever his reasons, he's got to be stopped because whatever he's doing is surely contrary to this or that national interest. Or corporate interest. Or religious interest. In most countries, all three are the same. And in all those meetings not one single person will raise a hand and say, "Why don't we just ask him?"

And this brings us to a question that is all the more basic. Is Harry even aware of this prophecy? Possibly no, but just as possibly yes. He avoids the Middle East, but he keeps up to date. He's probably wondered where it came from himself, never dreaming that the source might be under his nose.

And that Aisha might not live to reach sixteen.

He picked up his phone and punched out a number. It rang only once. Harry's voice came on.

He said, "Yitzhak, you just caught me. I'm on my way out. But I bet I can guess why you're calling."

TWENTY SIX

It was nine in the morning before Haskell realized that the mogul and the banker had betrayed him. The mogul had the trots. Couldn't come down to breakfast. That was the story that the banker had returned with.

He'd asked the banker, "Any sign of Howard Leland?"

The banker answered that the mogul said he'd gone jogging.

"He saw Leland go out?"

"About an hour ago, yes."

The mogul said he'd gone for an early stroll himself and he saw Howard Leland come down the front steps dressed in his old Princeton sweatshirt and shorts. He was heading toward the old logging road.

Gone jogging? Really? With a head that must be pounding? He'd been over served, as they say, last night while laughing it up with that canoe group.

The banker said that the mogul was surprised as well. The banker stifled a belch as he spoke. He said the mogul could see that Leland was hurting. As Leland went by him Leland smiled a rueful smile and said to the mogul, "Never again." He didn't stop to explain. The mogul said there was no need. He knew a hangover when he saw one. Death warmed over. Pallid even with his sunburn. Hair askew, unshaven, well, you'll see for yourself. He should be back before long. The banker said, "If I were Leland, I'd stop at the fitness center and try to sweat it off in the sauna."

The banker belched again. It was followed by a fart. The banker said, "Oh, my. I hope I'm not getting it." He asked, "Last night, did you have the oyster stew? No you didn't. But we did. That must have been it." The banker was squirming. "You'll have to excuse me. Oh, my. I hope I make it up the stairs."

Haskell had to hand it to him. It was a good performance. The logging road was one nice touch to his story. It formed a loop. One could jog it and be back within an hour and a half. An hour had passed. Half an hour to go. The idea was to get him to sit for that long waiting for Leland to return. He's still not here? He's running late? Perhaps he did stop at the fitness center. That was another nice touch.

Haskell did get restless. He did take a walk. He walked to a point where he was able to see both the logging road and the fitness center. No sign of Leland. He turned back toward the cabin. The lobby was empty; there was no one at the desk. The clerk who was normally there at all times must have eaten the oyster stew as well. He climbed the stairs and, moving quietly on the carpeting, he approached the door of Howard Leland's Room 3. He listened, heard nothing. He knocked lightly. No answer. He turned the knob and stepped in.

And there was nothing. No Leland. No befouled Saudi prince. And, of course, no suicide note. No bent shower head, no damage to the plaster. He touched his thumbnail to the plaster. It was still soft. No luggage, no clothing, the bed freshly made, fresh linen, fresh towels, the scent of pine disinfectant. The roll of toilet paper folded neatly to a point. A fresh terry robe on its hanger. He felt sure that there would be no fingerprints either. Only his own on the doorknob.

He took a single Kleenex from its dispenser. He used it to wipe the door's outer knob after he had closed it behind him. He stepped from Room 3 to Room 5 farther down, the room of the missing Saudi prince. He used the Kleenex again to open the door, but he already knew what he'd find there. Not a thing. Another freshly cleaned room. No bottles of Jack Daniels sitting on the wet bar. No sign that there had been a recent occupant.

He went on to Room 7, that of the mogul. This time he didn't bother with the Kleenex. No mogul, but his personal effects seemed all there. The room hadn't been tidied: the maid hadn't come, yet the bathroom smelled fresh as a daisy. Some trots. He tried the banker's room next. No banker there either. His clothing and wherewithal were still where they should be. Except for his laptop. No laptop.

He recalled the banker's story of one of the workers who got himself hung from eave. The mogul had seen him, found the vision indecorous, and placed a call to the maintenance chief. No more worker. He was never seen again.

Good man. Well done. Haskell made a mental note. Go meet that chief before this is done with. Just the sort of man he needs on his payroll.

But the banker and the mogul. Where would they be right now? They'd be outside the gate where Leland's Lincoln was parked and where Leland's security team has been housed. Leland wouldn't have called his two agents just yet. He'd still be listening to whatever proposition the mogul and the banker were presenting to him. Would they have shown him the note? Almost certainly, yes. And they would be saying, "This was all Haskell's doing. We are your friends. He is not."

See here? It's the prince's suicide note. Read it. You can see what Charles tried to do. See this lighter? Watch. I am now going to burn it. There. Nothing left if it. It never existed.

Except that it's a copy that they would have burned. They would not have destroyed the original. They'd have made a color copy off the banker's laptop, then folded it and crinkled it where the sash would have crushed it. They'd have added some facsimile of the prince's sweat and drool stains plus some approximation of his smell. Not hard to do. Simply wipe your ass with it. Further dampen it with bourbon and voila!

They'd say go home now, back to Washington; none of this ever happened. Today's Wednesday; this was to be your last day here anyway. You have our word that this episode will leave you untouched. Where is the prince? You have no idea. The last time you saw him was when he drove past you. As far as you know, he never came back. He ran off in Lisbon as the banker's plane refueled or perhaps he made his dash when it reached Sacramento. Troubled man. That's the last that's been seen of him.

So you see? It never happened. We've seen to that for you. We'll expect, however, a small favor in return. Only one. Just that disk. Then we're out of your life. Unless, of course, you're still interested in becoming a Bohemian. No, strike that. Bad timing. Put it on the back burner. Your comfort level isn't what it might be.

Well, there you have it, thought Haskell. Outsmarted again.

"Or so it would seem."

Yes, it certainly would.

"Well?"

Well, what?

"What's your next move?"

Mine? None at all. The ball's in their court. The mogul and the banker will now come back and say, "Yes, Charles, we've done this and it's for your own good. We still need each other; we can still work together, but from now on we're doing things our way. You've lost it over this whole Kessler business and you don't understand men like Leland."

He'll let them talk. He might even let them try it their way. It won't work, of course. They'll get nothing from Leland. Howard Leland now has a five-hour plane ride during which to gather his thoughts. Will he be grateful to the mogul and the banker? Perhaps just a bit. For the first fifteen minutes. Then he'll realize that those two would have at least made a copy. It will sink in that he can now expect to be blackmailed for as long as he is of the slightest value. He'll get back to Washington at around dinner time and will probably run straight to Roger Clew.

He'll unburden himself. He'll tell Clew all that happened. He'll recite the contents of the prince's note, especially the part that threatens to bring the wrath of Islam down on Belle Haven, Virginia. Oh, to be a fly on the wall during that conversation.

Will Clew alert Kessler? Of course. He will have to. What will Kessler do? Come after Charles Haskell? No, not for another ten days at least. Not while the Bohemian Club is in session. He'll wait. But well before these ten days are up, he's going to have much bigger problem than this. Whistler's house is likely to have gone up in flames.

But how will that happen if the damning document is now in the hands of Leland's protectors? The mogul and the banker will keep it for themselves. They'll say, "Charles, you can't have it. You're out of control." They'll say, "Look at you, standing there talking to yourself, reciting our lines, putting words in our mouths. No fair. You must try to listen."

Well, no. They won't say that. Do they know that he does that? No matter. They'll have plenty more to say.

And, indeed, he will listen. Very calmly and politely. The mogul will say, "Howard Leland will play ball. He'll get us the disk and wash his hands of the matter. He'll do so because I have won his trust, which is something that you could never do."

The banker will say, "He really has no alternative. It's the price of our silence and a small price to pay. If this became front page news, humiliation aside, he would have to resign in disgrace."

The mogul would add, "I know that you don't understand this, but a man like Leland would never permit his family name to be stained. He'd no longer be welcome at his clubs."

Would the mogul actually say that? Yes, he probably would. Yada yada yada yada yada.

He, Charles Haskell, will be hard pressed not to say to them, "Guess what? That note? The one you let him see you burn? The one whose original you've stashed away someplace? Well, you saw what a mess the prince made as he was writing it. If you think that one's bad, you should see the first draft. Yup, he wrote it twice. I kept the first one."

They won't believe it, so he'll show them. "See all the scratch-outs? Twice as many on that one. More words misspelled. More gauges through the paper. I wanted something more legible, but now that I think of it, this one looks even more like a suicide note written by a desperate drunk."

Well, he won't show them all of it. Perhaps just a glimpse. The first one did go a bit over the top. While he was dictating that one to the prince, he was extremely pissed off at Elizabeth Stride. He'd promoted her to Nasreen-in-Chief. He named her as first among the lesbian whores who corrupted and then murdered nice Muslim girls so that they'd be her sex slaves in hell when she got there.

But even the prince had trouble with that one. He'd asked, "Who is this Elizabeth Stride?"

"Never mind. Just write it. She deserves it."

The prince said, "This is true if she's a lesbian whore. But you say that in hell there are sex slaves?"

"It's in the hadiths. Volume three, I believe."

"In my life," said the prince, "I have never heard this."

"Your clergy has been keeping it quiet."

"So in hell, whores have whores? This means women for women?"

"Yes, but don't worry, they're all ugly and diseased." He could have added, "You'll see for yourself in ten minutes," but that would have ruined the surprise. The prince started to write what he'd said about Stride. Haskell stopped him. "Scratch that out. We'll take care of her later."

Pissed though he was, one ought to be fair. Yes, she's fucking Kessler or at least one assumes so. Making bad choices doesn't make her a whore. And maybe what's between them isn't sexual at all. More of a partnership. A union of convenience. Perhaps they even have separate rooms. Perhaps Kessler doesn't sleep in the main house at all. Perhaps she has him sleep over the garage.

"Charles… get a grip."

"This is none of your business."

"Then I shouldn't have to listen to it either."

"But you see what she does to me? How she gets into my head?"

"Take a deep breath and focus. Keep your eye on the prize. Let's get back to your two friends who betrayed you."

Yes. You're right. Where was I? Oh, yes. After he's shown them parts of the note, he'll show them all the pictures that go with it. Yes, he has photos. About fifty in all. Yes, he broke the rules. He brought a camera to the Grove. Couldn't help it. It's part of his cell phone.

Yes, still again. He'd brought a cell phone to the Grove. Rolled up in a pair of white socks just in case. Hundreds of members must have done the same thing. Just be sure it doesn't ring and don't be seen using it. The prince did and look where it got him.

Stupid shit.

What was it Leland said? "You've insulted a prince." That shows how much Leland knows about princes. This turkey was a prince because his father was a prince. No intrinsic merit there. It's an accident. Six thousand Saudi princes, but let's break that down. Take any group of six thousand men. Take their average I.Q. and fully half, minus one, must be below average in intelligence. The lowest tenth will be functional illiterates. If they weren't princes they'd be sweeping the streets.

Another tenth of any group, especially this one, will have serious personality disorders. The full range of sociopathic behavior. Pathological liars. Inveterate sneaks. Sexual predators of every stripe. The full range of all the other perversions.

No big surprise there, but how about this? Another tenth will be atheists. Twice that number, agnostics. All day long over there it's Allah this and Prophet that and kneeling on their prayer rugs five times a day while many don't believe a damned word of it. It's not hypocrisy, though. It's called going with the flow. When in Rome and all that. Another tenth or so are going to be gay although none, of course, will come out; they'd be beheaded. Most of the rest will jack off watching re-runs of Baywatch except when they're flying up to Cairo or Marbella to bang every blond hooker in sight.

How did he get on this?

Oh, yes. The dead prince. Lowest tenth.

One wouldn't think that it would have been so hard to starve a brain that small of its oxygen. Haskell thought he'd never stop bucking and kicking. On the other hand, we mustn't be too hard on ourselves. It was, after all, our first strangulation. The sash wasn't doing it. He'd needed a lever. He'd looked around for something to insert in the loop. He saw that dumb little trophy that Leland had won for blasting away at clay pigeons. He dragged the prince within reach of it. Not the ideal shape, but it did the job. The prince's sounds were reduced to a squeak.

After he'd finished winching him up to hang him from the base of Leland's shower pipe – which was no mean feat either – all flaccid dead weight – he'd set about taking lots of pictures. His two slippery friends had seen that room before they had it all tidied up. Well, gentlemen, guess what. Now you can see it again. He must have photographed every square inch.

There are a dozen or more of the bathroom alone with special attention to the prince. From various angles. And in various poses. You saw the pose that I finally settled on. I liked the one with his purpling face looking out at you and his ghutra slapped back on his head. Next, Leland's bedroom. His unmade bed. His monogrammed briefcase and most of its contents. State department memos and various documents. Secret stuff? He didn't know. He didn't take time to read them. The same with his notebook that sat along side of it. Then the clothing in his closet and in his dresser drawers and, of course, Leland's slightly bent trophy. Did you know that Leland is bothered by hemorrhoids? Yes, the contents of his toilet kit as well.

He'd also snapped Leland's entry in the guest book downstairs. It showed his name and his title and the date of his arrival. The guest book was an afterthought. And not really needed. Barely worth the risk of being spotted with a camera. But events have proven it to be serendipitous. What'll you bet that that page has since been doctored? What'll you bet that the staff has been told to say that Leland never stayed in this cabin?

Was he even at the Grove? Oh, they wouldn't have gone that far. Too many people saw him and he's in the club's computer. So is the prince, for that matter. It will be enough for it to show that they both checked out on Wednesday and of course their rooms were then vacuumed and scrubbed.

Good man, that maintenance chief.

As for the disk, he knew that he'd never get it. The mogul and the banker won't either. Clew will probably get it. He'll share some of it with Leland. He'll keep some to himself because he's trickier than Leland. He'd know valuable trade goods when he sees them. He'll help wring substantial quid pro quos from the Saudis in return for... well, if not for restoring all of those funds, at least not making public the names of the skimmers. More than one thousand thieves. A lot of them royals. They're all traitors, you know. They intend to go AWOL. And they're family, for God's sake. How embarrassing.

Clew will probably call a meeting of that network of his. Harry Whistler and Yitzhak Netanya in particular. Kessler, too; they can't very well shut him out. Which means Stride as well. She is sure to have her say. Not Leland, however. They'll deal with him later.

They'll all sit down and they'll draw up a wish list. Washington, first. What do we want from Washington? Howard Leland keeps his job no matter who's president. Ditto Roger Clew, but he's already immune. Clew knows where too many bodies are buried. Or he's thought to know. Same effect. Harry Whistler would smile if he heard it said that the Bohemians think they run the world. He probably wouldn't remark on the boast. But he might say to himself, as Clew surely would, that we'll show those codgers who does.

Labyrinthine.

That's the word Leland used.

He said, "You have a labyrinthine mind, Charles."

You want to see Labyrinthine? Okay, here it is. What's the next best thing to having that disk in terms of getting the Saudis to owe me? Need a hint? It's in the note. The prince's suicide note. It's in showing the Saudis that Whistler and friends are the source behind everything that ails them. By the way, we've also photographed both versions of the note. We'll decide which one we're going to post on Saudi web sites along with some of those other photographs. That decision will depend on how generous he's feeling toward Elizabeth Stride at the time.

The note says that it's Whistler who funds the Nasreens. Bet you never suspected that, did you? Through them, he's been stealing your marriageable daughters in order to emasculate their prospective grooms by leaving them at the altar. And to blackmail their fathers. He learns all the family secrets. He threatens to splash them all over the internet unless they agree to do his bidding. He's turned them into spies, double agents in your midst. And not just yours, either. The entire Middle East. Hell, the whole Muslim world.

And what's worse? The prophecy. He's behind that as well. He hopes to turn all your women against you in order to profit from the chaos that ensues. How? I'm not sure yet. You figure it out. You've no shortage of paranoid conspiracy theorists. Oh, but I know one way. Almost forget. He intends to flood the world with cheap Caspian oil, forcing you to cut your prices to the bone.

Keep in mind though that I, Charles Haskell, am your ally. I'm showing you the enemy. I'm telling you where to strike. You know that I am a true friend of Islam because there it is, in the prince's own hand, and I have sworn to avenge him. Oh, and yes, I am prepared to convert, so let's show a little gratitude, shall we? To me and to Trans-Global Oil.

But let's first make them pay. Make every one of them pay. Including my two erstwhile friends who've betrayed me. Not yet, though. We still need them. They can wait.

I know you have that bounty on Elizabeth Stride, but don't touch her. I'll fix her myself in my own good time. That one's personal. She's had her chance.

"Um… Charles…"

Okay, not really, thought Haskell, but she could have, in time. I would very much like to have known her.

"So now you're going to have her killed? That would seem to dim the prospect. Why not simply eliminate the competition instead?"

Her defiler? Oh, I will. He'll be first.

"She'll survive him? By how long?"

Long enough to feel the pain.

"But she'll be in need of comfort, will she not?"

What are you saying?

"Well, of course, I don't know how you'd manage it, Charles, but a void in her life is a door left wide open. You just said it. You're the one who she could have been with, given time and with no one else filling that void."

Forget it. Too late for that now.

"Why is it too late?"

The fanatics will soon swarm all over Belle Haven. She'll probably go down with the ship unless...

"Unless what?

Unless I can save her before that. Let me think. When is this party that Gilhooley mentioned?

"What's today? Wednesday? It's this evening."

Well, that's it, then, thought Haskell. He'll show them a party. A real surprise party. One for the books. He punched a button on his cell phone. He scanned its stored numbers. It was time to have a chat with the Irishman.

He'd tell Gilhooley, good news, you get to use your expertise.

An enormous blast. Turn them all into cutlets. All the smoke and the fire. People screaming and running. Perhaps we'll find a way to lure Stride toward the front. She emerges unscathed. Well, perhaps a popped eardrum. And in shock as she realizes that all those in the back...

Oh, she'll get over it. Give her time.

And get this on tape. He'll want to watch it. Slow motion. He'll want to watch it over and over again. He'll tell Gilhooley, bring a video camera.

Rats.

Not good enough.

He wanted to be there.

"Um... Charles... be where? You can't mean in Belle Haven."

I want to see their faces as they arrive and as any survivors come staggering out."

"Charles, they'll see yours."

See my what?

"Your face."

No, they won't. I'll be on the other side of the street. I'll be watching from behind Gilhooley's truck.

"Still too big a risk. Everybody seems to have a camcorder these days. And the media are certain to rush to the scene. If you should be spotted, how would you explain..."

Good point. Okay. I'll wear a disguise.

"As what? Another handyman?"

All I'd need is a dark business suit and a briefcase. And a Wall Street Journal tucked under my arm. I'd look like any other Belle Haven executive coming home from a day at the office."

"Dumb."

Why is that dumb?

"You'd look just like you."

All you do is find fault. Make a useful suggestion.

"Here's a sensible suggestion. Stay here at the Grove. You just finished saying you're unreachable here. Wait for the video. Give a copy to the Saudis."

Along with that suicide note. Good idea.

"So you'll stay?"

Uh-uh. Got to see it.

"I don't."

Oh, where's your sense of adventure?

TWENTY SEVEN

Kessler, early that morning, had been wearing his new bathrobe when he opened the message from Netanya. The bathrobe was a first. He'd never owned one before. Elizabeth bought it for him and insisted that he use it. Brown with a hood. It made him look like a monk. This robe went almost down to his ankles.

Before that, he would normally walk around in short pants after making morning love to Elizabeth. Sometimes twice. So the prospect of an encore argued against any rush to get more encumbered by clothing. The impetus wasn't lust, or at least not entirely. The impetus was these blue pills he was taking. They had restored a function that he thought had been lost when a dose of radiation almost killed him.

The "sometimes twice" was making up for lost time. He had also regained much of the weight that he'd lost and his face was no longer so gaunt. His curly brown hair had long since grown back in and his teeth, therefore his smile, were brighter than ever because many of them were replacements. His face had picked up a couple of new scars in Angola, but he'd had them reduced by a Tel Aviv surgeon so that they hardly showed. He'd kept the v-shaped scar that bisected his right eyebrow. That one was much older. He liked that women liked it. So did Elizabeth, although she'd never say so. But lying face to face, she would touch it sometimes. Her touch had always been more tender than her words. His stamina, overall, was back near its peak, thanks to good food and frequent visits to the gym. Even so, the blue pills were a miracle.

There were, however, four girls in the house. Aisha's bedroom and Rasha's were just down the hall. The Darvi sisters bedrooms were directly above. All four were usually up at dawn to say their prayers. Accordingly, one must be discreet. One must try to keep the climactic groans to a minimum. One must not walk around dressed in such a way that one's readiness is sometimes all too apparent. Shahla, the eldest, seemed especially abashed by any such physical display by a man. He had no trouble understanding the reason. He tried to be extra careful in her presence.

On reading the message from Yitzhak Netanya, he had felt no particular sense of alarm. He'd recognized Netanya's email address; it was the one Netanya used from his home. Wednesday, thought Kessler. He still takes Wednesdays off. And he doesn't send anything very sensitive on Wednesdays, certainly not unencrypted.

So Netanya knows about the four Muslim girls. That in itself didn't come as a shock. His Mossad had contacts among the Nasreens. They'd helped each other on this or that matter. This "mutual friend' is most likely a Nasreen. She had told some

361

agent, for whatever reason, that the girls were living with them for a while. Until three could be placed. No great rush.

But why would this "friend" have reason to think that the girls might make trouble for Aisha? Netanya says don't let them use their computers. They're "involved in something." Well, in what? The destruction of Israel? Insider trading? Have they mentioned Aisha's name when they've emailed their friends? Such emails can't be traced, not to Harry's machines, but even if they could be, so what? Aisha's presence in Belle Haven was not meant to be a secret. She'd be starting school here in September.

Today, however, her name isn't Aisha. On this day she is known as Birthday Girl. First a special breakfast prepared by young Rasha, then an hour of tennis to work up a sweat, then they'll all cool off with a dip in the pool. After that, time to shop. Just Aisha and Elizabeth. Aisha will be getting a real grown-up outfit which she'll wear at the party tonight. He himself had learned the words to the song, Sixteen Candles, from a CD he found in Harry's library. He will sing it as a special surprise. He can't sing, but who cares. It's the sentiment that counts. There won't be a dry eye in the house.

Except on Harry Whistler. He'll be laughing himself silly. Roger Clew would more likely hide his face in his hands. No matter. It's nice that Harry called to say they're coming. Elizabeth had been hoping that they could.

The only fly in the ointment this morning was this email. "Problems for Aisha," Kessler muttered to himself. A bit more loudly he said, "This is typical Netanya." The man is a show-off. Always was and still his. He's a man who likes to tease you with snippets. Well, two can play that game.

Kessler started to compose his response, but he realized that his coffee mug was empty. He got up from his desk in the first floor study and walked back to the kitchen to replenish it. Aisha was busy setting the table while Rasha was preparing to make pancakes. Rasha was still in her ankle-length nightgown, but she wore it for comfort more than modesty. She was shuffling about in her fluffy pink slippers. The kitten he'd got her had crawled under the nightgown and was busy attacking the slippers. The two Darvi girls weren't down yet.

Elizabeth sat in the breakfast nook, absorbed by the Washington Post crossword. She and Aisha had already dressed for their tennis. Kessler stood for a moment admiring Elizabeth as he did at least five times a day. She was stifling a yawn, but her whole body moved. Every part of it seemed to coil very slowly and, just as slowly, relax. She was more like a cat than the kitten.

She felt his eyes on her and she knew what he was thinking. She gave him a soft little smile. He sighed. "You are such a magnificent creature. But I suppose I might as well dress."

His use of such language caused Rasha to blush, but not because she was embarrassed. Expressions of affection from a man were still new to her. Not so from a woman, however.

"Sweetie," said Elizabeth, speaking to Rasha, "I'll fix the batter. You go and get Shahla and Niki."

He knew her reason for volunteering. Rasha and pancakes were a worrisome combination. One never knew what she'd mix in. Too late, though. The batter was already green. He saw an opened can of chopped spinach. Now Elizabeth saw it. A sigh of surrender.

She asked Kessler as Rasha rinsed off her hands, "Did I hear you mention Netanya?"

That's Elizabeth, thought Kessler. Ears like a bat. Even from two rooms away. "It's nothing," he told her. "He's just keeping in touch."

"He's the one who'll get touched the next time I see him."

A bat, thought Kessler, with an elephant's memory. "I'm sure that's why he's been reluctant to drop in unless I've locked up all the cutlery."

Little Rasha raised an eyebrow upon hearing this exchange. She knew that Yitzhak Netanya was Mossad. She knew that Netanya was his friend, if not Elizabeth's. Friendship with a Jew had been an alien concept for the first fifteen years of her life. It was not an active prejudice and it wasn't her fault. It was more of a reflex. A conditioned reflex. She'd never heard a single good word about Jews until Elizabeth began opening her eyes. And, of course, the Nasreens.

Elizabeth had told her, "Clear that crap from your mind. I've worked with them, I've known them, I respect them on the whole. Except Yitzhak Netanya, who's a shit."

Kessler tried to defend him. "He's been a good friend."

"Wrong," said Elizabeth. "He's Israel's friend and that always comes first. Who knows that better than you do?"

"Of course it comes first. That's his country; that's his job. All loyalties are local. Look at ours."

"We're not shits."

This was not a dispute that would be easily resolved. He'd once asked her, "How can you not admire a man who wears loud Hawaiian shirts, some with Elvis? This was not a testament to his sartorial tastes, but rather a salute to his boldness. An assassin could spot him from a mile away. He'd have a clear shot because nobody else would walk within ten feet of Yitzhak Netanya while he was wearing such a shirt.

This wasn't really true. Netanya rarely wore them. Except to the beach and, even then, not an Elvis. He'd just thought that it might soften her image of Netanya. It didn't. She'd said, "Then he's an idiot."

One result, however, of having that discussion was improving Rasha's grasp of scatological English. "We're not shits" became something of a personal mantra. For her, it seemed to define who we are. He'd heard her use it once to scold Niki Darvi who had said or done something ungenerous. "We don't do that," she told her. "We're not shits."

Rasha had been up the stairs and back down. She asked him, "Mr. Kessler? How many pancakes?"

He looked again at the batter. "You are... very creative."

"It's spinach. You can add almost anything."

"Maple syrup, most commonly," said Kessler, "and butter. Spinach pancakes are a new one on me."

Elizabeth caught his eye. She gave a small helpless shrug. It was she who had introduced Rasha to pancakes. Also to peanut butter and jelly. For Rasha, this was a new world to be explored. And yes, she'd made peanut butter pancakes.

"I've eaten, thank you." He lied. He had not. He told Elizabeth, "I'll give Yitzhak your regards."

Kessler didn't linger to await her response. He returned to the study and sat down at his desk top. He clicked on Netanya's home email address. He thought, where were we? Ah, yes. We're doing snippets. He wrote, "Tell this mutual friend not to worry. All is in place. The day is at hand." Kessler hit send and sat back.

The answer came. "What day? The day of her coming? Are you telling me you know about this?"

See that? Always cryptic. The man can't help himself. Kessler wrote, "Spinach pancakes. And then sixteen candles. The world will be a better place for it." He thought of adding "We're not shits," but he didn't.

"Some of it might. But you might not live to see it. Martin, is your scrambler connected?"

Kessler answered, "Give me one minute."

He connected a box that Harry had shown him to the modem port of his computer. It's LED lit up. It showed a series of codes speeding by in rapid sequence. He didn't know what they meant. Harry said he wouldn't have to. The box would choose the right code.

He wrote, "Done, I think." He hit send.

A reply popped on. For an instant it was gibberish. In a blink, it turned into English.

Netanya wrote, "What day is at hand? Is Aisha turning sixteen? Are you saying that she's reached full womanhood?"

I certainly wouldn't go that far, thought Kessler. "Sixteen candles, Yitzhak, make a lovely light. The world could use such a light, don't you think?"

He replied, "I don't believe this. You're letting this happen? Is Elizabeth still with you? Does she know what you're doing?

Kessler wrote, "Okay, Yitzhak. Enough is enough. Tell me, plain language, what you're talking about or I'll start with spinach pancakes again." But before he could hit send, a new message popped on. Netanya wrote, "Stay available. I need twenty minutes. Don't move. Stay at your machine."

Kessler took a sip from his mug. He clicked on his solitaire game.

It wasn't twenty minutes; it was nearer only ten when Netanya's next email popped on. It said, "I just got off the phone with Sadik. He wants to come and see you. I have agreed. Right now he's on a flight to Geneva where he's going to hitch a ride with Harry Whistler. I have cleared this with Clew so that he's not detained when he lands in D.C."

Kessler stared. He wrote, "You mean Rajib Sadik? Is Rajib this mutual friend?"

"I think a better friend than you know," wrote Netanya. "He is trying to save Aisha's life."

"Yitzhak… what the hell are you talking about?"

"Is Elizabeth near? First go get her."

He heard Rasha asking, "Apple or Orange juice?" Three young voices answered "Apple" in unison. Elizabeth said, "Me, too. Thank you, Rasha." Kessler got to his feet and walked into the kitchen. He said to Elizabeth, "Come in here, please. There's something I need you to see."

Elizabeth saw his eyes. She saw no trace of good humor. She asked, "What is it?"

"Just come in."

She said to the girls, "Don't wait for me. Eat." She followed. He closed the door behind her.

For the first five minutes, they sat watching the screen. Kessler would ask another question now and then, but mostly they read the words of Netanya. After that, through Netanya, they read those of Sadik. Elizabeth wasn't much quicker than he had been to grasp what Netanya was telling them.

Elizabeth said, "Sadik. Don't I know that name? There's a Rajib Sadik with Hamas."

"Same man."

"Well, he's not coming here. Not Hamas."

"It's okay," Kessler told her. "You must trust me on this. I've known him longer than I have known you."

"Does he know that I'm here? That I walk down the street here, unarmed, by myself? Martin, there's still a bounty on me."

Kessler thought, unarmed maybe, but not by yourself. Harry Whistler had made certain quiet arrangements. Someone's almost always watching for who else might be watching. But to tell her that would have destroyed the illusion that her life here was normal once again.

He said, "It won't be a problem. You'll understand when you see him. Now hush. Just read, then we'll talk."

They read the text and the provenance of the old Berber prophecy. They read that in the opinion of Sadik and Netanya, the source of its recent revival was Belle Haven. More specifically, the source was the three Muslim runaways, the two Darvi sisters and the princess. And possibly a fourth. Perhaps Aisha.

They read about the messages from the "handmaidens" who've been spreading "She is coming" all over the world. How they'd managed to penetrate Saudi Overseas Charities and had frozen more than ten billion dollars.

"This can't be right," said Kessler to Elizabeth. "Ten billion?"

She shook her head uncertainly. "Impossible."

She read about the disk that must be in their possession. Yes, their possession. Not that of the Nasreens. Rasha had clearly kept a copy.

Netanya wrote,"This is flight money mostly, not charity money. It's the Saudi princess, Rasha, who froze it."

"You're certain?" asked Kessler.

"Who else?" replied Netanya. "But if it isn't, so what? She's the one they'll come after. The Saudi's will pressure your government to find her. Your government, if you're lucky, will begin with Roger Clew, but it won't give Clew more than a couple of days before it pulls out all the stops. The Saudis, meanwhile, will be sending their own if they manage to find out where you are. Nor, by the way, is it only the Saudis. They'll all come, and not just the Muslim fanatics. Every Muslim regime where this prophecy has caused problems will be taking a bead on your town. Especially Iran. Sadik has met with them. He thinks he's bought you some time, but not much."

Kessler started to type another question for Netanya, but Netanya was still listing the belligerents.

"There was a banker, an Englishman, in Riyadh with the prince. This was on Monday, two days ago. The banker was after that money as well. Sadik says he's from the Bohemian Club. Do you know about the Bohemian Club? Very powerful; they own half the world. Ten billion dollars should be pocket change to them. A lot of them work in big oil which is trillions. Do you begin to get the picture? This is all about oil. You won't survive a fight with big oil."

Kessler asked Elizabeth, "The Bohemian Club?"

"I've heard of it," she told him. "I don't know much about it. Netanya talks as if it's some kind of mafia. I've never heard anything like that."

"How big? How many members?"

"Maybe two or three thousand."

"Too many," said Kessler, "to be of one mind. But there are always clubs within clubs." He wrote, "Who is this banker? We need names."

"Sadik says he knows," came Netanya's reply. "Also the names of the banker's associates, both of whom are Bohemian Club members. He won't give me the names. He says nothing for nothing. This is how he got me to get him to Belle Haven. He says he'll tell you the names and maybe you will tell me. Do I have your word that you will?"

"If I can."

"Martin, maybe you were joking about changing the world. If not, you've bit off more than you can chew."

Elizabeth looked at Kessler. "Changing the world?"

"Said in jest," he told her, "before I knew about this."

"This is all news to you? Be straight with me, Martin."

"Elizabeth, I knew nothing that you didn't know. I knew that Rasha got out with some material on a disk. Here's Netanya saying that she kept a copy. If so, she broke faith with the Nasreens who saved her. Does that sound like Rasha to you?"

"No, it doesn't. But never mind that for now." She reached past Kessler, her fingers on the keyboard. She typed, "Yitzhak, it's Elizabeth. What's this about Aisha? Why would they want to hurt Aisha?"

He replied, "Elizabeth? Did you know this was happening?"

"No, damn it," she wrote, "and neither did Martin. Answer my question. Why Aisha?"

"The prophecy, Elizabeth. The Lady of the Camel in that prophecy is Aisha. If you don't know Muslim history, think Joan of Arc. Think what happened to her when she was betrayed. The English called her a heretic and they burned her."

She wrote, "I know Muslim history, but I don't know this prophecy. You say it's all over the internet?"

Netanya replied, "You can look for yourself. Do a search and you'll see. It's already making half the world crazy."

She said to Kessler. "Let's get the girls in here." But before she could open her mouth to call them, she saw the name Shahla appear on the screen. Netanya had written, "To show Shahla Darvi the harm she has done, you can tell her that her friend, a girl named Farah, died for her. This is true. Sadik was with her when she died."

Kessler read it. "Let's do this one at a time."

"Shahla first," said Elizabeth. "Let her see this."

TWENTY EIGHT

On Wednesday, Roger Clew had gone back to his office. He still had most of his day to kill before Harry's plane landed at Reagan. Harry's ETA was 3:50 PM. He decided that he'd better brief Howard Leland on all these exchanges with Harry and Yitzhak. Perhaps he wouldn't mention Sadik just yet, least of all that he was being smuggled in. He had placed a call to Leland's security detail. They would pass the message in to Leland.

It would be something more than a courtesy briefing. He wanted to know whether Haskell bought Leland's promise that Stride would find that disk for him. Also, Leland had said that he had reason to suspect that Haskell might know where Stride and Kessler are living. If Haskell does, he's almost surely got some people in Belle Haven. Maybe Leland has learned something more. He wanted to be alone in his office if and when Howard Leland returned his call. He didn't want to take it on a cell phone.

To kill some of that time, he sat through two briefings. Both, as it happened, were Mideast-related and both mentioned, as a footnote, the disquieting effect of the prophecy throughout the region. A paper in Bahrain, the English language Tribune, had run a recent feature that included a drawing of what the reborn Aisha might look like. Also of Qaila, Aisha's guardian angel. Aisha on her camel. Qaila hovering, sword in hand.

The briefer had seen State's copy of the paper. She hadn't thought it worth bringing to this meeting because it was only some artist's impression. A footnote to a footnote, so to speak. She hadn't thought that the drawing would interest him, but he saw that it had clearly interested her. She was able to describe it in detail.

The Aisha depicted was beautiful, she said. Very young and with enormous dark eyes, her expression serene and yet determined. Her eyes seemed to be looking into the soul of anyone reading that paper. She was dressed, as expected, in a flowing white robe, but the garment had been girdled at her waist and at her wrists as it might be if she were preparing for battle. Her head was wrapped in a white linen turban. The wrap's end had been brought down under her chin and then thrown back over her shoulder.

There was nothing serene, said the briefer, about Qaila. Flame-haired wasn't a color; it was actually on fire. So was the sword that she held in both hands. From the look on her face she seemed itching to use it on anyone who looked at her cross-eyed. Clew's briefer had heard that thousands of readers had made multiple copies of the drawing. They were faxing it well beyond the borders of Bahrain. It was said to be hanging in women's lavatories as far away as Malaysia.

Normally, the daily Bahraini Tribune was available in Saudi Arabia. Not this week, said his briefer. It's been banned since that drawing. Even so, a few issues had managed to slip through, carried over the connecting causeway by truckers. The Saudi censors had already been busy trying to block any reference to the prophecy.

Clew had to smile. They were always blocking something. The Saudis had thousands of low-level clerks whose job it was to run a black Magic Marker through any article that seemed critical of the regime or of its religious establishment. The job was highly labor-intensive. They'd black out the article in every single copy of every newspaper or magazine before allowing them to reach Saudi newsstands. Even Time or Newsweek. There were no exceptions. But usually not the whole edition.

The blacking-out, thought Clew, was exquisitely dumb. All it did was call the reader's attention to an article that otherwise might have been ignored. And all the reader had to do was hold the page up to the light and easily read the text underneath. Or the interested reader could find it on the internet. The Saudi censors did a fairly effective job of restricting internet access. But it was a losing battle in a wired world. Too many Saudis had satellite dishes even though they were technically illegal. Those with dishes were able to download the internet from one of the many satellites overhead. The Saudi authorities didn't dare seize those dishes because every Saudi prince had one, often several, one at each of his homes and at his office. And the dishes were sold at every shopping mall.

Clew told the briefer to bring him State's copy of the Bahrain Tribune. He knew that the drawings were only composites. They were probably closer to a thousand other women than they were to our Aisha and Elizabeth. But perhaps too close for comfort, given all those faxed copies. He thought he'd best see for himself.

The second briefing was just winding down, this one by a small team of analysts. He'd had a tray sandwiches brought in. Clew saw the light of his private line blinking. He peered at the read-out. It was Howard Leland. He asked the briefers to excuse him, take their sandwiches with them.

He picked up and said his name. He heard only a hum. Then a smacking of lips and a clearing of the throat. The hum, it turned out, was from the jet engines of Leland's State Department C-4. Leland was on his way back. Clew glanced at his watch. It was already after two. After ten on the coast. Leland had left a few hours earlier than planned.

"Sir? Are you there?"

He heard a deep sigh. "Yes, Roger. I'm here."

"Sir, I'm glad you called. I have a number of questions."

When Leland spoke again, it was as if he hadn't heard. He said, "Roger, I want you to record what I say to you. Or are you recording already?"

"No, I'm not, sir."

"Begin recording when I say 'now.' Stop recording when I say, 'We'll talk again later.' After that, we'll have a private discussion."

Clew shrugged. "Should I be silent while I am recording?"

"By no means. It must be clear that I'm speaking to you. You'll have questions, but please try to keep them to a minimum. I'm doing this to try to convince... you, to start with... that

I was not a willing participant in… well, you'll hear it all in a minute."

"I'll say the 'now' for you." Clew reached for a button. "You're being recorded starting… now."

Clew listened as Leland identified himself and gave his oath that what follows is the truth as he knows it. That said, he recounted the events of that morning. The Saudi prince in his shower. Made to look like a suicide. Almost certainly a murder. The role of Haskell's friends, the mogul and the banker, in hustling him away from the scene of the crime. Leland, himself, becoming complicit by allowing himself to be removed. Leland knowing full well that those two had arranged for a clean-up crew to obliterate any evidence that a death had occurred.

"Including the body? This is Roger Clew asking." Clew added his title, the date and the time.

"Thank you, Roger. I'm not thinking. Should have logged this myself."

"You're welcome, sir. What about that dead body?"

"Gone. Disappeared. I don't think it will be found. All that remains is a suicide note. I've seen it. I've read it. I watched it being burned. Or more likely, a facsimile thereof. I will now recite its contents from my memory of it. I wrote it down while I was being driven to the airport. I believe I have it almost verbatim."

Clew listened in growing astonishment as Leland read from his notes. Harry Whistler, Martin Kessler, the Nasreens and himself, and, of course, Howard Leland, all enemies of God and corruptors of Muslim wives and daughters. Harry Whistler "pulling the strings." All this done behind the walls of Harry's house in Belle Haven. So Haskell has known all along.

It gets worse. They're also thieves. Ten billion dollars stolen. Taken from some vast Saudi poor box. And spreaders of false prophecy – no doubt the Aisha prophecy – with the help of Sadik who is now… Netanya's mole? They're all involved in this enormous conspiracy. All evil-doers. Can't trust a one of them. Who can you trust? Charles Haskell, that's who. Everyone else should be killed.

Clew wondered if he'd heard right. "Ten billion dollars?"

"Yes, billion. With a B. Perhaps more."

"Holy shit."

Leland added, "This Sadik. I don't know that name. I don't know how he's involved."

"I'll… check out the name with Netanya."

Leland asked, "Have you heard from Elizabeth Stride?"

"No, I haven't," said Clew. "Did you tell Haskell that you spoke to her?"

"I did, but I think he knows I did not. Is she still in Belle Haven? Was he right about that?"

Damn, thought Clew. "For the moment."

"The Saudi princess as well?"

"For the moment."

"Why do you suppose… never mind. Not important."

"All of this is important. What were you about to say about the princess?"

"Oh. Not her. I was thinking of Stride. Why would she be left out of this list of transgressors? It's as if she'd been given a pass."

Clew pondered for a moment. He asked, "Haskell's words, right?"

"In the prince's handwriting. But the text could only have been Haskell's."

Clew shook his head. "I have no idea." He said, "Let's get back to this murder."

"Haskell's two associates seemed as shocked as I was to find the prince dead in my shower. I don't think it was an act. I think their shock was genuine. I'm quite sure that Haskell did it, or that he had it done, without either man's prior knowledge."

"Maybe. These other two. Who are they?"

"The banker is Sir Reginald Leeds. He's chairman of InterBank, Limited of London. His bank financed Trans-Global's early expansion. Branches all over the Mideast. The other, their spokesman on this occasion, is Huntington Bentley, the media giant. Right wing, an elitist in the extreme, divides the world into two different groups, the Bohemians and everyone else. I assume their names are not unfamiliar."

Clew jotted them down. "I've heard of Leeds. Can't recall much about him. But everyone knows Huntington Bentley."

"Then you know the extent of his media empire. It reaches a quarter of the world's population. Certainly all of the English-speaking world and, through his several satellite stations, almost everyone whose language is Arabic."

Clew was well aware it. He knew Bentley's reach. He also knew that the largest of those satellite stations, the one that broadcast out of Dubai, was a regular booster of Trans-Global Oil. It tried to hammer home that only Trans-Global had the technical competence to keep the oil flowing regardless of political uncertainties. If he checked, thought Clew, he'd probably find that InterBank Limited was similarly touted as the only bank competent to handle their revenues. They made for a very cozy threesome.

Clew wondered in passing whether Huntington Bentley also owned that Bahraini newspaper. Probably not, he decided. It would not seem to be in that threesome's interest to publicize Aisha's second coming.

"He has real power, Roger. He can make or break anyone."

"So they say. But, I gather, not you."

"Bentley promised to insulate me from all this. He made it clear how I might return the favor."

"He wants the ten billion? He thinks it's in Belle Haven?"

"Wherever it is, whoever has it, they want it. By 'they', I mean the three of them, Bentley, Haskell and Leeds, although it seems clear that a rift has developed. By 'it,' I mean a disk. The money's all on a disk."

Clew listened further as Leland explained what all he understood to be on the disk. Names of key Saudis who helped themselves to funds intended for legitimate charities. All in off-shore accounts. Flight money, certainly. Account numbers, access codes; everything. That those names, and not the money per se, were what Haskell and friends wanted most. How the prince's daughter got out with that disk. How she, only days ago, sent word to her father that she'd doctored the original files. How that disk was not only the sole record of those names, but the only means of accessing those funds by either Haskell's friends or the Saudis.

Clew told him, "I'm finding this hard to believe."

"Roger, I was there. Horse's mouth."

"Why the wild accusations of that suicide note."

"Haskell's mouth," said Leland. "Those words were his. Somehow he got the prince to write them down in my notebook. To me, the 'why' is obvious. Misdirection."

"And I'm one of the plotters?"

"In your capacity as my lackey."

"Yes, sir. I caught that." Clew couldn't help smiling. He asked, "And the prophecy? How does that figure in?"

"At the very least, it's a wonderful diversion. We know that Haskell has some scheme in the works and that it involves Saudi oil. Haskell, however, knew nothing of the prophecy. I was standing there the first time he heard of it. But give the man credit. He's fast on his feet. It's clear to me from the language of the suicide note, that he saw it as a way to keep Kessler diverted."

"Diverted from Haskell? Howard, I told you…"

"That he has no interest. Yes, Roger, I heard you. But Haskell thinks he does and that's all there is to it. What sweeter way to get even with Kessler – to say nothing of Whistler who pulls Kessler's strings - than to pit him against the whole Muslim world. Or half of it anyway. All the husbands and fathers."

"Sir…"

"Oh, I know," said Leland. "Not half. A tiny fraction. But it's still no small number. A few thousand fanatics. Enough for one hell of a diversion."

"While Haskell ingratiates himself to the rest?"

"That would seem to be his hope." Leland paused. He cleared his throat. He added, "Roger, I'm on my way home. You and I will talk again later."

Clew heard the emphasis. He shut off the recording. He said to Leland, "We're clear, sir. Go ahead."

He heard another heart-felt sigh on Leland's end. Leland said, "If only I'd listened to you. If only I'd followed those tail lights."

"If you had, I wouldn't know any of this."

"I will submit my resignation on Friday," said Leland. "My position is no longer tenable. I will then go public with all that I know. I will release the tape you just made. Doing so is the only way I can think of to thwart Haskell from using that suicide note."

"There's thwarting and there's thwarting," said Clew.

"Meaning what? Have him killed?"

"Let me deal with this, sir."

"Then what about Bentley? What about Leeds? These are three exceedingly powerful men. I suppose you could always nuke the whole Grove. That way, you'd be sure of getting all three. Reduce them all to scorched floating molecules. All copies of that note would be vaporized as well. That way, I'd be able to go merrily along without fear of being blackmailed or pilloried in the press."

"Sir…"

"Of course it would trigger a world-wide recession. All those dead CEO's. A panic on Wall Street. That might not be so bad if we time it just right. We could buy a few shares on the cheap."

"Sir, I'm going to ask you to say nothing further to anyone else on this matter. You said Friday; today's Wednesday. Give me those two days."

Another long silence. Then, "Could it be true?"

"Um… what part of it, sir?"

"Could Haskell be right? Could it be Harry Whistler? Could Whistler be moving against the Saudi royals? Could he be in competition with Haskell after all?"

"No."

Leland's voice strengthened. "Just no? You're that sure? He has those girls in his house. He has Aisha in his house. How do you know he's not using that prophecy to distract the Saudis—no, the whole Muslim world—while he pursues a scheme of his own?"

It was Clew's turn to sigh. "I'll look into it."

Clew could hear Leland drumming his fingers. When he spoke again, his voice had a weariness to it.

Leland said, "I will hope to hear from you, Roger, before I hand my letter to the president. Whatever the truth, there's one fact that's inescapable. I have dishonored myself and the office I hold by not summoning the authorities to that room at once."

Clew could have argued, but it would have been no use. He could see in his mind the ghost of Howard Leland's father standing at the shoulder of his eldest son. He was saying, "You must do what is expected of you, Howard. You must always do the honorable thing."

But Clew saw his own father materializing and saying to the other, "What is it with you people?"

Then Leland's father lifting his chin and saying, "I beg your pardon?"

"Your son was set up. You want him to roll over? I've got news for you, pal. You get hit, you hit back. You play to win. Look at my kid. He's a devious little bastard, Can't fight worth two shits man to man, but he wins. I remember one time..."

"Pop... shut the fuck up."

"Roger?" Leland's voice. "Did you just say something?"

Oh, Christ. "I said buck up, sir. We'll talk when you get here."

"I won't be stopping at the office today. I need to spend some time with my wife."

"By all means. We'll talk tomorrow. Until then, sir."

Clew sat back in his chair. He replayed the recording. Leland wants to release this? In a pig's ass. He looked at the time. He saw that he had almost an hour before he had to leave for the airport.

He called the researcher who'd given the first briefing. She's a good one. Name's Tatiana. Twenty years in foreign service. She, and both her parents before her.

He read off the names, Haskell, Bentley and Leeds. "I want everything we have. All their holdings, where they live, where they work, where they play."

"Tax records?" asked Tatiana. "For those I'll need your signature."

"Come and get it. Oh, and add Rajib Sadik." He spelled the name. "Find good recent photos of all four. And don't forget that issue of the Bahrain Tribune."

"I'm on it. How soon?"

"You've got less than an hour."

"Sir?"

"Can't help it. Things are starting to pop.

TWENTY NINE

If Elizabeth had been asked to guess who had caused this, she supposed that she would have guessed Shahla. Frightfully abused at the hands of her father. Abused by a system that allowed him to pimp her. Abused by two weekend "husbands," business contacts of her father's, who saw not a person, but a firm young body. He'd told both of them that she was a virgin. Shahla's mother was too weak to stop it. Or as the Nasreens had put it, too ground down.

The scars that this left were still plain to see. Shahla often tensed up in the company of men unless at least two other women were present. But Shahla had the tools to get even.

Shahla, of the two, was the serious one. At nineteen, she'd already reached her senior year in college. She'd carried two majors, Journalism, Social Sciences. She'd had several essays published on the need for reform and especially on feminist issues. The papers that printed them kept getting shut down, but she'd achieved a measure of celebrity. In Iran, these days, reformist journalists are like rock stars. Nearly half the population's under twenty. She'd been arrested twice, treated roughly, then released. The arrests only added to her stature.

Shahla's father, some minor official, had apparently been pressured to control her or else. That's probably when he started renting her out. After the first time, she applied to the Nasreens. She was accepted, but not before the second. She gathered the usual insurance material concerning some of her father's business dealings.

Whatever the reason, all arrangements had been made for her to get out of Iran. The time and place of the rendezvous was set. But Niki, her sister, had followed her there and threatened to blow any chance of escape unless Shahla agreed to take her with her. The Nasreens didn't want her. They were ready to abort. They thought that Niki was just another sullen teenager. Immature, self-absorbed, an indifferent student, perhaps jealous of her more accomplished sister.

Shahla told the Nasreens that she understood. They hadn't bargained or planned for her sister. But Niki had apparently burned a few bridges making sure that they couldn't go back. Shahla told the Nasreens that they'd try on their own. If they could reach the border and get past the minefields, they would cross into Kurdish Iraq. The Nasreens relented. They took Niki.

Elizabeth brought Shahla into the study and sat her in front of the computer screen. Shahla asked, "What is it? Do I have some mail?" She showed no hint of unease.

Elizabeth told her, "Just read."

Shahla saw the name Farah. It caused her to smile. But then as she read the message that spoke of her, the color drained from her face. She covered her mouth. She couldn't speak.

"She died for refusing to say where you are. They knew that you'd been emailing your friends in Tehran even though you were warned against doing so." Elizabeth reached past her to scroll through the messages. She said to Shahla, "Keep reading."

Shahla did so. Blinking. Rapidly blinking. Her head began shaking from side to side as in disbelief at the words on the screen.

Elizabeth said to her, "Let's hear it."

She said, "I... don't know what you want me to say. I never knew any of this."

"You did write to your friends, did you not?"

Shahla looked up at her. "Never. Not once."

Kessler said to her, "Shahla... you signed your name. These were all your friends. You not only told them that the prophecy was real, you claimed to be the handmaiden of 'she who has come.' There doesn't seem much point in denying it."

A low moan arose from deep within Shahla. She began rocking back and forth in her chair. The moan increased in volume. It went up in pitch. First a wail. Then a scream. The scream was "Niki!!"

It was Niki. Always Niki. And acting alone. Within the hour, they'd pieced it together, having gathered all four girls in the study. First came the prophecy. How had that started? The beginning, it seems, was entirely innocent. Just four girls chatting. It occurred soon after the sisters and Rasha arrived at the Hilton Head facility. Aisha had been assigned as their counselor. Rasha had asked Aisha if she'd heard of the prophecy, her name being Aisha and all. Aisha remembered hearing about it while she was a child back in Cairo. Aisha and Rasha were both aware that a lot of Sunni girls are named Aisha. And many of their mothers would have told them the story of Mohammed's young warrior wife. Some of those mothers would have told them of the prophecy.

Rasha said, "It was never, 'Hey, maybe it's you.' It was more about being proud of the name and being guided by Aisha's example."

How is it that Rasha knew of this prophecy? She had come across it back in Riyadh. She was doing a paper on the Berbers for school. She got interested in Muhammad ibn-Tumart because he believed in women's' rights. Within limits. She says she never thought much more about it.

But then she met Aisha, the first Aisha she'd known. Now she remembered little clues in the text that seemed to fit her new friend. Aisha was young, not yet at full womanhood. Aisha was dressed in white when they met and was usually in tennis clothes thereafter. Then, of course, there was that East and West business. On top of all this, she thought Aisha was beautiful. The text did not describe her as such, but physical beauty is assumed in such cases. "Pure of heart" also seemed to fit the bill. As did Elizabeth, Aisha's friend and protector. Protectors are like guardian angels.

To Aisha and Shahla, this was just conversation. To Aisha, it was also embarrassing. Especially the part about how beautiful she was. She could have done without the "Pure of heart" as well. This led to some ribbing, according to Rasha. She said none of them took it to heart. Niki, however, had asked Shahla at one point, "Don't you wish this was true?" She asked, "Don't you wish you could be there when she comes to Tehran and calls our dear father to account?" But Shahla had no wish to revisit that subject. She thought that was the end of it. It wasn't.

Niki had asked Rasha where she found the text. Niki told her of a web site, some Moroccan museum. Nike found it later on her own computer. On a whim, she started to spread it. She sent it first to an Internet Café that she'd used a few times in Tehran. But it was Shahla who'd used that café the most often. It's where she'd written and distributed her essays. Most other girls who used it were her friends, not Niki's.

Niki was never a popular kid. Even girls of her own age thought her to be sly. Being overweight didn't help either. Shahla had many friends. Her sister did not. Niki sent this mail to Shahla's friends, all of whom she knew, and pretended that she was Shahla. She knew that they wouldn't take it seriously from her, but they'd believe a message from Shahla.

Niki was quaking as she made this admission. She kept her eyes on the floor. She could not look at Shahla.

But no harm was done at first. The authorities took no notice. At the start, Niki's messages got lost in the crowd of a millions of messages on thousands of sites. Weeks went by before it started to snowball. Did Shahla's friends believe it? Perhaps. More likely not. But for some it was fun to consider and pass on. Niki did prime the pump and she did keep it flowing, but it quickly took on a life of its own. Soon on some of those web sites there were clerics and scholars debating the prophecy's legitimacy and some of them were actually confirming it. On others, Muslim women were arguing with each other over who needs Aisha's help and who doesn't.

Now the authorities were forced to take notice. Arrests were made at the Internet Café. If it wasn't the source, it's from where it was spread. The source was found to be a young woman named Shahla who claimed to be the first among Aisha's handmaidens. Her friend Farah was arrested, lashed out of her mind. Did Farah believe it? Perhaps not at first. Sadik said that, in her pain, she began to hallucinate. Aisha, he thought, became real to her. She was also determined not to betray this handmaiden who she thought was her childhood friend, Shahla.

It was Niki as well who stole the ten billion. Or rather, primarily Niki.

The Darvi sisters and Rasha had first met in France, at a Nasreen safe house in Toulon. They stayed there for two or three days. While there, they were encouraged to email their families to say they were safe but would not be coming back.

Both Shahla and Rasha brought computer disks with them. They both turned them over to the Nasreens because that was part of the agreement. They told the Nasreens, in broad strokes, what was on them. The Nasreens checked them out on the safe house computer, but only to see that they were readable.

Elizabeth said to Kessler, "That's all they do with them. As a rule, they never make use of them unless…"

"Unless they need the leverage, I know."

And that was that. Or that seemed to be that. A few days later, all three were in South Carolina. A few weeks after that they had moved to Belle Haven. Each girl was given an on-line computer. This was for home schooling primarily. They were given a list of firm do's and don'ts. The biggest 'don't' was letting anyone know where they were. No contact with friends or family back home unless it went through the Elizabeth and then the Nasreens.

Which Niki ignored.

Well, in fairness, not entirely, thought Kessler. She insists that she never said where she was. But she did do a search of several Islamist web sites to see who, if anyone, was looking for them. All she did was type in each of their names. The only hits she got were in reference to Rasha. The source, she said, was one of Rasha's male relatives who was apparently directing the search for her. He'd eventually enlisted the Wahhabi Hasheem. The cousin listed several places where she might have been taken. One was the safe house on Hilton Head Island. It was, however, well down the list because it was thought to be more of a dispersal point than any sort of permanent location.

Even so, she decided that was getting too close. She should have told Elizabeth, but she didn't. She told Rasha, however. She brought her up to her room. She showed her all the traffic between this cousin and the Saudi sheik who heads the Hasheem. This would not have been possible on an ordinary computer, but this was Harry's system. It was not ordinary. Niki asked Rasha what made her so important that they'd send the Hasheem after her. She knew that Rasha was a princess. She also knew that in her case that was not so big a deal. Was all this because she'd been promised to this sheik? It seemed there had to be more than his wounded pride at stake for such a wide hunt to be justified.

She then asked Rasha what was on the disk that she'd given the Nasreens in Toulon. Rasha told her about Saudi Overseas Charities. Hundreds of numbered off-shore accounts, much of that money embezzled. She said her father knew that she'd copied those files because she'd told him when she emailed him from Toulon. She'd promised that she wouldn't tell anyone she had them unless any harm should come to her mother and as long as he left her alone.

But now all bets were off as far as Niki was concerned. The problem was that the Nasreens had the disk. Rasha hadn't kept a copy after all. They could go to Elizabeth, have Elizabeth get it back. But Niki thought it was probably useless by now. The Saudis would surely have hidden that money or at least changed the passwords to get into their system. Rasha agreed that somebody might have, but not her father; he wouldn't know how. Nor did she think he'd tell anyone else. If he did, he knew they'd crucify him. Well, not crucify, thought Kessler. They don't do crosses. But beheading was not out of the question.

Niki said that if it's true that no-one else has changed the passwords, maybe Rasha could still get into those files. As she'd seen, Harry's system could get in almost anywhere. Rasha didn't want to try it without clearance from Elizabeth, but Elizabeth, at the time, and this was only last Saturday–had gone out to the gym, as had Kessler. Niki said, 'Let's at least see if it's still there.' Rasha agreed to go only that far. The web address hadn't changed for Saudi Overseas Charities. In short order she saw that the passwords hadn't either. Rasha saw that almost nothing had changed except that some of the balances had grown larger.

Niki asked Rasha whether she could get at it. Could they help themselves to some of that money. Rasha said that she could, but she wouldn't. For one thing, some of those accounts were legitimate. Rasha wasn't sure which was which. For another, although a transfer was possible, transfer it where? She had no place to put it. She had no account of her own. Niki's answer?

She said, "But Martin does. And Elizabeth does. And Elizabeth has no love for the Saudis."

Rasha says that she told her, "Not all Saudis, Niki. Only men. And only some. Don't forget that my mother's a Saudi."

She said that Niki answered, "I have a mother, too. And mine didn't do a thing to help Shahla. She wouldn't have stood up for me either."

"Well, mine has done everything for me."

Rasha, aware that this could well hurt her mother, told Niki to leave it alone. She wasn't about to take their money. Niki, however, had a suggestion. She was looking at columns, names, numbers and amounts, and asked Rasha if Rasha could scramble them herself. Rasha said that she could, but what good would that do? Niki said that way she'd have the only original. She could let her father know what she'd done. She could tell him that she'd put them back as they were if he promised to call off the hunt.

Rasha wasn't convinced. Her father's promise would be worthless. Niki argued that it was still worth a shot. After all, if Rasha's family did manage to track her, they'd have found Niki and her sister as well. The hunters might decide that in order to get at them, they'd need to kill Elizabeth and Martin.

This last was almost enough to sway Rasha. An idea of her own put her over the top. She would insist that her mother arrive safely in Toulon before any of these funds could be touched. She scrambled the accounts. It took her only ten minutes. In that time, she changed two of the passwords as well. She deleted all the names and the bank codes. But first she downloaded the original file so that it could be restored if her father behaved. In the meantime, that ten billion was frozen. She then sent the message to her father. She sent it through this cousin who was handling the search. She included the address of an Islamic website that routinely took personal messages. She said she would watch for his answer.

There was no reply yet. Nothing as of this morning. She'd hoped for at least a progress report regarding the arrangements for her mother's departure. In the meantime, Niki was busy.

The scrambling had been done on her computer, not Rasha's. As soon as Rasha was out of the room, Niki downloaded the file once again. She now had the new passwords. She changed two of them again. She had her own plans for these new ones. She left the first one so that others could get in, but only far enough to see the message, "She Is Coming."

She entered that message and a lot more. Niki knew that someone would check right away to see whether Rasha had done as she'd claimed. Next they'd try to circumvent the new passwords. So Niki, on her own, planned an ambush. According to Netanya, the next person who tried was some banker who showed up in Riyadh with her father. Niki was ready for them.

She identified herself as one of Aisha's handmaidens. She implied that this was done at Aisha's direction. She called them hypocrites and thieves. She said that when Aisha comes, which could be any day now, she'll begin by taking back the ten billion.

Elizabeth asked Niki, "Where is that disk now?"

She barely whispered her answer. "On my hard drive. In my room."

"How many copies? God help you if you lie."

"Only one. I made a back-up. Not for any bad purpose. It's a good idea to always..."

She said, "Martin, please go with her. Take Rasha. Make sure." She said, "Shahla, my apologies. I judged you too quickly."

Shahla waved it off. "I could see how you would."

Elizabeth spread her arms. Shahla entered them. They hugged. Elizabeth said, "Niki, go to the library. Shut the door. Sit and think. Do not set foot out of that room."

Niki asked her, chin quivering, "Will you send me away?"

"Just get out of my sight," said Elizabeth.

Niki left them, shoulders hunched, racked with sobs.

Aisha, all this time, had said hardly a word. Now she asked in a halting voice, "Will they... think that I am Aisha reborn? If they do, they'll think you must be Qaila."

She said, "Don't worry. We're going to fix this. We'll decide what to do when Harry gets here with the others." She added, "In the meantime, today's still your birthday. Go and change. It's too late to play tennis, but we're still going shopping. We'll have some time alone. Just the two of us."

Aisha left. Walking slowly. She closed the study door behind her. Shahla said to Elizabeth, "She's scared."

"I could see that."

Shahla said, "Yes, but I'm not sure you know why. Did you know that her mother comes to see her in her dreams? Did you know that they have long conversations?"

"She's told me."

"Aisha dreamed of her last night. She was telling us after prayers. She said her mother was telling her that today would be special. Special beyond anything Aisha could imagine. Her mother told her how proud she is of her."

"Referring to Aisha's sixteenth, though," said Elizabeth. "Not about all this other nonsense."

"No, no mention of the prophecy. No mention of the money. That would really have been spooky if there were. Aisha thought that she meant her party at Mangiamo. She already knew it would be extra special when she learned that Mr. Whistler would be flying in for it. That's why she asked her mother what more was going to happen that would be beyond her wildest dreams. All her mother would say was, 'Wait and see.' My first thought was that maybe you'll be teaching her to drive. You can drive at sixteen in Virginia."

Elizabeth nodded. "We did have a learner's permit in mind. Martin planned to start teaching her this weekend."

"Well, that's all I wondered. But you saw what came next."

"You said no one was serious when you talked about the prophecy."

Shahla answered, "We weren't. Least of all Aisha. But here's all this happening today, on her birthday, right down to the tennis whites she's wearing. Here's Aisha – she can't help it – she's starting to wonder whether this is what her mother was talking about."

Elizabeth made a face. "It was only a dream."

"She was staring at you after you scrolled back and read the text of prophecy aloud. The angel Qaila doesn't turn up out of nowhere. She's been there all along. She's been guiding her, protecting her until she comes of age."

"Uh-huh. And on that day, Qaila springs it on the kid that she is the Lady of the Camel?"

"On her birthday," said Shahla. "Maybe this one."

Elizabeth waved a hand. This was just too ridiculous. She said to Shahla, "She's too bright to believe that."

"She is very bright. She's other things, too. She's a kid, but a very spiritual kid. And… don't laugh, but she's almost too pretty to be real. Perfect teeth, no fillings, big brown eyes like a deer. Have you noticed her skin? Not a mark. Not a blemish. If I were to imagine Aisha reborn, our Aisha is what I would imagine."

"Angels shouldn't have any blemishes either. I've got enough for the two of us."

Elizabeth checked her watch. Harry wouldn't get here until five at the earliest. Not much time to meet. The party's at seven. But still plenty of time to go shopping with Aisha. There's a Lord & Taylor up at Landmark Mall. Aisha could use the distraction.

She said to Shahla, "I was thinking of a whole new look for her. A grown woman's look. A black cocktail dress. One that shows off a little of that skin that's so perfect."

Shahla brightened. "With high heels. She says she's never had heels."

"And light on the accessories. A silver herringbone chain. Silver earrings with black onyx. Or maybe black pearls. Simple. Understated. Less is more."

Shahla said, "Just don't let her pick anything white."

"I think she's got the message," said Elizabeth.

"Would you like me to come? It might put her more at ease."

"No, you stay here and keep an eye on your sister. I'd feel better if you all stay inside."

And out of sight, thought Elizabeth, from anyone watching. She'd had a feeling, several days now, that she'd had a shadow. That old pickup truck. Seen in too many places. She'd seen it again Monday when she left Mangiamo. She'd seen it through the mirror of her compact. To make sure, she'd changed her route, made a random turn. When the driver didn't follow, she felt a bit silly. No one uses a pickup for a tail. But there was that other one. The silver Ford Escape. She'd also seen that one in too many places. But at one time it looked like it was following the pickup. It probably wasn't. She'd been at this too long. Too much looking over her shoulder.

Elizabeth's face took on a wistful expression. Shahla saw it. She asked, "Is something else wrong?"

"Just thinking," said Elizabeth. "Who would believe this? Who would believe that one girl did all this?"

Shahla dropped her eyes. There seemed nothing to say.

"One girl with a computer, the whole world within reach. One girl might be turning that whole world upside down. Who's going to believe it? Would you?"

Shahla sighed. "Not if I hadn't seen it,"

"You like to write essays? There's the subject for your next one. One girl. A good computer. Too much time on her hands."

Talk about doomsday devices.

THIRTY

"You rascals," said the note that Haskell had left. "We must have a good long talk when I get back."

Haskell had left it at the front desk, to be given to either the banker or the mogul when next they returned to the cabin. They had gone there promptly after seeing Leland off. They had rehearsed what they hoped would be a rational discussion concerning the actions they had taken.

"Back?" asked the mogul. He was speaking to the desk clerk. "Back from where? Did he say where he was going?"

"All I know is to the airport. He asked to be driven."

"Sacramento?"

"Yes, sir. He has his corporate jet there."

"So do most of us," said the mogul, "but does he intend to use it? Did he call from your desk to have it readied?"

"No, sir, but he could have done that from the limo. He only stopped long enough to dash off that note. I assumed that some urgent business matter had arisen. But I think he's only gone for the day."

"Why is that?"

"All he carried was a briefcase. No overnight bag. And he'd changed into a dark business suit."

"I see," said the mogul. He said, "Thank you," to the clerk. He took the banker aside. He lowered his voice.

"I'd have thought that Charles, having realized what we've done, had rushed off to try to catch Howard Leland. Show Leland that the note's not destroyed after all. Charles would have made a copy of his own."

"Except for…"

"I know. The business suit and the briefcase."

The banker nodded. "And taking the time to change. That would seem to rule out chasing Leland."

"So he has flown off somewhere. Still, why the suit? One dresses for function or one dresses for effect. I'm sure it's an elegant well-tailored suit, but who on earth would Charles be hoping to impress any more than he would in what he's worn here?"

"Perhaps not to impress. Perhaps more to fit in."

"To not seem out of place?" asked the mogul. "That makes sense. Who and where, though?"

"Well, it's not to call a meeting of his board of directors. He's gone to see someone who could further his cause."

"You're thinking Kessler?" asked the mogul. "To try to deal with him directly?"

"Telling him, 'Here's the note. Get me the disk or I release it.'"

"He'd release it regardless. Kessler would know that, as would Harry Whistler. Besides we still come back to the question of that suit. I doubt that Kessler enforces a dress code."

The mogul pondered. "If not those two, perhaps Roger Clew. Fly to Washington; show Clew what he has on Clew's boss. Perhaps even getting there before Leland. A nice suit would certainly fit in at State. He'd do this hoping that Clew is sufficiently loyal to bail Leland out by delivering that disk."

"Or getting Clew to get Kessler to do so."

The mogul growled within himself. He didn't like this at all. If they'd had the chance to sit down with Haskell, they might have persuaded him to listen to reason. And then, if this works, to forgive and forget. But that chance is blown. Haskell's off on his own. Haskell now has all day to reflect on their "rascality." Don't bet on him forgiving and forgetting… unless…

"Tell you what," said the mogul. "Let's assume he's back tonight. I'll wait up for him; you needn't. I know the man better and I know that he unnerves you. Leave Charles Haskell to me."

"You and Charles? Alone?"

"You and I will talk at breakfast."

"Tomorrow morning?" asked the banker.

"First thing," said the mogul. "Clearer heads. A few things settled."

"I… suppose you're right," said the banker. "You don't need me. You truly are so much better with Haskell than I am."

The mogul heard the hesitation. He said, "Listen to me. You and I need each other. The question is, do we need Charles Haskell? His companies have no shortage of ambitious executives who would readily fill any void. As a matter of fact, I have one in mind. My good friend at Scorpion Systems."

"The man whose firm you found for Haskell? Would he turn against him?"

"Against him? My dear man, he's never been for him. He reports to me. Always has."

The banker could only stare.

The mogul said, "We must face it. Charles is out of control. And if we play our cards right, he's superfluous."

"Are you saying…?

"You need to hear it in plain language? Very well," said the mogul. "We get him before he brings us down with him. And certainly before he gets us."

The banker felt his stomach rising into his throat. My God. What now? First, it's the prince who was no longer needed. Now it's Charles Haskell who's superfluous? And as for the two of them needing each other, that is no longer true either. His own role had been to get at those Saudi names and then siphon that ten billion off through his bank. To then launder the money through his several Mideast branches. But the money that had sat in Saudi Overseas Charities isn't there anymore for all practical purposes. Whether or not they get their hands on that disk, he is now the least needed of the three.

Oh, dear, thought the banker.

Still another thought struck him. This one even more troubling. He remembered what the mogul had once said of Roger Clew. Unlike Charles, his stock in trade isn't killing people off. It's in getting rival factions to do the job for him. Could it be? Is it possible? Is he pulling the strings here?

No. Don't be silly. Get hold of yourself. There's no unseen hand. They're doing all this to themselves.

"Are you all right?" asked the mogul.

"Hmm? Yes, quite," said the banker.

"Well? Did you hear me? Did you hear what I said?"

"Before he gets us. Yes, quite plainly."

"Do you agree?"

"You know best. You always do. But this sort of thing isn't..."

"Your cup of tea. I know that. Leave this to me."

"How would you... when would you...?"

"All in good time. I'll talk to Charles when he returns. I'll calm him. Reassure him. Then I'll make the necessary arrangements."

The banker's thoughts had gone beyond his own fear of Haskell. He was almost more afraid of the mogul. He now wondered whether he would ever see breakfast. Whether he, himself, would be found in his shower. Whether he'd be found at all, for that matter. Whether his room would be all squeaky clean as if it had never been occupied.

Would they dare? A second time? Two calls in two days to the Maintenance Chief?

Crazy.

Impossible.

Not a member of his standing. He was Reginald Leeds. Sir Reginald Leeds. He wasn't some minor Saudi prince.

Nor, for that matter was Huntington Bentley and Bentley could end up deceased just as easily if Haskell should see through his "reassurance."

Oh, dear indeed. This doesn't bode well. Yes, he'd sleep, wait 'til morning, but he wouldn't sleep here. He'd find a bed in a cabin half a mile away. Or a lobby couch. A laundry pile if need be.

He said to the mogul, "By all means, you deal with him."

We'll see which of us makes it to breakfast.

THIRTY ONE

Gilhooley was about to make a pass of the house as he'd done a few times every day. One never knows what one might see. As he approached the curve that would put it in view, he happened to glance in his rear view mirror. He spotted what looked like the Greek's Ford Escape. It was some three streets behind him.

He slowed. It slowed. Yes, it's probably the Greek. He looked ahead, and damn it, there's the green Subaru just now coming out through the gate. He saw two women in it, or a woman and a girl. The blond at the wheel was definitely the one in whom Haskell has such a great interest. She turned left, away from him. He couldn't very well follow with that little prick behind him. The Greek must be headed for that house.

Mulazim's full attention was on this Gilhooley. He saw Gilhooley slow. Had he been seen? Perhaps not. Gilhooley's head didn't seem to have moved. He was looking at the road straight in front of him.

Now Mulazim saw it. The green Subaru. It suddenly appeared. It was not there before. It must have come from one of the houses nearby. Which one though? It could be one of several, all big.

He cursed Gilhooley for slowing when he did. If he hadn't, Mulazim would have seen from which driveway it came or at least from which side of the street. Is it one of the two that have white columns in front? Is it the one brown shingles? Is it the one of brick and stone with wooden beams and a gate? He could see two... no, three that have gates. Mulazim growled within himself. There was no way to know. But at least he had narrowed his search.

The green Subaru had now turned out of sight. Gilhooley hadn't followed. He'd turned off to the left. So, Mulazim wondered, why had he come here? He didn't know the answer, but one thing was certain. This Gilhooley was going to be a problem for him. If the opportunity presented itself, he'd be tempted to get rid of him once and for all.

But, no, another dead man would not be good. Not so soon. So be patient. Be calm.

Gilhooley turned to see whether the Greek would follow either him or the green Subaru. The Greek had done neither. No sign of him. The next time he saw that Greek's Ford Escape, he'd make sure that it needed a tow.

He was still on that thought when his cell phone vibrated. There was no need to see who was calling. It could only be Haskell.

He answered it, "Gilhooley."

"New instructions," said Haskell, "Buy a video camera. One that goes from wide angle to zoom."

"Buy one? I got one. Right here in the truck."

"Records audio as well? My own voice while I'm taping?"

"Records anything within fifty feet or so."

"That should do it," said Haskell. "How much Semtex do you have?"

"With me? Almost two kilos."

"That's what? Four pounds? It doesn't sound like very much."

Gilhooley was beginning to get a bad feeling "Not enough for Whistler's house, if that's what you're thinking."

"I'm not. We're not vandals. It's too nice a house."

"So that rules out swastikas sprayed on its front wall."

"Gilhooley… are you trying to be funny?"

"Just trying to get on the same page, Mr. Haskell. If you're thinking their cars, I've got plenty for that. I could rig them any time I see them parked around town."

"No," said Haskell, "that's too willy-nilly. I'm thinking in terms of a gathering place. Do you have enough for that restaurant?"

"For Mangiamo? Yeah, I guess, but…"

"You're going to blow it," said Haskell. "Actually we are. I'm on my way there. I should be landing in D.C. around five-ish, your time. What's it like across the street from that restaurant?"

"Just… regular commercial. One and two stories. There's a real estate office. A law firm. A bakery."

"Is there a place of concealment from which we could tape it?"

"Tape… what? The bar?"

"Well, yes," said Haskell. "That's the whole idea. Tape who shows up for this party they're having and tape the whole building collapsing on them."

"You want to hit a birthday party? A party for kids?"

"These are not just kids. They are enemies of Islam. That is to say they are enemies of God. Paradise awaits those who slay them."

What is this, Gilhooley wondered? Has he gone fucking nuts?

But Haskell had expected a degree of reluctance. He said, "Okay, that God part was over the top. The main thing is that Kessler will be there. And you'll never guess who else. Roger Clew is coming. So is a meddler named Rajib Sadik. And, best of all… are you ready for this? Harry Whistler himself will be joining them."

Gilhooley knew about Whistler. He'd heard the bartender say it. But it's the first he'd heard about Clew and some Arab. He asked, "Who told you this? Leland?"

"No, he didn't. Nor would he. He's been less than a friend. But happily we have our little birds."

Gilhooley took that to mean he had someone at State. People in Clew's position don't go out for a haircut without leaving word where they can be reached.

He said, "Look… I'm on a cell phone. It isn't secure. This might not be a private conversation."

"Not to worry," said Haskell. "It's secure on my end. Our words are not floating out there in the ether. I'm assured that only gibberish could be overheard. It's spatial harmonics. Or something like that. I leave the tech nitty-gritty to others."

"If you say so."

"Vantage points, Desmond. You still haven't answered."

"Well, let's see. There's not much. There are always parked cars. Not directly across though because there's a bus stop. But the bus stop has one of those shelters with a bench. It's maybe thirty yards down the street."

Haskell asked, "Glass enclosed? Or is it solid?"

"Solid except for one side that's plastic."

"So that those waiting can see the bus coming. That might do very nicely. Meet me there at six o'clock. You will have planted the explosives in the back among those tables. I'm relying on your vaunted expertise."

"I'll think of something."

"We'll work the logistics out when I see you. Oh, one more thing. Elizabeth Stride. I've decided that she is to be a survivor. She's not even to be smudged if we can help it."

Gilhooley grunted. "I wondered why you didn't mention her. I thought maybe she wouldn't be there."

"Count on it. She'll be there. I have other plans for her. I know how we might spare her. Tell you later."

A click.

Gilhooley stared at his now lifeless cell phone. Haskell's actually coming? He wants this on tape? He wants to kill Whistler, Kessler and Clew, not to mention those four Muslim girls and the Arab. That's a hell of a hit. World class. Lots of headlines. If there's even a whisper about who's behind it, where does Haskell think he can hide? Does he think he's some kind of national treasure just because he supplies oil?

My "vaunted expertise," thought Gilhooley.

Shit.

Blowing up is blowing up. It does not get selective. But Haskell wants this thing fucking choreographed so his dream girl gets out without a scratch. He has other plans for her? She might have some for him. Haskell hadn't told him hardly anything about her, but if she hangs out with Kessler and that crowd she's got to be more than some groupie. Could he possibly think she'll just waltz off with him? She'll turn him into a grease spot.

But, okay. He'll plant the charge. He knows a good spot. He'll meet Haskell at six with his video camera. Maybe he can get Haskell to understand the basic concept of overkill. Not to mention the concept of survival.

Failing that, okay, we blow the bar, he makes his movie. Maybe Stride survives it, maybe she doesn't. He, Gilhooley, won't know if she does or not because he won't be hanging around to find out.

Once that blast goes off, he is gone.

THIRTY TWO

Elizabeth had seen the black pickup again. It had almost seemed to be waiting down the road for her to drive out through the gates. But it hadn't followed. It slowed, then turned off.

A tail only does that when there are at least two. The spotter, the pickup, then radios ahead for some other vehicle to take it from there. The other vehicle would then appear in her mirror unless its driver was good at the job. A good one would have pulled out a block or more in front of her, watching her while she's watching behind her. A good one would also be a woman, quite possibly. In an unremarkable car, blue or tan. No one ever seems to look for a woman.

But there was no one. She was sure of it now. She had gone two full miles, made a number of turns, and had seen no sign of surveillance. She reached her left hand to the door's side compartment. She felt to make sure that the weapons she kept there were unencumbered by road maps. Her Ingram Mac-10, a light machine pistol. She also fingered the hilt of her knife, a twin of the one in her purse.

Aisha didn't know that the weapons were there. Or knew and kept silent. The former, most likely. But Aisha saw that she was driving with uncommon alertness. She asked outright, "Are we being followed?"

"No, honey. It's me. I'm just a bit spooked. An hour ago, not a care in the world. You didn't need this on your birthday."

Aisha was silent for another mile or so. Elizabeth broke the ice. She said, "Shahla told me about your dream. About what your mother said to you."

"She tells me a lot of things, Elizabeth."

"But… you do understand that they're only dreams?"

"I guess, but I don't choose to think of them that way. I like feeling that's she's with me. That she's watching out for me. I like wanting her to be proud of me."

"I'm sure that she is. More than proud."

A small smile. "You think that she would be. Not that she is. I know that you're not buying into this, Elizabeth. I don't think you believe that there's anything else out there. Or are you hoping that there isn't?"

"Better not be. I've run up quite a bill."

"And you'll be weighed in the balance and found wanting? Is that it? That won't happen. You're kind, Elizabeth. You're strong, but you're kind. You and Martin defend people who aren't so strong. That will tip the balance, believe me."

"We'll see."

"In these dreams, my mother tells me what's already in my heart or at least at the back of my mind. But she does throw in a surprise now and then. She says there is tennis in heaven."

"Oh, good."

"She plays with my father in a group that they've formed. Do I really believe that? I do and I don't. But it is a pretty thought, so I'm keeping it."

Aisha said nothing for another half mile. Elizabeth wasn't sure how to broach the other subject. She said to Aisha, "Go ahead. Ask me."

Aisha shook her head. "I don't need to, Elizabeth."

"Because you trust me?"

"With my life."

"Well, you'd trust Qaila, too. So ask. Get it out of your system."

Aisha took a breath. She said, "Okay. Let's suppose you were Qaila."

"Uh-huh. Let's suppose. Would I know that?"

"Well, sure."

"I don't and I'm not, but let's say I am. I'm now revealing it to you right here in this car. I'm telling you that you're Aisha reborn. What happens right now, right this minute?"

"I don't follow."

"Remember the language of the prophecy," said Elizabeth. "It says you'll know that it's true because a veil will be lifted. It does not mean tomorrow. It means now as I speak. Do you feel a veil being lifted?"

"A weight off my shoulders. Does that count?"

"A veil is not a weight. Besides, there's more. Will you be reaching full womanhood today?"

"You're my idea of full womanhood, Elizabeth."

"Keep that thought. You've got twenty years to go."

That made Aisha smile. She was starting to relax. But the smile came and went. "Would you lie to me, Elizabeth?"

"Never have. Never will."

"Not ever? You promise?"

"There are things that I might elect not to tell you, but this, you may be sure, isn't one of them."

Another silence. Another few blocks. Aisha said, "When we get to Lord & Taylor, I'm going to shoplift some jewelry."

"Say what?"

"I'll be really bad at it, so I'll promptly get busted. I'll make a big scene. I'll smash the display case. What I need is a criminal record. And a mug shot."

"Because Aisha reborn doesn't shoplift. I get you," said Elizabeth. "Come to think of it, that's not a bad plan."

"I like it."

"Could you wait, though," said Elizabeth, "until we've actually bought things? We'll be running tight on time as it is."

"It depends. We won't be shopping in Junior Miss, will we?"

"Not a chance."

"Can I get heels?"

"They're already on the list," said Elizabeth. "Shiny black ones. And a black cocktail dress with spaghetti straps, bare shoulders. Would Aisha reborn be caught dead in that outfit?"

"Not a chance."

"Well, there you have it. Case closed?"

"Case closed."

The Landmark Mall was just coming into view.

Aisha reached a hand to Elizabeth's arm.

She said, "I love you, Elizabeth. So does God. Or he will."

"Ask your mother to put in a good word."

THIRTY THREE

Clew was waiting on the tarmac with his Lincoln stretch limo when Harry Whistler's Gulfstream rolled to a stop near one of the more distant hangars. Clew stepped out of the limo, his briefcase in hand, drumming one finger against it.

There could be no mistaking Harry Whistler's several aircraft. They all bore his initials in red trimmed with gold. On the Gulfstream they stood five feet high. Nor was there any mistaking Harry Whistler when he appeared in the hatchway. A great bear of a man with a Hemmingway beard. Wearing a blazer the same shade of red, monogrammed of course, blue pants, western boots. All this topped off with a Tyrolean hat that had a silver medallion on its side with a fan of feathers rising out of it. He'd worn that same hat all the years Clew had known him. Fifteen years now. Even then Harry Whistler had been larger than life. Deliberately and enjoyably so.

He was preceded down the stairway by one of the twins. Either Donald or Dennis. No way to tell which. Tweedledum and Tweedledee, always identically dressed, choosing clothing that would make them barely noticeable depending on where they were working. He knew that he probably would not see the other, or, if and when he did, he still wouldn't know which. The other would probably stay out of sight and make his own way to Belle Haven. They seemed half Harry's size. He'd heard people call them "cute." But they were utterly devoted to Harry and just as utterly deadly. Especially the one who you always failed to see because you were watching the other.

The next man out, close behind Harry Whistler, had to be Rajib Sadik of Hamas. He had the look of a fifty-ish business executive except for a considerable stubble on his face that looked like about a week's growth. No, not a businessman. Clew had almost forgotten. Sadik was a doctor, a surgeon. He'd emerged with his medical bag in one hand and only a toiletries case in the other. He must not have had much time to pack.

Clew had thought he looked familiar when he saw the photos his researcher had gathered. Now even more so, seeing him in the flesh. But Clew still couldn't place where he'd seen him before. Most likely in some earlier briefing on Hamas.

Harry Whistler approached him, Sadik at his side. Harry did the introductions. Sadik offered his hand. As Clew took it, Harry was watching his eyes for some sign that he recognized Sadik. Harry's look seemed one of amusement.

Harry settled the question. He said, "Yes, you've met. Dinner party. Geneva. Twelve years ago. Kessler knows him, too, even back before that. Stride met him later, but she wouldn't remember. She was mostly in a coma at the time." He touched a finger to two spots on his abdomen. "My friend here dug two bullets out of her."

"Wait a minute," said Clew. He was looking at Sadik. "Yes, I remember. Weren't you Harry's doctor?" The name was Emil something. It wasn't Sadik. It was a Swiss name. Or German.

Harry said, "That'll keep. We'll get caught up soon enough." He gestured toward Clew's briefcase. "Done some homework?"

"Oh, indeed," Clew told him. "I'll have to go through this with Kessler and Stride, but we have forty minutes; let's use them."

He signaled his driver who was also his bodyguard. The driver opened the limousine door.

Harry and Sadik both sat facing forward. Clew took the seat opposite, facing the rear. The twin sat up front with the driver. Clew had opened the electronics-laden work table that folded out from under his seat. He drew a micro disk out of his briefcase and inserted it into the work table's slot. He played both recordings that he'd made.

The first was the one he'd already sent to Harry, his first conversation with Leland. It was filled with speculation, short on hard information. He'd hesitated before playing the second, the one that gave the text of the suicide note, the one in which Leland said he'd have to resign. Harry told him, "No secrets from my friend here."

"Well, he's also a friend of Yitzhak Netanya, to say nothing of Abbas Mansur of Iran."

"As for Netanya, this cat's out of the bag. As for Mansur, we'll deal with that later. Go ahead and play the tape, Roger."

Clew did so. Harry listened. When they got to the wording of the suicide note, Harry had him back up and repeat it. Clew said, "I've transcribed it. I have several copies." Harry said, "I still want to listen."

He heard all the names of those accused by the prince. He asked, "No Elizabeth? Why no Elizabeth?"

"No idea," said Clew. "But your friend here's dead meat."

"We'll deal with that as well. Play the rest of the tape."

Next came Leland's recital of the names of the conspirators. He said to Clew, "I assume you have files on these three." Clew patted his briefcase. "Right here."

Harry took a moment to chide Sadik. These names were what Sadik had promised Netanya as the price of Netanya getting him to Belle Haven. Harry said to him, "See? We didn't need you after all." Sadik answered him, saying, "You will."

Clew had already reached into his briefcase. He took out his Beretta and set it aside. Sadik eyed the weapon with distaste. Clew drew out three folders. "I have more than names. I have the whole lives of all three."

In fact, he'd brought dossiers on more than the three. He also had a file on Rajib Sadik, but that one was considerably thinner. No reference to any past connection with Harry. No reference to him ever being… Emil… Emil…

Freundlisch? Yes, that was the name he'd heard in Geneva. Dr. Emil Freundlisch. He remembered.

He said to Sadik. "Aren't you Dr. Freundlisch?"

"Sadik. Dr. Rajib Sadik."

"So you've converted to Islam?"

Harry raised a hand before he could answer. Harry said, "Long story. I'll fill you in later." He tapped the work desk. "Let's see what you've got."

Clew set down the three folders facing Harry and Sadik. Each of them had photographs clipped to its cover. He said, "I didn't have time to put these on a disk. Otherwise I could have shown them on the limo's computer."

"This is better," said Harry. He spread them out side by side.

Harry touched the first of these with his finger. "Charles Haskell," he said. He was talking to Sadik. Haskell was posing in a hardhat and jumpsuit on one of Trans-Global's offshore rigs. It had been clipped from an annual report.

Clew told them, "That one's the best we could find. These were pulled together quickly. We're looking for more. I don't think he likes to be photographed."

Harry Whistler asked Clew, "Have you ever met him?"

"Not really. He's shown up at a couple of receptions at State. He didn't pay any attention to me. He was there to get his hooks into Leland."

Sadik asked Harry, "You've not met him either?"

A shake of the head. "But I know his reputation. Let nothing surprise you with this one. He rewrites the book on abnormal psychology. Some say he's bi-polar. Some say that's too easy. Some say he's not real. That he invented himself. And in doing so, he's managed to purge himself of all ethical and moral restraint. Utterly dogged in pursuit of his goals, even those that he has little chance of achieving. I'm not sure what drives him. I don't think it's greed. I rather think… never mind. Let's go on."

Sadik said, "Wait. You have an insight? Please share it."

Harry Whistler rocked a hand. "This is only my impression. I think he does what he thinks Charles Haskell would do. I think there's still someone else in there someplace." He paused. "But that's no insight. We all do that, don't we? We are what we've become, but we still have our longings. Forget it. Not helpful. Here's the next one."

He moved his finger to the photo on the second dossier. "Huntington Bentley, the media giant. His papers reach much of the literate world. His radio stations reach those who don't read. Haskell uses him, but he also uses Haskell. Egocentric. Very much an elitist. Count on him to look to own interests first. He'll follow Haskell, or not, as it suits him."

"And this one," said Sadik, pointing at the third photo, "is the banker who came to Riyadh with the prince. Sir Reginald Leeds. This one didn't impress me. I'd say he's the weak link of the three."

Sadik spoke to Clew. "All three are now at the Bohemian Grove?"

Clew nodded. "And they'll stay there, cloistered, while this thing blows."

"Cloistered?"

"No communication with the outside, the better to disclaim any knowledge of what happens. We probably can't get at them, if that's why you're asking. Not even on suspicion of murdering the prince. All we have on that is the suicide note and its wording exonerates Haskell."

"And… your estimation of Haskell's intentions?"

"My guess? Try a trade. The original for the disk."

"And failing that?"

"Either way, he'll still publish it. He hates Kessler. He hates Harry. He'll tell Bentley to run it on every front page and most people who see it will believe it. If Bentley should balk for whatever reason, he can splash it all over the internet himself."

Sadik nodded, agreeing. "To the whole Muslim world."

"Sure," said Clew, "but don't think only Muslims. To all western governments, all intelligence agencies. It is in their urgent interest to find out if it's true that we, all the people named in the note, are behind the social upheaval that's happening where most of the world's oil is. And that's just about the prophecy. There's also the ten billion. The Saudis are going to want their money."

"Which Kessler has," said Harry, "according to Yitzhak. Kessler only learned he had it this morning."

"But on a disk," said Clew. "On some sort of record. He doesn't have the actual money."

"The actual money's a few key strokes away. The point is that, right now, only he can get at it. He could also, if he chooses, make the money disappear. Gone in a blink. Unrecoverable. You've heard the expression, a finger on the button? That's a hell of an insurance policy."

"And he'll need it," said Clew. "But don't count on it buying more than a few days once Haskell releases that suicide note.

Belle Haven will be swarming with reporters, federal agents, dozens more from foreign intelligence services, to say nothing of the curious who might come by the busload."

Did he say the curious? How about the religious? A Blessed Virgin outline appears on some wall and hundreds of people flock to see it. How many would come to see Mohammed's wife reborn? How many would call her a pretender, a heretic, and see it as their duty to kill her?

"Which reminds me," said Clew. He reached again into his briefcase. He drew out State's copy of the Bahrain Tribune. He opened it to a page that he'd marked with a post-it. There, in vivid color, centered on that page, was an artist's impression of Aisha and Qaila with a heading that asked, "Is She Coming?" Aisha sat astride a camel that was pawing the ground like a bull getting ready to charge. She was clad all in white head to toe. There was Qaila, hair on fire, eyes on fire, sword on fire, hovering above and behind her. The rest of the page contained dozens of comments, pro or con, many heated, from the web sites.

Clew asked Harry Whistler, "See anyone you know?"

"I'll be damned," said Harry. "It's them."

He was looking at the faces of Elizabeth and Aisha. Not some artist's impression.

Their actual faces. In Elizabeth's case, it was a bit less precise. You'd have to catch her in one of her don't-fuck-with-me moods to see the face shown in this drawing. That of Aisha, however, was near photographic. Those big eyes, those high cheekbones, the set of her mouth. Eyes looking right into your soul.

Harry seemed dumfounded. "How could this be?"

425

He touched a finger to one side of her face. He said, "See this dimple on her left cheek? The artist got her right down to that dimple. Wrap a white turban around our Aisha's head, extend it under her chin; she's dead-on."

Sadik, yet to meet her, asked Roger, "This is true?"

Harry answered for him. "It's true."

Clew drew their attention to a small notation at the end of a column of comments. "This says that the drawing is based on descriptions by women who claim to have seen them."

Harry seemed doubtful. "That would make these composites. These are way beyond composites. This would almost have me believing."

"Can this car go any faster?" asked Sadik.

THIRTY FOUR

On returning with Aisha, approaching the house, Elizabeth watched for the black pick-up truck. She didn't see it, but she saw something else. A gray van, tinted windows, was coming from the opposite direction. It had a plumbing firm's signage on its side. She thought that it was moving just a little too slowly, a few miles under the limit. Service vehicles usually move with dispatch when going from one call to the next. The two men in it were faced straight ahead, so they weren't driving slowly to spot an address.

On the other hand, it probably meant nothing at all. It passed her. It kept going. No increase in speed. Jumpiness did not become her.

Two minutes later they were inside the gates, gathering their Lord & Taylor shopping bags. It was almost four o'clock. Harry would be arriving. She wanted to see what else Martin had learned.

To Aisha she said, "Honey, take these bags to your room. Try on some things. See what suits you." They'd bought the black dress and the black high-heeled shoes. But Aisha seemed embarrassed when she saw herself in them. Wearing heels took a little getting used to as well. So she ended up with two alternate outfits. One a pretty yellow sheath that was much less revealing. The other was called a safari ensemble, with a belted beige jacket and brown slacks with patch pockets. Elizabeth would have bought that one for herself if Aisha hadn't got to it first.

She said, "Bring Shahla with you. She'll help you decide. When you're ready, I'll come in and fix your hair."

Once inside, Shahla didn't need to be asked. She saw the bags. She mouthed the words, "Did you buy it?" Elizabeth answered with a nod and then a shrug to convey that the issue was not yet resolved.

With that set in motion, she climbed the main staircase. She cleared her throat to let Martin know she was home if he hadn't already heard the chime that rings when the front gate is opened. He hadn't. Moreover, he was still in his robe. He and Rasha, who had dressed in a turtleneck and jeans, had pulled two chairs up to the computer.

"Hi," they said in chorus without looking up.

"Hi, yourselves. Aisha's done. What's new here?"

Kessler touched a few keys. "Not much, I'm afraid. Rasha has been trying to identify those accounts that she knows to be legitimate Islamic charities. She was able to point out quite a few that she remembers, but there must be a hundred she's not sure of."

"So there's no way to well which ones have been skimmed?"

"Assume all of them," he told her. "Even Sadik's. His clinics, by the way, aren't lumped with Hamas. That way none of it goes to the militants."

"Perhaps."

Kessler turned in his chair. He seemed annoyed that she was doubtful. He glanced at Rasha in a way that suggested that he'd have more to say to her in private.

Elizabeth asked, "Any more about Niki?"

Rasha said, "She's been crying on and off since you left. She's in the library. She hasn't stepped out. I brought her my kitten and the litter box, too. I hoped that you wouldn't mind."

Nice thing to do, but more than she deserved. Elizabeth didn't say that, only thought it. "I was asking about all these emails she's sent."

"Nothing new there. A lot more of the same. Except..." He hit some keys. "Who is Bernice Barrow?"

"Bernice? She runs the office at the tennis academy. Niki's been emailing Bernice?"

Kessler shook his head. "More the other way around. Bernice only wanted to send Aisha a gift. Had you given this Bernice our address?"

"Not the street address. Harry's post office box. And only to Bernice. She's reliable."

"Even so..."

"Martin, I had to have a way to get mail. My house is being sold. There would be documents to sign. Then there's bank statements, credit card bills and the like. I used to have a life down there, you know. All of your stuff can go through Harry's system. Mine can't."

He raised his hands. "Easy. No argument from me. If Bernice sent a gift, we'll have to pick it up tomorrow. The post office closes at five."

She softened. "You're right. That was a mistake. I could have rented a box a few towns away."

"No harm done," he told her. "How is Aisha?"

"Not as scared. Right now she's got her new outfits on her mind. Shahla's with her. She's helping her decide."

Kessler turned to Rasha. He said, "Would you please excuse us, my princess? I would like a few minutes with Elizabeth."

He said to her, "Those bullets you took. That drive-by in Romania by those Hezbollah gunmen. You know how close you came to dying."

Her hands, involuntarily, went to her abdomen. She said to him, "Martin, that was twelve years ago. Why would you bring that up now?"

"Do you know who saved your life?"

"You did. And you found them." She folded her arms. "You threw their leader out of a hotel window. What is this? Have I never thanked you?"

"You have. In your fashion. In many ways. But I didn't save you. All I did was get help. That help was provided by Harry Whistler. He flew down from Geneva with a surgical team."

"I know that. I've thanked him as well."

The chief surgeon's name was Emil Freundlisch at the time. Do you remember anything about him?"

A shake of her head. Only drug-befogged images. She asked, "Martin, where is this going?"

"Emil Freundlisch, my darling, is now Rajib Sadik. At some point he decided that he'd done enough patching of Harry's ever-widening circle of friends. He gave up his practice. He joined Doctors Without Borders. His work with them eventually took him to Jordan and from there to Hebron on the West Bank. That is where he decided that he was most needed. He and Maryam both. Maryam is his wife. She was part of your surgical team. Her field is obstetrics/gynecology."

"Why…" She stopped herself. So many questions. "Why have you never told me?"

"Two reasons. First, there seemed to be no point. It wasn't likely that you'd ever see him again. Second, when you were on your way to recovery, you were told that he had to remove more than bullets. You were told that you could never bear a child of your own. Your reaction to that was understandable, Elizabeth. It was also extremely ungenerous."

She knew what he meant. She'd blamed the surgeon, not the shooters. She remembered that she'd called him a butcher. He had neutered her. He had defeminized her.

She said, "A good surgeon… should have put me together."

"And you see," said Kessler? "A third scar remains. I've wondered whether your altered condition led to your maternal behavior toward Aisha. Whether I'm right or wrong, that was only for the good. The two of you needed each other."

"Was... Sadik a Muslim when he operated on me?"

"He was, and, yes, he knew who you were. He could have let the Black Angel die. No one would have been the wiser, even me; I was watching. Instead, he and Maryam worked for nine hours to save your life and to try to save the rest of you as well. If there was a way, they would have found it."

She was silent for a moment. She still hadn't quite absorbed this.

"By the way," said Kessler, "What does Freundlisch mean in German?"

"In German? I believe it means friendly."

Even as he spoke, she remembered her Arabic. "Sadik," she said. "It means the same thing."

"And perhaps that's how you'll treat him when he gets here," said Kessler. "He is very much my friend. He should be yours."

Elizabeth wanted to admit that he's right. To assure him that none of those ill feelings remained. But she knew that she still was enough of a woman to ache inside for what might have been. She knew that Martin was right. The scar remains.

She said, "Isn't it time you got dressed?"

Rasha was waiting near the top of the staircase. She said, "May I speak to you, Elizabeth?"

She looked at her watch. "Sweetie, I've got an awful lot on my mind. Could it wait until…"

"It's important. Two minutes."

Rasha sat down on the carpeted step. She gestured for Elizabeth to sit with her. She did. Rasha said, "I brought my kitten to Niki because I heard her crying. I heard her saying 'I'm so worthless, I wish I could die.' She's really very sorry, Elizabeth."

"Sorry doesn't cut it. Not this time."

Rasha picked at some cat hairs that had clung to her turtleneck. She asked, "Do you think Shahla's pretty?"

"What's that got to do with…? Never mind. Yes, I do. I think she's a handsome young lady. And bright."

"Niki isn't as bright. And she isn't as pretty. I mean, she's not homely; don't mistake me. She would have a nice face if she could manage to soften it. And she'll lose the weight. She's still growing."

Elizabeth sighed. She started to rise. Rasha reached for her hand to keep her in place. "When she was only twelve she heard her father tell her mother that he would never find a good husband for her. If he did, the payment would be very small and the husband would be of no importance. The father never spoke to her except to belittle her. He made it clear that she was unwanted and that no one else would ever want her either. He'd say that Shahla was at least worth her keep."

"Worth her keep because…?"

"Let's not talk about that."

"You're right. We needn't. Go on."

"It was more than that," said Rasha. "He'd demean her to everyone. And I heard this from Shahla, not from Niki. If you grow up believing that you have no value, you do things… I don't know… to get attention. It's sort of like it is with those suicide bombers."

"Um… that's apples and oranges. Rasha."

"Yes, but okay… I'm just making a point. Not many of them do it for those seventy-two virgins or whatever silly things some clerics promise. Muslims aren't all stupid. We know bullshit when we hear it. Excuse me, I should not have used such language."

"You're excused. What does this have to do with Niki Darvi?"

"Believing that you're nothing. That you'll never be anything. The people who recruit the suicide bombers understand this feeling and they use it. They'll say you'll be remembered. You will have mattered. They'll hang posters with your picture all over your village saying what a hero and martyr you are. They'll tell you that people will brag about knowing you. They'll name children after you. They'll name a street after you. And you want that. You want to have mattered."

"Yes, I know. We see the same thing over here. That's why some kids walk into their schools and start shooting. It's not just that they snap. A lot of hatred builds up."

"Yes, of course," Rasha answered, "but hatred of whom? Of everyone who has more? Or is it hatred of themselves for not amounting to more. That's what my mother thinks. I've seen it myself. No one ever forgets even small humiliations. But most, even you, don't go out looking for revenge. Certainly not against the innocent."

"Glad you added that last part," said Elizabeth.

"We're not shits. It's because we're not shits."

"Um… Rasha."

"That one's okay to say, is it not? Isn't it one of your slogans?"

"I wouldn't call it slogan. It depends on the context."

"Well, the context in this case is not holding grudges. My own father never wanted a daughter either, but I had my mother and I had friends in school and then I had Aisha and the Nasreens."

That, and being a princess, thought Elizabeth. A princess rates quite a few perks.

Rasha read her mind. She said, "I know what you're thinking. But my title was my only value to him. He was giving me in marriage to a cleric of some influence who had promised, in return, to get his income increased. Niki Darvi wasn't worth even that. Not even the Nasreens wanted Niki."

Elizabeth said, "Granted. She's had a tough time. A lot of us have. We get over it. Didn't you?"

"No, but I'm trying. So is Niki. Aren't you?"

Great kid, thought Elizabeth. With a very big heart. But there such a thing as being too damned perceptive. She took her hand back from Rasha. She rose to her feet. She said, "I haven't decided about Niki."

"There's one other thing that I've wanted to say to you." Rasha pushed herself up as well. "It's about Muslims in general."

"Let's hear it."

"They're not all like my father. They're not all like Niki's father. Most are very decent. Most love their families dearly. And most of them believe, or want to believe, that there is one God who cares about them. Do we understand everything? No, Elizabeth, we don't. We just live our faith the best we know how."

Elizabeth said to her, "There's one thing I've wondered. I assume that your mother's marriage was arranged."

"At fourteen. A year younger than I am."

"To a prince. Her family must have gotten a deal."

"There is always a contract in such cases."

"Fourteen, though," said Elizabeth. "Only a schoolgirl. How did she manage to get educated? How did she become so fluent in English that she later went on to teach it?"

"Because she too had a family. It was all in the contract. Her family believed in education for women. Her family saw to my education was well. My father had no choice but to permit it."

Elizabeth heard the chime of the front gate being opened. She bent down and could see a stretch limousine coming in. She saw that its left rear window was down. She could see Harry's face. No mistaking that hat. He was holding a set of keys in one hand. He must have used one to open the gate.

Rasha saw him, too. "And there's one of the twins."

One of them. Whichever. He'd popped out the right front while the car was still moving. Carrying a small satchel. Weapons, most likely. Carrying something else. It looked like a wrapped gift. He disappeared toward the garage.

Elizabeth said, "Rasha, I'll go down and greet them. We'll meet in Niki's room. We shouldn't be long. I want you and the others to stay out of sight until I get the lay of the land here."

"They're coming to the party?

"I'm sure they will, yes. I'd like that to be the first they see of Aisha."

THIRTY FIVE

Haskell's corporate jet had landed at Reagan. It taxied to a slot that, to his amusement, stood wingtip to wingtip with Whistler's Gulfstream. Two maintenance men were just washing it down. The late afternoon sun caused it to gleam brightly, especially those red and gold initials. He resisted an impulse to key it.

"Very childish."

Oh, shut up. I wasn't serious. I'd have needed a ladder.

He'd told his air crew to stand ready for a prompt departure when he returned in three hours. He'd told them that he was meeting with some business associates who were waiting at the main terminal. Nor had he arranged for a car and driver. A taxi could be taken anonymously. He took a short jitney ride to the terminal. He put on a pair of half-frame reading glasses, tousled his hair, and climbed into a cab. He spoke to the driver with a guttural honk that he intended to sound vaguely European.

He'd forgotten to account for D.C. evening traffic. The ride to Belle Haven took nearly an hour. He'd hoped to do a pass of Whistler's Tudor on the way, but had to forego it due to the time. As it was, the driver took another ten minutes to locate the complex of which Mangiamo was a part. Haskell, of course, hadn't mentioned that name. His destination, as far as the driver was concerned, was the across-the-street real estate office that Gilhooley had told him about. He still got there shortly before six.

He dismissed the driver and proceeded to the bus stop where he sat on the bench of its shelter. He took his Wall Street Journal out of his briefcase and slid his reading glasses a bit lower on his nose. There, while pretending to be reading the charts, he took in the rest of his surroundings.

Looking over his glasses, the restaurant, Mangiamo, looked smaller than it did in the photos he'd seen. Narrower, anyway. But considerably deeper. It was a wood frame structure, probably quite old, and probably not built as a restaurant at first. A shop, more likely, whose owner lived upstairs. The roof was peaked, but it had a dormer window. There seemed sufficient room for living quarters.

There were similar buildings on the left and the right. One housed an art gallery, the other a liquor store. Both were still open for business. None of them had any parking of their own, only narrow service alleys between them. Several traffic cones had been placed in the street directly in front of Mangiamo.

"For the guest of honor, no doubt."

No doubt. Space had been reserved for three cars.

The restaurant did have that relaxed homey look that was typical of neighborhood bars. Its clientele would be mostly locals. It was painted a quiet red with green trim. Italian colors. The same shades as their flag. The sign above the entrance was flanked by a collection of various antique copper pans. From his angle he could see nearly all of the bar through the large picture windows on both sides of the door. Toward the rear, he was able to see the first letters of what had to be a Happy Birthday banner. It hung over a mural of one of those villages that dot Italy's Amalfi Coast.

And now he could also see Gilhooley.

Gilhooley appeared, squeezing out between customers. He was headed toward the front entrance. Once outside, he lit a smoke and tossed the match to one side, never glancing in Haskell's direction. With studied insouciance he idled for a bit before ambling to the opposite side of the street. He paused at the bakery near the real estate office. He started to enter, but backed up a step. He stood holding the door for a woman, then exiting, carrying a large white box in both hands. Haskell watched her cross the street to the service alley where she disappeared into the restaurant's side door. Must be the door to the kitchen, thought Haskell. Probably the birthday girl's cake.

Gilhooley had gone into the bakery, emerging minutes later, a white bag in one hand, with which he strolled over to the bus stop. Gilhooley was munching a Danish.

"Great disguise," said Gilhooley, not looking at him. "You mussed your hair and put on glasses. That's it?"

"It's not as if I had time to buy a fright wig," said Haskell. "Beside, you saw the crowd in that bar. Fully half of them are dressed just as I am." He asked, "Is it always that busy?"

"Nope. Just tonight. And not just for the party. Harry Whistler seems to have a lot of friends around here. Word got out that he's back in town."

Then we'll make it a night to remember, thought Haskell. He asked, "Have you planted the explosives?"

"I have. Why are you talking funny?"

"Oh. Sorry. I'd been practicing an accent."

Gilhooley turned his head. He looked up at the sky. Haskell knew that he was probably rolling his eyes. Haskell didn't bother explaining. He asked Gilhooley, "Well? Where did you plant them?"

Gilhooley said without gesturing, "See the service alley? See that metal trash bin? That's where it is, between the bin and the wall."

"Not inside? I specified among those back tables."

"While they're back there decorating? Hard to do. You also said you'd leave it to my vaunted expertise. That metal bin helps to direct the charge. It'll blow that whole wall. It's a bearing wall. The top floor and the roof should come down."

Hmm. A great scene. The Saudis will love it. "A fireball rising?"

"Two hundred feet maybe."

"You'll have earned my lasting approval."

Gilhooley placed his white bakery bag on the bench. The bag made a solid-sounding clunk. Gilhooley said, "I got you a cheese Danish. I put my video camera in the bag with it. There's also a cell phone. I've pre-programmed a number. All you do is hit send and it blows."

"Umm… what blows, exactly? How much of it blows?"

"At least the kitchen and that back dining area."

"But not the bar," said Haskell. "Correct?"

"Not that much, I don't think. At least not the front half. It will get some concussion and a whole lot of smoke. The concussion should blow out those front windows."

"Yes, but you'll be safe if you duck behind the bar where it curves to the left on this end."

"I'll be safe," said Gilhooley, "because I won't be in there."

Haskell ignored him. He peeked into the bag. He said, "I assume this is not your only cell phone."

"That's just the trigger. Use and discard."

"So you still have your own?"

"The one you called me on, sure." He touched a hand to his belt.

"I've told you that I've chosen to spare Ms. Stride. When they're all gathered… What's for dinner, by the way? Are they slaughtering a lamb? Served with hummus? Stuffed grape leaves?"

"You're serious?"

"My report to the Saudis. They're fond of details. Falafel patties? Kabobs?"

"Not about the damned menu. I mean about me. You seriously expect me to be in there?"

"Here's what happens," said Haskell. "You'll watch them all enter. I'll be taping them from here. It will probably take them at least a few minutes to work their way through that bar crowd. Friends of Whistler's, you say. There will be some glad-handing. When they're all in the back and the party starts in earnest, you'll call me and say that it's show time."

"But…

"No, Desmond, just listen. Here's what happens next. I'll call you back, you'll put the phone to your ear. You'll say her name aloud. Elizabeth Stride? You'll pretend that the caller is looking for her. Says it's very important. Can't wait. Life or death. You'll ask the bartender to send someone back for her. When she comes back out and is almost upon you, you'll give me a signal, a wave of the hand, and I will detonate your little package. You will seize Stride and drag her to the floor, sheltered in the lee of the bar."

Gilhooley, dumfounded, managed to say, "Mr. Haskell… no fucking way."

"Desmond… I need you to keep her from harm."

"So that later she can ask me who made the call? And why would that call have been made to me? I'm just some handyman, remember?"

"There won't be any later. We'll depart in the confusion. We'll go just as soon as the fire engines get here. I want footage of their hoses being turned on the flames."

Gilhooley reached into his pocket. He pulled out his cigarettes and with them his matchbook. He placed the red and green matchbook on Haskell's bench. "This matchbook is Mangiamo's. Two phone numbers on it. One for the office and one for the bar. The bar phone's all the way up at the front. I don't call. You call. A guy named Sam will pick up. He tends bar, but he's the owner. Tell him there's some bad news for one of the girls. He'll get Stride up there, guaranteed."

Hmm, thought Haskell. Yes, that could work, too. What news, though? The prince? Hate to ruin Rasha's evening. He'd say he wished we could talk about something more pleasant, but..."

"Charles..."

I've never heard Stride's voice. I've only imagined it. I'd like to hear it at last.

"Charles, all you'll hear is 'Who's calling? What's happened?' It's not as if you'll get into a chat."

Yes, but I can record what there is of it. I'll be videotaping while I'm talking to her. If she does ask what's happened, I'll say 'This is what's happened," and wham, I set off the explosion.

He saw that Gilhooley was looking askance. "Mr. Haskell? You okay? You just went someplace else."

"Give me a few seconds, Desmond."

She's never heard his voice either, thought Haskell. But it might seem familiar when they finally meet. So he'll disguise it. A new one. Something Arabic-sounding. A parting shout of Alahu Akbar just before the roof flattens Kessler and restores her to the singles scene again.

He said to Gilhooley, "We'll do it your way. But I still need you there to tell me when they've seated."

"You'll make the call?"

"I'll handle it, Desmond."

"When I see her come up, I'm gone, Mr. Haskell. Someone else can keep her from getting all smudged."

"You're not much of a gentleman, are you."

THIRTY SIX

Kessler had gone to the master bedroom to quickly throw on some clothing. He returned to the foyer inside the front door. There was Clew with his briefcase, Harry doffing his hat, and Elizabeth making nice with Sadik.

Now she was all warmth. All sweetness and light. She was saying, "A thank you is so long overdue. Both to you and to your lovely wife Maryam."

Sadik blinked once or twice as if he'd scarcely remembered. He returned the courtesy in what seemed a rote manner. He said, "It's good to see you looking so well," all the while staring at her face. His eyes then shifted. He was scanning the interior. He asked, "Where is Aisha? Is she here?"

Kessler thought he knew what the stare was about. So did Elizabeth. Her smile disappeared. She said to Sadik, "She is in her room dressing. When you see her, you'll only be seeing our Aisha. Don't look at her as if she's a specimen."

446

"Of course," said Sadik. "I understand perfectly."

"I hope so."

"I would very much like to speak with her. May I?"

"On this subject? No. Not a word, not today. And never just the two of you alone. For this visit, you are Doctor Emil Freundlisch again. You're not Sadik, you're not Hamas, you're not even Muslim. You're just an old friend who once patched me up. You're here as an old friend of Harry and Martin. You happen to be here on her birthday."

"This party. I may come?"

"Just remember what I said."

So much for sweetness and light, thought Kessler. He told them. "Upstairs. Let's get started."

They'd begun with the recordings. Clew handed out copies of the suicide note as the second tape was being played. The note came as a surprise both to Kessler and Stride. Elizabeth asked, as the second tape ended, "Is that true? Rasha's father is dead?"

"You heard Leland," Clew answered. "Haskell killed him."

"I got that part, Roger." Not much there, she realized, between Rasha and her father. Even so, it might not go down easily. "But the note points the finger at you three and Leland."

"Kessler, too. Not you, though. Feel neglected?"

"She'll get over it," said Harry. "Let's move on."

Next came the dossiers. Haskell, Bentley and Leeds. After those, they gathered around the computer as Kessler brought up the Saudi files.

"This is the scrambled version, but you see all those names. You see it's ten billion and counting."

Sadik said, "I see mine. I have twenty-six million?"

"No. That's the scramble. You have two million and change. You want it? I can transfer it myself."

Harry said to Sadik, "That can wait."

Clew said, "I'll want a copy of the unscrambled disk."

"You won't get one," Kessler told him. "All copies stay with us. Later, however, I'll give you a quick look. Just enough so that you can say that you've seen it to anyone who doubts that we have it."

"Who else has one?" asked Clew. "The Nasreens?"

"Safely held."

That wasn't true and Elizabeth knew it. The Nasreens had their copy, but not the new passwords. Nor were the original and its copy safely held. But they would be shortly. After this meeting ends. Until then, having all of it in this one room amounts to a ticking bomb in their midst.

Roger Clew's cell phone vibrated. He saw the call was from his office. He said, "Time out. I'd better take this."

He put the phone to his ear. "Tatiana? What's up?"

He listened, first nodding, then with his eyes widening. He said, "Both magazines? On their covers? When?" He listened further. He sighed. He muttered a curse. He said, "Thank you, Tatiana. Stay on it."

He said to the others, "Time and Newsweek magazines. They're both planning to run cover stories on the prophecy. Both issue dates are a week from next Monday." He said to Harry and to Sadik, "One guess what they're using for the cover."

He said to Kessler and Stride, "I was just getting to this." He reached into his briefcase for the Bahrain Tribune. He said to Elizabeth what he'd said to the others. "Anyone here look familiar?"

She knew in a flash why Sadik had stared at her and why he was so eager to see Aisha. She said to Clew what Harry had said. She asked him, "How could this be?"

"I don't know. We don't know. We were equally shocked. Tatiana says the banner on the Newsweek edition is going to read, 'Is She Coming?' She's working on getting advance copies of the text. It's all about the world-wide effect."

Elizabeth ran a finger to the bottom of the page. She looked up at Kessler. "This says it's based on descriptions by those who have seen her."

He said nothing. His expression was enough. The answer had come to them both in that instant. Niki had provided the descriptions.

"Excuse me," said Elizabeth. "I have some business downstairs."

Kessler asked, "What's the point? To rub her nose further? Yes, she got carried away with details. She didn't know that a drawing would be made of them."

Sadik asked, "Do I take it that her handmaidens described her?"

449

"Not handmaidens," said Kessler. "One girl."

Another cell phone chimed. It was Elizabeth's.

She answered distractedly. "Who? Oh, Sam. We're running a bit late. I'll have to call you." She listened further. "Uh-huh. Harry's here. Oh, really? I'll tell him." Again she listened. He had more to say. She made a slow circling motion with her free hand as if wishing that he would get on with it. "Sam, I have to go. Oh. The count? Hold on." She asked Harry, "Both twins?" Harry held up one finger. She understood. Only one at a time. She said, "Sam? Figure ten all together."

She broke the connection. "Sam Foote," she said to Harry. "Your retired leg-breaker."

"You insult him. That's the least of what he was."

"Sorry." We're not shits. "He's been great."

She punched in the number of Shahla's cell. She said, "Shahla? Elizabeth. Are you done with Aisha? Good. Now go tell your sister to get dressed." She listened for a beat. She said, "Yes, she's included. We can't leave her here." Another beat. "No, Shahla, I'm no longer angry. Rasha stuck up for her. Rasha... explained her. Tell Niki she's got twenty minutes."

Sadik asked her, after the call was concluded, "Niki Darvi was the one? She did all this by herself?"

Elizabeth, still distracted, waved off the question. She asked Kessler, "Are we crazy to go ahead with this now?"

"My vote would be to do it. For the girls, it's good medicine. For everyone else, it gives all this time to settle. However, this should be your decision."

She asked Harry Whistler, "Do you have an opinion."

He said to Clew, "The prince's murder. That was only this morning?"

"That's when Leland found him," said Clew.

He said to Kessler, "Do a search. See if anything's appeared yet."

Kessler typed in all the keywords he could think of. It took less than a minute for the search to be completed. Kessler said, "I see nothing at all."

Elizabeth said, "We might be under surveillance. One old black pick-up. And perhaps a gray van."

Harry said, "An old pick-up? A poor choice for surveillance. Would the van be of a plumbing concern?"

"It would. Are they yours?"

"They're Yitzhaks's Mossad. They're down from D.C. He asked me if I'd mind. I said, sure, why not? He would have sent them regardless."

"That shit."

Harry only smiled. He was not touching that one. He clapped his hands to sum up the discussion. "So the threat is not an imminent threat. If this thing is going to blow it won't happen right away. Even if Haskell has gone to the media, we won't see the first mention before tomorrow at the soonest. And even jihadists need time to plan and to get from one place to another."

Clew shook his head. "They won't be the first. Our intelligence services, our own, not theirs, will mount a raid as soon as they get their first whiff. The FBI will claim jurisdiction, but some of the others won't wait for a ruling. They'll bust in wearing SWAT gear through every window. They'll worry about warrants some other time. They'll cart off all your computers."

Elizabeth asked, "Even knowing that you're here?"

"Leland's lackey? I'm one of the conspirators."

Elizabeth said to Harry, "We can't stay here. I know that. You don't want your house ripped apart."

"Now it's me you're insulting. It's only a house. But Roger's right about the computers."

Elizabeth asked him, "How long do we have?"

"A day, perhaps two. But we must assume less. This house should be vacant by this time tomorrow."

She took a long breath. She said to Kessler, "So it doubles as a bon voyage party. I guess I'm with you. Let's do it."

She said to Harry, "Besides, your fan club is down there. Sam apologized for it. He said he only mentioned to one or two people that High-stepping Harry would be there for Aisha's party. He said word got around. They're now two deep at the bar. He said he had to ask a cop friend of yours to fill in as a second bartender."

"Which cop is that?"

"The lady cop. Karen."

Harry smiled. "He'll go broke. She pours heavy."

"Oh, and another friend of yours is in town." She paused to remember. "Zeke the Greek? "

Harry squinted. "Zeke the Greek. No last name? Only that?"

"He said something about shipping. You use Greek ships, don't you?"

"I do. I guess I'll know him when I see him." Harry looked at his watch. He said, "Elizabeth, please take Roger and the doctor downstairs. Martin and I will be just a few minutes." Harry sat down at the keyboard.

Both Clew and Sadik were reluctant to leave. Harry was busily typing. Sadik asked him, "Why can't we see what you're doing?" A wash of symbols was cascading down the screen. It stopped abruptly. Harry hit Enter. "Just some added insurance. Don't worry."

Elizabeth looked at him questioningly. He told her, "The dog. I'm letting him out." She nodded to show that she understood him. She said to Kessler, "We'll gather the girls." She said to Sadik, "Let's go, Dr. Freundlisch. This is your chance to meet Aisha."

"Safely held?" asked Harry, once they were alone. "When were they going to be safely held?"

"About now," Kessler told him. "I'd have done what you're doing."

"All the files that matter are now in Geneva. The dog will eat everything else."

The word "dog" referred to a built-in device, a powerful magnet the Mossad had developed. They called it a Caanan. That's a wild desert dog. Harry simply called it the dog. The device was installed in all Israeli computers that might be at risk to fall into wrong hands, certainly the computers on their warplanes. It renders any hard drive unreadable in seconds. Also VHS or DAT tapes. Also Zip disks and back-ups of any description. The result was a complete annihilation of memory followed by the destruction of itself.

"If there's a raid," said Harry, "all they'll get is scrap metal. This one's done. We'd best do them all."

"Especially mine. That whole exchange with Netanya."

"And then let's go enjoy ourselves, shall we?"

THIRTY SEVEN

Haskell had almost had to change his position. Two busses had stopped, several passengers got off. The busses took their time moving on. While idling, they were blocking his view. Then there were the people who were waiting for busses. He'd forgotten that people ride busses.

One man wandered by to check the bus schedule that was posted at one end of the shelter. He had a sense that this man was looking him over. An odd little man dressed in work clothes like Gilhooley. As it turned out, however, the man's only interest was in Haskell's half-eaten Danish pastry. It sat atop the white bakery bag that still held the camera and cell phone.

He asked, "Where'd you get it? This bakery right here?"

Haskell answered, "That would seem the way to bet."

"They sell coffee in there?"

He said, "One would assume so."

"Thanks. I'll go take a look."

He was gone none too soon. The first guests were arriving. Haskell pressed Record on the video camera. He held it, chest level, in his right hand with his left hand placed over it for concealment. He began his narration with the words, "Part One. The lambs being brought to the slaughter."

The big bartender had stepped out the front door and was waving a stretch limo into its space, picking up traffic cones as he did so. "This would be Harry Whistler in the limo," said Haskell.

But it wasn't. Two girls emerged, then a third, then two women, all but one of them bearing wrapped gifts. The limo's driver had opened the rear door for them. The bartender helped them climb out. The sight of Stride in the flesh caused a stirring inside him. There she was, standing tall, looking up and down the street. Alert, but not skittish. She would never be skittish. It was just one more thing to admire about her. Her scan of the street took in Gilhooley's truck which was parked several car lengths further on. But it was only a glance. Her attention did not linger. No more so than it did on other vehicles. The limo's driver indicated that he'd stay with the car. Haskell thought that he was probably armed.

He recognized three of the others from their photos. "Correction," said Haskell into his camera. "These are none other than the handmaidens who stole from your wonderful charities." He named them as he recorded them. There was Rasha, the princess, now a traitorous apostate, in a cardigan sweater, a blouse and a skirt. By her standards, that was probably daring. Standing with her were the two sisters from Iran, the older one dressed in a stylish sheath, the younger one wearing the sort of chemise that women wear when there's a little too much of themselves. Everyone smiling, their party faces on. Well, not all. Not exactly. The younger sister seems to be a bit slower than the others to get into the spirit of the thing.

Speaking of which, where is Aisha, Haskell wondered? And who is that other woman with Stride?

Oh, wait. That's no woman. "That's her. That's Aisha." And, thought Haskell, she looks utterly smashing. Form fitting black dress, low cut in the back, her hair styled in a twist that flowed over one shoulder. Both shoulders were otherwise bare. Only sixteen years old? Not in that dress. That's a full grown woman inside it.

"That's her," said Haskell into his camcorder. "No question about it. That's her. That's the heretic who claims to be Aisha reborn. A Nasreen, of course. Another lesbian whore. Just look at her in that sluttish black dress. Well, you won't hear any more out of her."

Haskell watched the bartender-owner. He's so struck by what must be this new look for her that he's actually standing there applauding. Aisha seems abashed. She draws back toward the limo as if to escape. Elizabeth stops her. Encourages her. The bartender offers Aisha his arm, asking her, "May I have the honor?"

Whistler must have decided that the birthday girl deserved to show up in his limo. Aisha and the bartender led the way in. More than escorting, he was steadying her. She did seem a bit wobbly, thought Haskell. She also seemed taller than she did in her photos. Ah, it's the heels. She must not be accustomed to heels. More applause greeted her as she entered the restaurant. He could hear shouts of "Wow" and a chorus of whistles. He could see the bartender waving his hand as if saying, "That's enough. You're embarrassing her." Even Gilhooley had joined in the clapping. Had to seem one of the gang.

The black Mercedes sedan pulled up next. Still no Harry Whistler. That's Roger Clew driving. Haskell tried to make himself smaller, but Clew never glanced in his direction. Clew's passenger, now emerging, was… could that be Sadik? Not Kessler, for sure, unless he'd aged since Angola. He was a courtly-looking man, well tanned, well dressed although in need of a shave. He didn't look much like an Arab to Haskell, but he knew that had to be Rajib Sadik. He said so into the camera.

"This is the mole the prince told you about. Rajib Sadik. Wormed his way into Hamas. Spies on them for the Zionists. The man with him is his handler, Roger Clew. "

The third car was a good three minutes behind. It was the green Subaru, Martin Kessler at the wheel. His passenger, no question, Harry Whistler himself. No mistaking that beard or that Tyrolean hat. There was not enough room left in front of the restaurant. The bar owner hadn't figured on the stretch. So Kessler pulled into the service alley. He had to stop at the curb cut, let Whistler out first, before he could squeeze the car in. He parked and locked not ten feet from the bomb. This was almost too perfect to be happening.

A third man was with them, He got out behind Whistler. Small, pear-shaped. He seemed vaguely familiar. Haskell started to zoom in, but the third man had somehow melted away. Never mind. Stay on Kessler and Whistler.

He named them, but he'd forgotten what the note called them. He had to reach into his inside jacket pocket where he carried both versions of the suicide note. One with Stride, one without. He'd go with the second. He could always change his mind later.

Ah, yes, here it is. He read from it aloud. "Harry Whistler, a great enemy of God who pulls so many strings from Geneva in Switzerland."

Hmmph. Should have made that much stronger, thought Haskell.

He continued, "And his puppet, the German, Martin Kessler, who mocks Islam from Harry Whistler's house in Belle Haven."

That one could have used more specifics as well, but let's remember that the prince was thoroughly blotto and kept scratching holes in the paper. Can't use that excuse to the Saudis, of course. Charles Haskell wasn't there. He only found the poor man later. The proof? Here it is. In his illicit cell phone. All the photographs he took of the suicide scene. The prince with his blackening tongue sticking out. Leland's bathroom and the rest of Room 3 as it was before his fair weather friends had it tidied.

"Their day of judgment is at hand." said Haskell, for the benefit of his audience-to-be.

All of them. Including Bentley and Leeds.

But all in good time. First things first.

Gilhooley watched them enter from his up-front location. First Stride and the girls. Their progress was slow. The lady cop, Karen, tending bar to help Sam, leaned over the bar and stopped the traffic herself to tell Aisha how terrific she looked. Her dress, her hair, her black pearl pendant earrings.

Gilhooley turned up his faux hearing aid in time to hear the one called Shahla chime in. Saying to Aisha, "Didn't I tell you?" Karen saying to Aisha, "I'd kill for that skin. Me, I spend a fortune on makeup." Aisha blushed while asking, "Do you think this is too much? Shahla insisted on doing my face." Karen asked, "What? A little lip gloss? A little eye liner? No, I think it's just the right touch." The small one in the sweater saying to Karen, "Do you like Niki's dress? She looks really good, too." Karen picking up on the hint. "You're like fairy tale princesses. All four of you."

This caused Aisha to give the small one a nudge. All four of them smiled. Must be some inside joke.

They hadn't progressed more than halfway back when Clew, the guy from State, came through the front door along with a man who seemed somehow out of place. Sadik, thought Gilhooley? Must be.

The girls, at least, had reached the back room, passing under the Happy Birthday banner. The three carrying presents placed them on a table where a few were already displayed. Stride lagged behind. She was talking to Sam. Gilhooley had stretched to see Kessler and Whistler turning into the alley in the green Subaru. Whistler getting out while Kessler drove further in. Haskell's got to love where he parked it, thought Gilhooley. Scratch one green Subaru.

Suddenly through his earpiece, he heard his name spoken. He looked back toward the rear. Sam was looking right at him. So was Stride.

He looked away quickly, mouthed some words to people near him, pretending to be in conversation with them. But he listened. Getting fragments. They were talking about his truck. Stride must have asked him whose pickup it was. Sam told him. Gilhooley. Down there at the end. Stride must have spotted him and his truck, maybe making one pass too many. But whatever her concern, Sam did not seem to share it. Gilhooley heard him say, "Does odd jobs. He's all over." The answer seemed satisfactory to Stride. But Sam said, "I'll keep an eye on him anyway."

Great, thought Gilhooley. He's already a suspect. The sooner he's out of here, the better.

Whistler was barely through the front door when another round of greetings erupted. "Harry, you old pirate. How long are you staying? Hi, Martin. Get him in here. What are you drinking?" Karen was ahead of them. She was holding up a bottle of Glenlivet 18. Must be Whistler's drink of choice, thought Gilhooley. Without waiting for a nod, she poured two glasses, neat, and had them passed to Kessler and Whistler. Now Sam spotted Whistler. He was pushing through the crowd. This seemed a good time to take a smoke break.

Haskell saw him exit, saw him take out a cigarette, saw him patting his pockets for the book of matches, forgetting that he'd left it on the bench. He motioned for Gilhooley to come over.

"Smoking's bad for you, Desmond, but do you know what's worse? Abandoning your post is what's worse."

Gilhooley explained the slow progress toward the tables. He mentioned the fish-eye that he'd got from Stride. He also noticed the red light on the video camera. He asked, "Do you have me on that thing?"

"I'm awaiting your signal. That's part of the narrative. Without you, this report would look choppy."

"Oh, Christ."

"Now, that," said Haskell, "I will have to edit out. Don't mention Christ again. Don't bless yourself either. The Saudis might find that jarring."

Gilhooley's miffed response was to turn his back to him and stand, arms folded, foot tapping.

Haskell took the moment to check the camcorder and make sure it had plenty of juice left. Having done so, a movement to his left caught his eye. He looked out through the shelter's plastic window. What had caught his eye was the man who had asked him where he had got his cheese Danish. He was exiting the bakery with a larger white bag and seemed about to cross the street toward Mangiamo. That was odd. The man had seemed to be waiting for a bus. Perhaps the baker prevailed on him to bring some extra goodies to the celebrants.

The man looked to his own left and paused at the curb when he saw that a car was approaching. The car was moving slowly as if searching for a space. The man with the bakery bag waited. Now Haskell saw that the driver of the car, a man wearing a red baseball cap and green jacket, seemed more interested in cars that were already parked. His head had turned toward Gilhooley's black pickup. Creeping by, the driver brought his right hand to his window and looked as if he was... what?... aiming something at the pickup?

He crept forward and now he was doing the same as he passed the stretch limo and the restaurant's entrance and Harry's Mercedes sedan. His brakes gave a screech as he passed the service alley where Stride's Subaru had been left. He'd slowed to a crawl. Haskell could see that his lips were moving as if he were talking to himself. The little man with the baked goods was watching this as well. He hadn't yet left the curb. He stood casually munching on a donut from his bag, powdered sugar falling onto his jacket. But his interest was short-lived. He gave a shrug, turned and entered the bar.

At that moment it struck Haskell where he'd seen that car before. It was among the photos that Gilhooley had sent him. It was the silver Ford Escape that Gilhooley had seen prowling. He'd offered no other information. Haskell had dismissed it as being unimportant. A burglar. That was it. That was what he'd assumed. Casing houses and parked cars to burgle.

Haskell said to Gilhooley who hadn't been watching, "Have you learned any more about this one?"

Now Gilhooley saw him. He had not seen Gilhooley. And now they both saw what the driver had been pointing. Another video camera. A mini.

"Yeah, the Greek," said Gilhooley. "He's been hanging around. He showed up in Mangiamo one night last weekend. Looking for Whistler. Says he knows him from Piraeus. He does know Piraeus. I quizzed him a little. Says he does some shipping for Whistler."

Gilhooley's voice had trailed off as he said this. "But what the hell's he doing with that camera?"

Haskell watched as the Ford Escape passed on by. "Broken tail light," he said, "Did you do that, by chance?"

"Too many silver or white SUVs. Made this one easier to spot."

They watched as it continued to the end of the street, then made a U-turn and came back just as slowly. The car pulled over some fifty yards in. The Greek double-parked it, got out, didn't lock it. He seemed to have left the engine running. He walked up the street close to other parked cars, his eyes fixed on Mangiamo's front entrance. He was a scrawny non-descript little man. He walked with the slow measured stride of a heron. Or more aptly, that of a stalker.

"Friend of Whistler's?" asked Haskell. "Somehow I don't think so. He looks like he buys all his clothes in Ohio."

"Well, he knows Harry's here. Let's see if he goes in."

He didn't. He got to the service alley where he raised his mini camera again and aimed it at Stride's Subaru. His lips again moving. Now Haskell understood. This man was narrating as well.

He leaned forward for a close-up of the Subaru's plate. As he did so, the back of his jacket pulled tight.

"Got a gun," said Gilhooley. "See? Small of his back."

"An automatic pistol. I saw it."

"Bounty hunter, maybe?" asked Gilhooley.

"After who, though? Stride?"

"There's a bounty on Stride?"

Haskell caught himself. He shook his head. "I meant to say on Stride's Muslim girls."

"Whoever," said Gilhooley, "The thing is, he's alone. He'd have to be crazy to try anything tonight. No chance that he'd get out of that restaurant alive. My guess? He's here scouting for somebody else. That would explain why he's taping."

As they watched, the man had turned his camera around and now he was taping himself. He looked into the lens, grinning, for a good twenty seconds, adding more commentary as he did so. It was the sort of corny thing a tourist might do in order to involve himself in the scene. For whose benefit, though? The Saudis? Very likely. They've long since been hunting their princess.

They watched as he started to move down the alley, pausing only to spit on Stride's car. That seemed proof. They watched as he neared the side service door. There he paused, his camera still at the ready. He opened the door. He peeked inside. His camera came up to eye level. At this, the sounds of the party spilled out. Someone singing off-key, but unabashedly so. A man's voice. Vaguely German. Must be Kessler. He was trying to get through the song, "Sixteen Candles" amid much hooting and laughing.

The Greek, if that's what he was, did not reach for his weapon. Nor did he even check to make sure it was free. From the look of it, all that he wanted to achieve was to get a little footage of the party. If so, he never got much past the door. A white coated woman, clearly one of the cooks, had taken the uninvited guest by the arm and was leading him back into the alley. Politely, but firmly, she was pointing the way toward the main entrance out on the street. He seemed apologetic, clasping his hands. She closed the door. He shook a fist at it.

The Greek stood for a minute as if deciding whether or not to go in the front door. In the meantime, he decided to vent his frustration by kicking at the front of Stride's car. They could hear the crunch of his heel against its grill, followed by a second and more tinkly crunch. He'd taken out one of her headlights.

"Must be too many green Subarus," said Haskell dryly.

"No, he's just pissed off."

"Yes, I got that," said Haskell.

"Look at this, though. The Greek's going to tape it."

The Greek had backed away from the car. He aimed his camera at the damage he'd caused. His smile indicated satisfaction. He slipped the camera into his pocket and with lightened pace, emerged from the alley and turned right toward the entrance. He was going inside after all.

As he entered, the man from the bakery came out and was once again idling in front. Haskell noticed that he'd cleaned off the front of his jacket. It occurred to Haskell that he looked very much like the man who'd arrived with Whistler and Kessler. Couldn't be, however, unless they were… twins? Oh, get with it, Charles. The brass ring's inside. He said to Gilhooley, "It's show time. Get in there."

"What for? You heard the singing. They're all in the back."

"So is Stride. Have you forgotten?"

"No, I have not, but you don't need me to signal. You can zoom from here and see the whole front. Make your call; she walks up; you press the button."

"Alas," said Haskell, "There are several new wrinkles. You saw what your Greek friend did to that car. One assumes that he harbors ill-feelings toward Stride. You'll be there to see that they're not acted upon."

"Mr. Haskell… bullshit. I quit."

"You saw that he was taping the damage he did. You and I are nicely framed in the background. Not good."

Gilhooley fell silent. No denying it.

"Therefore we want the camera that moron was using. Aside from the fact that our faces are in it, I want to see what-all else is in it and I want to hear what he's been saying. You'll relieve him of it in the confusion."

"You're saying after the blast."

"He'll be easier to handle."

"I still quit," said Gilhooley. "This is just too damned nuts."

"Worth a bonus."

"How big?"

"Twenty thousand," said Haskell. "But only if you also get that video camera. I want the only record of this thing to be mine and I will decide who gets a viewing."

"Twenty thousand is chump change to you, Mr. Haskell."

"Okay, name it."

"Fifty. And no more crap assignments."

"Done. Scouts' honor. Get in there."

THIRTY EIGHT

Haskell watched through the zoom lens of the video camera as Gilhooley entered the bar. His reappearance got the immediate attention of the bartender working that end. Now he's questioning Gilhooley. Asking, very likely, where he'd gone off to. A casual inquiry? Nope. Not at all. They've definitely had their eye on him.

So had the Greek, now not five feet away. The Greek reached up and snatched that cap off his head. He turned away and shrank down as if avoiding being seen. He must also be suspicious of Gilhooley.

Haskell took the trigger phone out of the bag and rested it on his thigh. He took his own cell phone and punched out the bar number, all the while aiming his camera. The bartender picked up. Haskell repeated what he'd rehearsed. He attempted a Mideastern accent. The bartender seemed either doubtful or reluctant. He began asking questions. Haskell feigned desperation. "Please. There's no time. Life or death."

And it worked. The bartender set the phone down on the bar and turned to walk back toward the rear. Haskell was expecting a thumbs-up from Gilhooley, but Gilhooley seemed troubled. He raised a hand while mouthing "Wait."

Now Haskell saw the woman bartender bearing a tray of what looked like champagne flutes. She was passing them out to all at the bar while making some sort of announcement. He heard what sounded like "These are on Harry." Those who'd taken the flutes were moving back toward the rear. As their bearer moved forward, he could hear her more clearly. She was saying, "We're all going to sing."

What would Stride do? Let him wait while they sang? And that's what they were doing. They were singing Happy Birthday. Haskell swung the zoom lens back on Gilhooley who was standing, looking back there, still signaling "Wait." But then, a thumbs-up, a vigorous nod. Haskell saw her now. She was coming after all. She was shouldering her way through the crowd, her face showing both annoyance and concern. Gilhooley could no longer be seen. He had dropped beneath the bar's overhang.

Off to Haskell's left, another bus was approaching. Within seconds it would be blocking his view. Now or never, thought Haskell. He wouldn't wait to hear her voice. He put down his cell and picked up the other. Still taping, he hit the Send button.

The blast stunned Haskell even though he had braced for it. A loud "Whomp" from the alley. A ball of red flame. A cloud of gray smoke rushing toward him. Sounds of creaking and collapsing like a dozen trees falling. Window glass peppering the

Mercedes and the limo and spraying all over the street. The shock wave tried to lift Haskell's bus shelter as if it were a sail in a storm. It slapped his newspaper into his face, but he managed to keep the camera going. He felt a sting on the top of his head. He touched it. He was bleeding. He kept taping.

The billowing flame rose upward and outward. It rolled over the Subaru, engulfing it fully. Haskell heard a loud clang against the pavement very near him. He turned the camera toward it, not knowing what it was. His first thought was that it might be the Subaru's hood, but its shape was or had been rectangular. It must be the lid of that trash bin.

More cracking and snapping, more ripping and tearing. It was, he thought, how a farm house must sound while being ripped apart by a tornado. He'd heard human voices, first as yelps of surprise, but now they'd risen into a chorus of screams. Hysteria. Panic. All recorded. Great stuff.

He couldn't see a thing in the alley itself because of the flames and the smoke. He swung the camera to where he'd seen Stride coming forward. He couldn't see her either. Nor anyone else. The entire interior was a cloud of white smoke. It poured out through the frames of the now glassless windows, curling out and up toward the sky.

He saw the first people staggering out. The white smoke was thinning. He could see more of them. Almost all of them blackened, most coughing and retching. Most helping others. Some out for themselves.

He saw people coming from other directions. From the liquor store, the gallery, the real estate office and everyone who worked in the bakery. Others came from the bus that had screeched to a stop the moment the Semtex went off. Some had rushed forward to help those coming out. Others held back, gaping, afraid to go near. Still others scattered to the left and the right, intent only on getting to their cars and away before there was another explosion. One man, and then a woman who had been on the bus stopped in the middle of the street to take pictures. The woman had a digital camera to her eye, snapping photos in rapid succession. The man had a video camera.

"Told you so," said the voice in his head. "Everyone has a camcorder."

Shut up. Not now. Where is Stride?

He still didn't see her among those streaming out, many soaking wet from the sprinklers. But he now saw Gilhooley. There's Gilhooley among them. He'd pulled his denim jacket over his head and one hand was covering his face. Injured? No. Doesn't seem to be. He must have spotted those two taking pictures. Without looking up, he raised his right and waved it in Haskell's direction. Haskell saw the small rectangular shape of what must be that Greek's mini camera. A man, some man, was reaching for Gilhooley. Where did he come from? Not from inside. Must have come from one of the neighboring businesses. He seemed to be trying to guide him to the street. He seemed to be trying to help him.

Gilhooley is trying to squirm from his grasp. The man won't have it. He's determined to help. He's gripped the collar of Gilhooley's denim jacket, pulling it even further over his head in his effort to lead Gilhooley to safety. Gilhooley resisting. He slips out of the jacket. The mini camera, apparently, goes with it, stripped from the palm of his hand. Haskell couldn't see it. Did it fall to the sidewalk? Gilhooley looking down, looking this way and that. Gilhooley doesn't seem to see it either. The man, the Samaritan, stands holding his jacket, offering it back to Gilhooley.

Suddenly, the Greek appeared, staggering out. He seems to have been blinded by the smoke. One hand is pressed against the side of his face. He's bleeding. Profusely. Blood oozing through his fingers. That's probably, thought Haskell, where Gilhooley cold-cocked him, probably with the nearest beer bottle. The other hand comes up. It's holding that pistol.

Gilhooley must have thought he was down for the count and chose not to take the time to relieve him of it. Now Gilhooley has cause to wish that he had. Gilhooley is backing away further. The Greek, reeling, does not see Gilhooley. He probably can't see much of anything. Gilhooley breaks into a run, going straight up the street, headed, no doubt, for his truck. No, he isn't. He's running right past it. He's leaving it.

The Samaritan waves his jacket. Must be asking, "Don't you want this?"

Guess not.

Gilhooley keeps going.

"Very sensibly," said Haskell's inner voice.

The Samaritan turns toward the staggering Greek. Again he reaches out and... crack... he flies backward. Did the Greek just shoot him? Yes, he did. Did he mean to? He must have thought that the man was Gilhooley. The Greek is standing over him, trying to focus, amid shouts of "Look out. That man has a gun." The Greek is now aware that the man's not Gilhooley. Oblivious to the crowd that is scattering, shouting, and oblivious to the people who are now steaming out, he looks up and down in his search for Gilhooley. He concludes, apparently, that Gilhooley's still inside. Or if not Gilhooley, whoever else he might be here for. He turns and plunges into the smoke.

Damn, thought Haskell. Where is that mini camera? Probably in the folds of Gilhooley's denim jacket, still clutched by the man who got shot. Well, so much for Gilhooley's fifty thousand dollar bonus which he's not going to live to see anyway.

Ah. That will keep. Here comes Stride. Haskell zeroed in with his zoom lens. She was coming, he saw, from well back in the restaurant, not from where Gilhooley last saw her. She must have rushed back through that wave of white smoke and now she was coming back out again, unharmed, but dripping wet from the sprinklers.

Who was that with her? Two blackened survivors. Damn, thought Haskell. One of them is the princess. How the hell could she have survived? The other is the younger Iranian sister. Both of them soaked to the skin. Right behind came the older one, equally soaked, but otherwise not much worse for wear. She was helping a woman who was cradling her arm. Must be one of the Mangiamo regulars.

But no Aisha. Where was Aisha? Inside dead or dying? There's no way that all four could have made it.

The bartender appeared before Stride reached the sidewalk. He's steering people toward the front door. She sees him; she's handing all three girls to him. She seems to be saying, "You take care of these while I go help the others." She's speaking with both hands over her ears. Her ear drums must have taken a beating. Didn't slow her down, though. What a woman.

Haskell thought that he should have heard more shooting by now. If not by the Greek, then at him. Perhaps he's hiding in there someplace, lying in wait. But for whom? Still Gilhooley? Not for the princess. She's already out. For the fourth one? The birthday girl? For Elizabeth Stride? Those two must be still in the back. As are Kessler and Whistler. As are Clew and Sadik. Please God, we at least got those four.

Nope. Not Whistler. Shit, shit, shit. Here he comes. Alive, limping badly, lost his hat. Smoke was seeping from his wet clothing. He has a phone to his ear. He steps into the street, still trying to speak into it. Must be too noisy inside. Beside him was that odd little man who had lingered with Haskell at the bus stop. The one who'd then gone into the bakery and later crossed over into the restaurant after the Greek coasted past.

Whistler got through to whoever he's calling. He's barking orders into the phone. Haskell heard him say the word "bomb." He said it not once, but at least two more times. He heard him say the words, "Get them down here. My house." Sounds like he's calling up the reserves. To his house, though? Not here? He probably wants them to cover his house to make sure there aren't more bombs planted there.

See that? That should show Harry Whistler's true nature. He'd walked past the girls with hardly a glance, pausing only to touch Rasha's shoulder. Not even noticing the man who was shot. Never pausing to offer a helping hand to anyone he'd passed along the way. Some of his houseguests are still in there somewhere and all that the great Harry Whistler cares about are his own property interests.

Up the street, a gray van, tires squealing appeared. Whistler waved it forward. It screeched to a stop. The van had the logo of some plumber on its side. Haskell heard the driver ask, "Where do you want us?" He couldn't hear much of the rest of the exchange, but Haskell could have sworn that he heard the driver speak the name of Yitzhak Netanya. Shame he wasn't invited, thought Haskell.

The van sped off. Guess they weren't needed. Whistler probably sent them to his house as well. Surprised he didn't go with them. But Whistler is going back in after all. Probably to look for his hat. But first he gave an order to the little man with him while gesturing toward something down the street. The little man seemed reluctant to leave him, but Whistler had said to him, "Go. Check it out." He seemed to be gesturing toward the Ford Escape that the Greek had left idling, double-parked.

Sensible, thought Haskell. It was certainly suspicious. In a bombing, the first bomb is sometimes a decoy. The next one drives up, takes out any survivors. Also anyone who'd come to their aid. But that was highly unlikely in this case, thought Haskell. Whatever the Greek's intention had been, he was in no condition to drive.

For now, though, Haskell returned to his coverage. More people milling around outside, others still trying to squeeze through the door that didn't want to stay open for some reason. It looked a bit crooked. Must be damaged. There's the younger Iranian running up to it, the bartender calling, "Niki, stop." She's grabbed the door, she's holding it open, freeing the way for those bunched up inside. Now she's pulling at it, looking up at a hinge that was no longer flush with the frame. She'd trying to rip it away. Not strong enough, but there goes her sister. And there goes the princess, but the bartender grabs her. The two sisters have gripped it below the top hinge and tugging mightily; they don't have the strength. But now the bartender lends both his big hands and the door is torn free and dragged away.

Haskell got it on camera, but he couldn't use it. Heroics by runaways are not in the script. He would edit that out at his leisure. For now he zoomed in on the sign above the entrance. It, too, had come loose. It had partly fallen. One end was dangling over the doorway just enough to cause some to duck under it. That thing falling, if it did, would make a great visual. Splice it to the end. A signature shot.

This is no good, thought Haskell. He was missing too much. That man and that woman who come off the bus were getting much better pictures. They had a better angle and were free to improve it. Get out of this shelter. Get closer than this. Even better, go inside and work your way to the back. That's where the real carnage should have been.

"Charles... No!"

Sorry. Got to see. That's too many survivors coming from the back room. Soot blackened, dazed, perhaps going into shock, but few of them seem badly injured.

Haskell felt a slow trickle moving down across his forehead and gathering at his right eyebrow. He wiped at it. Blood. It was that sting he'd felt. Must have been from a flying piece of glass. The cut was nothing, a mere breaking of the skin, but head cuts always bleed beyond their worth. Now his face was smeared and that could be good. He'd look more like a victim than they did.

"Sirens, Charles. Do you hear those distant sirens?"

Distant. Still distant. He had time.

"They are racing to the scene with the press close behind them. Charles, you can't be here. They have cameras."

Yes, he can. He'll have faded into the background. Just another safe-distance on-looker by then. And it's all the more reason to get his own pictures now. While he's at it, even better, he'll give Stride a hand. Let her see what he's made of, ignoring his own hurt. Five minutes. That's all it should take.

"Charles… are you out of your fucking mind?"

Besides, I need to get that Greek's camera.

"Charles, I beg you. Do not…"

Beg all you like. He'd stopped listening to himself. After all, no one in there would know him from Adam. He was across the street in five seconds.

He kept his own camera running, but he held it low lest it seem his primary interest. He passed Stride's Subaru. It was no longer green. It was fully ablaze, black smoke pouring from it. He could smell the upholstery melting. Its gas tank ought to go up any time. No loss. He'd buy her a Ferrari.

Whoa. There it goes. Not explosively, however. More like a giant match being struck. The tank must have been nearly empty. But the flames that licked up were being sucked into the building. That must be what they call a backdraft. He approached the bartender who'd gathered the three girls. Haskell asked him, "How can I help?"

The bartender saw the blood he'd smeared on his face. He said, "You could use some yourself."

"There are many much worse. Tell me what I can do."

The bartender had his arm around a shivering Rasha. He said, "She's cold. You can lend her your jacket."

Jacket, jacket, thought Haskell. He'd almost forgotten. He turned to where he'd seen the Samaritan fall. There he was, not moving, Gilhooley's jacket half under him. He'd get to that in a second.

"Of course," Haskell answered, slipping out of his own. "Poor little thing. Here you go."

"Charles..."

Not now, thought Haskell. He placed his suit jacket over her shoulders. She looked up at him. So trusting. "Th-thank you, sir," she said shivering. Lovely moment. But not in the script either.

He knelt with her wiping some grime from her face. A part of him wanted to hold that pose long enough for Elizabeth to see it. They'd meet again someday. Perhaps someday soon. And she would remember him as the man who, in total disregard of his own painful head wound, gave aid and comfort to Rasha.

"Charles... the prince's note. His suicide note!"

Oh, shit. His breast pocket. He said to Rasha, "Excuse me." He reached in and retrieved it the two copies that were in there and his camera cell phone as well. All those shots of her dangling father. He slipped them into the pockets of his trousers.

"And no posing, either. Get away from here, Charles. You might even pick her up and take her with you."

Who, Rasha? Good thought. It would be a splendid coup. He could commandeer one of these cars that are leaving. To the bartender, he said, "She's still very cold. Let me take her across and put her on that bus." Once behind it, out of sight, he'd keep going.

The bartender, now more anxious, had seen the flickering glow through the smoke that resulted from the Subaru's eruption. He said, distractedly, "They want to wait here."

Rats, thought Haskell. Who cares what they want? He wouldn't get to videotape who's dead inside, but he'd have the little princess to deliver. All he'd have to do is get rid of this man. If he could, who's to stop him? These two sisters?

He asked, "Wait for what? Oh, their parents, of course."

"Not their parents. Their friend. The girl this party was for."

"I'd go find her except I don't know what she looks like. You can go. I'll stay here and watch these three."

The bartender hesitated, but only for a beat. He said to the three, "You stay here with this man. Elizabeth should be out in a minute."

And with that he was gone. Into the smoke. Still confusion all around them. Everybody distracted. Good a time as any to retrieve Gilhooley's jacket. He walked over to the dead man. Oops. Not so dead. He moaned softly as Haskell tugged the denim jacket free. Haskell fingered its folds and... yes... there it was, the Greek's mini camera. It had been caught up in the middle of the jacket's right sleeve. He extracted it, palmed it, and folded the jacket, placing it under the Samaritan's head. Good move in case anyone's watching. Haskell slid the mini into his pocket along with his cell and the suicide notes. His left hand still held his own camera.

At that moment, there came another shout of his name. Not "Charles" this time. The voice shouted "Haskell." And it wasn't coming from inside his head. It was coming from all that black smoke.

Haskell blinked. He peered inside. He saw several shapes approaching. The nearest, stumbling over a fallen bar stool, was pointing a finger straight at him. Haskell knew that face underneath the wet soot. Roger Clew. But how could Clew have recognized him? They'd been at the same event only once, maybe twice, and hadn't so much as traded nods.

Whatever, thought Haskell. Take the bull by the horns. Calling out, "Wait. Let me give you a hand," he bounded through the door frame toward Clew. While appearing to reach a helping arm around his shoulders, he swung the hand that held the video camera against the side of Clew's head. Clew's legs promptly buckled and he started to fall onto a tangle of bar stools. Haskell caught him, stopped his fall, and lifted him bodily. He carried him out to the sidewalk.

Clew wasn't unconscious. He was struggling against him. But Clew was no match. Would not have been at best. Clew wasn't so much fighting as flailing. Haskell shifted Clew's weight. He wrapped an arm around Clew's neck. He squeezed hard to stop the flow of blood to Clew's brain and at the same time crush his voice box.

The older sister called, "Sir, what are you doing?"

"Convulsions," said Haskell. "He's gone into convulsions. I'll handle it. I know CPR."

Haskell saw that no one else was paying much attention. They were either absorbed by the scene inside or attending to their own discomfort. His intention, his plan, off the top of his head, was to drag Roger Clew between the nearest parked cars and silence him for good with a choke hold. The nearest spot that he saw with no cameras pointing at it was between the Mercedes and the stretch limousine.

He heard a woman's voice repeat the same question. She called out, "What are you doing?"

Without looking back, he said, "He's choking. The smoke."

A male voice said, "I'll take him. I'm a doctor."

Haskell turned his head, intending to say, "No need. I'm a doctor myself." He saw Sadik. Then he saw who was with him. The woman's voice had come from Elizabeth Stride. He saw that half her hair was burned off. Her appearance must have caused him to weaken his grip because Clew was flailing again. He wormed loose enough to turn his head toward them. He gagged the words, "Haskell. It's Haskell."

Confusion from Stride. She couldn't quite hear him. She'd cupped a hand to her ear. Clew's voice became stronger. He gripped Haskell's shirt. He cried out, "Haskell did this. This is Haskell."

Sadik's eyes widened. He said to Elizabeth at a level she could hear, "Roger's right. That man is Charles Haskell." He'd remembered the face from the offshore rig photo, the smear of blood notwithstanding. But the improbability, Haskell being at Mangiamo, caused him to freeze momentarily.

Not an instant's worth of hesitation from Stride. She vaulted past the doctor, made a skip and a hop, and threw a spinning kick at Haskell's knee.

He let out an "arghh." He had felt the knee pop. He dropped Clew and feinted a jab with his right while swinging the camera at her face with his left. She ignored the feint; she ducked under the camera. The eye-piece end of it glanced off her skull. He swung it again, back-handed this time. Too late. She was on him. She kicked at his crotch. An explosion of pain and he was down.

"Elizabeth… Elizabeth." Haskell choked out her name. "This isn't… it's not what you think."

Staring coldly, she asked Clew, "This is Haskell? You're sure?"

Clew was rising. "And he did this. You can bet your life on it."

Haskell managed, "Wait. You don't understand." He tried rising himself. "All I wanted… why I'm here… I did not want you hurt… it was only to free you from Kess…"

Another kick came. This one to his mouth. It toppled him backward. Elizabeth moved in. She kicked him twice more. She was about to drive a spiked heel through his eye, when Sadik rushed to grab her. He pulled her away.

He said, "We'll have questions for this one."

Elizabeth's response was to stomp on his stomach. It doubled him up. She rolled him onto his side. She patted his pockets. She extracted his wallet. She opened it and held it up to the light. "Charles Barrington Haskell. It's him."

Elizabeth put a hand on the stretch limousine. She asked Clew, "Where's your driver? Have you seen him?"

"Inside. He's helping the others."

She moved quickly to the driver's side window. In almost the same motion, she put her heel through it. She reached through the hole and opened the door. She found the trunk latch and released it.

"Good idea," said Sadik as the trunk lid popped open. He reached in to retrieve his medical bag. It was why he'd come out in the first place. Clew did the same with his briefcase. Sadik said to Clew, "Help me lift him. Be careful. I don't think he's finished."

Together, they hoisted him into the trunk. He was, in fact, not quite finished. He struggled against them, trying to kick loose. He said to Elizabeth, his voice catching in his throat, "All I want... I came... I came to make peace. A trade. All I want is a trade."

Elizabeth ignored him. She was checking the trunk lid. It had a yellow safety release. She used the heel of her ruined right shoe to disable it. She reached to close it on Haskell.

He saw his last chance. He tried to grab at her. She bounced the trunk lid off his forearms. He recoiled with a yelp. She reached to shut it again. Her foot touched his dented video camera. She picked it up. She threw it in with him.

Sadik said, "His cell phone. Don't leave him with a phone."

She saw it on his belt. She reached in and snatched it. But she had no pockets, no place to put it. She tossed it to Roger Clew.

Haskell screamed, "Elizabeth!! Please listen. Don't go." And then, as if yelling at somebody else, he snapped, "No. Shut up. I need to tell her... Shut up." Then to Stride, "You're too good for... they'll betray you. He'll betray you."

Clew said to her, "Not me. He means Kessler."

Haskell called out once more, his voice hoarse and pleading. His words were, "All I wanted... you're Elizabeth Stride. All I wanted... Elizabeth... Oh, if we could talk."

Sadik said to Haskell, "Talk about what? How you'd kill four young girls just to meet her?"

He sank back. His voice became a little boy's whine. He said, "Elizabeth... to save you. I can give you so much more. We could... we could... play tennis."

Elizabeth stood blinking. Her eyes went to Clew. He remembered what Harry had said of this guy. Wrote the book on abnormal psych. He said, "Don't even try to understand that."

She slammed the trunk shut. She could still hear Haskell. And Haskell was still whining, but at somebody else.

She also heard the sirens. They were now very near. She had no time to wonder who was in there with Haskell.

She said to Clew, "Get your driver. Him or the keys. Get this limo out of here now."

"Take it back to the house?"

"If it isn't burning. Either way, stay with it. I'm going back in to help Martin."

THIRTY NINE

Four were killed or mortally injured outright. That number could easily have been forty. Almost everyone suffered from smoke inhalation in addition to cuts, burns and bruises. Many had been deafened by the blast temporarily. Most of these were expected to recover.

Many of the injured were treated at the scene in either of three emergency vehicles, assisted by a certain Dr. Freundlisch. About a dozen required hospital care. These were mostly from smoke inhalation. Of these injuries, many could have been avoidable. Most were patrons who had refused to leave until they saw their friends safely out. Not all were that selfless. Only most.

The dead included two cooks and a waiter. The fourth wasn't found until later. The two cooks were crushed when the alley wall collapsed and with it that part of the roof. One had died instantly; the other soon after. Both had also been seriously burned. For a time, it was hoped that the waiter might live. He, too, had been burned, but to a lesser extent. But his station had been near the door to the alley. The blast blew the door and the waiter with it almost to the far side of the room.

A large commercial stove was thought to have deflected the greater part of the blast. It had the effect of shaping the charge more back into the alley than intended. It still took down most of the wall. Another factor, identified later, was that the alley's trash bin had been empty. It was hollow. That, too, had dispersed the effect.

But the biggest of these factors had been Harry's gesture of buying champagne for the house. Once all glasses were filled, he led them in a toast to be followed by them singing Happy Birthday to Aisha. There was no room in the back for all those at the bar. The girls and their hosts, therefore, had to come forward. They gathered in the archway, decorated with vines, that marked the divider between the bar area and the reserved dining area. It was the extra strength of the archway that kept that section of the ceiling from collapsing. Otherwise, it fell on the tables. It fell on platters of half-eaten antipasto, temporarily abandoned when the toast was announced.

Some there had called it miraculous.

Aisha had been fully shielded from the blast by the bodies of those standing around her. The toast was to her, the singing was to her, so she'd been guided, blushing with self-conscious modesty, into a center stage position. She'd stood with Rasha, flanked by the sisters, five adults standing behind them. The five were Harry Whistler who was leading the song, Kessler, Clew and Sadik, plus one of the Beasley twins. Whichever. Not Elizabeth, however. She just been called forward to take what was said to be an emergency phone call.

Harry had been struck in the hip by a piece of brick and mortar that flew in from the wall. It knocked him into the row of four girls, dragging three of them to the floor as if tackled. The Beasley twin assumed that this was deliberate so he threw himself on the fourth, which was Niki. Kessler had been knocked down as well, although not by a projectile, the shock wave. While falling, he'd grabbed onto Clew and Sadik. It wasn't deliberate. It was a reflex. No bodily shielding was intended by any with the single exception of the twin. Not that they would not have. They simply did not. Even so, no matter what the denials, the belief would persist that Whistler and Kessler had been ready to give their lives for the others, and for young Aisha in particular.

Another miracle. Of a sort. In later telling.

The overhead sprinklers had come on at once, drenching everyone there, front and back. Thick smoke rolled over them, first high and then settling. Stride had instantly plowed back through the crowd. Over it, actually. Most were down. She and Kessler, she frantic, were unscrambling the pile to determine who was hurt and who wasn't. Stride's first interest was the girls and in getting them to safety. She reached Rasha first, telling her to stay low. It was then that she realized that her hearing was affected, even having been so far up front. She could barely hear her own voice. She took Rasha and Niki, each by an arm and again stepped over the bodies of patrons who were too slow getting up. Shahla reached down to help one of these whose arm had clearly been broken.

Elizabeth shouted for Aisha to follow. Kessler, by this time, had Aisha in his arms and he had his own deafness problem. He was urging Elizabeth and the others to stay. He was saying that they might be safer where they are if this was a deliberate attack.

He said that someone might be waiting to see who survives, ready to finish the job. She would have understood him if she could hear. All she saw was a time-wasting mouthing of words. She shouted, "Bring Aisha. Let's go." She went on, expecting that he would follow.

Kessler wasn't certain that this was an attack. It could have been a kitchen explosion. A gas leak. He released Aisha, told her to stay put, and made his way over to the kitchen, staying low. He saw the wall. Blown in, not blown out. This was no kitchen explosion. He found the two cooks, one of them beyond helping. A part of his skull torn away. The other, a young woman, didn't look much better, but she was trying to rise. She was naked, waist up, except for her bra. The rest had been blown or burned off. The steady spray from the sprinklers was at least cooling her, but it made her harder to grip. He lifted her and, half-carrying, half-dragging her, he bought her closer to the shelter of the archway.

Harry was gone. The twin was gone. Clew had left as well, but no further than mid-bar where he was helping some of the dazed and confused. There were more than a dozen still inside. Kessler heard Sam's voice telling Clew to get out. "Get some air. Clear your lungs. Clear your head." Apparently, Clew was of limited use, but at least he had good intentions.

Sadik, however, had been careful to stay low and he had chosen to stay back with Aisha. The wet smoke, now turning black, was settling on them both. He saw that Aisha and Sadik were kneeling beside the fallen waiter. Kessler saw his foot moving. Perhaps he was only stunned. Kessler called Sadik, he called him by name, telling him that the cook needs him more. Kessler realized his mistake on seeing Aisha's confusion. But this was no time for explanations. Sadik came over. Aisha stayed with the waiter. She was holding his hand, speaking softly to him, rocking back and forth as she did so.

Sadik assessed the condition of the young cook. Her breathing was labored, she was coughing up blood, but she seemed to be almost fully conscious. He said he must go and get his medical bag. He took Kessler aside and out of her hearing. He said, "Her chest has been crushed. That blood's from her lungs. All I can do is ease her pain."

"Can she live?"

"I don't think so. Too much damage inside." Having said this, he cursed, he gritted his teeth. He said to Kessler, "That makes two in three days."

Kessler knew what he meant. He meant Farah. Shahla's friend.

Sadik stood and was about to enter the archway when Elizabeth returned from the street. She was holding her nose. She was blowing and swallowing, still in the process of clearing her ears. She told him that Sam had the girls. She said to him, "Why is Aisha still here? I told you to grab her and go."

Aisha either couldn't hear her or chose not to hear. She continued rocking and whispering softly. She still held the hand of the waiter. Kessler noticed that Aisha's new dress was torn and that part of her black bra was showing. She'd also lost her shoes in all the tumbling and scrambling and her new panty hose was in shreds. Like the rest, she was wet and streaked with soot.

Kessler glared at Elizabeth, annoyed by her tone. "Oh, you told me, did you? Open your eyes. Can't you see…"

He didn't finish because it was at that moment that the Subaru's gas tank erupted. A sheet of flame rolled across and above them, licking at the ceiling's sagging tiles. It quickly receded, leaving only glowing embers, but its heat was enough to sear Kessler's face and Aisha's bare shoulders as well. Elizabeth, standing, got the worst of it. Smoke rose from her hair where it was singed. The fabric on her blouse puckered. But she barely flinched. Her concern was for Aisha.

She said, "Aisha… now. Get out of here now. More ceiling could come down any moment."

Aisha answered, "Elizabeth, it will drop on them, too. We're not hurt, but they are. I'm staying until we get help."

Elizabeth growled. An expression of frustration. But her eyes showed pride more than anger. What anger she felt, she took out on Sadik. She said, "You heard her. Let's get them some help." Before leaving, however, she spotted a cabinet in which the white table linens were kept. She reached in, took a table cloth, and shook out its folds. It was one of the big ones, banquet size. She draped it over Aisha's head and shoulders.

This was, although no one realized it at the time, the third miracle in the making. Or perhaps it was more of a curse.

She and Sadik were gone for no more than a minute when Kessler thought he heard Haskell's name being called. Clew's voice? Yes, he thought so. Sounding choked. And there it was again. Clew's voice. The name Haskell. Suddenly the sprinkler system shut off. Now he heard a lot of shouting and banging. He heard a man's voice. It sounded in pain. He peered out through the smoke. It had thinned a good deal. He could make out Elizabeth, Clew and Sadik. They were standing at the open trunk of the stretch. He couldn't tell what was happening out there. Had Clew decided to announce to the world that Haskell and his bunch were responsible for this? Not impossible, but what made Clew think so?

He saw Sadik coming with his medical bag. Kessler asked him, "What was that all about?"

Sadik said, "That can wait. It's under control." He knelt beside the cook and got to work.

Harry Whistler appeared, his red blazer now gray. For once, he blended into a crowd. He said, "I'm leaving. We're taking the limo. It can't be here when those sirens arrive. I'll take the three girls with me."

Sadik said, "Take Martin. He's done all he can. I'll stay and watch over Aisha."

Harry left. Kessler didn't. He'd watch Aisha himself. But then he heard several shouts from the bar. Among them a woman's. "That man has a gun." He thought that this warning must be related to the shouting and banging that he'd heard outside. But this wasn't outside; it was inside. He looked through the thinning smoke and he saw faces turned to a man who was groping along the far wall. That part of it was mostly intact. The man seemed to be trying to feel his way, not toward the front, but toward the rear. He had reached the ruined mural and the Happy Birthday banner which had long since fallen in a tangle. In his right hand, he held a Glock pistol.

No idea who he was; he'd never seen him before, nor was Kessler aware there'd been a shooting outside. Kessler didn't see him as much of a threat, but a gun was a gun so he took it away.

No struggle, he simply took it out his hand and stuck it into his belt.

"Just like that?" Roger Clew would ask later.

"This man was a zombie. One eye halfway out, cheek the size of a grapefruit, blood all over one side of his face. As I say, though, a gun is a gun."

He said it took this man perhaps two or three seconds to realize that the weapon was no longer in his hand. He looked around to see if he had dropped it. He sank to his knees feeling through the debris. Kessler wanted to get out to the girls and decided to drag this man along. He reached to seize him by the collar of his jacket. Just then, he saw Elizabeth coming back in, intent on retrieving Aisha. He saw that she was bleeding from a cut on her scalp and that she'd lost the heel of one shoe.

He asked again, "What was all that outside?"

She answered with one of those satisfied smiles that he'd get whenever she aced him at tennis. "Show you later," she said. "A surprise."

He was about to ask her if it rhymes with rascal, but the man in his grip cocked his head when she spoke. He suddenly stopped struggling and turned his good eye in the approximate direction of the sound. He went rigid. He seemed to recognize her. Suddenly he let out a squeak like a mouse and tore himself loose from Kessler's hand. Now he was clawing through the sodden debris in an even more desperate search.

Kessler said to the man, "It's not down there. I have it." He touched his fingers to the butt of the Glock. He asked, "What did you have in mind?"

The man was frantic. He tried to lunge at the weapon, but his feet got no traction; he fell in a splash. Elizabeth, meanwhile, had shown little interest. She knew that he could deal with… whatever this was. As she continued on her way, this man's good eye followed, all the while trying to find the snap would open the sleeve of his jacket. All the while snorting and gasping. By this time, as far as this man was concerned, he, Kessler, was no longer there. Elizabeth had disappeared through the archway, this man scrambling after her, crab-like. He was making new sounds or perhaps saying words that were unintelligible to Kessler.

Right then, Elizabeth reappeared in the archway. She'd heard the sounds that this man was making. She looked at the man. She looked at Kessler. She said, "That was Arabic, Martin."

"Saying what?"

"That I'm a slut. And a lesbian whore."

Kessler said, "Go. I'll take care of this."

Certainly, this raised questions that ought to be asked, but he doubted that this man could process any thoughts beyond his opinion of Elizabeth. He was more than half out of his mind. So enough was enough. They could sort this out later. For now, get him out of the way.

Kessler picked him up by his belt and looked around for a place where he might put him. He decided that the nearby men's room would do. It seemed unlikely to be needed for some time. As he dragged him through the door and threw him into a stall, the man was still tearing at the cuff of his sleeve, fumbling for something inside it. Another weapon, thought Kessler, more than likely. Kessler lifted him, turned him, stripped the green jacket off him and saw the knife that was taped to his arm. Kessler banged the man's head against the tank of the toilet in order to settle him down. He went limp. He peeled the knife loose and examined it. A cheap throwing knife from a sporting goods store. A cutting edge had been ground on one side. He'd made a graspable handle using band-aids.

"With this," Kessler asked him, "you'd go after Elizabeth? You would take on Elizabeth Stride?"

The question was rhetorical. The man was unconscious. Perhaps he thought that a slut and a lesbian whore would fall all to pieces at the sight of this toy. No more time for this, however. Kessler left him.

"That's it?" Clew asked later, "You just left him?"

"I severed his Achilles. He'd be going nowhere else. I left his knife stuck in the ceiling."

The young cook had succumbed before the ambulance got there. Sadik had stayed with her to the end. He'd given her morphine. Perhaps enough. Perhaps more. No one seemed willing to ask.

The waiter lived a few hours longer. The EMT medics worked to stabilized him before lifting him onto a stretcher. They found him conscious, in good spirits and in little or no pain. He told them, "I'm all right. Don't bother about me." He was talking to them, but he was looking at Aisha. She'd been holding his hand all the while.

But she had to let go when they carried him out. Elizabeth would not let her follow. In the ambulance, they learned later, he'd repeated his assurance that he was not badly hurt. He said he'd thought he was, but he wasn't anymore after Aisha knelt with him and prayed with him. He'd told them that she was an angel. He'd made it to the intensive care unit where he died of massive trauma to his skull and his spine. And yet he'd never suffered. Not while he was with Aisha. Her name was on his lips when he died. That, at least, was the story.

Another miracle? Or was it a trick of his brain, anesthetized by soothing and comforting words, to say nothing of the flood of endorphins released when the body goes into deep shock. This was Elizabeth's preferred explanation. "That's all we need, damn it," she said with disgust, "is anyone thinking she's a healer."

Elizabeth was actually mad at herself for the way she'd left the restaurant with Aisha. It turned out to be the frosting on the cake.

As she and Aisha walked out the front door, there must have been twenty flashing cameras. There were also the strobing blue lights of the police cars, the red lights of fire trucks, the amber lights of the EMT vehicles and of ambulances still lining up. There was no room as yet for the TV mobile units, but these were waiting on the next side street. Their reporters, however, had come forward on foot and were lining up witnesses to be interviewed.

Those twenty or so flashing cameras outside recorded every person, not already out, as they appeared in the doorway on foot or on a stretcher. They did, however, miss Rajib Sadik who certainly had no wish to have his face on news broadcasts. They ignored him, assuming he was just another doctor who'd arrived well after the event.

But the damnedest shot they got was of Elizabeth and Aisha. There was Aisha wrapped in a white table cloth that covered her from head to mid calf. Aisha, who'd worn hijab in the past, had arranged the tablecloth in much the same way. Not on purpose. Force of habit. Old habit. And there was Elizabeth, escorting her, protecting her, her mascara having run in such a way that there seemed a great fierceness about her. Add to that her hair, not burning, but burned, and still steaming from the residual water that still dripped from all over the ceiling. Elizabeth had grabbed a tablecloth of her own. For warmth. Not for modesty. She was feeling a chill. The air cooling system still functioned.

That shot would appear the next morning, Thursday, on page three of the Alexandria Gazette. The paper hadn't been able to get their names, but its reporter had learned from whatever source that they'd stayed to care for the dying. The accompanying caption said as much and it called them Angels Of Mercy. The shot wasn't quite a twin of that artist's rendering that appeared in the Bahrain Tribune. No camel, of course. And no flaming sword. But there was Aisha face with those same big eyes and with that same dimple on her cheek.

And looking radiant. Fairly glistening in the lights. Miraculously untouched by all the soot and the grime that had covered every single other person. How, one might ask, could this have been possible? She was, after all, in there almost the longest. The answer, of course, was the clean tablecloth, but that might not be enough for some people.

Still, there was cause to count a blessing or two. At least it hadn't made the front page. It was one of many that ran on a spread that covered the fourth and fifth pages. Most were quite small, maybe three inches high, and all part of a larger montage. It showed perhaps a dozen survivors in varying degrees of distress, several taking oxygen, others huddled under blankets. There was also a close-up of the burned-out Subaru and a number of interior shots showing the blast and water damage. The front page had been reserved for a wide-angle photo showing the exterior with its dangling sign and the gaping holes where its windows had been.

The Darvi sisters and Rasha were not shown at all. They'd been ushered by Harry into the stretch limo and were already long gone. The Mercedes, badly scarred, but entirely drivable, had moved several car lengths up the street where it waited beyond the art gallery. This was done at the direction of the fire department who needed it out of their way. The driver was one of the twins. There, it waited for Elizabeth and Aisha. Kessler had run interference for them, pushing several reporters aside. That didn't stop more shots from being taken as they climbed into the Mercedes. But none of these had appeared in the spread or on any of the late TV broadcasts. Of all the coverage, there was only that one single photo of the two "angels" emerging. And since that was only one among many, perhaps Aisha would be lost in the crowd.

Roger Clew, like Sadik, had escaped being photographed as did Harry Whistler himself. They'd already left the scene in the limo, Charles Haskell still in the trunk. The presence of State's Director of Intelligence would have attracted the notice of the media world-wide. Bad enough that the bombing itself had already. It was among the leads on several internet news sites within ninety minutes of the blast. There would be no hope of containing this.

And yet speculation was curiously muted as to the cause of the explosion. Few even used the word "bomb." Terrorism was mentioned, but generally dismissed. No one could think of any possible motive for targeting this restaurant in particular. None realized that any at the party were Muslims, let alone being runaways brought out by the Nasreens. Haskell's scheme notwithstanding... and Aisha's photo notwithstanding... no one drew a connection between this attack and either the prophecy or the Saudi ten billion. This was true of the media. Largely true of the police. Their interest was local. Their interest was personal.

One of them had been helping tend bar.

FORTY

The policewoman, Karen, full name Karen Hoffman, had witnessed a good deal both inside and out. Her first instinct had been to get people to safety. She did so while calling 911. Her biggest concern had been for the girls. She shouted to Harry asking if they're okay. He'd shouted back through the din. "We all seem to be, yes. Martin's checking on the staff. We'll need ambulances."

"They're coming," she told him. "I can hear them."

Karen had been in and out several times, giving aid wherever she saw the need. She was in when the struggles with Haskell occurred. They'd only lasted for a minute or two. She was out when Harry appeared with the twin, first making at least one call of his own. She seen him send the twin for the Ford Escape that had been left idling down the street. She knew it wasn't Harry's. It belonged to the Greek. She saw the twin drive it to the next street up where there was a building under construction, but with no workers present at that hour. She saw the twin – not that she knew he was a twin - step out of the car, having left it in gear, and walk back as the Ford Escape kept going, finally coming to rest between a pile of sand and a heavy construction site dumpster.

That was all the attention she'd had time to give it until perhaps a good hour later when the body of the Greek was discovered.

A fireman had found him in the men's' toilet stall. He promptly called in the nearest police in the person of Karen and her sergeant, Dave Ragland. They'd been out taking statements from witnesses while avoiding saying much to the press. The sergeant was in uniform. Karen was not. She still wore the grimy white shirt and stained slacks that she'd put on to help with the party. But she wore her badge on her belt. The Greek had bled out from a wound to his face and from one deep cut through his Achilles. They saw the throwing knife stuck in the ceiling. They saw fresh blood on the side that had been sharpened. They saw the bandages on the dead Greek's right forearm, some of which conformed to the shape of the knife. They found a Greek passport in his pocket. It gave his name as Zenobias Polykarpos. Within it they found a plastic key card with the name of a nearby motel. And they found a snapshot of a somber little girl who was dressed in Muslim attire.

The sergeant showed it to Karen. "Who's that look like?" he asked.

"Unless she has a sister, that's Rasha."

Karen's next stop, the sergeant at her side, was at the Greek's Ford Escape. Its right side had been deeply raked by the dumpster. Its engine had quit; it had probably stalled while struggling against the big sand pile. They started their search with the glove box.

In it, they found the car's registration and its proof of insurance. Both were in the name of one Bernice Barrow, of Hilton Head, South Carolina. The registration and the plate did not match.

They lifted the lid that concealed the spare tire. They could see that it wasn't seated properly. Sergeant Ragland removed the tire. He let out a breath, He said, "Son of a bitch." He was looking at the radio, taser and cuffs that had been taken from Eddie Fitch's body. He saw the extra clip from Eddie's Glock. Underneath, he found a plastic grocery store bag. In it was a tangled mass of junk jewelry and several of Bernice Barrow's credit cards.

They called for other officers to secure the scene and take photographs of all that they'd found. Their next stop was at his motel room.

In his closet they found an assortment of clothing, some of it still bearing price tags from Wal-Mart. On the closet shelf, underneath the extra blanket, they found a laptop computer. With it they discovered four cheap-looking cell phones, each of them pre-programmed to the same foreign number. These were throwaways, thought Ragland. Use once and discard. These hadn't been used, but there might have been others.

Hidden elsewhere, taped to the back of a drawer, they found more than four thousand dollars in cash and another passport, this one Saudi. The name on this one was Mulazim Jabir. He went to the end table next to the bed and found the room's telephone book. In the front he found the country code for Saudi Arabia. The code was 966, the same as those on the cell phones.

Karen said, "This is going to be a long night. I'd like to use this guy's shower."

"Do it," said Ragland. "Nice new clothes in his closet. You two are about the same size."

"A quick rinse," she told him. "Two minutes."

Within that time he'd read the email exchanges between Niki Darvi, the younger Iranian, and the owner of the car, Bernice Barrow. Her more recent messages struck him as odd. She'd used upper case letters for emphasis in others, but here they made no sense; they were on the wrong words. He told Karen what he found while she was toweling.

She said, "So this guy sent them after he stole it. Do we think that he would have left this woman alive?"

"No, we don't. I'd better call the Hilton Head cops. And then let's go talk to Harry Whistler."

Roger Clew had used the ride home in the limo to put in a call to Howard Leland. He wanted Leland to hear about all this from him before Leland saw it on the news. He reached for his cell phone, realized he had two. He'd almost forgotten that he had Haskell's. Elizabeth had taken it from him. He put it aside and used his own to call Leland. He caught him at his home in the Maryland suburbs, likely with a very stiff drink in his hand. He briefed Leland on the bombing attempt.

He told Leland that, yes, they thought Haskell was behind it. He said, no, they're all well, just some odd cuts and bruises. He told Leland that yes, Kessler did have the disk, but he truly hadn't known it before earlier that day. He said that it was safe, in good hands. He did not tell Leland that they had Haskell, that Haskell was locked in the trunk as they spoke, having been crippled by Stride. For one thing, the three girls did not know that either and they could hear every word Clew was saying. Happily, however, they couldn't hear Haskell except for an occasional dull thump. State limos were built to be soundproof.

"Sit tight, Mr. Leland. I'll be back in the morning. I'll brief you more fully when I see you."

Upon disconnecting, he picked up Haskell's phone. He went into the menu. He found Haskell's list of contacts. He saw the initials HB and RL who he presumed to be Bentley and Leeds. He'd get Haskell's full call record later. He noticed a read-out on its camera feature indicating that many photographs had been taken. He pressed a button to show them.

He scanned though some fifty that Haskell had taken in the room where the prince had been murdered. There were several of the prince as Haskell had left him. Clew was neither shocked nor surprised. It was the scene as Leland had described it. But there were close-ups of Leland's personal effects and the contents of his briefcase as well. Meant to serve as proof of Leland's involvement, but for what purpose? Extortion? Clew didn't think so. Haskell had to have realized that Howard Leland would sooner resign than submit to it. But that assumes that a man like Haskell would understand a man like Howard Leland. And that he'd never get the disk in that way.

No, these had the look of a slide presentation that Haskell would make to the Saudis. Followed, no doubt, by a videotape showing the destruction of all those responsible at the hand of Charles Haskell himself. All those named by the prince in his suicide note. And, for good measure, the source of the prophecy. The false Aisha and her lying handmaidens, the prince's "corrupted" daughter among them. It would have made him quite a hero to some.

The video tape? It's in the trunk with him. It's in the dented camera with which Haskell had attacked him and with which he'd tried to fend off Elizabeth. It's not going anywhere. It would keep. Clew closed Haskell's phone. He dropped it into his briefcase.

Harry had been watching him. "Something you plan to share?"

Clew let Harry see his eyes flick toward the three girls. "Later," Clew told him. "Not now."

The limo reached Harry's street. It wasn't the first. Clew saw that two cars sat flanking the gate on the strip of grass bordering the sidewalk. He saw another pulling up at the near end of the wall, announcing its presence with a flash of its brights. At the far end, he saw a gray van. All headlights were on. All engines running.

"They're ours," said Harry to the others in general. "I made a call from the restaurant." He flicked a finger toward the van. "Except for those. They're Mossad."

The gates swung open. The limo went through it. Clew saw two men standing on the front lawn, both with automatic weapons in their hands. Clew asked, "On the lawn? Shouldn't they be concealed?"

"A show of force, Roger, needs to be shown. They're there to discourage, not engage."

He said to the driver, "Please pull up in front." He said to the girls, "Go take nice long showers. When you're done, go to bed, get up early and pack. By this time tomorrow, we'll be landing in Geneva. You won't be coming back to this house."

Niki, who'd been silent throughout the ride home, said, "I'm not going with you."

Shahla said, "Niki, we'll talk later."

"No," said Niki, "I know what I'm saying. You all forgave me, but that was before. Did those people die in the back?"

"Yes," Sadik told her, "At least two so far. But it wasn't your doing, believe me."

"And you helped," said Shahla. "I was standing doing nothing. It was you who tried to take down that door."

Harry said, "Why don't we do this inside."

"No," said Niki firmly. "Here's what I'll do. I'll call the Nasreens. I have their California number. I'll tell them what I've done, how I've betrayed them and how I've almost killed all of you. Let them tell the world that there is no Aisha, there are no handmaidens; I've made it all up. After that, I'll go anywhere they send me."

"That," said Sadik, "is what you must not do. You want to make amends? There's a much better way. Take your shower. We'll talk when you're done."

The stretch limo had barely fit into the garage. It had to go in at an angle. There was room now that Stride's car no longer existed. But still room for Harry's scarred Mercedes. That car, bearing Aisha and Kessler and Stride, was just coming in through the gate. Clew directed it to the third garage door, formerly the Subaru's space.

Clew had intended to retrieve Haskell's camera, but he couldn't while Aisha was present. His jaw dropped when he saw how Aisha was dressed. And Elizabeth, too. Full length white abayas. He asked, "What's with… these?"

"What's with what?" asked Elizabeth.

It was only then, it seemed, that she realized how they looked. She fingered the fabric. "These are tablecloths, Roger. Aisha's burned and she needed to be covered."

"Burned badly?" he asked.

"No, but she'll blister. Let's get her inside so I can treat it."

Kessler cocked his head in the direction of the limo. He asked Clew. "Still in there?"

Clew nodded. He said "Still."

Kessler said, "At least he's quiet. Leave him. Let's go."

Clew said, "I'll be right behind you."

Sergeant Ragland had called from the gate asking Harry to open it up. He said that he had a few questions. He pulled up to the front in his Belle Haven squad car. Officer Karen Hoffman was with him. She looked as if she'd just dressed for golf. Harry, still limping, met them both at the door and directed them into the library. The sergeant carried a laptop computer.

Karen looked him over. "Are you sure you're Harry Whistler? You look like you've been living in a dumpster."

"Very funny. I'm waiting. We're low on hot water."

"All the girls are okay?"

"They're our problem with the water."

The sergeant said, "We saw the posse outside. Do you expect to be hit again tonight?"

"A few friends have dropped by. Just in case."

"I'll be straight with you, Harry. I'll tell you what we've got. We expect that you'll do the same for us."

"If I can"

"We might know who planted that bomb," said the Sergeant. He showed the Greek passport. "Do you know this man?"

Harry studied the face. He read the name. "Sam said that someone he called Zeke the Greek had claimed to be an old friend of mine. But no, I've never seen this one."

"Well, he isn't Greek, he's Saudi." Ragland showed the other passport. "His name isn't Zeke, it's Mulazim Jabir. We found cells in his room set to call a Saudi number. Did you see him at Mangiamo this evening?"

"Never laid eyes until now."

"Then why would you order his car to be moved?"

"What car was that? You mean the one double parked with its engine running? I just didn't like the look of it, Dave."

"Of him either, I guess. Did one of your people leave the Saudi on a toilet after bashing him and cutting his strings? I know it wasn't Sam. He'd have snapped him in two."

The sergeant didn't wait for an answer. He handed Harry the snapshot that the Saudi had on him. "This is Rasha, is it not? Was this Saudi after Rasha? Did Eddie Fitch spot him watching your girls play tennis? Were they there that night? Is that what got Eddie killed? Did that piece-of-shit kill Eddie with the knife we found stuck in the ceiling?"

Harry raised a hand. He said, "Dave, slow down." He was looking at the photo of Rasha in hijab. "Let me get Elizabeth and Martin in here. Hold your noses, however. They haven't bathed either. Then I'll ask you to take it from the top."

Kessler barely recognized the face in those passports as the man he'd disarmed and immobilized. The man had posed neatly groomed when he sat for the photo and not with one eye hanging out of its socket. Kessler only shrugged and said nothing.

A few minutes later, Elizabeth learned that the Ford Escape this man had been driving was owned by her friend, Bernice Barrow. Not only the car, but the laptop. She had asked Sergeant Ragland, "So he stole them from her?"

"Elizabeth… he killed her. She's dead."

Kessler reached to take Elizabeth's hand.

The sergeant said he'd called the Hilton Head's Sheriff's Department after leaving this man's motel room. She'd been found late Monday by people she worked with after failing to appear at her office. She'd been found in a closet, tied to a chair. She'd been strangled to death, but first she'd been tortured. She'd probably been dead since late Friday.

"They'd suspected a neighbor. A known drug user. But now I guess we know better."

Elizabeth dug her nails into Kessler's hand. She turned her head to look into his eyes. He knew Elizabeth. He knew what the look meant. It was partly a wish that she'd had a chance at him. And a hope that he'd made that man suffer.

Karen saw it. Ragland didn't. She looked Kessler in the eye. She said, "Witnesses reported seeing him with a gun. He used it to shoot a man on the sidewalk before stumbling back into the smoke." She opened her purse and, tilting it forward, displaying her own service pistol. "A Glock. Like this one. It has not been recovered. We think the gun they saw was Eddie's Glock."

"Then it might still turn up," Kessler told her.

"Maybe in my car if I leave it unlocked? Maybe shoved under my seat?"

"I've heard of stranger things happening."

Karen held his gaze. Her look was not disapproving.

Karen said to Sergeant Ragland, "I don't think he was the bomber."

"He would seem to be a viable suspect."

"For one thing, I saw him; he was inside when it blew. The first thing you learn on your first day of bomb school is to get a safe distance away. For another, a man who sounds like this character was seen videotaping the cars parked outside and talking into the camera. That sounds more like a surveillance to me."

Kessler hadn't seen any camera. Nor had he thought to check the man's pockets. He asked, "Did you find it? The camera?"

"When we do, we'll know what he was saying."

Karen said, "You know, I've been kicking myself. I saw him at the bar the night Eddie was found. He was sitting right there within reach."

The sergeant touched her shoulder. "You couldn't have known. I saw him myself the next day. I never checked him."

"Yeah, but..something else. There was something going on between him and Gilhooley." She paused to ask Kessler, "Have you met Gilhooley." His blank look was his answer. He had not. Elizabeth, however, squeezed his hand again. She had. Or she had knowledge of him.

Karen said, "All I noticed was some kind of tension. I don't know what else to call it." She turned to Harry Whistler. "When you made your toast. When everyone moved to the back of the bar. He didn't. He stayed up close to the door. I'm reaching here. You should know that I know that. But it's almost like he knew what was coming."

Harry asked, "Have you questioned him?"

"Couldn't find him. He's gone. And he left his truck. It's still where he parked it. Turns out it was stolen from a town in West Virginia a few days before he showed up here."

"You've searched the truck?"

"We will when we've towed it."

"And the laptop," asked Harry?

"We've only looked at the emails. Some were sent here when she was already dead. Two Hilton Head cops will be flying up to get it. They'll be taking the car back as well. We don't need them. They want them. They're evidence."

"And you brought it here because…"

"So we might leave it. Accidentally. It might have files that are nobody's business and have nothing to do with what happened to her. Someone might want to clean it up a little."

"Very thoughtful of you, Dave. I'll remember it."

Sergeant Ragland said, "We're almost done here." He asked Elizabeth, "You're not Muslim, are you?"

"I am not."

"But the girls were."

"They were," said Elizabeth, "and they are."

"Sorry, I just thought… they might have put it behind them."

"They have not. It's their faith. They're quite devout."

"Including Rasha?" he asked.

"Especially Rasha."

"Okay, no offense. What I'm trying to get at… she seems to have been the primary target. I've read that Muslims want to kill all apostates. I'm just wondering if that's what's behind this."

"A handful of Muslims feel that way, yes. So do a handful of Christians and Jews. All religions have their lunatic fringe."

"Fair enough. Can we speak to her?"

"Maybe tomorrow," said Elizabeth while rising.

"Sure," said Karen, rising with her, as did Ragland. "Maybe when we come back for the laptop."

Harry stood at the window watching them drive away. He said, "Good. Not a word about Haskell."

Kessler nodded. "Only about this man named Gilhooley." He said to Elizabeth, "You reacted to the name."

She told him that she'd seen him, was suspicious of him; she'd seen him or his truck once too often. She'd asked Sam Foote to keep an eye on him for her, but Sam seemed to think he was okay. "I'm not blaming Sam. but…"

"No post mortems," said Kessler. More likely, he thought, she was blaming herself for not confronting this man then and there. "You heard Dave and Karen. They both had regrets. I'm sure Sam has his own. They do us no good whatsoever."

Harry grunted. "You knew that Sam worked for me?"

"In Italy. Known as Bigfoot. I'd heard."

"You heard what? In a nutshell."

"That he never stops coming."

"Well, I suspect," said Harry, "that he's probably decided that he's had enough of retirement. He's going to want Gilhooley. And he'll find him."

Elizabeth said, "Haskell should know where he's gone."

"Yes, he might. And we'll talk to him. Not now. Let him cook. But assume that by morning some witness will remember seeing someone being thrown in Roger's trunk. Someone might even have it on video."

"If so, we say that it was one of your twins. They are known to ride in trunks, are they not?"

Harry started to say no. Dumbest thing he'd ever heard. It was true that in a car, one would always stay low if they had a task to perform. Normally in the back seat or in its well. They liked to avoid being seen both at once. Kessler's answer, on reflection, didn't seem so far-fetched. One might very well have ridden in the trunk.

Harry asked, "Where's Sadik, by the way?"

"In with Niki," said Elizabeth. "Settling her down. He's promised her a voice in what we decide to do with that Saudi flight money. He's told her that some good may yet come of this."

"Hmmph," said Harry. "A few more clinics, most likely. But that will have to wait until we get to Geneva. Everything's there. Nothing's here."

"Um… actually," said Kessler, "you sent copies to Geneva. I have kept an unscrambled original."

"You kept it because…?"

"Lest the dog eat it or some other misfortune. Mistrust was not an issue. Only prudence."

"Lest the earth should open up and swallow Geneva?" He said, "Never mind. I guess I'm glad that you did. We find ourselves with a working computer."

"The laptop, yes. But there is another. Clew's State Department limo comes well equipped. It folds out from under the seat."

"Yeah, we saw it. Don't go near it. Every keystroke on those units is recorded at State. Speaking of which, where is Roger?"

"Still outside, I believe. I'll go get him."

"I'll go," said Elizabeth in a voice that seemed distant. She said, "I could use some fresh air."

Kessler asked, with his eyes, whether she would like company. She answered with her own that she would not. Such unspoken exchanges were not new to them. He saw that she'd retreated into herself. He'd seen it before. Many times. For all that she was, she was still a woman whose emotions would sometimes come in conflict with reason. She would say, "I'm going to go for a walk," or, as in this case, "I could use some fresh air." He would offer to go with her, but only as a means of saying he was there for her if needed. Her need was to be by herself.

She picked up her purse from the chair where she'd left it. She said, "I might even go for a swim."

FORTY ONE

Clew had seen the police car. He'd stayed out of sight. There was still some chance that his name and position would remain unnoted by the local authorities and, by extension, the media. He saw them leave. He saw Elizabeth come out. He saw her pacing back and forth in front of the house, her arms tightly folded as if hugging herself.

As she walked slowly past one of the coach lights, he saw the glisten of a tear on her cheek. She turned away. Her back was now to him. He moved toward the front door as quietly as he could, not wanting to intrude on her moment. But she heard him. Or she sensed him. "They're waiting for you, Roger." She avoided showing her face.

Clew appeared at the door to the library. He had his briefcase in hand. Harry said to him before he could ask, "It was not an unfriendly visit, Roger. What have you been up to outside?"

Clew said, "You asked about Haskell's phone and whether I intended to share it." He produced it and set it on a leather-topped table. He explained what was on it, all those photos of the prince, all the others detailing Leland's room and his possessions. "You can look at them later. There's more."

Next, from his briefcase came a video camera. He said, "This is Haskell's. I just got it from the trunk. Apparently, he taped the whole thing. "

Whistler saw that it was dented and the eyepiece was gone. He asked, "It still functions?"

"It does. I've played it. Haskell wasn't alone. You'll see him talking to a man who he calls Gilhooley. He's telling Gilhooley how he wants this done. Otherwise, he's narrating what he tapes. He's structured this tape as a formal presentation, subject, I presume, to some editing. He paints himself as an avenger of crimes against Islam in general and against certain Saudis in particular. He names all of us as we arrive in our cars. He names the girls. He points out Aisha in particular. The Darvi girls are her handmaidens. He points out the prince's thieving daughter – his words. The tape shows Elizabeth, but he doesn't name her. Why? Stay tuned. That's coming up."

Clew reached into his briefcase again.

He produced two sheets of soiled notepaper that had been crumpled and folded, well worn. "Two versions of the prince's suicide note. One is a copy. That's the one you've seen. It's pretty much as Leland recited it. The other's the original of an alternate version. We wondered why the first made no mention of Stride. In this one, he does quite a job on her. It's just one extra paragraph. Want to hear it?"

Kessler leaned forward. "By all means."

Clew cleared his throat and read aloud:

"The worst of the worst is Elizabeth Stride. She is the lesbian whore who leads the Nasreens. This makes her a whore among whores, only worse. She kidnaps innocent young Muslim girls and rapes them in the way that lesbians rape so that they are forever lost to God. She then has them murdered which is why we can't find them. She murders them so that when she dies herself, they can serve as her sex slaves in hell."

Kessler wondered, idly, why slut was left out. He asked Harry, "If the men get seventy-two virgins, why must she provide her own sex slaves?"

"Well, at least," said Harry, "she got a promotion. Sadik's wife now works for her."

Clew signaled time out. "Can we hold the wisecracks? I don't think you'll hear Elizabeth laughing."

"No, we won't," said Kessler. "Proceed."

"Haskell had to have dictated both versions," said Clew. "I guess he was unhappy with her at the time. But, as you'll see when you play his tape, he had a big change of heart. You'll hear him place a call to the bar at Mangiamo in order to lure her up to the front where she wouldn't be harmed by the blast."

Harry asked, "He had these on his person?"

"Surprised me, too. You'd think he would have stashed them. But he really had to hustle to get here from the Grove if he wanted to catch all of us under one roof. Nor did he expect to get spotted by me because the blast was supposed to have killed me."

"And you took these from him? By yourself? Without help?"

Clew heard the implication that Haskell was beyond him unless Haskell was either dead or dying. He gave Harry a look. He said, "I managed."

Really!

Clew reddened. "I said I managed. I'm here. Let it go."

Harry smiled. "I begin to be very impressed by you, Roger. Unaided even by that Beretta in your briefcase?"

"I stuck it in his fucking mouth. Happy now?"

"Still impressed."

"Might I ask," said Clew, reaching into his bag again, "what you intend to do with that prick?"

Harry didn't answer. "What else do you have?"

Clew was groping for something at the bottom of his briefcase. He removed the dossiers on Haskell and the others in order to more easily find it.

Harry said, "I'll need those. Leave them with me."

"You're not going to tell me how you mean to use them?"

"It's a work in progress, Roger. Be patient."

"That limo goes back to D.C. in the morning."

"We'll be sure to disinfect it. Have no fear."

Clew stacked the three thick dossiers on the table. He found what he was looking for, another video camera, this one much smaller than Haskell's. "This was in Haskell's pocket. I don't know how he got it. It belongs to someone named – sounds like Moolazeem - or at least that's what he seemed to be calling himself. His narration was in Arabic. I don't speak the language. But I did pick up a word here and there. Rasha's name, for one. Stride's, for another. And he said the word 'Hasheem' more than once. The Hasheem are…"

"Saudi heretic hunters," said Kessler, frowning. "And that is to say, Aisha hunters."

Clew said, "In fairness, most Saudis detest them. They're no more fond of fanatics than we are."

"Then they'll be pleased to know that there's one less," said Harry. "That one's dead. Sergeant Ragland just told us."

Kessler said, "This is serious. Of all those who are seeking the source of the prophecy, the Hasheem would be the most zealous. That is true of all those seeking Rasha as well. Nor have they forgotten Elizabeth Stride. It's Hasheem that put the bounty on her. Ten years now, but she is still high on their list. If this man has reported that he's located them, believe me, many more will be coming."

Harry raised a hand. "Let's get a translation so we know what we're up against. Let's get Elizabeth back in here."

Clew said, "She looked a little fragile outside. It might be better if we have Sadik translate. Or is he still Emil Freundlisch? I lose track."

"He's Sadik," said Harry. He said, "Martin, please get him. While you're at it, get your disk. The night's young. We shouldn't waste it."

Clew asked, "You still have it? The master?"

"Thanks to Martin who is famously prudent."

"So… is this where I get that look that you promised?"

"You get to watch Martin, the good doctor and myself decide how to spend ten billion dollars."

Sadik read the alternate suicide note. "Has she seen this? No? Just as well."

Both of the video cameras were digital. He removed the memory cards from each and was about to play Haskell's on the laptop computer.

Kessler said, "No. The other one first. It's of more immediate concern."

Sadik played it, translating what seemed relevant as he went. He said to Kessler, "You're right; he's Hasheem. His sheik had sent him to Hilton Head Island, but according to this, no one knows that he's here. By here, I mean here in Belle Haven."

"You're sure?"

"He's reporting to his sheik by means of this tape. He's explaining why he hasn't used his cell phones. He refers to himself as Mulazim the Greek. Never as simply Mulazim. He's quite full of himself in a witless sort of way. He calls himself the hunter who never leaves trails. Well, he certainly didn't in this case."

Sadik said to Kessler, "As to your first concern, he says he's found Rasha and an 'even bigger fish.' He's found the Black Angel, Elizabeth Stride. There's no mention of Aisha, however. They can come and get Rasha and they can have Stride, but he wants a guarantee that he'll get half the bounty no matter how many they send. He also wants the reward the prince posted for

Rasha. Only then will he reveal the location to which he has tracked them. He insists that although he is loyal to Hasheem, God himself told him he should have those rewards. That it's God who's been guiding his hand."

"Say again," said Kessler. "No mention of Belle Haven?"

"He doesn't even say they've left Hilton Head."

"Nor will he," said Harry. "God got tired of guiding."

"So I had assumed. He was killed in the restaurant? This says he'd gone in to get some footage of his quarry, but the tape ends a few seconds later."

The camera had recorded the sound of the blast and it showed the effect of the shock wave. It knocked many down, Mulazim with them. He tried to get up. He was knocked down again. The camera recorded a squeal and a thud. His camera was still running, pointing this way and that as it might if Mulazim was thrashing about. For an instant it recorded his own twitching fingers until it rose up from his hand and moved off.

"Someone took it from him," said Sadik. "Was that Haskell?"

"No, Haskell wasn't there, but he did end up with it. Is there any indication that Mulazim knew Haskell or that this might have been a joint venture?"

"None whatever. He paid Haskell no notice. But Haskell noticed him and his video camera and must have sent someone to get it."

Harry said, "He did, but why would you say that? There's no reference to that on this video."

Sadik touched his finger to the rewind button. He was searching for a scene not far back. He hit Play. He'd found it. Mulazim in the alley near the service entrance door. The sound coming through is Kessler's rendition of the song he had threatened to sing, Sixteen Candles. Mulazim's angry at a cook who would not let him in. He takes it out on Elizabeth's car. It shows his shoe rising up to smash the Subaru's headlight. The camera backs up to take in the result. Sadik reached to touch the pause button.

Harry shrugged. "A fit of pique. What of it, Rajib?"

"Look past the car. Look across the street. Look who's taping this scene from that bus stop."

Harry looked. He smiled. "You have a good eye." He was looking at Haskell and Gilhooley.

He said to Kessler, "So this turkey worked alone. He's reported nothing. That's one less concern. But the Saudi Hasheem will learn soon enough that one of their number was killed in Belle Haven. Assume they'll send others if only to learn what might have led him here in the first place. It won't matter. We'll be long gone."

Clew asked Kessler, "That disk. Might the Hasheem be on it?"

"Hard to tell. But Rasha might know."

"Has she gone to bed?"

Harry said, "I would think that they all have by now. Martin, where's your disk? Let's get started."

Kessler drew a plastic sleeve from his pocket. He held it up for the rest of them to see. The label said: Roy Orbison. Greatest Hits from the Fifties. "Sixteen Candles," said Kessler. "This is where I learned the words. The sleeve seemed a handy place to keep ten billion."

Harry threw up his hands in a gesture of surrender. He said, "We really should have Elizabeth in here."

Kessler said, "Yes, we should. I'll go get her."

FORTY TWO

Kessler found her in the pool behind the main house. He didn't see her at first, but he did see her purse and the shoes she'd changed into. She'd left them on the rim at the deepest end. He felt a sudden stab of alarm. Could he have misjudged her state of mind?

But now he saw her. He saw why he'd almost missed her. She was sitting under the waterfall that washed gently down over natural rocks. The water came from the hot tub; it was comfortably warm. It flowed over Elizabeth's head and shoulders. She had taken off her blouse. He watched her dip it in the pool several times in order to rinse off the soot. Now she was raising it over her head in the act of putting it back on.

He was about to step backward, to allow her the moment. But she'd heard him. Or sensed him. Even under that cascading water.

She said, "Come in and sit with me, Martin."

He'd stepped out of his loafers and put his watch and wallet in them. He placed the album jacket beneath his shoes so that it was fully concealed. She hadn't yet looked in his direction. He used the ladder to ease himself into the water. He could have simply lowered himself from the edge, but that would have made a splash, however small. He didn't think he should disturb her with a splash.

Doing not much more than drifting, he moved in her direction until he felt the slope of the rocks underfoot. He slipped under the waterfall beside her. She didn't speak, but she did lean against him. He thought about putting his arm around her, but the idea that he had to think about doing so suggested that perhaps he should not. Her own hands remained on her lap.

She said quietly, "He wanted to play tennis."

Kessler felt sure that he understood her meaning. Sadik had told him what Haskell had said to her after he was thrown in the trunk. Sadik and Clew had lifted him. They'd shoved him in. And yet, according to Dr. Sadik, Haskell acted as if neither of those two were present. All of his attention was focused on her. He tried denying that he'd done what he'd done. Next he tried to explain why he'd done what he'd done. All he wanted was a trade. None of this had to happen. Then just as the trunk lid was slammed down on him, he said his hope was that they could play tennis. Strange man.

Now Elizabeth said, in that same quiet voice, "He has a home in Palm Beach."

It almost seemed that she wasn't speaking to him. It was more as if she were remembering.

"He says that it would suit me better than this one. He says this is a man's house. His is softer and prettier."

Kessler hadn't heard about this part of the exchange. Haskell was describing his house to her? It wouldn't seem to have been the most opportune moment to describe one's real estate holdings.

"It has two tennis courts. One is clay. One is grass. He asked me if I've played much on grass."

This seemed even more unlikely to Kessler.

"He has a yacht that he keeps there. He wasn't going to tell me. He only wanted to talk about tennis. It was as if he was arguing with somebody else about what I'd like most about living there. He wanted to take me there and show me."

Kessler was beginning to grasp what had happened. He asked, "Elizabeth, where did this take place?"

She answered with a small toss of one hand. The gesture was toward the garage. When she raised her hand to make it, he saw on her lap, the long thin blade of her curved Moroccan knife. It must have needed rinsing as well.

She said, "I looked at him and I saw Aisha's burns. I heard all the screams and the shouts and the sirens. I saw all of Aisha's presents soaked through by the sprinklers. They're still there. She never got to open even one of her presents. And this man's still talking about tennis."

Kessler said nothing. But he did take her hand.

She said, "It was just too much noise."

FORTY THREE

Roger Clew had gone out to look for them both. He returned, reporting what he had seen. He supposed they'd decided not to bother with a shower with a warm waterfall at their disposal. They were out there sitting under it. Talking.

Harry Whistler had just completed a phone call. He said, "It's just as well. I have someone driving down here who I'm going to need. You've met Hester Lazarus, haven't you?"

"Your forger? Formerly Yitzhak Netanya's?"

"You diminish her, Roger. The woman's an artist. She's still attached to the Israeli embassy, but I supplement her income considerably. She lives in Fairfax County. She'll be here within the hour. In the meantime, is anyone hungry?"

He hadn't eaten. None of them had. The three of them, Sadik included, retired to the kitchen where Clew put on some coffee while Harry and Sadik explored the panty and fridge. They found some cold lamb. They made sandwiches.

Clew said to Sadik, "As long as we're waiting, what's the story on how Dr. Freundlisch of Geneva became Dr. Sadik of Hamas? Were you already a Muslim when I met you?"

He wasn't. He said he'd been Lutheran if anything. He had been raised in a Swiss-German household by parents only casually religious. But then he'd met Maryam while at Medical school. She'd gone there on a scholarship grant. She'd won it in an open competition that is held every year in Amman.

"Maryam is Jordanian?"

"Palestinian," said Sadik. "And yes, she is Muslim. Her family is from Hebron, West Bank."

Sadik recounted the middle part of the story, hitting only on key highlights to do so. Graduating. Getting married during his residency. Joining a surgical practice in Geneva. Maryam, a year later, doing the same within her own specialty of Obstetrics. Maryam already pregnant herself. Meeting Harry when called on to patch one of his people. Patching Harry himself on two occasions. Later flying to Bucharest at Harry's behest where he took two bullets out of Elizabeth. That's where he met Kessler for the first time. Harry had known him for some years.

Harry said, "That's about when he got tired of patching."

Sadik shrugged. "I know. That's was the reason I gave. The truth was that both of us, Maryam and myself, had admired the good work of Doctors Without Borders. One's religious faith made no difference to them. Moving to Brussels, working with them, seemed very worth doing. We would give it two years."

"With your daughter?" Clew asked. He bit into his sandwich.

"What better education could she get?"

To cut some of the cords, they changed Freundlisch to Friendly. It wasn't intended as a disguise. It was more that they had begun a new chapter. It seemed a good idea at the time. All three traveled in the service of that organization throughout Africa and the Mideast. More and more the Mideast. More and more the West Bank. It was where he concluded that Maryam was right in what she'd been saying since before they were married. It was where both their skills were most sorely needed. Two years would not be enough.

They set up their first clinic. Harry contributed. They'd stayed in close touch with Harry. But it became clear that he would only be trusted by Muslims if he were a Muslim himself. He was, of course, well acquainted with Islam and was reasonably fluent in Arabic through his wife. He converted for practical, although not insincere reasons. He admired many aspects of Islam. He took a Muslim name. He chose Rajib Sadik. Friendly always seemed a good name for a doctor. It ought to work the same in any language.

For reasons that were equally practical, he and his wife joined Hamas. Hamas, being largely supported by the Saudis was where most of the money and the influence was. Using Hamas funds, they opened more clinics. Harry was still more than willing to help, but it was always best to use Muslim money. Saudi money in particular. All he could get. They had so much more than they deserved.

In order to do the most good for the poor, he had to try to ignore the more bloody activities of the militant wing of Hamas. He detested their attacks on Israeli civilians and yet he understood why they were done. Many hundreds of innocent Palestinians had died through Israeli shelling and strafing. Thousands humiliated every day of the week by their status as an occupied people.

"On that subject," said Sadik, "don't make the mistake of seeing this as unique to this particular conflict. All occupations are hateful."

"I know that."

"Israelis, British, Americans… doesn't matter. They must impose restrictions; they will be seen as bullies. Go here. Don't go there. Open that bundle. Making women lift their skirts; their husbands helpless to prevent it. Humiliation brings resistance which brings countermeasures. The occupiers have all the tanks and the war planes. The resistance never does. Their bombs must be hand-delivered or in cars or on bikes. How could anyone be surprised that this is so?"

"Can we get back to…"

"No, let me say this. Both sides kill the innocent. The occupier bombs a house; there is collateral damage; the bomb kills women and children. Someone retaliates with a suicide bomb. You believe that this someone is from Hamas because the Israelis tell you he is. As often as not, it's some father or brother who can't live with the shame of not avenging them."

"Yes," said Clew, "but who gives him his bomb?"

"Here's another surprise. Almost anyone, that's who. You think you are fighting one group in Iraq? It's more like a hundred.

You think they seem to spring up out of nowhere and they do. They spring up, they attack, their rage is spent and they're gone. That's why you can never defeat an insurgency. There's never one single head to cut off. It only ever ends when you get out."

"Point taken," said Clew. "But on the matter at hand…"

"I'm ranting. I know that. I just want the killing stopped. And another way to stop it is maybe, just maybe…" Sadik bit his lip.

"Aisha coming?"

"Never mind. Who knows? Let's get back to your question. You were asking about me and Hamas."

Hamas, Sadik told him, has been the only game in town when it came to helping Palestinians. Hamas, unlike the PLO, didn't steal. There was almost no corruption in Hamas. You never saw them riding around in new cars as soon as a new donation came in from the World Bank or whomever. But Hamas would have no credibility with the people unless it was willing to strike back in kind. A dirty business? Yes. Unending? He hoped not. There were reasonable people on both sides of the struggle. More and more of them. They were equally sick of it. Among them were people like Yitzhak Netanya whom he'd met years before through Martin Kessler.

Clew said, "Not to mention men like Abbas Mansur."

Sadik grunted. "I take it you've been making inquiries."

"I have. But I'm not clear on your relationship."

"I've known Mansur since college. The University of Geneva. We were roommates for two of those years."

"And he went on to become an alternate chairman of Iran's revolutionary Council of Guardians?"

Sadik shrugged. "Who knew at the time?"

Mansur, he said, could not have been called pious when they were rooming together. Respectful, yes, but not pious. Their many conversations, as with most college students, were about politics, religion, women and sports, but by no means necessarily in that order. He helped Mansur with his English and his German. Mansur, in turn, taught him some Arabic, using the Koran as a text. The Arabic he learned stood him in good stead when later, while attending medical school, he met the woman who would one day be his wife.

Clew paused to take a sip of his coffee. "Harry, Netanya, Mansur and Hamas. You've made some impressive connections."

"I've made friends. One can't have too many."

"Have you ever been accused of playing both sides?"

"Of course. And I do. It's not an afternoon tea. I play both sides all the time."

Clew had a question of immediate interest concerning Sadik's recent visit to Tehran. He'd started to ask it. Sadik waved it off. "Not so fast. Let's talk about my connections."

He told Roger Clew that it was due to those connections that he rose to his present rank in Hamas. He headed Hamas' Heath Services wing. It was one of five departments of Hamas, entirely distinct from the militant wing or even the political wing. Even so, he'd been asked many times to use his connections for various purposes. Among those purposes was tracking down women who'd bolted and especially those who'd been helping them to bolt. But he'd always refused. He said let them go. He'd said he'd willingly let his own daughter go if she were to choose to make a life somewhere else, assuming that she'd thought the matter out.

But he'd also been asked to intercede with Netanya to get this or that arrested Muslim operative released. Sometimes asked by Hamas. Sometimes asked by the Saudis. He'd done so, for some, but it was always a trade. He would want additional funding in return. More than that, he needed something to trade with Netanya. Netanya's motto was "Nothing for nothing."

And it worked both ways. One day, Netanya offered a Saudi arms smuggler in trade for two women who'd been imprisoned in Riyadh.

Sadik had asked Netanya, "Are they Mossad?"

"These two? No. These two are good Muslims. They have no connection with Israel."

Sadik asked Netanya, "Then why do you want them?"

"That's none of your business."

"Well, at least you must tell me what is their crime."

Netanya answered, "They are Nasreens."

Sadik was aware that the Nasreens existed, but had, until then, never given them much thought. What, in any case, would Netanya want with them?

It was no use asking Netanya again. But Sadik knew Netanya and he could guess. If Netanya wanted these two women freed, it wasn't so that they could resume their activities. It was so he could trade them to someone else for something else that he wanted.

Or perhaps he owed a favor to the Nasreens for some favor that they did for him. Who knows?

But he got them released and he took them to his home until a pick-up by Netanya's Mossad could be arranged. He got to know them a little and found that he liked them. Courageous, dedicated, entirely sincere. More than that, it turned out that his wife knew them well. Not these two. Not personally. But his wife knew their work. She was all for it. So was his daughter. They treated some injuries that they'd suffered in prison. Both Nasreens had probably been raped by the guards, but he, Sadik, had no need to ask. Not while there was a gynecologist handy. His wife and daughter had them take a good long soak in the bathtub while they went out and bought them new clothing.

The upshot of this was that after their release, the Nasreens knew who to go to when they needed a favor. Within months, his wife and daughter were full-fledged Nasreens. There's no membership committee. You don't get voted in. You become a member by helping where help is needed. Contributing some cash now and then doesn't hurt, but you can't just write checks; you must be active.

As for the prophecy, he'd paid little attention until he saw more women asserting themselves. Not rebelling so much. Not antagonism toward men. Or at least not toward men in general. It was more like saying to them, "There are changes in the wind." They would say, "Whether Aisha is coming or not, a lot of eyes and hearts are being opened. You're seeing it everywhere, even in Syria. People don't feel like sheep in some great flock anymore." And the men were listening to their wives and their daughters. Not all, of course. Some were totally dismissive. Especially the Saudis and some others he could name. But even there some were saying to their women, "You are right. It is in the wind. More than that, It's overdue. You deserve full respect and you shall have it. In time."

Overdue? And yet they still say, "In time?" This prophecy might be just the right medicine.

He'd known through Netanya and also through Kessler that Elizabeth had almost died once before. That was in Jordan, near the Saudi border. He knew that her life had been saved on that occasion by the woman for whom the Nasreens were later named. Stride might even have been one of their founders.

He'd known that she still had a price on her head. He'd known that she became tired of being hunted and had gone to America to start a new life. He'd known that she had somehow connected with a group of Nasreens in South Carolina. He'd heard that she, for some reason, had more or less adopted a young Egyptian fugitive named Aisha. He'd heard this from Kessler himself.

It struck him after reading the prophecy, that Qaila sounds a lot like Elizabeth Stride. Just a thought. A passing thought. Then one day he took a call from Abbas Mansur. Mansur wanted him to locate two Iranian girls who were thought to be somewhere in South Carolina, taken there by the Nasreens. Mansur asked because his old school friend was known to have close connections with the Nasreens. Sure he did. They lived under his roof.

Mansur, it seemed, had reason to believe that these same girls were involved in the prophecy. Or at least they were saying so over the internet. They were claiming that they'd actually seen Aisha. They said her "coming" was imminent. Mansur said that many of their friends had been arrested. If Sadik agreed to help, they'd be released.

Sadik declined when he was first asked, even though he had considerable regard for Mansur. His thoughts about Stride were no more than conjecture, even with South Carolina thrown in. The arrests, however, did trouble Sadik. He went on his computer to try to find out how widespread such arrests were. He found that there were many. Trouble all over. The web site for Amnesty International confirmed that some sixty had been imprisoned in Tehran alone. One had been sentenced to be flogged with a number of lashes that she wasn't likely to survive.

Clew asked him, "Is this when you flew to Tehran?"

"Not yet. Only sentenced. Don't get ahead of me. In the meantime, I had my own problems."

His main source of funding, Saudi Overseas Charities, seemed to have frozen his access to those funds. He flew to Riyadh to look into it. It was there that he saw what these "handmaidens" had done, never mind that it was really only Niki. Aside from announcing that this "coming" was imminent, they'd helped themselves to ten billion dollars.

"Moreover, as you know, Haskell's banker friend was there. And Rasha's father. They were out of luck as well. All at once, this was bigger than I had imagined." He looked at his watch. "We're still waiting for Kessler?"

"And Hester Lazarus. Get to Tehran."

"I called and tried to get through to Mansur. It was then that I learned that the flogging had begun. I rushed to Tehran and I... stopped it."

"Her name was Farah," said Clew. "I'm told that she died."

"She died in peace. Don't ask for details."

"But you spoke to her. Did she know that the Darvi girls were here? Did she know that Elizabeth and Aisha were here?"

No, Sadik, told him. Not specifically here. Nor did she seem to recognize Elizabeth's name. If he wondered, however, so might someone else. He decided that he ought to try to find out. If she wasn't involved, she might know who was. She might have an interest in containing this thing before her own Aisha came under suspicion and ended up as a target. At the very least, she ought to be warned.

He had no means of contacting Stride. He didn't know where Kessler was either, but perhaps he and Stride were still together. Netanya would know. Netanya always keeps tabs. Through Netanya he contacted Kessler.

His motive? His intentions? He found that they were evolving. First find Elizabeth. Through her, find the girls. Let Elizabeth know that they were playing with fire and many had already been burned.

"But the more I learned, and the more I considered it, this prophecy appeared to be a very good thing. Mansur himself said it. It made men stop and think. So perhaps we shouldn't be too quick to say that your Aisha's not the Aisha of the prophecy."

Harry raised a hand. He touched a finger to his lips. He said, "Hold that thought. I need a minute."

He got up, left the kitchen and, making no sound on the carpeted floor, he walked down the side hall to the nearest guest bedrooms. The first was Aisha's. The door was inches ajar. The room was dark and silent. He looked in.

He saw Aisha in her bed. She was lying on her stomach. The light from the hallway caught the glow of the salve that Elizabeth had dabbed on her arms and bare shoulders. Beside her, in the bed, was young Rasha, also still. Between them, a ball of gray fur, Rasha's kitten. Neither, he supposed, felt like being alone. Any dreams seemed unlikely to be pleasant.

He carefully eased the door closed. He returned to the kitchen where he said to Sadik, "I don't think they heard you. I wish I hadn't. Please tell me that you weren't serious."

"I said perhaps. Don't dismiss it too quickly."

"Is this the 'one way' you started to mention?"

"This thing could work miracles, Harry."

"But at what cost?" asked Whistler. "Having our Aisha hunted? Having our Aisha killed? Or do you prefer to use the word 'martyred?'"

"Harry... this is me. You're not talking to some nut. The least you can do is hear me out."

"No, the least I can do is end this discussion. You'd keep her hidden for... what? Five more years?"

"Harry, she's going to be hunted regardless. Sure, we could change her name, give her a new identity. Make her a Catholic. Say she's Spanish or Italian. But that means she can't be with Elizabeth Stride with whom she's now widely identified. Can you see Aisha agreeing to that? Can you see Elizabeth agreeing?"

Clew nodded. "He does have a point."

"Then we'll tell the truth. The whole thing was a hoax. Niki did this all on her own. The prophecy. The ten billion. All of it."

"Yes, it's the truth, but who would believe it? We still have trouble believing it ourselves and we know the truth beyond doubt."

Harry heard someone coming in the front door. He knew that it could only be Kessler and Stride. "Not a word of this to them. Not from either of you."

"We'll talk again later," said Sadik.

"No, we won't."

Harry rose from his chair. He left his half-eaten sandwich. "Not until we've given it more thought."

FORTY FOUR

They'd come in hand in hand, their clothing still dripping, Elizabeth carrying her shoes and her purse, both of them smelling of chlorine. Kessler apologized for holding them up. Harry told Kessler what he'd said to the others. Hester Lazarus was coming, no stranger to Kessler. Elizabeth didn't seem to be listening.

"May I hope," Harry asked him, "that Roy Orbison stayed dry?"

Kessler handed him the sleeve. "He's not a swimmer."

"Go change," Harry told them. "There's fresh coffee in the kitchen. If you have no objection, we'll get started."

Kessler said, "You needn't wait. But if you do find a moment, you might want to look in on Charles Haskell."

Harry saw, in Kessler's eyes, what hadn't been spoken. He saw that Elizabeth was still somewhere else. He would look in on Haskell when he found a spare moment. He felt sure that the need was not urgent.

Sadik touched a pencil to the screen of the laptop. He said, "A number of these have been starred. What are they?"

Harry leaned over his shoulder to look. "They're the ones Rasha says are legitimate charities. She put question marks where she wasn't certain."

"Well, she's mostly correct and I've noted others. Of the more than twelve hundred accounts on this list, roughly two hundred are legitimate."

Clew asked him, "What sort of charities?"

"Faith-based, Islamic, but not narrowly so. The Red Crescent, for example, the Islamic Red Cross. Some distribute the Koran in foreign language translations, but always accompanied by practical texts on subjects such as how to dig wells. The Koran is always part of a literacy program. No use sending it if they couldn't read it. Others fund the construction of local mosques where none existed before." He asked Clew, "Have you ever been in a mosque? I don't mean a tourist mosque. A real one."

Clew said, "I'm not aware of the distinction."

"A local mosque is important. It's not just good for preaching. Like most churches, it's also a community center and perhaps the only one for many miles. It's where food is distributed to those in need. It's where children get their vaccinations. It's where fishing and farming techniques are taught. It's where people meet their neighbors and become better neighbors. Very few are hotbeds for the radicals."

Clew sniffed. "One learns something every day."

541

Sadik curled his lip. "Are we being snide? A lot of nonsense is preached from your pulpits as well. Your faithful don't run home to get their guns."

"As a rule."

"Muslims are people. They just want good lives. Religion is important, but I'll tell you this. Give young Muslims a choice between taking up jihad and finding a good job and a decent apartment, they'll take the job and the apartment every time."

"Doc…"

"No job, no apartment, means you can't find a wife. No wife means no children. You are nothing without family. You want a hotbed? No hope? There's your hotbed."

"Doc, I get it," said Clew. "Let's move on."

Sadik grumbled a bit, but he got back to work. He touched his pencil to some of the entries. "An encouraging number have been set up for women, mostly funded by women although not entirely. These stress literacy and pre-natal care for the most part, but also practical skills for the workplace and other vocational training. Many provide limited medical services. Also nurseries, daycare centers, for women with jobs and even meals on wheels for the shut-ins."

"I'm impressed."

"You should be. Some good work is done there."

Clew asked him, "And these charities are all Saudi?"

"Yes, but not all are Sunni. And certainly not Wahhabi. It looks like… let me see… roughly one in five are Shiite and are based in the Saudi Eastern Province. The Shiites who live there call it the Hasa. They're a Saudi minority and are treated as such. They're obliged to take care of their own."

Clew nodded. Poorly treated. And yet that's where the oil is. A day of reckoning would not surprise him.

"You said about two hundred. What's their total in dollars?"

"Roughly two and half billion," said Sadik.

Harry asked, "It's just sitting there unspent?"

"They don't simply shovel it out," Sadik told him. "There's a lot of planning involved."

"On the presumption that they all have been skimmed, what adjustment would you make to that figure?"

Sadik shrugged. "I couldn't guess."

"Go ahead," Harry told him. "Take a shot."

Another shrug. "A billion? This comes out of thin air."

"But a nice round number. We'll go with that. We'll prorate it over the two hundred."

Sadik wasn't sure that he understood. "It comes from where?"

"I just told you. From the skimmers. When we're finished reviewing the names on this list, you can start making the transfers. Hester Lazarus will help you. She's due here shortly. She'll be making a few of her own."

Sadik said, "You haven't told us her role in this."

"Let's just say that she's very good at paperwork."

543

Sadik rubbed his forehead. "I must not be too bright. Say I've done as you suggest. Say I start moving money. How do these two hundred charities get at it?"

"Good question. Here's another. How do they keep it? What stops it from being re-skimmed?"

"Banking it elsewhere," said Sadik.

"Someplace neutral," said Harry. "My vote would be Credit Suisse in Geneva where I have friends on the board. As to how they'd get at it, they'd do so through you. You would control it. You'd approve all disbursals. You can surrender control on a case by case basis when you're assured that they'll be properly administered."

"Um …how will I say that I came by this money?"

"You didn't come by it. You rescued it for them. Not only that, you increased it substantially. I would think they be pleased to see that."

"Harry …I'll be asked how I did this."

"Yeah, I know, but hold that thought. We'll get to it later. First things first. Will you take this on?"

"Manage three and a half billion? Some two hundred accounts? Take it on when? My spare time? On my lunch break?"

"Well, someone has to do it. Otherwise the money sits. No new community centers."

"I'd need help," said Sadik. "An accounting staff certainly."

"Do you have one in mind?"

"Hamas has one. It's very efficient. And Hamas, by the way…"

"Doesn't steal. So you've said. I'll need to think about that. It would give them instant legitimacy."

"Hey." Sadik waved. "Do you see me standing here? Try to think of me as legitimate. Besides, we've been elected. Or do you not read the papers?"

"I said I'll consider it. What's next?"

"All the rest of the money," said Sadik. "This still leaves six and a half billion more spread over a thousand accounts."

"Flight money," said Harry, "for a thousand opportunists. They might have to re-think their retirement plans. Do you have any thoughts on what to do with it?"

"For a start, pay for some of the damage that's been done."

"You mean Mangiamo? Rebuild it?"

"And a car for Elizabeth. I know. I'm thinking small. But such things should not be overlooked."

"Understood. What else are you thinking?"

"Well, I owe four million to the government of Iran. No, wait a minute. That's not Iran's money. They made the Darvi girls' father cough it up. But I'll need more than that to fund my own work. My old well will probably run dry."

"The Saudis?" asked Harry. "You think they'll cut you off?"

"Don't say Saudis in general. There are many fine Saudis. But once they find out I've taken over these charities, I expect to be persona-non-grata with some. I'd prefer not to have to go begging."

"Suits me," Harry told him. "Take whatever you need."

"You trust me so much?"

"I might check in now and then."

"I see," said Sadik. He was drumming his pencil. "Would you object if I used some for political purposes?"

"You're thinking of running for office yourself?"

"Not me. Worthy candidates. I do what I do."

"These worthy candidates... they'd all be Hamas?"

"I'm thinking woman candidates. My daughter, for one. Good mind, good heart. She'll make a difference."

"I've no doubt of that. It's your call."

"As for the others, no militants. That I will promise. The need now is for those who can administer and build. The militants will one day be irrelevant."

"If you say so."

"Harry, like the Saudis, we have many good men. We have more than our share of good women. Beyond that, we have earned the support of the people through our own social programs that no one else gives them. You saw the elections. We got seventy percent. We exist for that seventy percent."

Clew said, "My government might take issue with that."

"Which part? That we exist for so many? You can give your government a message from me. Tell them, talk to me when they have a government, regardless of party, that exists for more than the five percent who write the biggest checks to their campaign funds. Tell them to kindly explain to me how this can be called democratic."

Clew raised his hands. "You tell them," he said. "But I'd wait until you've made it work."

Harry took another look at the list. He ran his finger down among the middle-range thieves. He asked, "Which of these would you say is most able to get Rasha's mother out of the country?"

"And safely to Switzerland?"

"Say by this time next week."

Sadik studied the names. He touched his pencil to one. "This one is that smuggler I told you about. He has his own fleet of planes. Netanya's men caught him. I got him released. He should be willing to do me a favor."

"Gratitude has a very short shelf life, my friend."

"This one, I assure you, will be more than grateful if we let him keep some of his money."

"You'll handle it?" asked Harry.

"As soon as we're done here. What's next?"

"You know the Hasheem has put a price on Elizabeth. Is it bankrolled by any of the names on this list?"

"I don't know," said Sadik, "but I can find out."

"When you do, you might try to get it rescinded. If he, or they, should fail to see it your way, put a bounty of five million on each of them."

"Happily," said Sadik. "Count it done."

"And another on that sheik who runs the Hasheem. He should learn how it feels to be hunted."

"I'll call it Rasha's dowry. Just kidding. I won't. But what about Haskell's two associates while we're at it? Why not put a bounty on them?"

"We'll get to them. They'll keep. Let's move on." He said, "The Nasreens have an earlier version of the disk. It's been scrambled, but it still has all of these names. I'm sure they'll give it up without compensation, but we still ought to make a contribution."

"Actually, that was Niki's suggestion. She's contrite about more things than you know. One of them is for threatening to expose the Nasreens when they didn't want to take her out of Iran. She says she didn't mean it. She says she would not have. Even so, she would like to make amends."

"Then she should do it face to face, not by getting them some money."

"She knows that. I told her that my wife would arrange it. My daughter, I'm sure, would accompany her. As I've told you…"

"They're Nasreens. Yes, I heard you."

Sadik paused. He said, "On that subject - compensation - what about the four girls? Shouldn't we do something for them?"

"Such as?"

"I don't know. An annuity? A college fund, maybe."

Harry shook his head. "I think you want to be able to say that none of them took a cent. We'll take care of them. They're not going to be hurting. As for Aisha, I'm told that she's pretty well fixed. Her parents left her a nice fortune in trust. She gets it when she comes of age."

Sadik's eyes widened. "Of age? What age would that be? Might it be when she reaches full womanhood?"

Harry hooded his eyes. "Screw the prophecy, doctor. It's whenever her parents' last will says she gets it. I would guess twenty-one, but I don't know that."

"This prophecy would seem to have some growth potential left. But as you wish, we won't belabor it. What else?"

Harry touched his finger to the top of the list. "Highlight those first three Saudi names."

"The three largest accounts?"

"Yes, do you know those names?"

Sadik looked. "Yes, of course. The first and the third are in the Saudi Oil Ministry. Not royals, but they're very high up."

"So they'd know Haskell?"

"No question about it. If he's doing business with Saudi oil, he would have to have paid them both off."

Harry asked him, "And the second? Who is he?"

"A mean one," said Sadik. "He's First Deputy Minister, Saudi Security. His office cracks down on all critics of the system."

"Is that job so rewarding? That's quite a nice nest egg."

"Persistent critics are labeled apostates. That can be a death sentence, so most flee the country. He confiscates their property and sells it at auction, often very cheaply to his own friends and relatives. Most of the proceeds do go to the treasury, but he keeps a nice commission for himself."

"A sweet deal," said Harry.

"For all but the critics."

"Okay. Don't touch those when you start redistributing. Leave those balances as they are, down to the penny."

Sadik raised an eyebrow. "That's almost a billion."

"I know."

"You're going to keep it?"

Harry Whistler almost smiled. "I have something else in mind. I'll tell you after Hester gets here."

FORTY FIVE

Clew took another call from Tatiana at State. She asked if he's been watching TV. She said the blast is on CNN and Fox News. She said, "No one's calling it a bombing so far. Just a mysterious explosion. Four dead, but no identities released. What makes it especially mysterious, however, is that a senior State official was there."

"Naming me?"

"No, not so far, but they've probably heard. The White House sure as hell has."

"You know that?"

"Not just the White House. Homeland Security... the intelligence services. Haven't you been checking your voice mail?"

"Been busy. I'll do that. I'll get back to you, Tatiana."

Clew's cell phone was a Blackberry Pearl. It had a feature called SpinVox that converts voice to text. The idea was to be able to read messages privately without being seen with a phone to one's ear or to risk having calls overheard.

Clew thumbed a button. The screen displayed a list of the incoming calls that his phone had recorded. He scanned through several, reading only the text. He got to the one from the White House.

He said to Harry Whistler, "All of these just this evening. Every agency you can name. This last one's from the White House, from the Deputy Chief of Staff. His name is Gerald Stickles. Do you know him?"

"Only of him."

"Then you know he's a pompous pain in the ass." Clew switched it back to voice mail and turned up the volume. He held the phone so that its speaker faced Harry. The voice that came through had the no-nonsense tone of a man accustomed to deference. Stickles felt no need to identify himself. Annoying. The arrogance of power.

"Was this a hit on Harry Whistler? Advise at once. If so, how does he intend to respond? How are Haskell, Bentley and Leeds involved? How is the Bohemian Club involved and where is Howard Leland at this time? Explain the involvement of Sadik of Hamas and Yitzhak Netanya's Mossad. Ditto this prophecy of Aisha's second coming. Ditto a considerable sum of money that the Saudi's seem to have misplaced. Report to me personally, soonest."

Harry sat tugging at the end of his beard. He asked, "How does Stickles know all this already? I gather that his source isn't Leland."

"No, Howard's lying low until I get back. He's not answering his phone or the doorbell. Stickles had to have pried this out of someone at State. He had to have been told that I pulled those four dossiers before I met your plane at Reagan. He'd know I took State's copy of the Bahrain Tribune. He'd know of my interest in the prophecy."

"His source at State also knew about the money?"

"No. I don't know how he heard about that. But Stickles said 'considerable.' He didn't say ten billion. If he knew, I think he would have said ten billion."

Either way, thought Harry, the word seemed to be out. Sadik had said that the Iranians, especially, were gloating. They'd heard that someone claiming to be Aisha's handmaiden had apparently raided Saudi Charities.

Clew said, "He might not know that Sadik is here. All he'd know is that I pulled his file."

"Could Haskell have someone at State on his payroll?"

"I don't like to think so, but he might."

"Well, I think he'd be remiss if he didn't. Either way, I don't want to get back to Reagan and find that my plane has been quarantined. Answer him, Roger. Tell him you're on top of it. Say you'll be in his office first thing in the morning to give him your report in detail."

"What am I to tell him?"

"Nothing, Roger, because you won't be there. And the rest of us should be airborne by then."

"If I don't give them some story, they'll come up with their own. Stickles needs to look as if he's handling this thing."

"They'll come up with their own no matter what we tell them, Roger. The simple truth is never simple to those people."

"Simple," Clew repeated. "You see this as simple?"

A shrug. "I think most of it is easily explained. That's if we were inclined to explain it."

Clew frowned. "Are you asking me to stonewall the White House?"

"Uh-huh. And tell Leland that he should as well. This business will not be laid at his door. Tell him that he has my word on it. Tell him further that he, by alerting you, has thwarted Charles Haskell's criminal ambitions and those of his two accomplices. He's done his country an inestimable service."

"Yeah, but what ambitions? What they were planning?"

"Well, you know it's oil-related. Saudi oil in particular."

Clew rolled his eyes. "No shit. But what exactly?"

"Roger... whatever. It's probably dead. It probably died with Charles Haskell."

"He's dead?"

"I have reason to believe that he has expired. Don't worry. He'll be gone within the hour. You, with my assistance and that of Howard Leland have ended a threat to our oil supply. When do you plan to see Leland?"

"Hold it," said Clew. "So you don't know what Haskell was planning?"

"I do. So do you. We're simply not saying. Whatever it is, you have it under control. Tell them they're going to have to trust you on that. I don't see that they'll have any choice."

"Except to fire my ass and throw it into a cell."

"Not a chance. You know too much. They won't want you to go off and write a book. If anything, you're more indispensable than ever. They know that you're their only link to me. And through me, to my friends in the Caspian oilfields. Drop the hint. It will make their mouths water."

"Yeah, your Muslim friends. Which include Hamas. And which might include a Muslim messiah that you and Sadik cooked up between you. That's what Stickles will be wondering."

"Roger, I can't help what he thinks. You can reassure him, however, on one score. On his question of how I intend to respond, you will tell him that I've agreed to stand down pending a green light from you. You're my control. You have been for years. No, make that you and Leland. Without the two of you holding fast to the reins, my many good friends would be running amok in their eagerness to please me by avenging me. Gerald Stickles might not be safe either."

"Why Stickles?"

"He says 'ditto,' said Harry. "That's reason enough. No, it isn't. He's rude. His voice mail was rude. Don't let him get away with that again."

"Don't let him because... I'm holding the reins?"

"Perception is everything, Roger."

Hester Lazarus's car had pulled up outside. Harry got up to let her in. She was a severe-looking woman in her forties. No sign of Make-up, hair practically a buzz cut, no jewelry except for a small Star of David and an oversized, multi-functional wrist watch. She carried a laptop computer of her own and a diplomatic attaché case that had a chain running from it to her waist.

She offered no greetings. She asked, "Where do I work?" Harry gestured toward the library desk where he'd left the dossiers of Haskell, Bentley and Leeds and Bernice's laptop computer.

He asked, 'Do you need privacy?"

"Doesn't matter," she said.

He asked, "How long do you think this will take you?"

"Forty minutes. Maybe less. If you stand watching me, maybe longer."

He said, "You might have questions in sorting this out."

She gave him a look as if he'd insulted her. She unchained her briefcase and plugged in her laptop. She ran a cable from that one to the back of the other and adjusted them, side by side facing her.

Clew took Harry aside. "What's she going to do?"

"Create some accounts. Move some money around. After that, she'll help Sadik move some more."

Harry picked up his phone. He punched in the number of Yitzhak Netanya. As he waited, the phone at his ear, he said, "In the meantime, I'll look in on Elizabeth. Why don't you and the doctor get some air?"

Outside, Clew gestured toward the garage. He asked Sadik, "Are you at all curious?"

"Not so much. But you can't stand it. So let's look."

Clew pushed the outside button. The door rolled up. Clew was startled to see that the trunk was wide open. His hand darted to the Beretta on his belt. Sadik touched his shoulder. "No, he's there."

Sadik produced a small pen light from his pocket. The beam washed over the crumpled mass and came to rest when it found Haskell's face. His mouth had fallen open and his eyes had filmed over. His expression struck Sadik as a curious one. People die with all kinds of expressions on their faces. Most often, one of shocked disbelief. Haskell's expression seemed more of a sadness. Sadik remembered his desperate pleading directed entirely at Elizabeth Stride. It appears that she rejected them. Once and for all.

He saw the marks on his face where Elizabeth had kicked him. He could see no sign of blood elsewhere. His necktie was bunched and its knot was pulled tight, but not nearly tight enough for strangulation.

He asked Clew, "The necktie. Was that from your grappling encounter with him?

"I don't think so. I was mostly on my knees."

Sadik looked closer. Now he saw some fresh blood. Not much, but it was under the knot. He reached his fingers behind it. They found the fresh wound. He said, "The Black Angel worked with a knife, did she not? Long and thin with a bit of a curve?"

"Yeah, she did."

"And still does, it seems, when the occasion arises. I can't imagine what sort of discussion took place beyond the lunacy we both witnessed earlier. But I can imagine her explaining to him why his interest in her would remain unrequited. An inch at a time. This was not a quick thrust. She wanted him to know that he was dying. And why. My guess is that he still would not accept it."

A pair of headlights washed over them suddenly. They turned to see the gray van approaching from the direction of the gate. They heard Harry's voice. He was nearing the garage. Harry said, "Our two plumbers will dispose of Mr. Haskell." He said to Clew, "They'll steam clean the trunk."

Clew stood back as they lifted him out and rolled him up in a tarpaulin. They lifted him into the van.

Clew asked Harry, "Will he ever be found?"

"I haven't decided. I'll speak to Elizabeth. She might have some thoughts on the subject."

"Didn't you just go see her? How is she?"

"I did peek in. I tiptoed back out. She and Kessler are wrapped in each other's arms, their wet clothing in a heap by their bed. A private moment. Much needed, I think. Let's get back. We have much more to do."

FORTY SIX

On their return to the house, they passed the library's windows. Sadik was able to see Hester Lazarus. She had papers scattered all over the desk. Her fingers flew over a keyboard. He said to Harry, "May I now know what she's doing?"

"She's opening three new off-shore accounts in the names of Charles Haskell and his friends."

He said, "You'll recall those top three accounts. She transferring the money from those. Haskell gets three hundred and eighty one million plus a few hundred thousand and some. I forget the exact figure, but it's down to the penny. Huntington Bentley gets some twenty million less. Sir Reginald Leeds gets three hundred five million and so on and so on plus fifty-two cents."

Sadik didn't understand. "They're getting new accounts?"

"They're easy enough to open on-line, especially in places like Panama. She has everything she needs in each of their dossiers.

Their addresses, their assets, their whole financial lives, plus specimen signatures from their tax returns."

Sadik's expression remained blank. "I still don't get it."

Harry Whistler said, "Oh, and the prince. She has his formal signature from the suicide note. The prince will be named jointly on all three accounts, but there's a ceiling on the amount he's allowed to withdraw. I believe he tops out at fifty million." He said, "She won't be long. She's done this before. Then you can go in and get started."

"Sorry," said Sadik, "My brain must not be working. Are you going to tell me why you're doing this?"

"When she's done, she's going to give you the details. The bank, it's location, account numbers and such. You'll get the password that's used for checking the balance, but not the one that's used for transfers or withdrawals. You, Rajib Sadik, will then contact these three Saudis and tell them that you, through your many connections, have learned who took their money and where it has gone."

"So that... they will come after Bentley and Leeds?"

"And Haskell. And the prince. But not Rasha. Not now. Apparently the prince put one over on them. He wasn't as inept as they thought."

Sadik glanced skyward. "Please be patient with me. Isn't the prince buried in some California forest or weighted down in some lake?"

"It's anyone's guess where they disposed of him."

Sadik's eyes had narrowed. "Are you being cavalier or are you pulling my leg? One does not expect whimsy in this situation."

"I'm just trying to answer your questions."

Sadik asked, "Do you intend to kill Bentley and Leeds?"

"No, I'm not bothering with them."

"I see that I must phrase my questions precisely. Why not? No, wait. Answer this question first. What keeps them from denying that they took it?"

"They'll try. But there it is. Down to the last penny. Your three Saudis will see it when they type in the password. Those two probably won't live very long. Or the three Saudis won't. Whoever's first."

Sadik was still squinting. "Unless these two give it back."

"They can't. They won't have the second passwords."

Sadik understood. Or at least was beginning to. He asked, "This method, is it normal for you? I mean, setting your enemies at each other's throats? It seems to me that I've heard this about you."

"I've found that to be a convenience."

"Nice for you," said Sadik. "Saves time. Saves trouble. But at the cost of almost a billion dollars? You'd be leaving this money to their heirs."

"The heirs won't get it. That money's only bait. Hester's setting up an automatic transfer to a charity in the event of their deaths. Don't ask which charity. She will have invented one. A real one has procedures. It might ask too many questions. Each of their balances will revert to that charity within hours of their bodies being found and identified."

Sadik touched the fingers of both hands to his temples. "Okay. Simple question. It should get a simple answer. Do we get the money back from this charity?"

"Every dime."

Sadik had been at the computer for an hour. Harry Whistler had retired into the kitchen to make a few more telephone calls. The longest had been to his wife in Geneva. He'd briefed her on all that had happened. She'd already heard a good deal of it from Yitzhak who'd called her on his own to reassure her.

Reassured, but annoyed, she said, "You couldn't have called?"

"Not until I could give you the time you deserve. I've been rather in the thick of things, my darling."

"You've been there, what… only five or six hours? That's the last time I let you out alone."

"Kate, I have the twins with me. And Kessler and Stride."

"All of whom should be dead from the looks of that restaurant."

"It's on TV even there?"

"It's everywhere, Harry. Never mind that for now. What do you need from this end?"

He'd asked her to prepare for the arrival of the girls and arrange for their transport to the lodge in Chamonix directly upon landing in Geneva.

"Including Kessler and Stride?"

"And one kitten."

She'd said, "You might have trouble getting out of D.C." She said, "I'll have a back-up, unmarked, no initials, waiting at the Baltimore-Washington Airport. I'll call you back with the details."

With that, he made a fresh pot of coffee.

Hester smelled it. She came in. "I could use some of that."

"Help yourself," he told her. "How is Sadik doing?"

"He has trouble believing that these numbers are real money. It's not every day he moves billions."

"But he's doing it?"

"Yes. How are you holding up?"

"I don't do this every day either."

She found a mug. She filled it. "I'm not talking about the money. You look... I don't know... a little wiped. You okay?"

"Nothing that a hot bath won't fix."

She took a sip and placed her mug on the counter. She stepped behind him and began massaging his shoulders. She said, "See that? You're as tight as a drum." Her strong fingers worked their way to his neck.

She said, "I could hear you talking to Sadik. I could hear some of what you were saying to Roger. You seemed, as always, very much in control."

"But?"

"No 'but.' You were being Harry Whistler."

"Being Harry Whistler can be tiring, Hester. In my next life, I think I'd like to be a Shih Tzu."

"I'd adopt you," said Hester. "But you'd have to eat kosher. While you're thinking that over, let's talk about the money. Up to six and a half billion is going to remain. What does Harry Whistler intend doing with it while he is still Harry Whistler?"

"No idea."

"So you're going to keep it?"

"Sadik's welcome to it."

She continued her kneading. "Have you thought this out? If Rasha's father stole it in league with this Haskell, how will you explain how you got it?"

"I won't."

"Good," she said. "Why confuse them with the truth? So it will be assumed that you took it from them, but not before they took almost a billion off the top. You saw to it that another three and a half billion went back where it was intended. What was your motive? Simple decency? Justice? Talk about hard to believe."

"Hester, I didn't do a damned thing. This time yesterday, the biggest thing I had on my mind was what I felt like having for lunch."

"Maybe, but that's equally hard to believe. Even for me. And I believe you."

"You want simple decency? It's in the next room."

"Yes, Sadik, but through you. You handed it to him. And this will add greatly to his stature in Hamas. Why would Harry Whistler want such a thing? Does he intend to add Hamas to his formidable network? Wrest control from the Saudis? Make his own peace? Then buy up a few miles of beachfront in Gaza to create a Palestinian Eden?"

"Hester... I'm just trying to get through the day. I understand what you're saying, but I have no control..."

"Sure you do. You're Harry Whistler. You're always up to something and you're always pulling strings. If that's the perception, and it is; you can't change it. You might as well make the most of it."

"Harry Whistler is open to suggestions."

"Not so much about the money, but if you don't want it, you could always give it back to the Saudis."

"Which Saudis?" he asked. "Those who stole it?"

"No, to their treasury. In return for whatever. Sooner or later, they'll know Sadik has it. You know that they'll make the first claim on it."

Whistler shook his head. "What claim can they make? If the remaining money came from skimming and from bribes, it would have come from foreign companies doing business with them."

"And foreign governments."

"I know that," he told her. "This government included. But none of it would have come from Saudi pockets."

"Might be true," said Hester, "but the skimmers will want it. Some of them are bound to come after him for it. No one walks away from so much cash."

"Sure, but how would they account for having it in the first place? This is flight money, Hester."

"Yes, it is. So the first thing they'd do is take flight. Once safely abroad in their flight money havens, they'd start looking for a bargaining advantage. They'll start looking for something to trade."

She was right. It was true. He had not thought this out. That "something to trade" would be Sadik's wife or daughter. They'd have to go into hiding.

"Your advice?"

"Get rid of it. Give it away. Okay, not to the Saudis, but give them a disk that shows only the names and the current cash balances. That keeps some of the skimmers from coming after you because the royals will have had them beheaded."

He nodded. "More than likely. And the money?"

"To charity," she answered. "Sadik's on a roll. Let him tell the Saudis and let him choose who gets it. If it all goes to Muslims, how upset can they be? Charity's one of the five pillars of Islam. Sadik's smart enough to let them take credit. They might even sweeten the pot."

"That region could use a few more doctors like Sadik."

"And new medical schools. If that's your preference, tell Sadik."

"Hester, that's just a thought. They could use almost everything."

"I know that," she told him, "but your instincts are sound. All we hear about are profligate sheiks and emirs. For millions of Arabs, their idea of wealth is having children who live past the age of five."

"Which brings us back to doctors," said Harry.

"Sadik would need a great deal of organizational help. Not Hamas, though. Hamas would limit its charity to its own turf. Don't your companies endow a number of foundations that give educational grants? Sadik's own wife went to medical school on a grant from one such in Jordan."

Whistler said, "She competed. She got one of only six."

"Only six," said Hester, 'and we're talking thousands. Ten thousand new doctors from poor Mideast families. All they need is the smarts and the desire. I changed my mind, though, about strictly Muslims. I'd include a percentage of Christians and Jews, whatever that percentage is where they live. That way, it's not so much Muslim as Mideastern. I'd try for a quota, half men and half women. You won't get that many women, but try. In return they must all pledge five years of their lives working with the poor where they came from."

He smiled. "I'm so glad I thought of this, Hester. What are some of my other ideas?"

She slapped his shoulders indicating that the rubdown was over. She crossed to the opposite side of the counter and pulled up two stools facing his. She climbed onto one of them, turned her head, and called out, "Sadik. It is time for a break. Come sit with us in the kitchen."

Whistler started to rise. He said, "You don't need me to sell this to Sadik. Do it. It's decided. It's time for my bath."

She planted her elbows, her chin in her hands. She said, "Sit. New subject. The prophecy."

FORTY SEVEN

It took them a while to get to that subject. Sadik went from being dazed to being dazzled at the prospect of controlling all that money. His concerns, and there were several, kept being dwarfed by the prospect of having ten thousand new doctors.

He was doodling on a notepad, playing with numbers. Ten Thousand? Twenty thousand was possible, he said. Or ten thousand plus a thousand local clinics. At least twenty million vaccinations a year paid for by the interest alone.

Whistler used the time to make more calls to Geneva to confirm that the various foundations Hester spoke of were equipped to deal with such amounts. The answer was basically, "We don't see why not." The founders of Microsoft have established foundations that total four times as much. They would arrange a meeting of all the directors to be held on the following Monday. Sadik should plan on attending that meeting. He'll be asked to take a seat on the board.

Hester was calling him back into the kitchen. She repeated, "Now the prophecy. Come sit."

He'd heard Sadik's arguments over the good that even the talk of this prophecy might do. He was not greatly interested in hearing them again, except that here was Hester, an Israeli Jew, who seemed to have embraced it as well. He was curious as to her reasons.

Besides, he felt he owed her. Not least for the massage. She had just relieved him of a major headache. A six and a half billion dollar headache.

The main argument was an old one, centuries old, but revived with a vengeance by the prophecy bloggers on thousands of internet sites. A great many Muslim thinkers had been critical of Islam. This once brilliant culture of scholars and poets, consummate builders, mathematicians and astronomers, had gradually allowed itself to be mired in a bunkered long-ago past. Unlike Christianity, it's never had a Martin Luther to spark a self-examining Reformation. It's never had a Jean-Jacques Rousseau to plant the seeds of a Renaissance.

Sadik said, "But of course, that's not strictly true. There were plenty of reformers, progressives and liberals. Like Luther, most were branded as apostates and heretics by a clergy that saw its authority threatened. The only movement that ever really got off the ground was one that went backward, not forward."

"The Wahhabis?"

"Uh-huh. Fundamentalist Sunnis. Got in bed with the patriarch, Abdul ibn Saud, who was then just a run-of-the-mill tribal leader who eked out a living raiding caravans. They'd support him if he'd support them. He'd accept their Islam as the only true

570

Islam. In return, they'd give him a religious dispensation that permitted him to rob any non-Wahhabi, which meant everyone else in the world."

"That would seem to come in handy for a bandit," said Whistler.

"You got it," said Hester. "It also worked for the mullahs of Iran who snatched most of that country's GDP for themselves."

Sadik winced as she said it. "They're not all like that."

She said, "No, they're not all like your old college roomie. But even Abbas Mansur has to watch what he says. But, okay, let's stick with the Wahhabis." She said to Harry, "Aside from being anti-modern, anti-all things western, even banning sunglasses there for a while, they were a disaster for women. They said a woman's only function was to breed more men. There were plenty of women who thought, 'Well screw you,' but they didn't dare say it out loud."

"Until the internet."

"Yes. That's where this thing got its wings. There are some who've been calling her a Muslim Joan of Arc but that's exactly what we don't need. No one's looking for the kind who'll lead armies into battle. But we'd love to see a champion arise and speak out, both to women and to fair-minded men. And we need a voice that cannot be silenced."

"This Aisha," said Sadik, "has only one message. She says read the Koran. You don't need a cleric to interpret it for you. They've twisted its teachings long enough. All through it, it tells women, 'Be the best you can be.' Within limits? Yes. Because family is important. But it spelled out women's rights that western women wouldn't get for another twelve hundred years."

Harry said to Hester, "You said we need a voice. Just so I'm clear, who is we?"

"Women," she answered. "All women. Jews included. Read the blogs. Some of the most heart-felt are from Hindu women. The Wahhabis, not to mention the Pakistanis, want the Hindus just as dead as the rest of us."

Sadik said, "Speaking of that part of the world, do you want to know who doesn't feel the need for a champion?"

Harry waited.

"It's the Muslims with whom you do business, Harry. All the Muslims of the Caspian republics. Neither Sunni nor Shiite, these are Hanafi Muslims. They are the least fundamentalist of all Muslim sects."

Hester chimed in. "And their women are regarded as a equals, not as property, and nearly all are at least high school graduates. Literacy, both sexes, stands at 99 percent. Middle east Muslim countries average half that. How come? Those countries were Soviet Republics. The Soviet Union's educational system stressed the sciences regardless of gender. It encouraged talent regardless of gender. They are not cowed by clerics. They think for themselves. They interpret the Koran for themselves."

"And their women," Sadik added, "still manage to raise children while designing roads and bridges and pipelines."

"Okay, I get it." said Harry. "Education is key. Let's get back to this Aisha reformation…"

"Good name for it," said Hester. "Good thinking."

"The protestant reformation was hardly peaceful," he reminded her. "The medieval Catholic church, unless I'm mistaken, was just as intolerant of dissent."

"Until Martin Luther. Until Rousseau. Until they freed people to follow their hearts."

Harry had to smile. "Nice thought, but not true. They were merely divided into warring camps of Catholic and Protestant armies. I assume you've heard of the Thirty Years War. They proceeded to slaughter each other."

"Harry," said Sadik, "warring camps need warring leaders. All these leaders were men. That's what's going to be different this time."

"Um… how so?"

"Aisha, to begin with, doesn't divide. You heard Hester. Her message unites. And as Hester said, she cannot be silenced. If a Muslim Martin Luther were to spring up, they'd cut his throat before you could say boo."

"They could cut our Aisha's throat just as quickly," said Harry. "That's where you lose me on this."

Hester asked, "She is safe, is she not?"

"She'll be out of reach soon. But not forever." He said. "Look, we've all dodged a bullet today. That suicide note was only written last night. Haskell had time to fax a copy to the Saudis with a promise that he'd kill us all."

"He didn't," said Sadik. "I'm named in that note. The first Saudi who read it would have picked up the phone and asked

Hamas to arrest me just in case. I can assure you that my wife would have heard. She would have called me by now."

"That's the Saudis," said Harry. "What about the Iranians. Mansur asked you to track down the prophecy. You're in Tehran one day and in Belle Haven the next. The Iranians, who get CNN by the way, might be able to add two and two."

Sadik said, "You leave the Iranians to me. I promised Abbas Mansur that I'd report and I will. I'll give him my word that Elizabeth Stride's Aisha had no role whatsoever in the spread of this prophecy. He'll believe me because it's the truth."

"Niki Darvi sure did. What will you say about her?"

"I'll tell him, if asked, that his suspicion was correct. The younger Darvi sister made some mischief. She's been punished by Elizabeth; she's no longer in Belle Haven. She was not, however, the original source. There were already references to the prophecy on Google. Thousands of others must have seen them and discussed them long before Niki sent her first email. This is also the literal truth."

"Some mischief?" asked Harry. "That's what you'll call it? She claimed to be Aisha's handmaiden, for Pete's sake. She claimed to have seen her in the flesh. She claimed to have taken that ten billion dollars so that Aisha could give it to the poor."

"Juvenile mischief. You took it. She didn't. You took what was left of it and gave it to me so that I could give it back to the poor. Maybe she overheard what you were planning to do and decided to pretend that Aisha did it."

Hester raised an eyebrow. "That's pretty damned thin."

"Perhaps," said Sadik. "but what can he say? It didn't start here and it won't end here either. But no more of it will be coming from Niki."

"He'll have heard about the bombing. What will you say about that?"

"Not related," said Sadik. "It was the act of a man who had a personal grudge against some of the people in that restaurant. I can place my hand on the holy Koran and swear that it was not about the prophecy."

Whistler was doubtful. Sadik saw that on his face. He said, "Listen to me, Harry. This was Mansur's big question. Is this prophecy part of a Western conspiracy to cause turmoil in the oil-producing countries? I can look him in the eye and say that it is not. Will some try to take advantage? Of course. Some always do. But because, when you come down to it, all it really is, is gossip, there is nothing for them to try to crush."

Whistler asked Hester, "Would you say we're home free?"

"From whom? The Inquisitors? Muslim heretic hunters? I would say maybe. For a time. With some luck."

"A most comforting answer. Thank you, Hester."

She said, "Washington, I think, might make a pest of itself. But not for long. You're Harry Whistler. You find oil."

He rubbed his eyes. He said, "Okay. Let's get back on the subject. You haven't told me what you want me to do about keeping the prophecy alive."

"Who said keep it alive?" Sadik asked. "Just don't kill it."

"Explain."

Sadik said, "Only what you're already planning to do. Keep these girls, all of them, out of sight for a while. Keep an eye on Niki especially. You don't want her, as she's threatened, to spill the beans and tell the whole world that this was a hoax – which is, incidentally what Mansur has in mind for her. Many Muslim women would be made to look foolish. Those awakened might go right back to sleep."

"Um… isn't it already being labeled a hoax?"

"Labeling isn't knowing. And besides, she's really come. Aisha's spirit is already out there. I've been working on Niki to make her understand that she has actually done some real good. But only if she never speaks of it."

"Go on."

"The second," said Sadik, "is for you to keep silent. You know that this part of it began as a lark. You know that it grew out of four girls talking. We're simply asking that you never say so. Not even if the president asks you."

"That's all you're asking? That I don't derail it?"

"Deny, if asked, whether you are behind it. I know. You don't deny. You don't tell them a thing. But in this case, we don't want it said that an infidel…"

"This infidel will deny all involvement."

Hester and Sadik exchanged satisfied smiles. This was easier than either had expected.

Harry said, "Not so fast. There are conditions."

"That it never touch Aisha?"

"If anyone I know should so much as hint that our Aisha is the Aisha of the prophecy, I'll call a press conference myself. I will give my word that she has not, and never pretended to be, the Aisha of the prophecy reborn."

"Fair enough," said Sadik. "But you won't say it's false?"

"The prophecy? Who am I to say such a thing? I'll only say that it must be some other Aisha."

Sadik hesitated. He was rubbing his chin.

"Rajib?"

He said, "It's agreed. She is not the new Aisha. A small part of me, however, can't help wishing that she might be. She'd have more than an angel to protect her."

"Okay, you've said it. Can you now put it out of your mind?"

Sadik offered his hand. "My word on it. Done."

Harry took it. He said, "Let us hope so."

They spoke for a while on a number of subjects. Harry still wasn't sure that he understood why Hester would ally with Sadik. Sadik is Sadik, but Hamas is Hamas. And the bedrock raison d'etre of that organization's charter is the final destruction of Israel. That would seem to be an obstacle to peace.

Another, even stronger, is in the Koran. The language is very specific. You may not, repeat not, make peace with an enemy who has taken your land. One could argue all day about whose land it is and who had the greater historical claim. One could argue about which was the chosen of God. One could note that fully a fifth of all Israelis were Muslims with full rights of citizenship.

But the fact remained, at the end of the day, that many more had either been driven from their homes or not permitted to return.

Sadik had asked him, "You've read the Koran?"

"I re-read it on the plane coming over."

"Next time read more carefully. That's not all it says. It says we must either drive them from our land or else let them stay and pay tribute."

Harry seemed to recall that it did, in fact, say that. Hamas' charter, however, does not offer that option. Sadik then pointed out that the Koran takes precedence over any political document.

Harry asked, "Then why bother including it?"

"To get Saudi backing. You don't get Saudi backing without Wahhabi backing. Israel's there to stay. We all know that," said Sadik. "No one's driving them into the sea."

"As long as they pay tribute? That would seem… unlikely."

"It would?" asked Sadik. "They're already paying. Israel has paid millions in reparations to Muslims whose land they have taken. Over here, you call that eminent domain. You take homes where you need to build a highway."

"That's compensation," said Harry. "Not tribute."

"Semantics," said Sadik. "Israel is paying. But from their point of view, they are making an investment. Not a pay-off, not a bribe, but a legitimate investment. The Palestinian work force is far and away the most educated and industrious in all the Mideast. In that regard, the two peoples have much in common. They're already trading partners on quite a large scale."

"We buy their grain," said Hester, "their fruits and their vegetables. We buy copper and potash and sulfur from their mines. You know this new wall that you hear so much about? All its concrete comes from Palestinian companies that were more than happy to sell it. We also buy about a third of our fresh water from them. All this can only increase."

Harry remained doubtful. "Trade still isn't tribute."

"It is if we say it is," said Sadik.

Hester added, "But of course no one says it out loud. This is just to quiet the die-hards. It allows them to believe that they've not only won something, but have satisfied Allah's primary requirement. More investment, meanwhile, provides jobs and good lives. What will those who have them say to the die-hards? More and more, they will say, 'Oh, shut up.'"

"More and more," asked Harry, "over how long a period? The pace of change has been less than breath-taking."

"Not as slow," said Hester, "as your civil rights movement. Your blacks had been citizens for almost a century before they began to be treated as such. Why then? Because their own Martin Luther stepped forward. The writer, James Baldwin became their Rousseau. All Palestine had was Yasir Arafat who never missed an opportunity to miss an opportunity. But then, of course, he was…"

"Only human?" asked Sadik.

"And a man," Hester answered.

"Two encumbrances," said Sadik, "that Aisha's spirit doesn't share. Perhaps she can pick up the pace."

FORTY EIGHT

Two helicopters were waiting on the tarmac in Geneva. The alternate aircraft that Kate Whistler had chartered touched down a few minutes after sunset.

Harry's Gulfstream had, as he'd suspected, drawn a reception committee at Reagan. There were cameramen among them, but not from the media. Gerald Stickles had intended to be photographed interdicting Harry Whistler and the terrorist, Sadik, as proof that he was in full command. The Gulfstream's pilot had warned Harry off as soon as he saw the line of black cars race up and block the aircraft from moving. Clew's limo proceeded to Baltimore.

The crew of the Gulfstream had been detained and denied further access to telephones. But they couldn't be held for more than a day. It was only after they were once again airborne when Harry learned that his Gulfstream had been standing wingtip to wingtip with a Trans-Global Oil & Gas corporate jet signed out to its CEO, Charles Haskell. The world seems to get smaller by the day.

The two helicopters were five-seat Bell Rangers. They had waited well away from the passenger terminal but under a bank of bright floodlights. The helicopters were painted a candy-apple red and, as with the Gulfstream, Harry's initials stood outlined in gold, this time only two feet high on the fuselage. A Humvee waited near the Bell Rangers, this one gold with Harry's initials in red.

"So much for our new low profile lifestyle," said Elizabeth as their unmarked aircraft rolled to a stop.

"Harry is Harry," said Kessler.

She saw Kate Whistler standing by the gold Humvee. No airport officials, no customs officials were anywhere in sight. She assumed that Harry had a standing arrangement that certain arrivals with certain guests would remain officially unnoticed.

Elizabeth unbuckled. She went to rouse the four girls. They had slept through much of the crossing. Rasha and her kitten were easily wakened, as were Shahla and Niki. All three yawned and stretched and, realizing where they were, excitedly pressed their foreheads to their windows. Aisha seemed almost unwilling to wake up. She'd been dreaming, no doubt, of her mother again, telling her, perhaps that she had been right. It had been a birthday to remember.

She told the girls, "All six of us are staying aboard until Harry's helicopters are ready to go. We'll wait until those damned lights go off. "

Shahla asked her, "Aren't we staying in Geneva?"

"No, we're going to France. The French Alps."

Harry himself had passed some of the flight in the co-pilot's seat, on the radio with Clew or watching video replays on one of two cameras that the twins brought aboard. These were not the cameras of Mulazim and Haskell. They were the cameras of commuters who had come off the bus and who had taped the chaos, the smoke and confusion that followed the explosion at Mangiamo. The twins, upon establishing that Harry was safe and that no serious harm had come to the girls, set about relieving those commuters of their cameras. Harry didn't ask by what means they had done so. He assumed that the owners of the cameras had been left looking much like all the others in need of first aid.

Disconcerting for them, but they'll get over it, thought Harry. He was glad to have their cameras because they had in fact recorded Elizabeth's dismantling of Haskell. They'd also recorded Haskell's nearly successful strangulation of Roger Clew. Poor Roger. Not much of a fighter, but he tried. Harry would erase his awkward flailing. He would also erase the footage that showed the late Charles Haskell being stuffed into the trunk of a limo bearing State Department plates.

One of the twins had also recovered his hat. It was in need of professional care, but it had suffered no permanent damage. That alone would be worth a nice bonus.

Sadik had spent nearly all of the flight quietly working with Mossad's Hester Lazarus on the two laptop computers. The Humvee was for them. Kate Whistler would be driving. One twin would go with her. She would take them to the family villa in Geneva where, by week's end, they intended to complete the transfer of several billions more.

The lights were turned off, the Two Bell Rangers were ready. The other twin escorted the girls into one. She and Kessler and Harry would fly in the other. They took off into the night.

After a flight of less than two hours, they approached the lights of the helipad of what Harry referred to as his ski shack. It overlooked the Chamonix valley from the western slope of Mont Blanc. In architectural style, it was a chalet that could have passed as a four star hotel. Three stories high, twenty bedrooms and suites, surrounded by eight hundred acres, all forested, except for a half dozen ski trails, all private. Kessler and Elizabeth knew the place well. Elizabeth had once convalesced there.

She'd said to Whistler as they passed over Chamonix, "Tell me you haven't painted it red."

"I'm only that Harry Whistler when I want to be, Elizabeth. No, it's the same. It's all wood and stone. A retreat is a retreat, not a showcase."

"You're full of it, Harry. I bet Kate put her foot down. Have I told you that you don't deserve her?"

He said to Kessler, "I see she's lost none of her charm." He said to Elizabeth, "Love your hair, by the way." He said, "No red Humvees either. The lodge comes equipped with two Saab SUVs. One is dark brown and the other dark green, the better to blend into trees. Both are highly powered; you'll need a light foot. Both are bullet resistant. In addition there are some new electronics since you last favored me with a visit. No unexpected guest can get near you undetected. It's even safer than the house in Belle Haven."

"What good are the cars? We can't go to town, can we?"

He said, "Not you with Martin, never together, even though Chamonix is always crawling with tourists. But singly, or with one, even two of the girls, by all means, go to movies, go shopping. I don't need to tell you not to use credit cards. How much cash do you have between you?"

"Not much," said Kessler. "A few hundred, American."

"Dollars won't attract notice, but Euros are better. My head housekeeper is French. Her name is Danielle. She keeps about fifty thousand on hand. It's there for guests who run short; use whatever you need; replenish it when you're able to transfer your own funds. Two armed guards with dogs are on patrol around the clock. Have you brought weapons of your own?"

"Only her knife," Kessler answered.

Harry asked Elizabeth, "No Ingram Mac-10? When have you ever been without it?"

"It burned with my car. But it's going to be found."

"And assumed to be yours. So what if it is? You're Elizabeth Stride. It would be laughable to charge you with possession."

He said, "Danielle will show you where our weapons are kept, ranging from handguns on up. You're not likely to need them. No guest ever has. On the other hand, it hasn't been often that I've entertained a Muslim messiah."

Elizabeth hissed, "Harry, Aisha is not…"

"You're not here because she is. You're here because there are people who might think she is. Don't worry. This will pass in due course."

It might, thought Elizabeth. It should. It had better. Unless Aisha, who's already been wondering about it, begins to believe it herself.

It was the next morning, a bright and beautiful Friday, before the girls got their first real look at the splendid scenery around them. Although it was July, the mountains were snow-capped. Aisha and Rasha were thrilled by the views. Neither had ever seen snow. The Darvi girls had. Tehran has cold winters. There were ski trails about an hour's drive north. Men and women had to use separate slopes, but the snow is pure and white, not like that of the city. In the city it would be covered with a layer of soot almost before it stopped falling. They had never really played in the snow.

Harry told them at breakfast, "Then you're all overdue. This morning we drive up Mont Blanc."

He was able to scrounge enough winter clothing and jump suits that had been left by other guests. Some fit Aisha and Shahla, both of whom were full grown, and some fit Niki Darvi who was nearly so. Rasha swam inside hers, but at least she'd be warm.

Elizabeth had put some fresh salve on Aisha's burns before she began to suit up. Happily, the burns didn't look bad at all. There was some minimal blistering, nothing likely to scar or discolor. In addition to the clothing, Harry brought from his ski room a pair of aluminum disks made for coasting and one well-waxed wooden luge. Rasha asked for first dibs on the luge.

Kessler went with them in one of Harry's SUV's, two pairs of skis on its rack. It had been too long since Kessler was on skis. Harry Whistler was counting on him being stale and that his ski legs would take a while to come back. He had never beaten

Kessler down a run before this. He'd bet a bottle of Cristal that he would.

A trip up above the tree line, more than anything else, just might be the best medicine for Aisha. A breath of fresh air, so to speak. By and large, she seemed her old self again. Certainly there were periods of reflective melancholy over the uprooting that had been forced upon them for the second time in three months. Forced on Elizabeth as well.

That much, however, was true of all four. But in Aisha's case there was also an awareness that she was very much at the center of all this. Not to blame for it. Not at all. But somehow responsible. So much, good and bad, had been done in her name. Well… not in her name, but we get the idea. And so much more was likely to be done. All we can do is try to help her to focus on the good, all those new doctors, for example. And on the courage that so many Muslim women have found. And on the many good men who are listening.

Elizabeth had chosen to stay at the chalet. The girls didn't need her. They could do with some fun. So could poor Martin and for that she blamed herself. She'd not been very pleasant since that email from Netanya. And even less so since people died at a party that she had insisted on going ahead with. She'd even groused at him for not giving her some time with that little insect from the Hasheem who he'd left in the men's room. The one who'd murdered Bernice. Totally unfair to him. He'd had no idea. And he'd been so very kind to her since. Sitting in that pool with her. Listening. Understanding. Taking her to their bedroom. Helping her to undress and dry off. Helping her into a warm nightgown. And holding her, just holding her, until morning.

Well, being such a bitch ends today, she decided. She'll make it up to him when he gets back. He'll want to take a shower and she'll climb in with him. There's nothing like a shower stall to shut out the world and to strip oneself of all other baggage. Left to her, she'd soap him up and screw his brains out. But Martin doesn't do that. He slows everything down. Lots of holding and whispering and feather-light touching. Where did he learn that? It wasn't from her. But because of it, he's got her for as long as he lives. And he'd better live for more than five years.

He will. He's strong. He gets stronger by the week. Doctors get it wrong all the time.

The girls had all urged her to come out and play with them, even offering to stay and really meaning it. Martin, too. She told them, "Tomorrow. We'll all go tomorrow. I'll find some red paint and some used Brillo pads. We'll make a snowman that looks like Harry Whistler."

See that? We're not shits, but she was being a shit. She still hadn't thanked Harry for all that he's doing. And speaking of the Brillo that they'd used for Harry's beard, that's exactly what her own hair now looked like. "Love your hair," the big ox said, flying down here on his Ranger. For that crack, he's got it coming. Well, she might let him off. But the fact remains, two thirds of it's gone. She'd better see what she can do with it.

For now, she'd enjoy the first solitude that she'd known since her walks on the Hilton Head beaches. Maybe she'd take a little nap. Maybe she'd have pleasant dreams. Maybe if she willed it hard enough, she'd get Aisha's mother to drop in. There were a few things she'd like to say to her. She'd say leave the kid alone. No more coming in her dreams. But if you do, if you must, don't be so damned Delphic. Say it flat out. It's not her.

Say, "Sorry to scare you, but it's true; you're not her. I know because I just had a chat with her."

This would perk Aisha up. She'd say "Really?"

"Yup. And it turns out you've got lots of time. She who's coming won't be coming for a while yet."

Aisha would ask, "But she's still coming?"

"Can't say for certain. She might be rethinking. I mean, why bother making the trip if half the world thinks she's down there already?"

"But what if some of them still think it's me?"

"Yeah, you'd better sit tight until this thing blows over."

"And if it isn't me, or if she's not coming through me, what was that about 'beyond my wildest dreams?'"

"What, that wasn't a hell of a party? People coming from all over? All those fireworks afterward?"

"Mom..."

"And tell Elizabeth that I thought you looked really good. Can't say the same for her. She looked like hell when she walked out with you. Hey, you know who she looked like?"

"The angel Qaila?"

"I was going to say more like a butch biker chick. If I were her, before I'd put any moves on Kessler, I'd think about getting a paper bag and putting it over my..."

Yeah, right, thought Elizabeth. If only.

She did work on her hair. Waste of time. It was hopeless. But Harry had a well-equipped exercise room that included a Jacuzzi and a sauna. She worked the Stairmaster, the bike and some weights before treating herself to a soak in the Jacuzzi. She'd put on some music. It was Bach. Chamber music. With the tub gently bubbling in time with the music, she was asleep in five minutes.

She'd slept well past noon. Danielle came in to wake her. She said, "I've fixed you some lunch." Danielle carried a tray containing soup and a sandwich and three folded sheets of copy paper. She set the tray down and reached for a towel. She said, "These are emails just in. First from Dr. Sadik. It is addressed to either you or Mr. Kessler. I review all correspondence. It's for everyone's protection. This one is good news for Rasha."

Elizabeth's eyes brightened. She sat up and reached for them, ignoring the towel that Danielle was holding for her. She opened the fold, dropping two of the sheets. She said, excitedly, "Sorry. Wet hands." She stepped out of the tub while reading the first. "We have robes here," said Danielle, "should you feel the need." Elizabeth gave no sign that she'd heard.

Sadik's email read:

"Rasha's mother, an hour ago, arrived in Toulon. Tell Harry that my arms dealer came through in return for the incentives we discussed. She's at the same Nasreen safe house where Rasha first stayed. For security reasons, she has not been told that you are at Harry's private retreat, only that Rasha is in excellent hands. I've emailed Harry separately with the Toulon number. Let Harry decide how best to make contact and how to reunite her with Rasha."

Elizabeth was thrilled. She couldn't wait to tell Rasha. No, better yet, let it be a surprise. Let her watch as one of Harry's Bell Rangers approaches. Let her see who climbs out of this one.

Danielle stood holding the two pages that she'd dropped. She said to Elizabeth, "Still mostly good. But not if these cause you to die of pneumonia. First the robe, then I give you the next one."

Elizabeth yielded to Danielle's sense of modesty before starting on the second of the pages. This one was from Roger Clew.

It read:

"Tell Harry that Bigfoot doesn't waste any time. It seems he visited some of Haskell's executives. One of them, while he was still able to talk, told him where Gilhooley might be found. There's a company called Scorpion Systems that Haskell's friend, Bentley controls. It has only one office and that's in Kuwait. Gilhooley's either there now or he's on his way. I told Sam to sit tight and let me look into it but I'm less than confidant that he will. I spoke to Netanya. He has people in Kuwait and he has his own interests. He says they're aware of Scorpion Systems as an oil field security firm that is thought to do Haskell's dirty work on the side. He says they'll watch for Gilhooley themselves and will advise when he's no longer an issue."

Hmmph, thought Elizabeth. Netanya has "interests?' Of course he has interests. He'll take Gilhooley not so much to save Sam the trouble as to keep Sam from queering an operation of his own. They've probably long since infiltrated that company. Either way, he's committed. Gilhooley will be found. Perhaps Netanya will send Harry one of his ears with that big hearing aid still hanging out of it.

Danielle said to her, "This last one might not be so welcome. Mr. Clew says that you might want to shop for a wig."

Elizabeth had to sit down as she read it. It was all about the upcoming editions of Time and Newsweek Magazines. The second coming of Aisha on both of their covers. One of them headlined with the question, "Is She Coming?" The other using that same illustration with "Riding The Internet Lightning" in a banner underneath. The treatment inside is similar for both. Reactions from all over the Muslim world including American Muslims. Interviews with clerics, most of them skeptical, but not willing to brush it off entirely. Pro and con lifts from Internet blogs which are running about ten to one pro. Photos of women holding vigils in Tehran and of other demonstrations throughout the Gulf states. This is under the sub-head, 'Millions Flocking To Her Banner.' There are also a few reports of claimed sightings including a possible in… Belle Haven.

Clew wrote:

"It's a shot of you and Aisha leaving Mangiamo. It appeared in Thursday morning's Alexandria Gazette. Very small in that paper. Part of a montage. But both magazines picked up on it. No names, but it's you, smoke coming from what's left of your hair, you and Aisha all hijabbed in those white tablecloths. Both magazine's noted that it's eerily similar to the drawing their using on the cover. All that's missing is a sword and the camel. And at least you've lost that helmet look that Newsweek says is catching on big time. Tatiana got both magazines to send galleys. I'll fax them as soon as I've read them. Both magazines to hit the stands in one week. International editions as well."

591

Danielle said, "International includes Chamonix. In French and in German and also in English. You cannot be seen with her in town."

No, thought Elizabeth. Not even in the week before they hit. And certainly not looking like this. "Wigs," she said. "Does the town have a wig store?"

"Quite a good one," said Danielle. "Every style, every color, from classic to funky. Also clothing stores for every taste, every age. All of you will need to buy new clothing."

Yes, they would, thought Elizabeth. Especially the girls. They came with only what they could carry. Harry can arrange to have the rest shipped, including their Korans and their prayer rugs. But whatever they'd worn in Hilton Head or Belle Haven ought not to be worn in Chamonix.

Danielle said, "This evening I'll write down all your sizes. Tomorrow, Saturday, I will shop for the women. What you don't like, I will return. I will bring Mr. Kessler because he's European. Between us we'll know what you'd like to wear, but also the things that you ought to wear."

Elizabeth made a face. "I suppose."

"I see… what? Reservations?" asked Danielle.

No, she saw concerns. There were plenty of those. Not least was how or whether to keep Aisha from seeing her name and her face on every news stand. The only way would be to keep her cloistered for a while, but even that wouldn't do any good because she'll hear about those issues eventually. No. let her see them. And then help her deal with them. But this wasn't what she said to Danielle.

"You see disappointment that I can't shop with them. Especially with Aisha whose new dress was ruined and whose wonderful party was blown all to hell. But… sorry. Never mind. You would not understand."

Danielle responded with a face of her own. "I am fifty years old. I've never known disappointment? I'm a woman. I don't understand shopping?"

Before Elizabeth could answer, Danielle said, "A new plan. I shop in the morning, but only for wigs. I come back with new looks for both you and for Aisha. You go back to town in one car with Rasha because she looks nothing like Aisha. Mr. Kessler goes in the second car and he shops with Aisha and the sisters. You start at opposite ends of the shops. You are never seen together as a group. You don't even acknowledge each other."

"Good idea," said Elizabeth. "Thank you."

"Tonight at dinner we'll decide more than sizes. New names for all of you, especially for Aisha. Don't be overheard calling her Aisha. In France there are many girls with dark hair. I recommend good French names like Dominique and Gabrielle."

"How about Christiane?"

"She might not be amused," said Danielle, who then shrugged. "Even so, it would certainly help to disguise her. But it's not enough. We need a total new look. I only wish that she was not such a beautiful young girl. Perhaps we can put some weight on her."

Not bad, thought Elizabeth. A sensible idea. Niki goes one way, knocks off twenty pounds, and the rest of us eat until we're morbidly obese. But no way. New looks will have to do.

593

For how long? There's no telling. She who's coming might be coming for another five years. Martin may or may not have five good years left in him. So how long? Three months. Maybe six, but not longer. Just long enough to grow out her own hair. She and Martin have some living to do.

She can't wait to get down to that wig shop herself.

Maybe something Dolly Parton-ish. Or maybe something Cher-ish. A total change from her normal low-maintenance cut. Martin likes it as it was, but he might like a sexy wig. She'll leave the final choice up to him.

Oh, no she won't.

Martin, remember, has a weird sense of humor. He'd probably claim to go for the Alpine peasant look. Golden blond with pigtails down to her butt.

No, wait. Oh, wait. Get one of those for Aisha. Or else something heavy metal. Streaked with purple. And a nose ring. She who's coming isn't coming looking like some rock groupie. Or a biker babe. Or a strung-out teen druggie.

This time shopping is going to be fun.

EPILOG

In Washington, another four days had passed. It was the following Wednesday, early evening.

Howard Leland, who had listened to Clew's arguments at length, and to others by Harry himself, had concluded that he must resign all the same. He felt that his honor required it. Clew then promptly met with the Deputy Chief of Staff. He alerted him that the gesture would be forthcoming and explained why it had best be declined.

The administration would lose more than an honorable man if Leland were to go public with his reasons. Its strongest supporters, its biggest contributors, were members of The Bohemian Club. They would be exposed to considerable discomfort. Think special prosecutors, think criminal indictments, think search warrants and corpse-sniffing hounds, think the dredging of their lake and their river. Think trying to explain to the Saudi government why the prince was there in the first place. Are most members innocent? Of this they are, yes. But how much scrutiny could many of them bear?

For these and other reasons, Stickles saw to it that Leland's resignation would be refused. He felt that as long as Leland retained his office, he would remain answerable to the White House. If he should leave, no longer bound by his oath of office, he might place his energies and his prestige in the service of Whistler's business empire which he saw as a rogue shadow government.

"Shadow government?" asked Harry when Clew called with the news.

"I know. That's a new one. You're up there with Big Oil."

"Should I expect to be invaded?"

"Nope. We got you to stand down."

"Who did?" asked Harry. "You and Howard?"

"Yup. You've promised to take no further action against the Bohemian Club's membership. You've promised that you would take no further action aimed at bringing down the Saudi regime – without prior consultation with the White House, that is - and you're going to keep your hands off their oil."

"Any discussion of the prophecy?" he asked. "Anything about Aisha and Elizabeth? I assume he's seen Time and Newsweek."

"The prophecy came up. I denied you're behind it. I wasted my breath; he doesn't buy it. Not that it matters, however. The White House doesn't want to go anywhere near this. It would be a no-win no matter which side they take. Say anything positive, piss off half the world's Muslims. Brush it off and risk losing half of this country's voters who are sympathetic toward the Muslim feminists. Unofficially, they hope you'll raise hell with it."

By the time these terms had been related to him, Charles Haskell's body had resurfaced. Haskell's gardening crew found it at his Palm Beach estate. They found it neatly posed in the umpire's chair that overlooked his grass tennis court. That's where Netanya's plumbers had left him after having him cleaned up and packed in ice for three days in order to make his death seem unrelated to the events in Belle Haven. Harry had specified the grass court.

Haskell's death, called murder, was widely reported in the world's business press and on the BBC and CNN. Elizabeth saw the coverage, but offered no comment. Harry found that somewhat disappointing. He thought she'd see the poetry of it. But in truth the pose had not been his idea. He would not have imagined that a private court would have such a thing as an umpire's chair. No, not even at a Palm Beach estate. Netanya's plumbers had made the delivery, saw the chair, and had found it impossible to resist. They'd tried to pose him, finger pointing, as if calling a foot fault. But Haskell, by that time, was sufficiently thawed that they'd have to have propped him up with cut branches and they'd have to have worked in the dark. They'd decided that it would probably never look right and besides, they needed to get back to D.C. They left him with his hands clasped together, his chin on his chest as if in prayer.

Clew had said, "They're still trying to dope out what that means."

Harry asked, "Dope out what what means?"

He said, "The message that you were trying to send by leaving him in that position. Not that you've been named, but that's the gossip."

The account that appeared in Business Week magazine called Haskell a "plunderer extraordinaire even by the freebooting standards of his industry." The umpire's chair, if one saw it as a throne, was seen to symbolize that ranking. The pose was described as depicting a man who'd been humbled and had been "possibly, although doubtfully, penitent," before the coupe de grace to his throat. Not much was said about his other injuries. They were all superficial. They did not suggest torture. He looked more like he'd been in a bar fight.

Clew said to Harry, "Speaking of gossip, it's an even bigger mystery how you managed to get to that banker."

The death of Sir Reginald might have been the last straw that led to Gerald Stickles feeling the need to protect the remaining Bohemians. Was his death, as was reported, from natural causes or was this the long arm of Harry Whistler at work?

The simple truth was that Leeds had a stroke.

Ah, said the gossip, but what brought it on? He was probably frightened to death. Some fellow Bohemians had described his demeanor as seeming to be terrified out of his wits upon learning of Haskell's demise and especially how Haskell had been found. They said that his behavior was increasingly bizarre over the several days preceding. Not willing to return to his assigned cabin. Sleeping on lobby couches or porch furniture elsewhere, inebriated much of the time. Running off at the approach of Huntington Bentley who seemed on the verge of panic himself, having taken a call from some Saudi acquaintance – an apparently very angry acquaintance – and was heard unconvincingly protesting his innocence to whatever he was being accused of. After which Bentley managed to catch up to Leeds. There were a few minutes of heated discussion. The color was seen to drain from Leeds' face. Leeds clutched his temples, let out a squeal, and the poor man dropped dead on the spot.

Harry Whistler, of course, knew what had them so upset. Sadik knew. And Hester knew, but nobody else. Two of them down. Two confirmed dead. Another seven hundred million will soon go to Sadik through Hester's off-shore machinations. Huntington Bentley should not be far behind. His time at the Grove is up this coming weekend. Perhaps Stickles will offer him a Camp David guest room in return for him throwing his media clout behind all of the president's policies. Whatever. He can't hide forever.

Sam Foote had returned to his home in Belle Haven. Harry had offered him his old job in Italy and had offered to finance a new restaurant there. Sam was torn. He loved all things Italian. He'd made, however, many friends in Belle Haven, none of whom knew of his colorful past. In Italy, he'd been feared. Here, not the least bit. He was inclined to rebuild.

"But," he told Clew, "something weird has been happening since those two magazines hit the stands."

"Other than attracting the curious?" Clew asked.

"Curious isn't the word for it, Roger. You ought to drive down here and see."

Sam went on to try to explain what he meant. It was not so much the story of the Aisha Prophecy and the effect that it was having world-wide. It was not so much what seemed a connection between the prophecy and the destruction of Mangiamo as suggested by that 'eerily similar' photo of Elizabeth and Aisha emerging. Some in Belle Haven had known Aisha and Elizabeth, if only by their first names. Many more knew their faces. They'd seen them in the restaurant and around town and playing tennis together. It was not so much that both of them had suddenly vanished. It was not so much the whispers about them that were spreading.

Whispers like, "Call me crazy, but they never seemed quite... human. They always seemed sort of... up there... sort of almost otherworldly. The older one... Elizabeth... ever noticed her eyes? An unusual color. Amber. Like a cat. And like a cat, she hardly made a sound when she moved. And the younger one, Aisha... that's what she was called. And that seems one hell of a coincidence."

They were a mystery. No question about that. And mysteries discussed are either solved or they deepen.

They deepened mostly among those whom the mystery attracted.

Muslim women.

They were coming by the dozens.

Just a handful at first. They appeared the same day on which Time and Newsweek were published. By the next day, they numbered about twenty. Most were young. Most were covered. Some were not. Some held copies of either magazine across their breasts. Others held copies of the Koran from which they'd read aloud, although softly. They would stand on the sidewalk across the street from what remained of the restaurant. Sam had seen them. He'd walked over to ask why they were there.

One told him, "We just wanted to come here."

"There's nothing to see. Just a boarded-up building."

"We don't have a better answer than that."

Sam decided to ask them outright. "Do you believe that the Aisha of the prophecy was here?"

"Not necessarily. Don't make us sound silly. It's more what we find ourselves feeling as we stand here."

"Might I ask what it is that you feel?"

"The love of God," said one.

Another said, "Hope."

Sam asked, "Hope for what? That she'll come back here to lead you? To free you?"

Some frowned at the question. Others smiled. One answered for them, "We don't need to be led. We don't need to be freed. But others do. We stand here for them."

By the third night there were twice that number. By the fourth, there were many more. Some came by car, some by bus, some came on bicycles. A few made the pilgrimage on foot. Sergeant Dave Harris called Sam at his home and asked what, if anything, he wanted done.

"They're still just standing?"

"Pretty much," said the Sergeant. "Some have brought flowers and candles. They leave the flowers and candles on your front step. Some break off a splinter or pick up a piece of glass and kiss them before putting them in their pockets. Some leave little notes or verses from the Koran and then they go back across the street."

"All women?"

"Mostly women. But they're not all Muslim women. Some want to make it clear that they're Christians or Jews and that this has become a solidarity thing. I've seen Karen with them a couple of times. I asked whether she was joining the movement. She told me it's none of my business."

"You say mostly women. How many men?"

"Not a lot," Harris told him. "But a few more each time. Karen says they seem to be just standing guard in case anyone tries to harass them."

Sam asked, "Has anyone?"

"Not yet, but we're holding our breath. A lot of Muslims out there see this as a heresy. But don't worry. If anyone so much as shakes a fist at them, he'll get busted the minute we get there."

That's when Sam called Roger Clew and made the suggestion that Clew come down and see this for himself. He said, "I think Elizabeth ought to know about this. And you know her a lot better than I do."

Clew told him, "I'll meet you. One hour."

"No, go alone. See what you make of it. Then call me. I'll buy you a beer."

Clew drove down to Belle Haven in his car, a white Buick, and pulled up several yards short of the bus stop. He sat doubled parked, his engine running. He could see the candles flickering out front. Others were held by the women themselves. They seemed mostly young, some as young as in their teens, but quite a few were considerably older. Mothers and daughters, perhaps.

There were about sixty, not counting the men. Three or four of the men stood mingled with the women, but most stood off to one side. They didn't seem to be part of the vigil as such, but none showed any sign of impatience, disapproval. Their faces showed, if anything, concern. Probably husbands and fathers.

The women had paid no notice of him, but a couple of the men to the side were more wary. One of these turned and said something to the others. They nodded in what looked like approval. He said what looked like, "Stay here. I'll see what he wants." He stepped into the street. He approached Roger Clew's idling Buick.

He said to him, "Good evening. Are you the police?"

"Good evening to you, sir. No, I'm not."

"A reporter?"

"No. Just a friend of the owner." He gestured toward the soot-blackened building. "If I seem to be intruding, that's not my intention. I'm told that no one else is going to bother you either. Least of all the police."

"You're a friend to those who were here on that night? Were you here yourself when it happened?"

No harm in it, thought Clew. Not if he didn't give his name. He nodded. "Yes. I was here."

The man hesitated. "May I ask… did you know her? Did you know the girl, Aisha, and her… guardian?"

"I did. I've known them both for some time."

"So you've spoken to them. To the girl as well?"

"Of course. On many occasions."

The man turned his head toward the gathering of women. He was making eye contact with one in particular. A woman in her thirties. It was probably his wife. He was motioning her to come over. She came. She brushed a lock of hair back under her scarf as if to see Roger more clearly.

Her probable husband said to the woman "This man tells me that you won't be disturbed." He asked Clew, "You have such authority?"

"Just enough to guarantee that you'll be left alone as long as you're standing here peacefully."

He said to the woman, "This man knows her. He was here."

Clew groaned within himself. Now he wished he hadn't come. The woman asked him, "What might you tell us about her?" But she asked it in a way that gave him a sense that she was afraid of his answer. Or at least of a flesh and blood answer.

He said what he imagined Sadik would have said. He answered, "She touched all our hearts."

The answer seemed to please her. "She's gone on to touch others?"

Clew left the question unanswered.

The woman said, "If you're wondering, we are not deluded. We don't know whether Aisha has been reborn. But she might have been. And she might have been here. That's what draws us. Her spirit. We're feeling it here. Do you know of a better place to look for it?"

"In here," said Clew. He touched a finger to his heart. It's what he thought Sadik would have done.

The woman fidgeted with the edge her scarf. She said, "I find I want to ask whether you're of our faith, but a voice inside tells me I should not."

"One should listen to one's inner voices," he told her. That sounded even more like Sadik.

The woman asked, "Have you touched her?"

Touched her? Sure, he had. She got a birthday hug from him. But he answered, for some reason, "Just as she has touched me."

Clew's left arm, in shirtsleeves, was resting on his door. His right arm rested lightly on his steering wheel. The woman eyes were on his right hand. She said, "If my husband should give me permission, will you allow me to touch the hand that touched her?"

The husband grumbled. "Since when do you ask my…?"

"I'm asking it now. This is not an ordinary man."

The husband said, "If he's willing, you have my permission. In return, will you promise to have something to eat?" He said to Clew, "They're fasting. Almost all of them."

Clew offered his right hand, it's palm facing downward. All he knew about offering a hand to a Muslim was that to offer the left hand was offensive. He wasn't sure about palm up or palm down, but in this case it didn't seem to matter. She took it in both of her own.

She closed her eyes. She rocked back and forth. He felt a shudder go through her. He said to her, "With that, I'm afraid I must leave you."

She released him. She asked, "Will you tell me your name?"

"It's not important. Goodbye. And please eat."

He drove away slowly, straight ahead. In his rearview mirror he could see that woman. She was showing her hand to the others. Faces turned in his direction. He could see their necks craning. Several stepped into the street to get a better look at the car of this man who knew Aisha.

What was it Sadik said about Aisha coming? He said no one can fight it because she's really come. He said her spirit is already out there.

And it is.

That's the power of faith and it's the power of myth. Aisha is here. The idea of her is here. Women like those women standing vigil back there back will probably soon start to organize. They'll form sisterhoods something like the Nasreens. They'll probably call them Aisha Societies. They'll start doing the work that Aisha would do. For Muslim women. Perhaps for all women.

Sadik was entirely correct. It was real. And this could only be a good thing.

And yet Clew still felt something eating at him. He knew what it was. A touch of guilt.

"This is no ordinary man," said that woman. And he made it worse by not giving her his name. Jack Smith. Ivan Goldberg. Any name would have done. Then poof, no more mystery. Just a townie passing through. What he's not is some other guardian angel who speaks in cryptics, who embodies love and kindness and who drives a three-year old Buick. The damned thing's even white. So is his shirt.

He should turn around.

But no, let it go.

Drive over to Sam's place. Kick back with a beer. And try to stop wondering whether Sam's ruined building has now become a permanent shrine because he didn't have the sense to keep his mouth shut. Whether sixty will soon be six hundred.

He'll wait a day or two. And then he'll check the internet.

He'll see how the word is spreading and whether he's part of it.

He'll see whether he's the angel of the Buick.

END

8929610R0

Made in the USA
Lexington, KY
14 March 2011